"**Don't you want to k...**

Kasey whispered the words to Eli's back, knowing that if he faced her, she wouldn't have the nerve to say them.

Eli stopped, half convinced that he'd imagined her saying words that he would have sold his soul to hear. Releasing the breath that had gotten caught in his throat, he slowly turned around.

"More than anything in the world."

"Then what are you waiting for?"

He could have said that he couldn't kiss her because, technically, she was still Hollis's wife. Or that he couldn't because he didn't want to take advantage of her, or the situation. There were as many reasons to deny himself as there were leaves on the tree by his window. And only one reason to do it.

Because he ached for her.

Dear Reader,

I have this thing about families. When I was little, I wanted three older brothers. Unfortunately, since I was the first born, no amount of my pleading seemed to rectify that. All my parents could give me were two younger ones. Now, because of our ages, I tell people they're my older brothers, so in essence, it all worked out. Once I began writing, I created those brothers (and sisters) that nature (and my parents) failed to give me. I became caught up in the worlds I was creating and just kept going. What began as a small family—and small town—kept on growing. Which is why Alma, who first appeared in the sheriff's story, suddenly was given siblings en masse by the time she got her own story (*Lassoing the Deputy*). I like large families and I like returning to them. So this is Eli's story, which shows how selfless love is ultimately rewarded. It's also a story about never giving up hope because if something is meant to be, it *will* happen.

I hope you enjoy this latest addition to the Forever, Texas saga. As always, I thank you for reading, and from the bottom of my heart I wish you someone to love who loves you back.

All the best,

Marie Ferrarella

A Baby on the Ranch

MARIE FERRARELLA

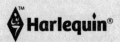

TORONTO NEW YORK LONDON
AMSTERDAM PARIS SYDNEY HAMBURG
STOCKHOLM ATHENS TOKYO MILAN MADRID
PRAGUE WARSAW BUDAPEST AUCKLAND

PLEASE RECYCLE
THIS PRODUCT IS RECYCLABLE

Recycling programs
for this product may
not exist in your area.

ISBN-13: 978-0-373-75414-4

A BABY ON THE RANCH
Copyright © 2012 by Harlequin Books S.A.

The publisher acknowledges the copyright holder
of the individual works as follows:

A BABY ON THE RANCH
Copyright © 2012 by Marie Rydzynski-Ferrarella

RAMONA AND THE RENEGADE
Copyright © 2011 by Marie Rydzynski-Ferrarella

This edition published by arrangement with Harlequin Books S.A.

For questions and comments about the quality of this book
please contact us at Customer_eCare@Harlequin.ca

® and TM are trademarks of the publisher. Trademarks indicated with
® are registered in the United States Patent and Trademark Office, the
Canadian Trade Marks Office and in other countries.

www.Harlequin.com

Printed in U.S.A.

CONTENTS

ABOUT THE AUTHOR

This *USA TODAY* bestselling and RITA® Award-winning author has written over two hundred books for Harlequin Books, some under the name of Marie Nicole. Her romances are beloved by fans worldwide. Visit her website at www.marieferrarella.com.

Books by Marie Ferrarella

A Baby on the Ranch

To Kathleen Scheibling,

for wanting to see more.

Thank you.

Prologue

"Eli!"

The loud, insistent pounding worked its way into his brain and rudely yanked Eli Rodriguez out of a deep, sound sleep. Eyes still shut, he sat up in bed, utterly disoriented, listening without knowing what he was listening for, or even why.

He'd fallen into bed, exhausted, at eleven, too tired even to undress.

Was he dreaming?

"Eli, open up! Open the damn door, will you?"

No, he wasn't dreaming. This was real. Someone was yelling out his name. Who the hell was pounding on his door at this hour?

The question snaked its way through his fuzzy brain as Eli groped his way into the hallway and then made his way down the stairs, clutching on to the banister. His equilibrium still felt off.

Belatedly, he realized that it was still the middle of the night. Either that, or the sun had just dropped out of the sky, leaving his part of the world in complete darkness.

His mind turned toward his family. Had something happened to one of them? They were all well as of the last time they'd been together, but nothing was stationary.

Nothing was forever.

"Eli! C'mon, dammit, you can't be *that* asleep! Wake up!"

The voice started to sound familiar, although it was still hard to make it out clearly above the pounding.

Awake now, Eli paused for a second to pull himself together before opening the front door.

And to pick up a firearm—just in case.

The people who lived in Forever and the surrounding area were good people, but that didn't mean that unsavory types couldn't pass through. There'd been an incident or two in the past five years, enough to make a man act cautiously.

"Dammit all to hell, Eli!"

That wasn't an unsavory type—at least, not according to the general definition. That was his friend, Hollis Stonestreet. Except right now, he wasn't feeling very friendly.

With an annoyed sigh, Eli unlocked his front door and found himself face-to-face with Hollis.

A one-time revered high school quarterback, the blond-haired, blue-eyed former Adonis had become a little worn around the edges. Though he was still considered handsome, the past eight years hadn't been all that good to Hollis.

Eli rested the firearm he no longer needed against

the wall. "You trying to wake the dead, Hollis?" he asked wearily.

"No, just you," Hollis retorted, walking into the front room, "which I was starting to think was the same thing."

"This couldn't wait until morning?" Eli asked, curbing his impatience.

Hollis was wearing his fancy boots, the ones with the spurs. They jingled as he walked.

Looking at the boots, Eli started getting a very bad feeling about this. What was Hollis doing here at this hour?

Last he'd heard, Hollis had been missing for almost a week now. At least according to his wife, Kasey. She'd said as much when she'd called him two days ago, apologizing for bothering him even though they'd been friends forever. Apologizing, and at the same time asking that if he wasn't too busy, would he mind driving her to the hospital in Pine Ridge because her water had just broken.

"The baby'll be coming and I don't think I can drive the fifty miles to the hospital by myself," she'd said.

He'd known by the tone in her voice that she was afraid, and doing her best not to sound like it.

His pulse had begun to race immediately as he'd told her to hang in there. Five seconds later, he'd torn out of his ranch house, dashing toward his Jeep.

That was the first—and the last—time he'd let the speedometer climb to ninety-five.

The following day, when he'd visited Kasey and her baby—a beautiful, healthy baby boy—he knew boys weren't supposed to be beautiful, but in his opinion, this one was—Hollis still hadn't shown up.

Nor had he come the next morning when Eli had gone back to visit her again.

And now, here he was, pacing around in his living room at 2:00 a.m.

What was going on? Why wasn't he with Kasey, where he belonged? He knew that *he* would be if Kasey was his wife.

But she wasn't and there was no point in letting his thoughts go in that direction.

"No, it can't wait," Hollis snapped, then immediately tempered his mood. He flashed a wide, insincere grin at him. "I came by to ask you for a favor."

This had to be one hell of a favor, given the hour. "I'm listening."

"I want you to look after Kasey for me."

Eli stared at the other man. If he wasn't awake before, he was now. "Why, where are you going to be?" Eli asked. When Hollis didn't answer him, for the first time in their long relationship, Eli became visibly angry. "Did you even bother to go *see* Kasey in the hospital?"

Pacing, Hollis dragged a hand through his unruly blond hair. "Yeah. Yeah, I did. I saw her, I saw the kid." Swinging back around, Hollis watched him, suddenly appearing stricken. "I thought I could do it, Eli, but I can't. I can't do it," he insisted. "I can't be a father. My throat starts to close up when I even *think* about being a father."

Eli dug deep for patience. Hollis had never thought about anyone but himself. Because of his looks, everything had always been handed to him. Well, it was time to man up. He had a wife and a baby who were counting on him.

"Look, that's normal," Eli said soothingly. "You're just having a normal reaction. This is all new to you. Once you get the hang of it—"

He got no further.

"Don't you get it?" Hollis demanded. "I don't *want* to get the hang of it. Hell, I didn't even want to get married."

No one had held a gun to his head, Eli thought resentfully. If he'd backed off—if Hollis had left town five years ago—then maybe *he* would have had a chance with Kasey. And that baby she'd just had could've been his.

"Then why did you?" he asked, his voice low, barely contained.

Hollis threw up his hands. "I was drunk, okay? It seemed like a good idea at the time. Look, I've made up my mind. I'm leaving and nothing you say is going to stop me." He started to edge his way back to the front door. "I'd just feel better if I knew you were going to look after her. She's going to need somebody."

"Yeah, her husband," Eli insisted.

Hollis didn't even seem to hear as he pulled open

the front door. "Oh, by the way, I think you should know that I lost the ranch earlier today."

Eli could only stare at him in disbelief. "You did *what?*"

Hollis shrugged, as if refusing to accept any guilt. "I had a straight—a straight, dammit—what're the odds that the other guy would have a straight flush?"

Furious now, Eli fisted his hands at his sides, doing his best to keep from hitting the other man. "Are you out of your mind?" Eli demanded. "Where is she supposed to live?"

The question—and Eli's anger—seemed to annoy Hollis. "I don't know. But I can't face her. You tell her for me. You're good like that. You *always* know what to say."

And then he was gone. Gone just as abruptly as he'd burst in less than ten minutes ago.

Eli ran his hand along the back of his neck, staring at the closed door.

"No," he said wearily to the darkness. "Not always."

Chapter One

When she turned her head toward the doorway, the expression on Kasey Stonestreet's face faded from a hopeful smile to a look of barely suppressed disappointment and confusion.

Eli saw the instant change as he walked into her hospital room. Kasey hadn't been expecting him, she'd expected Hollis. *Hollis* was the one who was supposed to come and pick her and their brand-new son up and take them home, not him.

"Hi, Kasey, how are you?" Doing his best to pretend that everything was all right, Eli flashed her an easy smile.

He had a feeling that for once, she wasn't buying it or about to go along with any pretense for the sake of her pride.

Kasey pressed her lips together as a bitter disappointment rooted in the pit of her stomach and spread out. When he left her yesterday, Hollis had told her that he'd be here at the hospital long before noon. According to the hospital rules, she was supposed to check out at noon.

It was past noon now. Almost by a whole hour. When the nurse on duty had passed by to inform her— again—that checkout was at noon, she'd had no choice but to ask for a little more time. She hated the touch of pity in the woman's eyes as she agreed to allow her a few more minutes.

Excuses came automatically to her lips. Life with Hollis had taught her that. "He's stuck in traffic," she'd told the other woman. "But I know he'll be here any minute now."

That had been more than half an hour ago.

So when the door to her room finally opened, Kasey had looked toward it with no small amount of relief. Until she saw that the person walking in wasn't Hollis. It was Eli, her childhood friend. Eli, who always came when she needed him.

Wonderfully dependable Eli.

More than once she'd wondered why Hollis couldn't be more like the man he claimed was his best friend. It went without saying that if she had asked Eli to come pick her up before noon, he would have been there two hours early, looking to help her pack her suitcase.

Unlike Hollis.

Where *was* he?

The disappointment evolved into a feeling of complete dread, which in turn spilled out all over her as she looked up at the tall, muscular man she'd come, at times, to think of as her guardian angel.

When her eyes met his, the fear she harbored in her heart was confirmed.

"He's not coming, is he?" she asked, attempting to suppress a sigh.

Last night or, more correctly, Eli amended, this morning, when Hollis had left after delivering that bombshell, he'd suddenly snapped out of his fog and run after Hollis barefoot. He'd intended to either talk Hollis out of leaving or, that failing, hog-tie the fool until he came to his senses and realized that Kasey was the best thing that had ever happened to him.

But it was too late. Hollis was already in his car and if the heartless bastard saw him chasing after the vehicle in his rearview mirror, Hollis gave no indication. He certainly hadn't slowed down or attempted to stop. If anything, he'd sped up.

His actions just reinforced what Eli already knew. That there was no talking Hollis into acting like an adult instead of some errant, spoiled brat who did whatever he wanted to and didn't stick around to face any consequences.

Eli looked at the young woman he'd brought to the hospital a short three days ago. She'd been on the very brink of delivering her son and they had *just* made it to the hospital in time. Had she waited even five minutes before calling him, Wayne Eli Stonestreet would have been born in the backseat of his Jeep, with him acting as an impromptu midwife.

Not exactly a notion he would have relished. He had a hunch that Kasey wouldn't have been crazy about it, either.

The doctor who'd been on duty that night had mistaken him for the baby's father and started to pull him into the delivery room. He'd been very quick to demur, telling the doctor that he was just a friend who'd volunteered to drive Kasey here.

He'd almost made it to the waiting area, but then Kasey had grabbed his hand, bringing his escape to a grinding haul.

On the gurney, about to be wheeled into the delivery room, Kasey had looked at him with panic in her eyes. "Eli, please. I'll feel better if you're there. I need a friend," she'd pleaded. Her own doctor was out of town. With Hollis not there, she felt totally alone. "Please," she repeated, her fingers tightening around his hand.

The next moment he'd felt as if his hand had gotten caught in a vise. Kasey was squeezing it so hard, she'd practically caused tears to spring up in his eyes. Tears of pain.

Kasey might have appeared a fragile little thing, despite her pregnant stomach, but she had a grip like a man who wrestled steers for a living.

Despite that, it wasn't her grip that had kept him there. It was the look of fear he'd seen in her eyes.

And just like that, Eli had found himself recruited, a reluctant spectator at the greatest show in town: the miracle of birth.

He'd taken a position behind Kasey, gently propping her up by her shoulders and holding her steady each time she bore down and pushed.

The guttural screams that emerged from her sounded

as if they were coming from the bottom of her toes and he freely admitted, if only to himself, that they were fraying his nerves.

And then, just as he was about to ask the doctor if there wasn't something that could be done for Kasey to separate her from all this pain, there he was. The miracle. Forever's newest little citizen. Born with a wide-eyed look on his face, as if he couldn't believe where he had wound up once he left his nice, safe, warm little haven.

Right now, the three-day-old infant lay all bundled up in a hospital bassinet on the other side of Kasey's bed. He was sound asleep, his small, pink little lips rooting. Which meant he'd be waking up soon. And hungry.

Eli took all this in as he cast around for the right way to tell Kasey what he had to say. But he hadn't been able to come up with anything during the entire fifty-mile trip here, despite all his best efforts. Consequently there was no reason to believe that something magical would pop up into his brain now as he stood in Kasey's presence.

Especially when she usually had such a numbing effect on him, causing all thought to float out of his head, unfettered. It had been like that since kindergarten.

So, with no fancily wrapped version of a lie, no plausible story or excuse to offer her, Eli had nothing to fall back on except for the truth.

And the truth was what he offered her, hating that it was going to hurt.

"No, he's not coming," he confirmed quietly. "Hollis asked me to pick you up because he said that the hospital was discharging you today." He offered her a smile. "Guess that means that you and the little guy passed the hospital's inspection."

His attempt at humor fell flat, as he knew it would. He hated that she had to go through this, that Hollis had never proven worthy of the love she bore him.

His attention was drawn to the sleeping infant in the bassinet. He lowered his voice so as not to wake Wayne. "Hey, is it my imagination, or did he grow a little since I last saw him?"

"Maybe." Kasey struggled not to give in to despair, or bitterness. She shrugged. "I don't know."

It was clear that she was upset and struggling not to let her imagination take off.

But it did anyway.

Still, Kasey tried to beat it back, to deny what she felt in her soul was the truth. Her last sliver of optimism had her asking Eli, "Is he going to be waiting for us at the ranch?"

Dammit, Hollis, I should have taken a horsewhip to you instead of just let you walk out like that. You're hurting her. Hurting the only decent thing in your life. She deserves better than this. Better than you, he thought angrily.

It hurt him almost as much to say it as he knew it hurt her to hear it. "No, Hollis isn't going to be there."

Suspicion entered eyes as blue as the sky on a summer's day, momentarily blocking out her fear. "Why? Why are you so sure?" she asked, struggling to keep angry tears from falling.

When Hollis had come to see her, not on the first day, but on the second, he'd been full of apologies and even more full of promises about changing, about finally growing up and taking responsibility for his growing family. All right, he hadn't held Wayne, hadn't even picked him up when she'd tried to put the baby into his arms, but she told herself that was just because he was afraid he'd drop the baby. That was a normal reaction, she'd silently argued. First-time fathers had visions of their babies slipping right out of their arms and onto their heads.

But he'd come around, she'd promised herself. Hollis would come around. It would just take a little time, that was all.

Except now it seemed as if he wasn't going to come around. Ever.

She felt sick.

"Why?" she repeated more sharply. "Why are you so sure?"

He didn't want to say this, but she gave him no choice. He wasn't good at coming up with excuses—with lies—on the spur of the moment. Not like Hollis.

"Because he came by at two this morning and asked me to look after you and the baby."

"All right," she said slowly, picking her way through the words as if she were navigating a potential minefield that could blow her apart at any second. "Nothing he hasn't said before, right?" Her voice sped up with every word. "He's just probably got a job waiting for him in another town. But once that's over, he'll be back." A touch of desperation entered her voice. "He's got a son now, Eli. He can't walk out on both of us, right?" Her eyes searched his face for a confirmation. A confirmation she was silently begging for.

More than anything in the world, Eli wanted to tell her what she wanted to hear. That she was right. That Hollis had just gone away temporarily.

But he couldn't lie, not to her. Not anymore.

And he was tired of covering for Hollis. Tired of trying to protect Kasey from Hollis's lies and his infidelities. Tired most of all because he knew that he would be lumped in with Hollis when her anger finally unleashed.

He looked at her for a long moment, hoped that she would find it in her heart to someday forgive him, and said, "I don't think that he's coming back this time, Kasey."

She didn't want to cry, she didn't. But she could feel the moisture building in her eyes. "Not even for the baby?"

The baby's the reason he finally took off, Eli told her silently.

Rather than say that out loud and wound her even more deeply, Eli placed his hands very lightly on her slender shoulders, as if that would somehow help soften the blow, and said, "He said he was taking off. That he wasn't any good for you. That he didn't deserve to have someone like you and Wayne in his life."

Yes, those were lies, too. He knew that. But these were lies meant to comfort her, to give her a little solace and help her preserve the memory of the man Kasey *thought* she'd married instead of the man she actually *had* married.

"'Taking off,'" she repeated. Because of her resistance, it took a moment for the words to sink in. "Where's he going?"

Eli shook his head. Here, at least, he didn't have to get creative. He told her the truth. "He didn't tell me."

She didn't understand. It didn't make any sense to her. "But the ranch—with Hollis gone, who's going to run the ranch?" She was still trying to recover from the delivery. "I'm not sure if I can manage that yet." She looked back at the bassinet. "Not if I have to take care of—"

This felt like cruelty above and beyond the norm, Eli couldn't help thinking, damning Hollis to hell again. "You're not going to have to run the ranch," he told her quietly.

Because this was Eli, she misunderstood what he was saying and jumped to the wrong conclusion. "Eli, I can't ask you to run the ranch for me. You've got your own spread to run. And when you're not there, I know that you and your brothers and Alma help your dad to run his. Taking on mine, as well, until I get stronger, would be too much for you."

He stopped her before this got out of hand. "You're *not* asking," he pointed out. "And I'd do it in a heartbeat—if there was a ranch to run."

"If there was…" Her voice trailed off, quaking, as she stared up at him. "I don't understand."

He might as well tell her all of it, this way he would pull the Band-Aid off all at once, hopefully minimizing the overall pain involved. As it was, he had a feeling that this would hurt like hell.

Eli measured out the words slowly. "Hollis lost the ranch in a card game."

"He…lost the ranch?" she repeated in absolute disbelief.

Eli nodded. "In a card game."

It wasn't a joke. She could see it in Eli's face. He was telling her the truth. She was stunned.

"But that was our home," she protested, looking at Eli with utter confusion in her eyes. "How could he? How *could* he?" she repeated, a note of mounting anger in her voice.

Good, she was angry, he thought. Anger would keep her from slipping into a depression.

"Gambling is an addiction," Eli told her gently. "Hollis can't help himself. If he could, he would have never put the ranch up as collateral." Hollis had had a problem with all forms of gambling ever since he'd placed his first bet when he was seventeen and lied about his age.

Stricken, her knees unsteady, Kasey sank back down on the bed again.

"Where am I going to go?" she asked, her voice small and hollow.

The baby made a noise, as if he was about to wake up. Her head turned sharply in his direction. For a moment, embalmed in grief, she'd forgotten about him. Now, having aged a great deal in the past ten minutes, she struggled to pull herself together.

"Where are *we* going to go?" she amended.

It wasn't just her anymore. She was now part of a duo. Everything that came her way, she had to consider in the light that she was now a mother. Things didn't just affect her anymore, they affected Wayne as well. Taking care of her son was now the most important thing in her life.

And she couldn't do it.

She had a little bit put aside, but it wasn't much. She had next to no money, no job and nowhere to live.

Her very heart hurt.

How could you, Hollis? How could you just walk out on us like this? The question echoed over and over in her head. There was no answer.

She wanted to scream it out loud, scream it so loud that wherever Hollis was, he'd hear her. And tell her what she was supposed to do.

Taking a shaky breath, Kasey tried to center herself so that she could think.

Her efforts all but blocked everything else out. So much so that she didn't hear Eli the first time he said something to her. The sound of his voice registered, but not his words.

She looked at him quizzically, confusion and despair playing tug-of-war for her soul. "I'm sorry, what did you say?"

He had a feeling she hadn't heard when she didn't answer or comment on what he'd just said.

This time, he repeated it more slowly. "I said, you and the baby can stay with me until we figure things out."

Eli wasn't making an offer or a generous gesture. He said it like it was a given. Already decided, Kasey thought. But despite his very generous soul, she wasn't his problem. She would have to figure this out and deal with it on her own.

As if reading her mind, Eli said, "Right now, you're still a little weak from giving birth," he reminded her. "Give yourself a few days to recover, to rest. You don't have to make any decisions right away if you don't want to. And I meant what I said. You're coming home with me. You and Wayne are going to have a roof over your heads for as long as you need. For as long as this takes for you to come to terms with—and that's the end of it," he concluded.

Or thought he did.

"We can't stay with you indefinitely, Eli," Kasey argued.

"We're not talking about indefinitely," he pointed out. "We're talking about one day at a time. I'm just asking you to give yourself a little time to think things through," he stressed. "So you don't make decisions you'd rather not because the wolf's at the door."

"But he is," she said quietly. That was the state of affairs she faced.

"No, he's not. I shot the wolf," he told her whimsically. "Now, are you all packed?" It was a needless question, he knew she was. He'd found her sitting on her bed, the closed suitcase resting on the floor beside her foot. Rather than answer, she nodded. "Good. I'll go find the nurse. They said hospital policy is to escort you out in a wheelchair."

"I don't need a wheelchair," she protested. "I can walk."

"Make them happy, Kasey. Let them push the wheelchair to the front entrance," he coaxed.

Giving in, she beckoned him over to her before he went off in search of the nurse. When he leaned in to her, she lightly caressed his cheek. "You're a good man, Eli. What would I do without you?"

He, for one, was glad that she didn't have to find out. And that he didn't have to find out, either, for that matter.

"You'd manage, Kasey. You'd manage." She was resilient and she'd find a way to forge on. He had no doubts about that.

He might not have any doubts, but she did.

"Not very well," she said in a whisper meant more for her than for him. Eli had already gone out to notify a nurse that she was ready.

Even though she really wasn't ready, Kasey thought, fighting a wave of panic. She did what she could to tamp it down. She wasn't ready to face being a mother all by herself. This wasn't how she'd pictured her life at this very crucial point.

A tear slid down her cheek.

Frustrated, Kasey brushed it aside. But another one only came to take its place, silently bearing testimony to the sadness within her.

The sadness that threatened to swallow her up whole, without leaving a trace.

Chapter Two

Kasey thought she was seeing things when Eli brought his vehicle to the front of the hospital and she caught a glimpse of what was in the backseat. She could feel the corners of her eyes stinging.

Leave it to Eli.

"You bought him an infant seat." Her voice hitched and she pressed her lips together, afraid that a sob might suddenly break free and betray just how fragile her emotions were right now.

Eli nodded as he got out of the Jeep and hurried around the hood of his vehicle to her side. The nurse who had brought the wheelchair had pushed Kasey and the baby right up to the curb and stood behind them, waiting for Kasey and her son to get into the vehicle.

Was Kasey upset, or were those happy tears shimmering in her eyes? Eli couldn't tell. Even though he'd grown up with Alma, he'd come to the conclusion that all women should come with some kind of a manual or at least a road map to give a guy a clue so he could properly navigate a course.

"I got the last one at the Emporium," he told her.

"I know that Rick would cut me some slack if I took the baby home without a car seat, given the circumstances," he said, referring to the sheriff. "It's not like there's a whole lot of traffic around here. But I thought you'd feel safer if Wayne was strapped into his own infant seat when he's traveling."

"I do," she said with feeling, her voice just barely above a whisper as she struggled to keep the tears back. What might have seemed like a small act of kindness to a casual observer threatened to completely undo her. "Thank you."

Never comfortable with being on the receiving end of gratitude, Eli merely shrugged away her thanks.

He looked down at the sleeping infant in her arms. It almost seemed a shame to disturb him, he seemed so peaceful. But they did have to get going.

While he was fairly adept at holding an infant, strapping one into an infant seat was something else. Eli looked from Wayne to the infant seat in the rear of the Jeep and then slanted a glance toward the nurse. He didn't like admitting to being helpless, but there was a time to put pride aside and own up to a situation.

"Um…" Eli dragged the single sound out, as if, if he continued debating long enough, a solution would occur to him.

The nurse, however, was in a hurry.

"If you open the door—" the young woman pointed to the side closest to the infant seat "—I'll strap your little guy into his seat for you," she offered.

Relieved, Eli immediately swung the rear door

open for the nurse. "I'd really appreciate that. Thanks," he told her heartily.

"Nothing to it." With a nod in his direction, the nurse turned her attention to the baby in her patient's arms. "If you're lucky," she said to Kasey as she eased the infant from her arms, "he'll just sleep right through this."

Cooing softly to the baby that Kasey had just released, the nurse leaned into the Jeep's backseat and very deftly strapped Wayne Eli Stonestreet in for his very first car ride. Eli moved closer, watching her every move intently and memorizing them.

"You're all set," the young woman announced, stepping back onto the curb and behind the wheelchair. She took hold of the two handlebars in the back. "Time to get you into your seat, too," she told Kasey.

Eli offered Kasey his hand as she began to stand. Feeling slightly wobbly on her feet, Kasey flushed. "I didn't think I was going to feel this weak," she protested, annoyed. "After all, it's been three days. I should be stronger by now."

"You will be," Eli assured her. Getting her into the front passenger seat, he paused to thank the nurse again. The latter, holding on to the back of the wheelchair, was all set to leave. Eli flashed her a grateful smile. "Thanks for your help with the baby. I figure it's going to take me a while before I get good at all this."

The nurse released the brakes on either side of the wheelchair. "It won't take as long as you might think," she told him. "It'll all become second nature to you in a blink of an eye. Before you know it, you'll be doing all that and more in your sleep." She smiled as she nodded toward the back of the Jeep. "These little guys have a habit of bringing out the very best in their parents."

He was about to correct the woman, telling her that he wasn't Wayne's father, but the nurse had already turned on her heel and was quickly propelling the wheelchair in front of her, intent on going back and returning the wheelchair to its proper place. Calling after her wasn't worth the effort.

And besides, he had to admit that, deep down, he really liked the idea of being mistaken for Wayne's father, liked the way someone thinking that he and Kasey were actually a family made him feel.

You're too old to be playing make-believe like this, he upbraided himself. Still, the thought of their being an actual family lingered a while longer.

As did his smile.

With his passengers both in the Jeep and safely secured, Eli hurried around the front of his vehicle and slid in behind the steering wheel. A minute later the engine revved and he was pulling away from the curb, beginning the fifty-mile trip to Forever. More specifically, to the small ranch that was just on the outskirts of that town.

His ranch, he thought, savoring the burst of pride he felt each time he thought of the place. He was full of all sorts of big plans for it. Plans that were within his control to implement.

Unlike other things.

Because he didn't want to disturb the baby, Eli had left the radio off. Consequently, they drove in silence for a while. There was a time that Kasey had been exceedingly talkative and exuberant, but right now she was quiet. Almost eerily so. He wondered if it was best just to leave her to her thoughts, or should he get her talking, just in case the thoughts she was having centered around Hollis and her present chaotic state of affairs.

If it *was* the latter, he decided that he needed to raise up her spirits a little, although what method to use eluded him at the moment.

It hadn't always been this way. There was a time when he'd known just what to do, what to say to make her laugh and forget about whatever it was that was bothering her. Back then, it usually had something to do with her verbally abusive father, who only grew more so when he drank.

Eli was about to say something about the baby—he figured that it was best to break the ice with a nice, safe topic—when Kasey suddenly spoke up.

It wasn't exactly what he wanted to hear.

"I can't let you do this," she told him abruptly, feeling woven about each word.

"Do what?" he asked. The blanket statement was rather vague, although, in his gut, he had a feeling he knew what she was referring to. Still, he decided to play dumb as he stalled. "Drive you?" he guessed.

"No, have me stay at your ranch with the baby."

She turned in her seat to face him. "I can't put you out like that."

"Put me out?" he repeated with a dismissive laugh. "You're not putting me out, Kasey, you're doing me a favor."

She looked at him, unconvinced and just a little confused. "How is my staying at your place with a crying newborn doing you a favor?"

"Well, you might remember that I grew up with four brothers and a sister," he began, stating a fact tongue-in-cheek since he knew damn well that *she* knew. Growing up, she'd all but adopted his family, preferring them to her own. "That made for pretty much a full house, and there was always noise. An awful *lot* of noise," he emphasized. "When I got a chance to get my own place, I figured that all that peace and quiet would be like finally reaching heaven."

He paused for a second, looking for the right words, then decided just to trust his instincts. Kasey would understand. "Well, it wasn't. After living with all that noise going on all the time, the quiet got on my nerves. I found that I kind of missed all that noise. Missed the sound of someone else living in the place besides me," he emphasized. "Having you and Wayne staying with me will help fill up the quiet. So you see," he concluded, "you're really doing me a favor.

"Besides," he continued. "What kind of a friend would I be, turning my back on you at a time like this when you really need someone?"

"A friend with a life of his own," she answered matter-of-factly.

"You're right," he replied with a nod of his head. "It is my life. And that means I get to choose who I want to have in it." He looked into his rearview mirror, angling it so that he could catch a glimpse of the sleeping infant in the backseat. "And I choose Wayne. Since he's too little to come to stay with me by himself, I guess that means that I have to choose you, too, to carry him around until he can walk on his own power," he concluded with a straight face.

Repositioning the mirror back to its original position, he glanced toward Kasey. She hadn't said anything in response. And then he saw why. Was he to blame for that? "Hey, are you crying?"

Caught, she had no choice but to nod. Avoiding his eyes, she said evasively, "My hormones are all over the map right now. The doctor who delivered Wayne said it's because I gave birth, but it's supposed to pass eventually."

She was lying about the cause behind the tears and he knew it. He could always tell when she was evading the truth. But for the time being, he said nothing, allowing her to have her excuse so that she could have something to hide behind. It was enough that he knew the tears she was crying were tears of relief.

Shifting and taking one hand off the steering wheel, he reached into his side pocket and pulled out a handkerchief. Switching hands on the steering wheel, he silently held out the handkerchief to Kasey.

Sniffing, she took it and wiped away the telltale damp streaks from her cheeks. Eli's offer of a place to stay had touched her. It meant a great deal. Especially in light of the fact that the man she'd loved, the man she'd placed all her faith and trust in, not to mention given access to the meager collection of jewelry her late mother had left her, had thought nothing of just taking off. Abandoning her at a point in time when she very possibly needed him the most.

And, on top of that, he'd left her and their newborn son virtually homeless.

If Eli wasn't here…

But he was. And she knew he was someone she could always count on.

"I'll pay you back for this," she vowed to Eli. "I'm not sure just how right now, but once I'm a little stronger and back on my feet, I'll get a job and—"

"You don't owe me anything," he said, cutting her off. "And if you want to pay me back, you can do it by getting healthy and taking care of that boy of yours. Besides," he pointed out, "I'm not doing anything that extraordinary. If the tables were turned and I had no home to go to, you'd help me." It wasn't a question.

"In case you haven't noticed," he continued, "that's what friends are for. To be there for each other, not just when the going is good, but when it's bad. *Especially* when it's bad," he emphasized. "I'll always be here for you, Kasey." It was a promise he meant from the bottom of his heart. "So do us both a favor and save your breath. You're staying at my place for as long as you want to. End of discussion," he informed her with finality.

She smiled then, focusing on his friendship rather than on Hollis's betrayal.

"I had no idea you could be this stubborn," she told him with a glimmer of an amused smile. "Learn something every day, I guess."

He caught the glimmer of humor. She was coming around, Eli thought, more than a little pleased. With any luck, Hollis taking off like some selfish bat out of hell wouldn't scar her. But then, above all else, he'd always figured that, first and foremost, Kasey was a survivor.

"There's probably a lot about me that you don't know," he told her as he continued to drive along the open, desolate road that was between Pine Ridge and Forever.

"A lot?" Kasey repeated, then laughed softly as she turned the notion over in her mind. After all, they'd known each other in what felt like close to forever. "I really doubt that."

He loved the sound of her laughter. Loved, he freely admitted, if only to himself, everything about Kasey—except for her husband. But then, he didn't have to love Hollis. Only she did.

It was because he'd accidentally found out that she loved Hollis that he'd kept his feelings for her to himself even though he'd finally worked up the nerve to tell her exactly how he felt about her.

But that was back in high school. Back when Hollis, the school's football hero, had attracted a ring of girls around him, all completely enamored with his charm, each and every one of them ready to do whatever it took to have him notice them.

Hollis, being Hollis, took all the adulation in stride as being his due. He took his share of worshipful girls to bed, too.

Even so, he always had his eye on Kasey because, unlike the others, while very friendly, she didn't fawn all over him. So, naturally, she was the one he'd had to have. The one he'd wanted to conquer. She'd surprised him by holding out for commitment and a ring. And he'd surprised himself by letting her.

One night, not long after graduation, drunk on far more than just her proximity, Hollis had given her both a commitment and a ring, as well as a whirlwind wedding ceremony in a run-down, out-of-the-way chapel that specialized in them, with no questions asked other than if the hundred-dollar bill—paid upfront—was real.

And just like that, Eli recalled, the bottom had dropped out of his world. Not that he felt he had a prayer of winning her heart while Hollis was busy sniffing around her. But Eli had honestly thought that if he bided his time and waited Hollis out, he'd be there when Kasey needed someone.

And he was.

It had taken eight years, far longer than he'd thought Hollis would actually last in the role of husband. More than anything, Eli wanted to be there for her. He'd take her gratitude—if that was all she had to offer—in place of her love.

At least it was something, and besides, he knew that unless he was dead, there was no way he wouldn't be there for Kasey.

He heard her sigh. This was all weighing heavily on her, not that he could blame her. In her place, he'd feel the same way.

"I want you to know that I really appreciate this and that I promise Wayne and I won't put you out for long."

"Oh, good," he quipped drily, "because I'll need the room back by the end of the week."

His words stopped her dead. Eli spared her a look, one that was a little long in length since he was fairly confident that there was nothing to accidentally hit on this stretch of lonely highway.

"I'm only going to say this one more time, Kasey. You're not putting me out. I want to do this. I'm your friend and I always have been and this is what friends do, they have each other's backs. Now, unless you really want to make me strangle you, please stop apologizing, please stop telling me that you're going to leave as soon as possible. And *please* stop telling me that you feel you're putting me out. Because you're not. It makes me feel good to help you.

"Now, I don't want to hear anything more about this. My home is your home for as long as you need a place to stay—and maybe for a little bit longer than that." He paused to let his words sink in. "Understood?"

"Understood," she murmured. Then, a bit more loudly and with feeling, she promised, "But I *will* make it up to you."

"Good, I'm looking forward to it," he told her crisply. "Now, moving on," he said deliberately. "You have a choice of bedrooms. There are two to choose from, pretty much the same size," he told her, then stopped when a thought occurred to him. "Maybe I should let you have the master bedroom. We can put the crib in that room, so you can have Wayne right there—unless you'd rather have him stay in his own room, at which point you can take one of the bedrooms and place him in the other."

Kasey felt as if she was still stuck in first gear, her brain fixated on something he'd said to start with. "The crib?"

Why did she look so surprised? he wondered. "Well, Wayne's got to sleep in something, and I thought a crib was better than that portable whatchamacallit that you had at your place. Or a dresser drawer," he added, recalling stories his father told him about his being so small to begin with, they had tucked him into the bottom drawer of a dresser, lined with blankets and converted into a minicrib. He'd slept there for a month.

Kasey pounced on something he'd only mentioned in passing. "You were there?" she asked eagerly. "At our ranch?" The *our* in this case referred to her and Hollis. When he nodded, her mind took off, fully armed to the teeth. "So that means that I can still go over there and get—"

He shook his head. The man who had won the ranch from Hollis had made it very clear that he considered everything on the premises his. Still, if she had something of sentimental value that she wanted retrieved, he would be there in less than a heartbeat to get it for her. The new owner would just have to understand—or be made to understand.

"The guy who won the ranch from Hollis is living there," he told her. "I had to talk him into letting me come in and get some of your things. Actually—" never one to take any undue credit, he felt he needed to tell her "—having Rick and Alma with me kind of gave me the leverage I needed to convince the guy to release your things so I could bring them to you."

"Rick and Alma," she repeated as that piece of information sank in with less than stellar results. "So they know? About Hollis leaving me?" she asked in a small, troubled voice.

He knew that she would have rather kept the fact that Hollis had walked out on her a secret, but secrets had a way of spreading in a small town the size of Forever. And besides, the sympathy would all be on her side for reasons beyond the fact that she was a new mother with an infant to care for. Everyone in and around the town liked her.

That couldn't be said of Hollis.

"They know," Eli told her quietly. "I figured they—especially Rick, since he's the sheriff—should hear it from me so that they'd know fact from fiction, rumors being what they are in this town," he added.

Kasey felt as if there was a lead weight lying across her chest. There was a very private, shy woman beneath the bravado. A woman who wanted her secrets to remain secrets.

"How many other people know?" she asked him.

"For now, just Rick and the deputies."

For now.

"Now," she knew, had an exceptionally short life expectancy. As Eli had said, rumors being what they were, she had a feeling that everyone in town would know that Hollis had taken off before the week was out—if not sooner.

It was a very bitter pill for her to swallow.

But she had no other choice.

Chapter Three

"I guess you're right. No point in pretending I can hide this," Kasey finally said with a sigh. "People'll talk."

"They always do," he agreed. "It's just a fact of life."

Fact of life or not, the idea just didn't sit well with her. She wasn't a person who craved attention or wanted her fifteen minutes of fame in the spotlight. She was perfectly content just to quietly go about the business of living.

"I don't want to be the newest topic people talk about over breakfast," she said, upset.

"If they *do* talk about you, it'll be because they're on your side. Fact of the matter is, Hollis more or less wore out that crown of his. People don't think of him as that golden boy he once was," Eli assured her. Over the years, he'd become acutely aware of Hollis's flaws, flaws that the man seemed to cultivate rather than try to conquer. "Not to mention that he owes more than one person around here money."

Kasey looked at him, startled. Her mouth dropped open.

Maybe he'd said too much, Eli thought. "You didn't know that," he guessed.

Kasey's throat felt horribly dry, as if she'd been eating sand for the past half hour.

"No," she answered, her voice barely above a shaken whisper. "I didn't know that."

If she didn't know about that, it was a pretty safe bet that she certainly didn't know about her husband's dalliances with other women during the years that they were married, Eli thought.

Hollis, you were and are a damn fool. A damn, stupid, self-centered fool.

He could feel his anger growing, but there was no point in letting it fester like this. It wasn't going to help Kasey and her baby, and they were the only two who really mattered in this sordid mess.

"Are you sure?" Kasey asked. She'd turned her face toward him and placed a supplicating hand on his upper arm, silently begging him to say he was mistaken.

It was as if someone had jabbed his heart with a hot poker. He hated that this was happening to her. She didn't deserve this on top of what she'd already gone through. All of his life, he'd wanted nothing more than to make life better for her, to protect her. But right now, he was doing everything he could. Like taking her to his ranch.

Dammit, Hollis, how could you do this to her? She thought you were going to be her savior, her hero.

The house that Kasey had grown up in had been

completely devoid of love. Her father worked hard, but never got anywhere and it made him bitter. Especially when he drank to ease the pain of what he viewed as his dead-end life. Carter Hale had been an abusive drunk not the least bit shy about lashing out with his tongue or the back of his hand.

He'd seen the marks left on Kasey's mother and had worried that Kasey might get in the way of her father's wrath next. But Kasey had strong survival instincts and had known enough to keep well out of her father's way when he went on one of his benders, which was often.

Looking back, Eli realized that was the reason why she'd run off with Hollis right after high school graduation. Hollis was exciting, charming, and fairly reeked of sensuality. More than that, he had a feeling that to Kasey, Hollis represented, in an odd twist, freedom and at the same time, security. Marrying Hollis meant that she never had to go home again. Never had to worry about staying out of her father's long reach again.

But in Hollis's case, "freedom" was just another way of saying no plans for the future. And if "security" meant the security of not having to worry about money, then Hollis failed to deliver on that promise, as well.

Eli had strong suspicions that Kasey was beginning to admit to herself that marrying Hollis had been a huge mistake. That he wasn't going to save her but take her to hell via another route.

Most likely, knowing Kasey, when she'd discovered that she was pregnant, she had clung to the hope that this would finally make Hollis buckle down, work hard and grow up.

Eli blew out a short breath. He could have told her that Hollis wasn't about to change his way of thinking, and saved her a great deal of grief. But lessons, he supposed, couldn't be spoon-fed. The student could only learn if he or she *wanted* to, and he had a feeling that Kasey would have resisted any attempts to show her that Hollis wasn't what she so desperately wanted him to be.

Eli tried to appear as sympathetic as possible. As sympathetic as he felt toward her. This couldn't be easy for her. None of it.

"I'm sure," he finally told her, taking no joy in the fact that he was cutting Hollis down.

Kasey shook her head. She felt stricken. "I didn't have a clue," she finally admitted, wondering how she could have been so blind. Wondering how Hollis could have duped her like this. "What's wrong with me, Eli? Am I that stupid?"

"No, you're not stupid at all," he said with feeling. "What you are is loyal, and there's nothing wrong with you." To him, she'd always been perfect. Even when she'd fallen in love with Hollis, he hadn't been able to find it in his heart to take her to task for loving, in his opinion, the wrong man. He'd just accepted it. "Hollis is the one who's got something wrong with him. You've got to believe that," he told her firmly.

Kasey lifted her slender shoulders in a helpless shrug and then sighed again. It was obvious that she really didn't want to find fault with the man who'd fathered her child. The man whom she'd loved for almost a decade. "He was just trying to get some money together to make a better life for us," she said defensively.

The only one whose lot Hollis had *ever* wanted to improve was his own, Eli thought grudgingly, but he knew that to say so out loud would only hurt Kasey, so he kept the words to himself.

After pulling up in front of his ranch house, he turned off the engine and looked at her. "Until you're ready, until you have a place to go to and *want* to go there," he added, "this is your home, Kasey. Yours and Wayne's. What's mine is yours," he told her. "You know that."

He saw her biting her lower lip and knew she was waging an internal war with herself. Kasey hated the idea of being in anyone's debt, but he wasn't just anyone, he silently argued. They were friends. Best friends. And he had been part of her life almost from the time they began forming memories. There was no way he was about to abandon her now. And no way was he going to place her in a position where she felt she "owed" him anything other than seeing her smile again.

"Don't make me have to hog-tie you to make you stay put," he warned.

The so-called threat finally brought a smile to her lips. "All right, I won't."

Feeling rather pleased with himself, at least for the moment, Eli unfolded his lanky frame out of the Jeep and then hurried over to Kasey's side of the vehicle to help her out. Under normal circumstances, he wouldn't have even thought of it. She'd always been exceedingly independent around him, which made her being with Hollis doubly difficult for him to take. Kasey couldn't be independent around Hollis.

Hollis enjoyed being in control and letting Kasey *know* that he was in control. That in turn meant that he expected her submission. Because she loved him, she'd lived down to his expectations.

Unlike Hollis, he was proud of the fact that Kasey could take care of herself. And also unlike Hollis, he liked her independent streak. But at the moment, that had to take a backseat to reality. It was obvious that her body was having a bit of difficulty getting back in sync after giving birth only a few days ago. Eli just wanted to let her know that he was there for her. Whether it meant giving her a hand up or a shoulder to cry on, she could always rely on him.

She knew he meant well, but it didn't help her frame of mind. "I don't like feeling like this," she murmured, tamping down her frustration.

Eli took her hand and eased her to her feet. "It'll pass soon and you can go back to being Super Kasey," he quipped affectionately.

Just as she emerged from the passenger side, the tiny passenger in the backseat began to cry.

"Sounds like someone's warming up to start wailing," Eli commented, opening the rear door. "You okay?" he asked Kasey before he started freeing Wayne from all his tethers.

She nodded. "I'm fine." A sliver of guilt shot through her as she watched Eli at work. "I should be doing that," she said, clearly annoyed with herself. "He's my responsibility."

"Hey, you can't have all the fun," he told her good-naturedly, noting that she sounded almost testy. He took no offense, sensing that she was frustrated with herself—and Hollis—not him.

The baby was looking at him, wide-eyed, and for a moment he had stopped crying. Eli took that to be a good sign.

"Hi, fella. Let's get you out of all those belts and buckles and into the daylight," he said in a low, gentle voice meant to further soothe the little passenger.

In response, the baby just stared at him as if he was completely fascinated by the sound of his voice. Eli smiled to himself, undoing one belt after another as quickly as possible.

Behind him, he heard Kasey say, "I'm sorry, Eli."

He looked at her over his shoulder, puzzled. "About what?"

"About being so short with you." He was being nothing but good to her. He didn't deserve to have her snapping at him.

"Can't help being the height you are," he answered wryly.

"I meant—"

He didn't want her beating herself up about this. God knew she had reason to be upset and short-tempered.

"I know what you meant," he told her, stepping back from the Jeep and then straightening. Holding Wayne securely in his arms, he changed the subject. "I can't get over how little he is. It's like holding a box of sugar. A wiggling box of sugar," he amended as the baby twisted slightly.

He saw that the infant's lips were moving. "Rooting," he thought the nurse had called it on one of his visits to hospital. It was what babies did when they were hungry and searching for their mother's breast.

"I think your son is trying to order an early dinner," he told her. Wayne had latched on to his shirt and was sucking on it. Very gently, he extracted the material from the infant's mouth.

Wayne whimpered.

Eli was right, Kasey realized. The nurse had brought her son to her for a feeding approximately four hours ago. She needed to feed him.

Kasey took the baby from Eli and Wayne turned his little head so that his face was now against her breast. As before, he began questing and a frustrated little noise emerged from his small, rosebud mouth.

"I think you're right," she said to Eli, never taking her eyes off her son.

She still wasn't used to Wayne or the concept that she was actually a mother. Right now, she was in awe of this small, perfect little human being who had come into her life. Holding him was like holding a small piece of heaven, she thought.

That her best friend seemed so attuned to her son made her feel both happy and sad. Happy because she had someone to share this wondrous experience with and sad because as good and kind as Eli was, she was supposed to be sharing this with Hollis. Her husband was supposed to be standing beside her. He should be the one holding their son and marveling about how perfect he was.

Instead, Eli was saying all those things while Hollis was out there somewhere, heading for the hills. Or possibly for a good time. And it was Hollis who had gambled their home right out from under them and then hadn't been man enough to face her with the news. He'd sent in Eli to take his place.

What kind of man did that to the woman he loved—unless he didn't love her anymore, she suddenly thought. Was that it? Had he just woken up one morning to find that he'd fallen out of love with her? The thought stung her heart, but she had a feeling that she was right.

Meanwhile, Wayne was growing progressively insistent and more frustrated that there was nothing to be suckled from his mother's blouse. All that was happening was that he was leaving a circular wet spot.

Glancing toward the protesting infant, Eli abandoned the suitcase he was about to take out.

"I'd better get you inside and settled in before Wayne decides to make a meal out of your blouse," he said. Nodding at the suitcase, he told her, "This other stuff can wait."

With that, he hurried over to the front door and unlocked it. Like most of the people in and around Forever, he usually left the front door unlocked during the daytime. But knowing he was going to be gone for a while, he'd thought it was more prudent to lock up before he'd left this morning.

Not that he actually had anything worth stealing, but he figured that coming into a house that had just been ransacked would have been an unsettling experience for Kasey, and he'd wanted everything to be as perfect as possible for her.

Despite their friendship, coming here wasn't going to be easy for her. Kasey had her pride—at times, that was *all* she had and she'd clung to it—and her pride would have been compromised twice over if she'd had to stay in a recently robbed house. If nothing else, it would have made her exceedingly uneasy about the baby's safety, not to mention her own.

She had more than enough to worry about as it was. He wanted to make this transition to his house as painless, hell, as *easy* as possible for her. That meant no surprises when he opened the front door to his house.

"Don't expect much," he told her as he pushed the front door open. "I'm still just settling in and getting the hang of this place. It'll look a lot better once I get a chance to get some new things in here and spruce the place up a bit."

Walking in ahead of him, Kasey looked around slowly, taking everything in. She knew that Eli had bought the ranch in the past couple of months. Though she'd wanted to, she hadn't had the opportunity to come by to visit. It wasn't so much that she'd been too busy to spare the time, but that she'd had a feeling, deep down, Hollis hadn't wanted her to come over. That was why, she surmised, he'd kept coming up with excuses about why he wasn't able to bring her over and he'd been completely adamant about her not going anywhere alone in "her condition," as if her pregnancy had drained all of her intelligence from her, rendering her incapacitated.

Not wanting to be drawn into yet another futile, pointless argument, she'd figured it was easier just to go along with what Hollis was saying. In her heart, she knew that Eli would understand.

Eli always understood, she thought now, wondering why she'd been such a blind fool when it came to Hollis. There were times, she had to reluctantly admit, when Hollis could be as shallow as a wading pool.

At other times…

There *were* no other times. If he'd had a moment of kindness, of understanding, those points were all wiped out by what he'd done now. A man who'd walked out on his family *had* no redeeming qualities.

She forced herself to push all thoughts of Hollis

from her mind. She couldn't deal with that right now. Instead she focused on Eli's house.

"It's cozy," she finally commented with a nod, and hoped that she sounded convincing.

He went around, turning on lights even though it was still afternoon. The sun, he'd noticed shortly after buying the ranch, danced through the house early in the morning. By the time midafternoon came, the tour was finished and the sun had moved on to another part of the ranch, leaving the house bathed in shadows. It didn't bother him, but he didn't want to take the chance that it might add to Kasey's justifiably dark mood.

"By 'cozy' you mean 'little,'" he corrected with a laugh. He took no offense. By local standards, his ranch was considered small. But everything had to start somewhere. "I figure I can always build on to it once I get a little bit of time set aside," he told her.

She nodded. "I'm sure your brothers would be willing to help you build."

"And Alma," he reminded her. "Don't forget about Alma."

His sister, the youngest in their family and currently one of the sheriff's three deputies, was always the first to have her hand up, the first to volunteer for anything. She was, and always had been, highly competitive. At times he had the feeling that the very act of breathing was some sort of a competition for Alma, if it meant that she could do it faster than the rest of them.

His sister had slowed down some, he thought—and

they were all grateful for that—now that Cash was in the picture. The one-time resident of Forever had gone on to become a highly sought-after criminal lawyer, but he was giving it all up to marry Alma and settle down in Forever again. He knew they all had Cash to thank for this calmer, gentler version of Alma. Eli could only hope that Alma was going to continue on this less frantic route indefinitely.

"Nobody ever forgets Alma," Kasey said fondly. Wayne, his cries getting louder, was now mewling like a neglected, hungry kitten. She began to rock him against her chest, trying to soothe him for a minute longer. "Um, could you show me where we'll be staying?"

Because Hollis had caught him by surprise, he hadn't had time to do much of anything by way of getting her room ready for her—or, for that matter, make up his mind about which room might be better suited to her and the baby. He was pretty much winging it. Stopping to buy the infant seat, as well as bringing over the baby's crib, was just about all he'd had time for before driving to the hospital.

"For now, why don't you just go into the back bedroom and use that?" he suggested. When she continued looking at him quizzically, he realized that she didn't know what room he was talking about. "C'mon—" he beckoned "—I'll show you."

Turning, Eli led the way to the only bedroom located on the first floor. Luckily for him—and Kasey—the room did have a bed in it. It, along with the rest of the furnishings, had come with the house. The previous owner had sold him the house on the one condition that he wasn't going to have to move out his furniture. That, the old widower had told him, would be one big hassle for him, especially since he was flying to Los Angeles to live with his daughter and her family.

Eli, who hadn't had a stick of furniture to his name, had readily agreed. For both it had been a win-win situation.

Opening the bedroom door, he turned on the overhead light and then gestured toward the full-size bed against the wall. It faced a bureau made of dark wood. The pieces matched and both were oppressively massive-looking.

"Make yourself comfortable," Eli urged. Stepping to the side, he added, "I'm going to go out and get your suitcase. Holler if you need anything."

And with that, he turned and left the room.

Kasey watched him walk away. With each step that took him farther away from her, she could feel her uneasiness growing.

I'm hollering, Eli. I'm hollering, she silently told him.

You're not the only one in the room, she reminded herself.

Smiling down at Wayne, she turned her attention toward quelling her son's mounting, ever-louder cries of distress.

Chapter Four

Eli kept looking at the door to the downstairs bedroom, waiting for it to open. It seemed to him as if Kasey had been in there with the baby for a long time.

Was that normal?

He debated knocking on the door to ask if everything was all right. But on the other hand, he didn't want Kasey to feel as if he was crowding her, either.

He didn't know what to do with himself, so he just kept watching the door for movement. He had no idea how long it took to actually feed an infant. Alma was the last one born in their family and since he was only eleven months older, he never had the opportunity to be around an infant.

Dragging a hand through his unruly, thick black hair, he blew out an impatient breath. No doubt about it, he'd never felt so out of his depth before.

When he glanced down at his watch, he noted that twenty minutes had passed. Again he wondered if he should be worried that something was wrong. Though she'd tried to hide it, Kasey had been pretty upset when she'd gone into the bedroom with the infant.

Not that he could blame her. The man she'd wanted to count on had abandoned her without so much as a shred of consideration for how she would feel about the situation. Hollis certainly hadn't had the courage to face her before he'd pulled his disappearing act.

She really was better off without him, but, if he said anything like that now, it might strike her as cold.

Frustrated, concerned, Eli ran his hand through his hair again, trying to think of a possible way to make things better for Kasey.

Maybe Hollis should have at least left her a letter or some sort of a note, apologizing for his actions and telling her that he just needed to get his head straight. That once that happened, maybe he could come back and do right by her. The more he thought about it, the more certain he became that Kasey would have taken comfort in that.

But there was no point in reflecting on that, since Hollis hadn't even been thoughtful enough of her feelings to do something as simple as that—

Eli stopped thinking of what was and began thinking of what should have been.

If it helped, why not?

He looked at the door again, and then at the old-fashioned writing desk butted up against the far wall in the living room. Weighing the pros and cons, he wavered for less than a moment, then quickly crossed over to the desk, took out a piece of paper, a pen and an envelope.

With one eye on the entrance to the living room,

watching for Kasey, he quickly dashed off a note of apology to her, doing his best to approximate Hollis's handwriting, then signed it *Hollis*.

He'd just finished sealing the envelope when he heard the bedroom door opening. The very next moment, he heard Kasey calling to him.

"Eli? Eli, are you down here?" Her voice sounded as if she was coming closer.

Stuffing the envelope into his back pocket, Eli raised his own voice slightly. "Out here. I'm in the living room."

The next moment Kasey walked into the room. Both she and the baby looked somewhat calmer.

"Well, he's all fed and changed, thanks to the disposable diapers in that little care packet the hospital gave me." Even as she said it, Kasey caught her lower lip between her teeth.

He was so tuned in to her, he could almost read her mind. She was already thinking ahead to all the things she was going to need, including a veritable mountain of disposable diapers.

"Well, unless we can get Wayne potty-trained by tonight, you're going to need more of those," he commented, taking the burden of having to mention it from her. "Tell you what, why don't you make up a list of what you'll need and I'll take a quick trip into town?" Eli suggested.

Kasey smiled, grateful for his thoughtfulness. How did one man turn out like this while another—

Don't go there, she warned herself. There weren't

any answers for her there and she would drive herself crazy with the questions.

"Sounds like a good idea," she agreed. Then her eyes narrowed as she saw the long envelope sticking out of his back pocket. "What's that?" she asked.

Appearing properly confused, Eli reached behind himself. He pulled out the envelope, looked at it and slowly allowed recognition to enter his expression.

"Oh, in all the excitement of bringing you and Wayne home, I totally forgot about this."

Kasey cocked her head, curious as she studied him. "Forgot about what?"

"When Hollis came over in the middle of the night to ask me to look after you, he wanted me to give this to you." And with that, he handed her the envelope.

She stared at it, then looked up at Eli. "Hollis left me a letter?" That really didn't sound like the Hollis she knew. He would have made fun of anyone who actually put anything in writing.

"I don't know if it's a letter or not, but he left something," Eli told her vaguely. "Here, why don't you let me hold on to the little guy so you can open the envelope and see what's inside." Even as he made the offer, Eli was already taking Wayne away from her and into his arms.

Really puzzled now, Kasey nodded absently in Eli's direction and opened the envelope. The letter inside was short and to the point. It was also thoughtfully worded. She read it twice, and then one last time, before raising her eyes to Eli's face. She looked at him for a long moment.

Swaying slightly to lull the baby in his arms, he looked at her innocently. "So? What did Hollis have to say?"

She glanced down at the single sheet before answering. "That he was sorry. That it's not me, it's him. He doesn't want to hurt me, but he just needs some time away to get his head together. Until he does, he can't be the husband and father that we deserve. In the meantime, he'll send money for the baby and me when he can," she concluded. Very deliberately, she folded the letter and placed it back in its envelope.

Eli nodded. "That sounds about right. That's more or less what he said to me before he left," he explained when she looked at him quizzically. "At least he apologized to you."

"Yes, at least he apologized," she echoed quietly, raising her eyes to his. Still looking at him, she tucked the letter into her own pocket. There was an odd expression on her face.

Did she suspect? He couldn't tell. There were times, such as now, when her expression was completely unreadable.

The next moment Kasey took her son back from Eli and sat with the infant on the sofa. A very loud sigh escaped her lips.

Eli perched on the arm of the sofa and looked into her face. Hollis was clearly out of his mind, walking away from this.

"Are you all right, Kasey?" he asked solicitously.

She nodded her head slowly in response. When she spoke, her voice seemed as if it was coming from a very far distance. And, in a way, she supposed it was. With each word he uttered, she closed the door a little further to her past.

He was about to ask her again when Kasey abruptly began to talk.

"I guess, deep down, I knew that Hollis wasn't the father type. As long as it was just him and me, he could put up with some domesticity, provided it didn't smother him."

Her eyes stung and she paused for a moment before continuing. She didn't tell Eli about the times she suspected that Hollis was stepping out on her, that he was seeing other women. There was no point in talking about that now.

"But then I got pregnant, and once the baby was here, it really hit Hollis that he might have to..." Her voice trailed off for a moment as she struggled with herself, vacillating between being angry at Hollis and feeling disloyal to him for talking about him this way. For once, anger won out. "That he might have to grow up," she finally said.

"First of all, you didn't just 'get pregnant,'" Eli corrected. "Last time I checked, it took two to make that happen. Hollis was just as responsible for this as you were," he pointed out.

Kasey smiled affectionately at him then. Smiled as she leaned forward and lightly touched his face. Both the look and the touch spoke volumes. But Eli had no interpreter and he wasn't sure just what was hidden behind her smile or even *if* there was something hidden behind her smile.

All he knew was that, as usual, her smile drew him in. There were times, when he allowed his guard to slip, that he loved her so much that it hurt.

It would be hard having her here under his roof, sleeping here under his roof, and keeping a respectful distance from her at all times.

Not that he would ever disrespect her, he vowed, but God, he wanted to hold her in his arms right now. And more than anything in the world, he wanted to lean over and kiss her. Kiss her just once like a lover and not like a friend.

But that was impossible, and it would ruin everything between them.

So he rose off the arm of the sofa and got down to the business of making this arrangement work. "If you could just give me that list of things—"

"Sure. I'm going to need a pen and some paper," Kasey prompted when he just remained standing there.

"Right."

Coming to life, Eli was about to fetch both items from the same desk he had just used to write that "note from Hollis" to her when there was a knock on the front door.

The first thing Eli thought of was that Hollis had had a change of heart and, making an assumption that Kasey would be here, had returned for his wife and son.

A glance at Kasey's face told him she was thinking the same thing.

As he strode toward the door, Eli struggled to ignore the deep-seated feeling of disappointment flooding him.

Kasey followed in his wake.

But when he threw open his door, it wasn't Hollis that either one of them saw standing there. It was Miss Joan and one of her waitresses from the diner, a tall, big-boned young woman named Carla. Miss Joan was holding a single bag in her exceptionally slender arms. Carla was holding several more with incredible ease, as if all combined they weighed next to nothing.

"Figured you two had probably gotten back from the hospital by now," Miss Joan declared. Her eyes were naturally drawn to the baby and she all but cooed at him. "My, but he's a cutie, he is."

And then she looked up from the baby and directly at Eli. "Well, aren't you going to invite us in, or are you looking to keep Kasey and her son all to yourself?"

Eli snapped to attention. "Sorry, you just surprised me, that's all, Miss Joan," he confessed. "C'mon in," he invited, stepping back so that she and the waitress had room to walk in.

He watched the older woman with some amusement as she looked slowly around. Miss Joan made no secret that she was scrutinizing everything in the house.

As was her custom, Miss Joan took possession of all she surveyed.

"I don't recall hearing about a tornado passing through Forever lately." She raised an eyebrow as she glanced in his direction.

Eli knew she was referring to the fact that as far as housekeeping went, he got a failing grade. With a shrug, he told her, "Makes it easier to find things if they're all out in the open."

Miss Joan shook her head. "If you say so." She snorted. "Looks like this could be a nice little place you've got here, Eli." Her eyes swept over the general chaos. "Once you get around to digging yourself out of this mess, of course." She waved her hand around the room, dismissing the subject now that she'd touched on it.

"Anyway, I got tired of waiting for an invite, so I just decided to invite myself over." Pausing, the older woman looked at Eli meaningfully. "Thought you might need a few things for the new guy," she told him, nodding at the baby in Kasey's arms.

"Oh, I can't—" Kasey began to protest. The last thing she wanted was for people to think of her as a charity case.

"Sure you can," Miss Joan said, cutting Kasey off with a wave of her hand. Then she directed her attention to the young woman who had come with her. "Just set everything down on the coffee table, Carla," she instructed. She shifted her eyes toward Kasey. "I'll let you sort things out when you get a chance," she told her. "Brought you some diapers and a bunch of other items. These new little guys need a lot to get them spruced up and shining." She said it as if it was a prophesy.

Miss Joan was right. She couldn't afford to let her pride get in the way, or, more accurately, Wayne couldn't afford to have her pride get in his way.

"I don't know what to say," Kasey said to Miss Joan, emotion welling up in her throat and threatening to choke off her words.

"Didn't ask you to say anything, now, did I?" Miss Joan pointed out. And then the woman smiled. "It's what we do around here, remember? We look out for each other." She nodded at the largest paper bag that Carla set down. Because she had run out of room on the coffee table, Carla had deposited the bag on the floor beside one of the table legs. "Thought the baby might not be the only one who was hungry, so I brought you two some dinner. My advice is to wait until you put him down before you start eating."

"What do I owe you?" Eli asked, taking his wallet out.

Miss Joan put her hand over his before he could take any bills out. "We'll settle up some other time," she informed him.

Kasey wasn't about to bother asking Miss Joan how the woman knew that she was here, at Eli's ranch, rather than at her own ranch. Even when things were actually kept a secret, Miss Joan had a way of knowing about them. Miss Joan *always* knew. She ran the town's only diner and dispensed advice and much-needed understanding along with the best coffee in Texas.

Joan Randall had been a fixture in Forever for as long as anyone could remember and had just recently given in to the entreaties of her very persistent suitor. She and Harry Monroe had gotten married recently in an outdoor wedding with the whole town in attendance. Even so, everyone still continued to refer to her as Miss Joan. Calling her anything else just didn't feel right.

Having done everything she'd set out to do, Miss Joan indicated that it was time to leave.

"Okay, Carla and I'll be heading out now," she announced, then paused a moment longer to look at Kasey. "You need anything, you just give me a call, understand, baby girl?" And then she lowered her voice only slightly as she walked by Eli. "You take care of her, hear?"

He didn't need any prompting to do that. He'd been watching over Kasey for as long as he could remember.

"I fully intend to, Miss Joan," he told her with feeling.

Miss Joan nodded as she crossed the threshold. She knew he meant it. Knew what was in his heart better than he did.

"Good. Because she's been through enough." Then, lowering her voice even further so that only Eli could hear her, she told him, "I ever see that Hollis again, I'm going to take a lot of pleasure in turning that rooster into a hen."

Eli had absolutely no doubts that the older woman was very capable of doing just that. He grinned. "Better not let the sheriff hear you say that."

Miss Joan smiled serenely at him. "Rick won't say anything. Not with Alma helping me and being his deputy and all. Your sister doesn't like that bastard any better than any of us do," she confided. Then, raising her voice so that Kasey could hear her, she urged, "Don't wait too long to have your dinner." With a nod of her head, she informed them that "It tastes better warm."

One final glance at Kasey and the baby, and the woman was gone. Carla was right behind her, moving with surprising speed given her rather large size.

"I didn't tell her about Hollis" was the first thing Eli said as he closed the door again and turned around to face Kasey. He didn't want her thinking that he had been spreading her story around.

Kasey knew he hadn't. This was Miss Joan they were talking about. Everyone was aware of her ability to ferret out information.

"Nobody ever has to tell that woman anything. She just *knows*. It's almost spooky," Kasey confessed. "When I was a little girl, I used to think she was a witch—a good witch," she was quick to add with a smile. "Like in *The Wizard of Oz*, but still a witch." At times, she wasn't completely convinced that the woman *wasn't* at least part witch.

He grinned. "Out of the mouths of babes," he quipped. "Speaking of babes, I think your little guy just fell asleep again. Probably in self-defense so that he didn't have to put up with being handled." He grinned. "Carla looked like she was dying to get her hands on him." He had noticed that the waitress had struggled to hold herself in check. "But then, I guess that everyone loves a new baby."

The second the words were out, he realized what he'd said and he could have bitten off his tongue.

Especially when Kasey answered quietly, "No, not everyone."

He could almost *see* the wound in her heart opening up again.

Dammit, he would have to be more careful about what he said around Kasey. At least for a while. "Let me rephrase that. Any *normal* person loves a new baby."

Kasey knew he meant well. She offered Eli a weak smile in response, then looked down at her son.

"I'll try putting him to bed so that we can have our dinner. But I can't make any promises. He's liable to wake up just as I start tiptoeing out. Feel perfectly free to start without me," she urged as she walked back to the rear bedroom with Wayne.

As if he could, Eli thought, watching her as she left the room.

The truth of it was, he couldn't start anything anywhere, not as long as she continued to hold his heart hostage the way she did.

Shaking free of his thoughts, Eli went to set the table in the kitchen. With any luck, he mused, he'd find two clean dishes still in the cupboard. Otherwise, he would actually have to wash a couple stacked in the sink.

It wasn't a prospect he looked forward to.

Chapter Five

Eli wasn't sure just when he finally fell asleep. The fact that he actually *did* fall asleep surprised him. Mentally, he'd just assumed that he would be up all night. After all, this was Kasey's first night in his house, not to mention her first night with the baby without the safety net of having a nurse close by to take Wayne back to the nursery if he started crying.

Granted, he wasn't a nurse, but at least he could be supportive and make sure that she didn't feel as if she was in this alone. He could certainly relieve her when she got tired.

Last night, when it was time to turn in, Kasey had thanked him for his hospitality and assured him that she had everything under control. She'd slipped into the same bedroom she'd used earlier. The crib he'd retrieved from her former home was set up there.

Her last words to him were to tell him that he should get some sleep.

Well *that* was easier said than done, he'd thought at the time, staring off into the starless darkness outside his window. He'd felt much too wired. Besides, he was listening for any sound that struck him as being out of the ordinary. A sound that would tell him that Kasey needed help. Which in turn would mean that she needed him, at least for this.

He almost strained himself, trying to hear if the baby was crying.

It was probably around that time that, exhausted, he'd fallen asleep.

When he opened his eyes again, he was positive that only a few minutes had gone by. Until he realized that daylight, not moonlight, was streaming into his room. Startled, he bolted upright. Around the same moment of rude awakening, the aroma of tantalizingly strong coffee wound its intoxicating way up to his room and into his senses.

Kicking off a tangled sheet, Eli hit the ground running, stumbling over his discarded boots on his way to his door. It hurt more because he was barefoot.

Even so, he didn't bother putting anything on his feet as he followed the aroma to its point of origin, making his way down the stairs.

Ultimately, the scent brought him to the kitchen.

Kasey was there, with her back toward him. Wayne wasn't too far away—and was strapped into his infant seat. Sometime between last night and this morning, she'd gotten the baby's infant seat out of the car and converted it so that it could hold him securely in place while she had him on the kitchen table.

Turning from the stove, Kasey almost jumped a foot off the ground. Her hand immediately went to her chest, as if she was trying to keep her heart from physically leaping out.

"Oh, Eli, you scared me," she said, struggling to regain her composure.

"Sorry," he apologized when he saw that he'd really startled her. "I don't exactly look my best first thing in the morning." He ran his hand through his hair, remembering that it hadn't seen a hint of a comb since yesterday.

"You look fine," she stressed. No matter what, Eli *always* looked fine, she thought fondly. She could count on the fact that nothing changed about him, especially not his temperament. He was her rock and she thanked God for him. "I just wasn't expecting anyone to come up behind me, that's all." She took in a deep breath in an attempt to regulate her erratic pulse.

"What are you doing up?" he asked.

"Well, I never got into the habit of cooking while I was lying in bed," she stated, deadpan. "So I had to come over to where the appliances were hiding," she told him, tongue-in-cheek.

But Eli shook his head, dismissing the literal answer to his question. "No, I mean *why* are you up, cooking? You're supposed to be taking it easy, remember?" he reminded her.

She acted mystified. "I guess I missed that memo. Besides, this *is* how I take it easy," she informed him. "Cooking relaxes me. It makes me feel like I'm in control," she stressed. Her eyes held his. "And right now, I need that."

He knew how overwhelming a need that could be. Eli raised his hands in surrender. "Okay, cook your heart out. I won't stand in your way," he promised, then confessed, "And that *does* smell pretty amazing." He looked from her to the pan and then back again. He didn't remember buying bacon. Maybe Alma had dropped it off the last time she'd been by. She had a tendency to mother him. "And that was all stuff you found in my pantry?"

"And your refrigerator," Kasey added, amused that the contents of his kitchen seemed to be a mystery to him. "By the way, if you're interested, I made coffee."

"Interested?" he repeated. "I'm downright mesmerized. That's what brought me down in the first place," he told her as he made a beeline for the battered coffeepot that stood on the back burner. Not standing on ceremony, he poured himself a cup, then paused to deeply inhale the aroma before sampling it. *Perfect,* he thought. It was a word he used a lot in reference to Kasey.

He looked at her now in unabashed surprise. "And you did this with *my* coffee?"

She merely smiled at him, as if he were a slightly thought-challenged second cousin she had grown very fond of. "Yours was the only coffee I had to work with," she pointed out. "Why? You don't like it?"

He took another extralong sip of the black liquid, waiting as it all but burned a path for itself into his belly.

"Like it?" He laughed incredulously at her question. "I'm thinking of marrying it."

Outwardly he seemed to be teasing her, but it was his way of defusing some of the tension ricocheting through him. He was using humor as a defense mechanism so that she didn't focus on the fact that he struggled not to melt whenever he was within several feet of her. Though he had brought her here with the very best of intentions, he had to admit that just having her here was all but undoing him.

"Really, though," he forced himself to say, putting his hand over hers to stop her movements for a second, "you shouldn't be doing all this. I didn't bring you here to be my cook—good as you are at it."

She smiled up at him, a thousand childhood memories crowding her head. Memories in which Eli was prominently featured. He was the one she had turned to when her father had been particularly nasty the night before. Eli always knew how to make her feel better.

"I know that," she told him. "You brought me here because you're good and kind and because Wayne and I didn't have a place to stay. This is just my small way of paying you back a little."

He shook his head. "This isn't a system of checks and balances, Kasey. You don't have to 'pay me back,'" he insisted. "You don't owe me anything."

Oh, yes, I do. More than you can ever guess. You kept me sane, Eli. I hate to think where I'd be right now without you.

Her eyes met his, then she looked down at his hand, which was still over hers. Belatedly, he removed it. She felt a small pang and told herself she was just being silly.

"I know," she told him. And that was because Eli always put others, in this case her, first. "But I want to." Taking a plate—one of two she'd just washed so that she could press them into service—she slid two eggs and half the bacon onto it. "Overeasy, right?" she asked, nodding at the plate she put down on the table.

They'd had breakfast together just once—at Miss Joan's diner years ago, before she'd ever run off with Hollis. At the time, he envisioned a lifetime of breakfasts to be shared between them.

But that was aeons ago.

Stunned, he asked, "How did you remember?" as he took his seat at the table.

She lifted her slender shoulders in a quick, dismissive shrug. "Some things just stay with me, I guess." She took her own portion and sat across from him at the small table. "Is it all right?" she asked. For the most part, it was a rhetorical question, since he appeared to be eating with enthusiasm.

Had she served him burned tire treads, he would have said the same thing—because she'd gone out of her way for him and the very act meant a great deal to him. More than he could possibly ever tell her, because he didn't want to risk scaring her off.

"It's fantastic," he assured her.

The baby picked that moment to begin fussing.

Within a few moments, fussing turned to crying. Kasey looked toward the noise coming from the converted infant seat. "I just fed him half an hour ago," she said wearily.

"Then he's not hungry," Eli concluded.

He remembered overhearing the sheriff's sister-in-law, Tina, saying that infants cried for three reasons: if they were hungry, if they needed to be changed and if they were hurting. Wayne had been fed and he didn't look as if he was in pain. That left only one last reason.

"He's probably finished processing his meal," he guessed. "Like puppies, there's a really short distance between taking food in and eliminating what isn't being used for nutrition," he told her.

With a small, almost suppressed sigh, Kasey nodded. She started to get up but he put his hand on her arm, stopping her. She looked at him quizzically.

"Stay put, I'll handle this." Eli nodded at his empty plate. "I'm finished eating, anyway." He picked Wayne up and took him into the next room.

She watched him a little uncertainly. This was really going above and beyond the call of duty, she couldn't help thinking.

"Have you ever changed a diaper before?" she asked him.

He didn't answer her directly, because the answer to her question was no. So he said evasively, "It's not exactly up there with the mysteries of life."

Changing a diaper might not be up there with the mysteries of life, but in his opinion, how something so cute and tiny could produce so much waste *was* one of the mysteries of life.

"This has got to weigh at least as much as you do," he stated, marveling as he stripped the diaper away from the baby and saw what was inside.

Making the best of it, Eli went through several damp washcloths, trying to clean Wayne's tiny bottom. It took a bit of work.

Eli began to doubt the wisdom of his volunteering for this form of latrine duty, but he'd done it with the best of intentions. He wanted Kasey to be able to at least finish her meal in peace. She didn't exactly seem worn-out, but she certainly did look tired. He wondered just how much sleep she'd gotten last night.

After throwing the disposable diaper into the wastebasket, he deposited the dirty washcloths on top of it. The latter would need to be put into the washing machine—as soon as he fixed it.

Dammit, anyway, he thought in frustration, recalling that the last load of wash had flooded the utility room.

Served him right for not getting to something the second it needed doing. But then, life on a ranch—especially since he was the only one working it—left very little spare time to do anything else, whether it was a chore or just kicking back for pleasure.

And now that Kasey and her son were here—

And now that they were here, Eli amended, determined to throw this into a positive experience, there was an abundance of sunshine in his life, not to mention a damn good reason to get up in the morning.

There! he thought with a triumphant smile as he concluded the Great Diaper Change. He felt particularly pleased with himself.

The next moment he told himself not to get used to this feeling or the situation that created it. After all, it could, and most likely *would,* change in a heartbeat.

Hadn't his life come to a skidding halt and changed just with Hollis banging on his door, abandoning his responsibilities on the doorstep? Well, just like that, Kasey could go off and find her own place.

Or Hollis might come back and want to pick up where he'd left off. And Kasey, being the softhearted woman she was, would wind up forgiving him and take Hollis back. After all, the man *was* her husband.

But that was later, Eli silently insisted. For now, Kasey was here, in his house with her baby, and he would enjoy every second of it.

Every second that he wasn't working, he amended.

Picking Wayne up, he surveyed his handiwork. "Not a bad job, even if I do say so myself," he pronounced.

Ready to go back out, he turned around toward the door with the baby in his arms. He was surprised to find that Kasey was standing in the doorway, an amused expression on her face.

What was she thinking? he couldn't help wondering. "Have you been standing there long?" he asked.

She smiled broadly at him. "Just long enough to

hear you evaluating your job," she said. Kasey crossed to him and her son. "And you're wrong, you know," she told him as she took Wayne into her arms with an unconscious, growing confidence. "You're being way too modest. You did an absolutely *great* job." There was admiration in her voice. "The nurse had to walk me through the diapering process three times before I got the hang of it," she told him with a wide smile. "You never told me you had hidden talents."

"Didn't know, myself," he freely confessed. "I guess that some people just rise to the occasion more than others."

She thought about him opening his home to her. They were friends, good friends, but that didn't automatically mean she could just move in with him. He had been under no obligation to take her in. She certainly hadn't expected him to do that.

Looking at him pointedly, she nodded. "Yes, they do," she agreed softly.

For one shimmering second, as he stood there, gazing into her eyes, he felt an incredibly overwhelming desire to kiss her. Kiss her and make a full confession about all the years he'd loved her in silence.

But he sensed he might scare her off. That was the last thing that either one of them wanted, especially him. He needed to put some space between them. He thought about his ever-growing list of things that needed his attention. Just thinking about them was daunting, but he needed to get started.

Eli abruptly turned toward the door.

"Well, I'd better get to work," he told Kasey. "Or the horses will think I ran off and left them." But instead of heading outside, the smell of a diaper that was past its expiration date caught his attention. "But the horses are just going to have to wait until I take care of this," he told Kasey, nodding at the wastebasket and its less-than-precious pungent cargo.

"Don't bother," Kasey said. "I'll take care of that." To make her point, she placed herself between Eli and the wastebasket. "Go, tend to your horses before they stampede off in protest."

Instead of getting out of his way, she leaned forward and impulsively kissed his cheek. "Thank you for everything," she whispered just before her lips touched his cheek. "Now *go*," she repeated with feeling.

His cheek pulsated where her lips had met his skin.

Eli didn't quite remember going upstairs to put on his boots or walking out of the house and across the front yard, but he figured he must have because when he finally took stock of his surroundings, he was on his way to the stable.

It wasn't as if she'd never kissed him before. She had. She'd kissed him exactly like that a long time ago, before she'd become Hollis's wife and broken his heart into a million pieces. But back then, she'd brushed her lips against his cheek, leaving her mark by way of a friendly demonstration of affection.

And the results were always the same. His body temperature would rise right along with his jumping pulse rate.

Just being around her could set him off, but that went doubly so whenever she brushed by him, whether it was her hand, her lips or the accidental contact of different body parts.

It made him feel alive.

It also reminded him that he loved her. Loved her and knew that he couldn't have her because it was all one-sided.

His side.

But he'd made his peace with that a long time ago, Eli reminded himself as he continued walking. It was enough for him to know that he was looking out for her, that he was ready to defend her at a moment's notice, Hollis or no Hollis. And because of that, she would be all right. If on occasion he yearned for something more, well, that was his problem, not hers.

During the day, he could keep it all under control, enjoying just the little moments, the tiny interactions between them as well as the longer conversations that were exchanged on occasion.

It was only in his sleep that all these emotions became a good deal more. In his dreams he experienced what he couldn't allow himself to feel—or want— during his waking hours.

But that was something he could never let her even remotely suspect, because in disclosing that, he'd risk losing everything, especially her precious friendship.

He wanted, above all else, to have her feel at ease with him. He wanted to protect her and to do what he could to make her happy. That couldn't happen if she thought he might be trying to compromise not just her but her honor, as well.

His own happiness, he reasoned, would come from her feeling secure. *That* he could do for her. For them, he amended, thinking of the baby.

Reaching the stable, he pulled open the doors. The smell from the stalls assaulted him the moment he walked in. Babies weren't all that different from horses in some ways. They ate, digested and then eliminated.

Mucking out the stalls would allow him to put changing a small diaper into perspective.

"Hi, guys," he said, addressing the horses that, for now, made up his entire herd. "Miss me?" One of the horses whinnied, as if in response. Shaking his head, Eli laughed.

Approaching the stallion closest to him, he slipped a bridle over the horse's head, then led Golden Boy out of his stall. He hitched the horse to a side railing so that the animal would be out of the way and he could clean the stall without interference.

"Well, I've got a good excuse for being late," he told the horses as he got to work. "Wait till I tell you what's been going on...."

Chapter Six

Eli worked as quickly as he could, but even so, it took him a great deal of time to clean out the stalls, groom the horses, exercise and train them, then finally feed them.

There were five horses in all.

Five horses might not seem like a lot to the average outsider who was uninformed about raising and training quarter horses, but it was a lengthy procedure, especially when multiplied by five and no one else was around to help with the work.

The latter, he had to admit, was partially his own fault. He didn't have the money to take on hired help, but that still didn't mean that he had to go it alone if he didn't want to.

It was understood that if he needed them, he could easily put out a call to one or more of his brothers and they'd be there to help him for the day or the week. He had four older brothers, ranchers all, and they could readily rotate the work between them until Eli was finally on his feet and on his way to making a profit.

But for Eli it boiled down to a matter of pride—

stubborn pride—and this kept him from calling any of his brothers and asking for help. He was determined that, as the youngest male in the Rodriguez family, he would turn the ranch into a success without having to depend on any help from his relatives.

Ordinarily he found a certain satisfaction in working with the horses and doing all the chores that were involved in caring for the animals. But today was a different story. Impatience fairly hummed through his veins.

He wanted to be done with the chores, done with the training, so that he could go back to the house and be with Kasey. He really didn't like leaving her alone like this for the better part of the day.

He sought to ease his conscience by telling himself that she could do with a little time to herself. What woman couldn't? His being out here gave her the opportunity to get herself together after this enormous emotional roller-coaster ride she'd just been on—gaining a child and losing a husband.

Not that losing Hollis was really much of a loss.

In addition Eli was fairly certain that Kasey wouldn't want him around to witness any first-time mistakes that she was bound to make with the baby. In her place, *he* certainly wouldn't want someone looking over his shoulder, noting the mistakes he was making.

Even if he wanted to chuck everything and go back up to the house to be with her, he couldn't just up and leave the horses. Not again. Not twice in two days. He'd already neglected their training segment yesterday when he'd gone to bring Kasey and the baby home from the hospital in Pine Ridge.

Not that he actually neglected the horses themselves. He'd made sure that he'd left food for the stallions and God knew they had no trouble finding the feed, or the water, for that matter. But the stalls, well, they were decidedly more ripe-smelling than they should have been. Breathing had been a real problem for him this morning as he mucked out the stalls.

Raising horses was a tricky business. He knew that if they were left on their own for too long, the horses could revert back to their original behavior and then all the hours that he'd put into training them would be lost.

Now they wouldn't be lost, he thought with a wisp of satisfaction. But he was really, really beginning to feel beat.

He was also aware of the fact that his stomach had been growling off and on now for the past couple of hours. Maybe even longer. The growling served to remind him that he hadn't brought any lunch with him.

Usually, when that happened, he'd think nothing of just taking a break and going back to the house to get something to eat. But he really didn't want to risk just walking in on Kasey. What if she was in the middle of breast-feeding Wayne?

The thought generated an image in his head that had him pausing practically in midstep as his usually tame imagination took flight.

He had no business thinking of her that way and he

knew it, but that still didn't help him erase the scene from his brain.

Taking a deep breath, Eli forced himself to shake free of the vivid daydream. He had work to do and standing there like some oversexed adolescent, allowing his mind to wander like that, wouldn't accomplish anything—except possibly to frustrate him even further.

Silver Streak, the horse he was currently grooming, suddenly began nudging him, as if clearly making a bid for his attention. The horse didn't stop until he slowly ran his hand over the silken muzzle.

"Sorry, Silver," Eli said, stroking the animal affectionately. "I was daydreaming. I won't let it happen again."

As if in response, the stallion whinnied. Eli grinned. "Always said you were smarter than the average rancher, which in this case would be me," he added with a self-deprecating laugh.

Since it was summer, the sun was still up when Eli fed the last horse and officially called it a day. He had returned all five of the quarter horses to their stalls and then locked the stable doors before finally returning to his house.

Reaching the ranch house, Eli made as much noise as he could on the front porch so that Kasey was alerted to his arrival and would know that he was coming in. He didn't want to catch her off guard.

Satisfied that he'd made enough of a racket to raise

the dead, Eli finally opened the front door and called out a hearty greeting. "Hi, Kasey, I'm coming in."

"Of course you're coming in," Kasey said, meeting him at the door as he walked in. "You live here."

Eli cleared his throat, feeling uncomfortable with the topic he was about to broach. "I thought that maybe you were, you know, *busy,*" he emphasized, settling for a euphemism.

"Well, I guess I have been that," she admitted, shifting her newly awakened son to her other hip. "But that still doesn't explain why you feel you have to shout a warning before walking into your own home."

He didn't hear the last part of her sentence. By then he was too completely stunned to absorb any words at all. Momentarily speechless, Eli retraced his steps and ducked outside to double check that he hadn't somehow stumbled into the wrong house—not that there were any others on the property.

The outside of the house looked like his, he ascertained. The inside, however, definitely did not. It bore no resemblance to the house he had left just this morning.

What was going on here?

"What did you do?" he finally asked.

"You don't like it," Kasey guessed, doing her best to hide her disappointment. She'd really wanted to surprise him—but in a good way. Belatedly she recalled that some men didn't like having their things touched and rearranged.

"I don't *recognize* it," Eli corrected, looking around again in sheer amazement. This was his place? Really?

The house he had left this morning had looked, according to Miss Joan's gentle description of it, as if it had gone dancing with a tornado. There were no rotting carcasses of stray creatures who had accidentally wandered into the house in search of shelter, but that was the most positive thing that could have been said about the disorder thriving within his four walls.

He'd lived in this house for the past five months and in that amount of time, he'd managed to distribute a great deal of useless material throughout the place. Each room had its own share of acquired clutter, whether it was dirty clothing, used dishes, scattered reading material or some other, less identifiable thing. The upshot was that, in general, the sum total of the various rooms made for a really chaotic-looking home.

Or at least it had when he'd left for the stables that morning. This evening, he felt as though someone had transported him to a different universe. Everything appeared to be in its place. The whole area looked so *neat* it almost hurt his eyes to look around.

This would take some getting used to, he couldn't help thinking.

The hopeful expression had returned to Kasey's face. She'd just wanted to surprise and please him. She knew she'd succeeded with the former, but she was hoping to score the latter.

"I just thought that I should clean up a little," she

told him, watching his face for some sign that he actually *liked* what she had done.

"A little?" he repeated, half stunned, half amused. "There was probably less effort involved in building this house in the first place." This cleanup, he knew, had to have been a major undertaking. Barring magical help from singing mice and enchanted elves, she'd accomplished this all herself.

He regarded her with new admiration.

She in turn looked at him, trying to understand why he didn't seem to have wanted her to do this. Had she trespassed on some basic male ritual? Was he saving this mess, not to mention the rumpled clothes and dirty dishes, for some reason?

"You want me to mess things up again?" she offered uncertainly.

"No." He took hold of her by her shoulders, enunciating each word slowly so that they would sink in. "I don't want you to *do* anything. I just wanted you to relax in between feedings. To maybe try to rest up a little, saving your strength. Taking care of a newborn is damn hard enough to get used to without single-handedly trying to restore order to a place that could easily have been mistaken for the town dump—"

She smiled and he could feel her smile going straight to his gut, stirring things up that had no business being stirred up—not without an outlet.

Eli struggled to keep a tight rein on his feelings and on his reaction to her. He succeeded only moderately.

"It wasn't *that* bad," she stressed.

She was being deliberately kind. "But close," he pointed out.

Her mouth curved as she inclined her head. "Close," Kasey allowed. "I like restoring order, making things neat," she explained. "And when he wasn't fussing because he was hungry or needed changing, Wayne cooperated by sleeping. So far, he's pretty low maintenance," she said, glancing at her sleeping son. "I had to do *something* with myself."

"Well, in case you didn't make the connection, that's the time that you're supposed to be sleeping, too," Eli pointed out. "I think that's a law or something. It's written down somewhere in the *New Mother's Basic Manual.*"

"I guess I must have skipped that part," Kasey said, her eyes smiling at him. His stomach picked that moment to rumble rather loudly. Kasey eyed him knowingly. "Are you all finished working for the day?" Eli nodded, trying to silence the noises his stomach was producing by holding his breath. It didn't work. "Good," she pronounced, "because I have dinner waiting."

"Of course you do," he murmured, following her.

He stopped at the bedroom threshold and waited as Kasey gently put her sleeping son down. Wayne continued breathing evenly, indicating a successful transfer. She was taking to this mothering thing like a duck to water, Eli couldn't help thinking. He realized that he was proud of her—and more than a little awed, as well.

He looked around as he walked with her to the kitchen. Everything there was spotless, as well. All in all, Kasey was rather incredible.

"You know, if word of this gets out," he said, gesturing around the general area, "there're going to be a whole bunch of new mothers standing on our porch with pitchforks and torches, looking to string you up."

She gazed at him for a long moment and at first he thought it was because of his vivid description of frontier justice—but then it hit him. She'd picked up on his terminology. He'd said *our* instead of *my*. Without stopping to think, he'd turned his home into *their* home and just like that, he'd officially included her in the scheme of things.

In his life.

Was she angry? Or maybe even upset that he'd just sounded as if he was taking her being here for granted? He really couldn't tell and he didn't want to come right out and ask her on the outside chance that he'd guessed wrong.

His back against the wall, Eli guided the conversation in a slightly different direction. "I just don't want you to think that I invited you to stay here because I really wanted to get a free housekeeper."

Kasey did her best to tamp down her amusement. "So, what you're actually saying is that I could be as sloppy as you if I wanted to?"

He sincerely doubted if the woman had ever experienced a sloppy day in her life, but that was the general gist of what he was trying to get across to her.

She could leave things messy. He had no expectations of her, nor did he want her to feel obligated to do anything except just *be*.

"Yes," he answered.

Kasey shook her head. The grin she'd been attempting to subdue for at least five seconds refused to be kept under wraps.

"That's not possible," she told him. "I think you have achieved a level of chaos that few could do justice to."

Somewhere into the second hour of her cleaning, she'd begun to despair that she was never going to dig herself out of the hole she'd gotten herself into. But she'd refused to be defeated and had just kept on going. In her opinion, the expression on Eli's face when he'd first walked in just now made it *all* worth it.

"How long did you say you've lived here?" she asked innocently.

He didn't even have to pause to think about it. "Five months."

Kasey closed her eyes for a moment, as if absorbing the information required complete concentration on her part. And then she grinned. "Think what you could have done to the house in a year's time."

He'd rather not. Even so, Eli felt obligated to defend himself at least a little. "I would have cleaned up eventually," he protested.

The look on her face told him that she really doubted that, even though, out loud, she humored him. "I'm sure you would have. If only because you ran out of dishes and clothes." Now that she thought of it, she had a feeling that he'd already hit that wall several times over without making any lifestyle changes.

At the mention of the word *clothes,* Eli looked at her sharply, then looked around the room, hoping he was wrong. But he had a sinking feeling that he wasn't.

"Where did you put the clothes?" he asked her, holding his breath, hoping she'd just found something to use as a laundry hamper.

"Right now, they're in the washing machine." Where else would dirty clothes be? Kasey glanced at her watch. "I set the timer for forty-five minutes. The wash should be finished any minute now."

She'd wound up saying the last sentence to Eli's back. He hurried passed her, making a beeline for the utility room.

"What's wrong?" she called after him, doubling her speed to keep up with Eli's long legs.

Eli mentally crossed his fingers before he opened the door leading into the utility room.

He could have spared himself the effort.

Even though he opened the door slowly, a little water still managed to seep out of the other room. Built lower than the rest of the house, the utility room still had its own very minor flood going on.

Right behind him, Kasey looked down at the accumulated water in dismay. Guilt instantly sprang up. She'd repaid his kindness to her by flooding his utility room.

Way to go, Kase.

Thoroughly upset, she asked, "Did I do that?"

"No, the washing machine did that," Eli assured her, his words accompanied by a deep-seated sigh. "I should have told you the washing machine wasn't working right—but in my defense," he felt bound to tell her, "I wasn't anticipating that you'd be such a whirlwind of energy and cleanliness. Noah could have really used someone like you."

"It wouldn't have worked out," she said with a shake of her head. "I have no idea what a cubit is," she told him, referring to the form of measurement that had been popular around Noah's time.

Although she was trying very hard to focus on only the upbeat, there was no denying that she felt awful for compounding his work. She'd only wanted to do something nice for Eli and this definitely didn't qualify.

"I'm really very sorry about the flooding. I'll pay for the washing machine repairs," she offered.

Kasey wasn't sure just how she would pay for it because she had a rather sick feeling that Hollis had helped himself to their joint account before leaving town. But even if everything was gone and she *had* no money, she was determined to find a way to make proper restitution. Eli deserved nothing less.

Eli shook his head. "The washing machine was broken before you ever got here," he told her. "There's absolutely no reason for you to pay for anything. Don't give it another thought."

There had to be at least two inches of standing water in the utility room, Kasey judged. The only reason it hadn't all come pouring into the house when he'd opened that door was because the utility room had been deliberately built to be just a little lower than the rest of the house—more likely in anticipation of just these kinds of scenarios.

"But I caused this." She gestured toward the water. None of this would have happened if she hadn't filled up the washing machine, poured in the laundry detergent and hit Start.

"I want to make it up to you," Kasey told him earnestly.

He had a feeling that he just wasn't destined to win this argument with her. Besides, she probably needed to make some sort of amends to assuage her conscience.

Who was he to stand in the way of that?

But right now, he really had a more pressing subject to pursue.

"You said something about having to make dinner?" he asked on behalf of his exceptionally animated stomach, which currently felt as if it was playing the final death scene from *Hamlet*.

"It's right back here," she prompted, indicating the plates presently warming on the stove. "And I don't have to make it, it's already made," she told him.

"That's perfect, because the washing machine was already broken. Looks like one thing cancels out the other." Satisfied that he'd temporarily put the subject to bed, he said, "Let's go eat," with the kind of urgency that only a starving man could manage. "And then I'll fix the washing machine," he concluded. "That way you get to keep Wayne in clean clothes," he added.

And you, too, she thought as she nodded and led the way back to the kitchen. *I get to keep you in clean clothes, too.*

She had no idea why that thought seemed to hearten her the way it did, but there was no denying the fact that it did.

A lot.

She smiled to herself as she placed his plate in front of him. If the smile was a little brighter, a little wider than normal, she really wasn't aware of it.

But Eli was.

Chapter Seven

"So how's it going?"

Busy taking a quick inventory of the groceries he'd placed in his cart, Eli glanced up. He was surprised to discover his sister standing at his side. She hadn't been there a moment ago.

Or had she?

He'd been completely focused on picking up the supplies Kasey said they needed and getting back to the ranch as quickly as possible. That described the way he'd been doing everything these past three weeks: quickly. He'd do what had to be done and then get back to being with Kasey and the baby. He was eager to get back to his own private tiny piece of paradise before it suddenly vanished on him.

Eli had no illusions. He *knew* that it wasn't going to be like this forever. Life wasn't meant to be cozy, soul-satisfying and made up of tiny triumphs and small echoes of laughter. But while it was, he intended to make the very most of it, to enjoy every single second that he could and count himself extremely lucky. These moments would have to last him once she was gone.

Alma had been taking her turn at patrolling the streets of Forever when she'd passed Eli's familiar Jeep. She'd immediately parked and gone into the Emporium looking for him. They hadn't talked since the day he'd brought Kasey back from the hospital when she and the sheriff had gotten some of Kasey's things, as well as the baby crib, out of the house that her no-account husband had lost in a poker game.

Her brother looked tired, Alma thought. Tired, but definitely happy.

Happiness didn't come cheap. She knew all about that. She also knew that when happiness showed up on your doorstep, you grabbed it with both hands and held on as tightly as possible.

"Alma Rodriguez, remember?" she prompted, pretending to introduce herself to him. "Your sister," she added when he just stared at her. "I know it's been a while, but I haven't changed *that* much. I recognize you," she told him brightly.

Not wanting to come back to the store for at least a week, Eli began to move up and down the aisles again, filling his cart. Alma matched him step for step.

"Very funny, Alma."

"No," she said honestly. "Very sweet, actually. All this domesticity seems to be agreeing with you, big brother." She examined him more closely for a moment, her head cocked as if that helped her process the information better. Eli continued moving. "Are you gaining weight, Eli?"

That stopped him for a second. "No," he retorted defensively although he really had no way of knowing that for certain. He didn't own a scale, at least not one for weighing people. Usually his clothes let him know if he was gaining or losing weight. For as long as he could remember, he'd worn jeans that proclaimed his waist to be a trim thirty-two inches, and they fit just fine these days, so he took that to be an indication that his weight was stable.

Although he wouldn't have really been surprised if he *had* gained weight. Kasey insisted on cooking every night, and that woman could make hot water taste like some sort of exotic fare fit for a king.

Seeing that her brother wasn't in the mood to be teased, Alma decided to back off. She knew first-hand what it felt like to be in a situation that defied proper description even though her heart had been completely invested.

She'd always had her suspicions about the way Eli had felt about Kasey and now, judging by what was going on, she was more than a little convinced that she was right. But saying so would have probably put her on the receiving end of some rather choice words.

Or, at the very least, on the receiving end of some very caustic looks.

Still, her curiosity was getting the better of her.

Watching his expression, she felt her way slowly

through a potential minefield. "I'm sorry I haven't been able to get out to visit you and Kasey—"

"Nobody was holding their breath for that," he told her quickly, dismissing her apology along with the need for her to make an appearance at his house. For the time being, he rather liked the fact that it was just the three of them: Kasey, the baby and him.

"Duly noted," she replied, then reminded him, "You didn't answer me." When he appeared confused, she repeated, "How's it going?"

He shrugged, as if he had no idea what she was waiting for him to say. He gave her a thumbnail summary. "I'm helping Kasey pull herself together. Hollis walking out on her like that really did a number on her self-esteem and her confidence. I'm trying to make her understand that she doesn't have to face any of this alone."

"How about the part that she's so much better off without him?" Alma asked.

"That'll come later. Right now, we're still gluing the pieces together."

And he felt as if he was making some serious headway. Kasey seemed more cheerful these days than when she'd first arrived.

"You're doing more than that," Alma pointed out. "You took her in."

He waited to answer his sister until Alice Meriwether passed them. Anything that went into the woman's ear instantly came out of her mouth. He nodded at Alice and then moved on.

"Yeah, well," he finally said, lowering his voice, "she didn't have any place to go and even though it's summer right now, she can't exactly sleep on the street."

"She wouldn't have," Alma assured him. "I'm sure Miss Joan would have happily put her and the baby up in her old house. She still hasn't gotten rid of it even though she moved in with Cash's grandfather."

Just saying Cash's name brought a wide smile to her lips. He'd come back for his grandfather's wedding and wound up staying in Forever for her. They were getting married in a little more than a month. And even though there was now a growing squadron of butterflies in the pit of her stomach, the fact that she and Cash were finally getting married was enough to make a person believe that happy endings did exist.

Which was, ultimately, what she was hoping that Eli would come to discover. His own personal happy ending with a young woman he obviously loved.

Alma crossed her fingers.

Her brother shrugged, doubting that moving into Miss Joan's house would have been a viable solution for Kasey. "Kasey would have felt like she was on the receiving end of charity. She really wouldn't have been comfortable accepting Miss Joan's offer," he told her.

Miss Joan was like everyone's slightly sharp-tongued fairy godmother—just as quick to help as she was to offer "constructive criticism."

"But she's comfortable accepting yours?" Alma asked so that her brother didn't suspect that she knew how he felt about Kasey.

"We've been friends since elementary school," Eli said. "That makes my letting her stay with me an act of friendship, not charity."

Alma congratulated herself on keeping a straight face as she asked, "So this is just like one great big sleepover, huh?"

Eli stopped short of coming up to the checkout counter. He pinned his sister with a deliberate look. "Something on your mind, Alma?"

"A lot of things," she answered blithely. "I'm the sheriff's deputy, remember? I'm supposed to have a lot on my mind."

His patience begun to fray a little around the edges. "Alma—"

"I saw you through the store window," she told him. "And I wanted to make sure that you were still going to be at the wedding." He'd gotten so wrapped up around Kasey, she was afraid that he'd forget that she and Cash were getting married. But before Eli could say anything in response, she deliberately sweetened the pot for him by adding, "You know that Kasey and the baby are invited, too, right?"

His instincts had prevented him from bringing up the subject of Alma's upcoming wedding and Kasey hadn't asked him about it. "She didn't say anything to me."

"That's because when the invitations went out, she

was still Hollis's wife and he kept her on a very tight leash. Most likely, he got rid of the invitation before she ever saw it," Alma ventured.

"She still *is* Hollis's wife," he pointed out, even though just saying it seemed to burn a hole in his gut.

"Which reminds me, Kasey can go see either Rick's wife, Olivia, or Cash to have them start to file divorce papers for her."

Both Olivia and Cash had had careers as high-powered lawyers in the cities that they'd lived in before coming here to Forever. In effect, they'd traded their six-figure incomes for the feeling of satisfaction in knowing that they were doing something worthwhile for the community.

"She's got the perfect grounds for it," Alma said when her brother made no comment. Didn't he want Kasey free of that deadbeat? He'd inherited the ranch they'd lived on from his late parents and had all but ruined it. He certainly had let it get run-down. "Abandonment," Alma said in case her brother wasn't aware of it.

But he was.

"I know that," Eli responded curtly.

Well, that certainly wasn't the reaction she'd expected from him. Alma tried to figure out why her brother seemed so short-tempered. Could it be that Kasey was still in love with that worthless excuse for a human being and had said as much to Eli?

Alma rather doubted that, not after Kasey had lived with Eli these past few weeks. Living with Eli gave the new mother something positive to measure against the poor excuse for a human being she'd been shackled to. For her part, she might tease her brother mercilessly, but she knew that the difference between Eli and Hollis was the proverbial difference between night and day.

"I never said you didn't," Alma assured him gently, then explained, "I was just trying to make myself clear, that's all. It's a habit I picked up from Cash." Her tone changed to an assertive one. "By the way, you're coming to the wedding." It was no longer a question but a command. "I've decided that I'm not accepting any excuses," she added. "Now, is there anything I can do for you or Kasey?" she asked. "I mean, other than shooting Hollis if he tries to creep back into town?"

Having reached the checkout counter, Eli had unloaded most of the items he'd picked up. He'd gotten everything on Kasey's list, plus a candy bar he recalled she'd been particularly fond of when they went to high school. Finished, he fished out his wallet to pay the clerk. That was when Alma had said what she had about Hollis.

The thought hit him right between the eyes. He'd all but convinced himself that Hollis was gone for good. "Do you think that he actually might…?"

There was really no telling *what* someone with Hollis's mentality and temperament would do. "I've found that it's really hard to second-guess a lowlife," she told her brother. "No matter how low your expectations, they can still surprise you and go lower. But in general, I'd say no, probably not." She knew that was what he wanted to hear and for once, she decided to accommodate him. Besides, there was a fifty-fifty chance she was right. If she was wrong, worrying about it ahead of time wouldn't help, and if she was right, then hours would have been wasted in anticipation of a nonevent.

Alma moved closer to him so that none of the customers nearby could overhear. She knew how much Eli's privacy meant to him.

"So then it's going well?" she asked for a third time.

He wasn't sure what she meant by *well* and he wasn't about to answer her in case Alma was too curious about whether something had blossomed between Kasey and him in these past few weeks. He knew how Alma's mind worked, especially now that Cash had come back and they were getting married soon.

Instead he gave her something safe. "She's learning how to survive motherhood and I'm getting the hang of changing diapers," he told her, then pointedly asked, "Is that what you wanted to hear?"

"I just wanted to know how you and she were getting along," she told him innocently. "And you getting the hang of diapering is bound to come in handy."

"Why?" He wasn't following her drift. Glancing at the total the supplies had come to, he peeled out a number of bills and handed them to the clerk. "Horses don't need to have diapers changed."

"No, but babies do." Her eyes met his, which were

hooded and all but unreadable. She hated when he did that, shut her out like that. "And you never know when that might come in handy."

His expression cleared somewhat as a light dawned on him. "You wouldn't be angling for a babysitter, now, would you?"

Actually she was referring to the possibility that he could become a father in the future—especially if he and Kasey finally got together the right way—but for now, she let his take on her words stand. It was a great deal simpler that way—for both of them.

"Not a bad idea," she told him. "I'll keep you in mind should the need ever arise down the line. Well, I've got to get back to patrolling the town—not that anything *ever* happens here," she said, rolling her eyes. *Boredom* happened here. Excitement? Hardly ever. "Give Kasey my love," she said as they parted company right beyond the front door. "Unless, of course, you've already given her yours." She winked at him and then turned on her heel to walk to her vehicle.

"You almost made it, Alma," he noted, calling after her. Alma turned around to hear him out. "Almost left without making that kind of a comment. I must say I'm impressed."

Alma laughed. "Didn't want you thinking that I'd changed *that* radically," she quipped just before she headed to the official vehicle she was driving. She had a town to patrol—and boredom to fight.

Eli watched his sister walk away. Shaking his head,

he was grinning as he deposited the various bags of supplies he'd just paid for into the Jeep.

HE WAS STILL GRINNING when he arrived home half an hour later.

He caught himself doing that a lot lately, he thought, just grinning like some sort of happy idiot.

Eli had never been one of those brooding men that supposedly held such attraction for all women, but there hadn't been all that much to be happy about, either: hard life, hard times, and then his mother had died. That took its toll on a man.

He wasn't like Alma. She was upbeat and optimistic to a fault. But he was, he'd always thought, a realist. Although, for the time being, ever since he'd brought Kasey here, the realist in him had taken a vacation and he was enjoying this new state of affairs just as it was.

Dividing the grocery bags, he slung five plastic bags over each wrist. He tested their strength to make sure they'd hold and moved slowly from the vehicle to the house. He brought in all the groceries in one trip.

Setting the bags down on the first flat surface he came to, Eli shed the plastic loops from his wrists as quickly as he could. But not quickly enough. The plastic loops bit into his skin and still left their mark on his wrists.

Rubbing them without thinking, Eli looked around for Kasey and found her sitting in an easy chair, the baby pressed against her breast.

It took him a second to realize that he'd done exactly what he'd always worried about doing: he'd walked in on Kasey feeding Wayne.

Breast-feeding Wayne.

His breath caught in his throat. He had never seen anything so beautiful in his life.

At the same moment it occurred to him that he had absolutely no business seeing her like this.

Even so, it took him another few seconds to tear his eyes away.

Then, hoping to ease out of the room without having Kasey see him, Eli started to slowly back out—only to have her suddenly look up from what she was doing. Her eyes instantly met his.

He'd never actually felt embarrassed before. He did now.

"I'm sorry, I didn't realize you'd be doing that out here. I mean—I'm sorry," he said again, his tongue growing thicker and less pliable with each word that he stumbled over.

"There's no reason for you to be sorry," she told him softly. "If anything, it's my fault for not going into my room with Wayne." She raised one shoulder in a careless shrug and then let it drop again. "But you were gone and he was fussing—this just seemed easier."

Belatedly, he realized that he was still facing her and that he still didn't know just where to put his eyes.

He immediately turned on his heel, so that he was facing the front door and had his back to her.

He couldn't let her blame herself. He'd walked in on her, not the other way around.

"It's my fault," he insisted. "I should have called out when I walked in," he told her.

"Why?" she asked, just as she had that first evening when he *had* called out before walking in. "After all, it's your house, you have every right to walk into it whenever you want to. If anything, I should be the one apologizing to you for embarrassing you like this. I'm the intruder, not you."

"You're not an intruder," he told her firmly. How could she even *think* that he thought that about her? "You're a welcomed guest. I didn't mean to— I shouldn't have—"

Eli sighed, frustrated. If anything, this was getting harder, not easier for him. He couldn't seem to negotiate a simple statement.

He heard her laughing softly and the sound went right through him. Right *into* him.

"It's all right, Eli. You can turn around now," she told him. "I'm not feeding Wayne anymore."

He sighed, relieved. "Thank God," he murmured, then realized that he'd said the sentiment louder than he'd intended. Swinging around to face her, he damned himself for his display of incredible awkwardness. He couldn't remember *ever* being this tongue-tied. "I'm sorry, that didn't come out right."

On her feet, still cradling the baby against her, Kasey crossed to him and then caressed his cheek as she laughed at his obvious dilemma.

"It's all right," she told him. "Really," she emphasized. "I know it was an accident and, like I said, it's my fault, not yours."

He was behaving like a jackass, Eli upbraided himself. Worse, he was behaving like an *adolescent* jackass. And Kasey was being wonderfully understanding. They were friends and friends sometimes had to cut each other some much needed slack.

"It's nobody's fault," he said with finality, absolving both of them.

Kasey smiled up at him. For the most part Eli had always known just what to say to make her feel better. She was happy to be able to return the favor, in whatever minor capacity that she could.

"I like the sound of that," she told him with approval.

He looked down at the baby in her arms. Wayne seemed to be growing up a storm. In the few short weeks he'd been here, the baby looked as if he'd all but doubled in size. If Wayne wasn't careful, he would be the first giant in kindergarten.

Ever so gingerly, he touched the downy head of blond hair. "Sorry, little guy, I didn't mean to interrupt your mealtime."

The infant made a gurgling noise as he stared up at Eli.

Kasey was delighted. "I think he recognizes your voice, Eli." Her smile broadened as she looked from the baby to him. "He's responding to you," she declared, both amazed and happy.

And he's not the only one, she added silently.

The very thought of *that* made her smile even wider.

Chapter Eight

"Godfather? Me?" Eli asked, staring incredulously at Kasey. "Are you sure that you want *me* to be Wayne's godfather?"

Morning was still in the formation stage, since the sun wasn't close to coming up yet. Eli had thought that he might start his day even earlier than usual so that, if everything went right, he could get to spend a little more time with Kasey and Wayne before the baby was put down for the night.

His plan was to just quietly slip out, easing the front door closed so that he wouldn't disturb or wake Kasey. But he should have known better.

She'd sensed the intended change in his schedule and she'd gotten up ahead of him. He'd come down the stairs to the smell of strong coffee and something delicious being created on the grill. Kasey was making him breakfast as well as packing him a lunch.

She'd been doing the latter ever since the second day she was here. She told him she did it so that he didn't have to go hungry or take the time to come back to the house to eat if he didn't want to.

Kasey always seemed to be at least one step ahead of him, or, at the very least, intuiting his every move, his every need.

Without making it official, they had slipped into a routine and become a family. The kind of family he used to daydream about having someday.

With her.

He used to envision what it would be like if Kasey agreed to marry him, to have his children—to have *their* children, he amended with feeling. And now, here he was, working the ranch, coming home to Kasey and the baby. It was all too good to be true—and he was more than a little aware of that.

He knew he was on borrowed time and he was trying to make the most of it without somehow scaring Kasey away.

Sometimes he'd quietly slip into the baby's room—which was upstairs now, right next to hers. They'd decided to move Wayne's crib into an adjoining bedroom so that Kasey could sleep a little more soundly. Slipping in, he'd just watch the infant sleep. Nothing was more peaceful and soothing than watching Wayne sleep.

As for their forming a family unit, he never said anything about it out loud because he was afraid of spoiling it, afraid that once he gave a name to it, the situation would change. He didn't want to take a chance on jinxing it. All he wanted to do was to savor every moment of it, knowing full well that it wouldn't last. That eventually, Kasey would become stronger, more confident, and want to move on.

But now this request of hers would forever bind them together. Being Wayne's godfather firmly placed him in Wayne's life and, by association, in hers.

Did she understand the full implication of what she was suggesting? He looked at her and repeated, "You're sure?"

She smiled at him, the kind of smile that always went straight to his gut. "I was never more sure of anything in my life," she told him. "Unless you don't want to," she qualified suddenly.

Until this moment it had never occurred to her that he might not be willing to do this. Though he kept insisting that he wasn't, maybe Eli *did* already feel burdened by having her and her son stay here with him. That meant that asking him to be Wayne's godfather was just asking too much.

"Because if you don't," she continued quickly, "it's all right. I understand. I mean, you've already done so very much for—"

She was talking so fast there was no space, no pause where he could stick in a single word. Eli didn't know any other way to stop her except to place his fingertips to her lips, halting their movement. She raised her eyes to his quizzically.

"Of course I *want* to. I was just surprised—and touched," he confessed, "that you asked. To be honest, I never saw myself as the type to be someone's godfather. That's a very big—"

Kasey was nodding her head. "I know. Responsibility," she said, thinking she was ending his sentence for him. She didn't want him to feel that she was putting any sort of demands on him, not after he had been so wonderful to them.

"I was going to say 'honor,'" he told her patiently. "Being a godfather is a very big honor and I just didn't think I was worthy."

Eli watched, fascinated, as her eyes widened. How many times had he felt as if he could literally go wading in those eyes of hers? Lose himself completely in those fathomless blue eyes?

It took a great deal of effort on his part to keep himself in check and just go on talking as if nothing was happening inside of him. As if he didn't want to just sweep her into his arms and tell her that he loved her, that he would always be there for her and for Wayne and that there was really no need for any formal declarations.

"Not worthy?" Kasey echoed. "I've never known a better man than you in my whole life and if you do agree to become Wayne's godfather, then we're the ones who will be honored, not you," she told him.

Eli shoved his hands into his pockets to keep from touching her face. He laughed in response to her statement, shaking his head.

"All right. Then consider yourself honored," he quipped. "I would *love* to be Wayne's godfather. Just tell me where and when."

"This coming Saturday," she told him. "We can go

to the church together. I'll just let the pastor know." She paused for a second, letting the first part sink in before she told him of her other decision. "I was thinking of asking Miss Joan to be his godmother." She watched his face for a reaction. "What do you think?"

Eli nodded, approving. He had a feeling that it would mean a great deal to the woman. "I think she'd like that very much."

Pleased, Kasey picked up the full pot of coffee. It had just finished brewing when Eli walked by the kitchen. She'd called to him, but she had a feeling that it was the coffee aroma that had lured him in.

"Well, that's settled," she said, pouring him a cup. "Now come and have your breakfast. I've already packed your lunch for you."

He doubted that she had any idea how good that sounded to him. He would never take this for granted.

"I keep telling you that you don't have to do this," he said, taking a seat at the table.

Admittedly his voice was carrying less and less conviction each time he told her that there was no need to get up and serve him like this. But that was because, beneath his protests, he was thoroughly enjoying sharing his meals with her. It would have taken nothing on his part to get used to a life like this.

Simple, without demands.

Just the three of them…

He knew he was dreaming, but dreams cost nothing, so for now, he indulged himself.

"And I keep telling you that it's the least I can do," she reminded him.

He stared at the plate that Kasey had just put on the table in front of him. There was French toast, sausage and orange juice, as well as the cup of black coffee. And over on the counter was his lunch all packed and standing at the ready, waiting to be picked up on his way out. Life just didn't get any better than this.

"If this is the least," he told her in appreciation, between bites, "then I don't think I'm ready to see the most."

She laughed, delighted. It occurred to her that she'd laughed more in these past five weeks than she had in all the years that she'd spent with Hollis. That could have been because with Hollis, there'd always been one problem after another, always something to worry about. All the bills—and finding the funds to pay them—had always fallen on her shoulders.

It wasn't like that with Eli. *He* was the one bent on taking care of her, not on being waited on, hand and foot, by her.

It was a completely different world. She had to admit that she rather liked it and could, so easily, get used to it....

"I'm working on it," she told him with a wink.

The wink set off its own chain reaction. Eli could feel his toes curling, could feel anticipation racing through him to the point that he could barely sit still long enough to finish his breakfast.

He couldn't recall *ever* being happier.

THE FOLLOWING SATURDAY, Eli carefully dug out the suit that he'd worn to Miss Joan's wedding. Brushing off a few stray hairs that had found their way to the dark, navy blue material, he put the suit on.

As Wayne's godfather, he wanted to look his best, he thought, carefully surveying himself from every angle in the mirror. He scrutinized his appearance with a very critical eye. The last thing he wanted to do was to embarrass Kasey by looking like some weather-beaten cowboy.

He was going for a dignified look. For that, he needed to wear a tie, but the thing insisted on giving him trouble, refusing to tie correctly.

Ties were nothing but colorful nooses, but a necessary accessory to complete the picture, and as such, he had to wear one.

Easier said than done.

When his third attempt at forming a knot turned out even worse than the first two, Eli bit off a curse as he yanked off the offending garment. He was never going to get this right. Alma had tied his last tie for him, but Alma wasn't here.

He had a hunch that all women were born knowing how to tie ties.

Impulsively, clutching the uncooperative tie in his hand, he went to Kasey's room and knocked on her door.

"Be there in a minute," he heard her call out.

He hadn't meant to rush her. "No hurry," he assured her. "I just wanted to ask if you knew anything about tying ties."

He should have just slipped his tie off over his head the last time he'd worn it. Then he'd be ready to go by now instead of walking around with his tie crumpled in his hand.

Just as he finished chewing himself out, Kasey's door opened. She wore a light blue-gray dress that stopped several inches above her knees.

The word *vision* throbbed in his brain.

"You look beautiful," he told her, his voice only slightly above a whisper.

She smiled at the compliment, finding his tone exceptionally sexy.

Her eyes lit up the way they had a tendency to do when she was happy. And as they did, he could feel his very soul lighting up, as well.

He ached for her.

"You're very sweet, Eli," she told him.

"And very inept," he concluded, feeling it best to change the subject and not dwell on anything that could get him into a whole lot of trouble. "You'd think a grown man could finally get the hang of tying a tie," he complained.

She didn't want him to get down on himself. "That grown man is too busy doing good deeds and trying to make a go of his new ranch while lending moral support to a friend. I'd say that tying a tie doesn't even make the top one hundred list of things that need to be learned." She stood in front of him for a moment, studying his tie, then said, "I'm going to have to stand behind you to do this—if you don't mind having my arms around you for a couple of minutes," she interjected.

Mind? Did she think he was mentally deficient? What man in his right mind would balk at having a beautiful woman put her arms around him under *any* pretext?

"No, I don't mind," he assured her, doing his best not to grin like a reject from a Cheshire cat competition as he said it. "Do whatever you have to do to get this thing finally on straight."

"I'll do my best," she promised.

The next moment she was behind him, reaching around his body to take hold of the two ends of his tie. Even though he was wearing a jacket, he was aware of her soft breasts pressing up against his back. Aware of the gentle fragrance of her shampoo as it filled his head. Aware of the hunger that coursed through his veins.

He took in slow, measured breaths, trying to reduce the erratic pounding of his pulse.

"I'm not making this too tight for you, am I?" she asked, her breath lightly tickling the skin that was just above his collar.

"No." He didn't trust himself to say any more words than that.

Within another minute and a half, Kasey was finished. With a tinge of reluctance, she stepped back, away from his hard, firm body, although not away from the sensations that contact with that body had created and left behind.

Eli was her friend. She wasn't supposed to think this way about him, wasn't supposed to react this way to him. More than anything else, she didn't want to risk losing his friendship. At times, knowing that Eli was there for her was all that kept her going.

Kasey came around to stand in front of him and examine her work.

She'd tied a perfect knot, a Windsor knot, it was called. "Not bad," she pronounced. And then, raising her eyes to his, she told him, "I think we're good to go. I'll go get Wayne."

He placed his hand on her arm, stopping her. "Let me," he offered. "After all, he's my godson—or my 'almost' godson. And once Miss Joan arrives at the church, I won't be able to get within shouting distance of him, much less hold him."

Kasey laughed at the exaggeration. "Right. Like you don't already hold him every chance you get," she teased, following behind Eli as he went to her son's bedroom.

Walking into Wayne's room, Eli went straight to the boy's crib.

Wayne was on his back, watching in fascination as his fingers wiggled above his head. Everything at his age was magical. Eli envied him that.

As he stood above the boy, Wayne focused on him and not his fingers. Recognition set in and Wayne began to get excited. This time when he waved his arms, it wasn't to watch his fingers. It was a form of supplication. He wanted to be picked up by this man.

Wayne didn't have to wait long.

Holding the infant to him, Eli picked up the thread of the conversation between them. He feigned ignorance regarding her last statement. "I don't know what you mean."

Oh, yes, he did, Kasey thought. He knew *exactly* what she meant.

"I hear you, you know. In the middle of the night, I hear you. I hear you going into Wayne's room when he starts to whimper. I hear you picking him up, rocking him, walking the floor with him sometimes. You're spoiling him, you know," she told Eli. Then she added with a wide grin, "And me."

Some people didn't get spoiled. Ever. She was one of them. "Never happen," he assured her.

Oh, but it's already happened, she couldn't help thinking. She'd gotten used to relying on him, used to experiencing the feeling of well-being that he generated for her.

Shaking herself free of her thoughts, she declared, "All right, enough fraternizing." She took the baby from him, tucking Wayne against her shoulder. "It's time to take your godson to church."

His godson.

He liked the sound of that. But then, he liked the sound of anything that came from her lips, he thought. He always had.

"Yes, ma'am," he said, pretending to salute her.

Squaring his shoulders like a soldier, Eli led the way out of the house and to his Jeep. The vehicle had been washed and polished in honor of the occasion.

Now if he could just keep it clean until the day was over....

THE BAPTISM ITSELF was a very simple ceremony, but touching nonetheless.

The solemnity of the occasion was interrupted when Wayne attempted to drink the drops of water that lightly cascaded from his forehead, his little tongue working overtime to catch as many drops as he could.

"The boy's got a sense of humor about him," Miss Joan declared with no small approval, nodding her head as she watched his failed efforts to make contact with the water. Because she wanted to hold the boy for a few more minutes, she allowed the moment to linger. Then, with a barely suppressed sigh, Miss Joan handed the boy back to his mother.

In her heart, she was reliving moments of her life when she'd held her own son this way, thinking how much promise was contained within the small boy.

She fervently hoped that the boy whose godmother she'd become today had a better, longer future ahead of him than her own son had had.

"All right," Miss Joan suddenly said, clearing her throat and raising her voice so that everyone in the church could hear her. "We've dunked him and promised to stand by him and stand up for him. Now let's all go and celebrate over at my place."

Her place, as everyone in town knew, referred to Miss Joan's diner. Forever's only restaurant had been suitably decorated to celebrate Wayne's christening. As with the Christmas holidays and the Fourth of July, all the women in town who'd been blessed with the knack had banded together and cooked up a storm, making everything from baby-back ribs to pies and cakes, some of which were so light Miss Joan's husband, Harry, claimed they had to be tied down to keep them from floating away.

The diner was soon filled to capacity. And then some.

Because it was warm, the establishment doors were left open and the party soon spilled out of the diner and onto the grounds surrounding it.

The celebration, fueled by good food, good company and boisterous laughter, continued until darkness overtook the sun, sending it away, and the stars came out to keep the moon company.

"I think we might have finally tired him out," Eli commented, looking at his brand-new godson. At close to six weeks old, the boy had miraculously taken to sleeping through the night—most nights, at any rate.

Kasey smiled her approval of this latest development. "I can take him home," she volunteered. "But you don't have to leave right away. You can stay here longer if you like."

He looked at her as if she wasn't making any sense.

"My mother always taught me to go home with the girl I brought to the dance."

"This wasn't a dance," Kasey pointed out, amused.

"Same concept," he told her. "Besides, why would I want to stay here without you—and Wayne?" he purposely added.

The smile she offered him stirred his heart—again. "I just wanted you to know you had options. I don't want you to feel I'm taking advantage of your kindness or that I'm monopolizing you."

He wondered what she would say if he told her that he *wanted* her to take advantage of him, *wanted* her to monopolize him to her heart's content.

Probably look at him as if he'd gone off the deep end, and he supposed he had. He couldn't think of a better way to go than loving Kasey until his last minute on earth was up.

But if he even so much as hinted at that, Kasey would probably be packing by morning. Not about to experiment and find out, he decided that it was for the best to just keep his feelings to himself.

"C'mon," he said, "I'll take the two of you home."

Tired, Kasey was more than willing to leave. She held the baby against her as Eli guided her out of the diner and toward his car. Without even realizing it, she was leaning into his arm as she walked.

Eli slipped his arm around her shoulders to help guide her, savoring the warm glow he felt.

Chapter Nine

Kasey supposed that she'd been feeling a little sad and vulnerable all day. She didn't know if it was because of all the couples at the christening, which in contrast made her feel isolated and alone, or because her hormones were still slightly off.

It could have also been due to her finally accepting that she would be facing life as a single mom.

Or maybe it was a combination of all three.

Whatever it was, her emotions were all very close to the surface. She did her level best to rein them in. The last thing she wanted, after he'd been so nice to her, was to burst into tears in front of Eli. He'd think that it was his fault, but it wasn't. After her son, Eli was the best thing in her life right now.

As they drove back to Eli's ranch, she felt an intense loneliness creeping in despite the fact that Eli was in the Jeep with her, as close as a prayer. Certainly close enough for her to touch.

Maybe she just needed to make contact with another human being, she thought. The sadness made her feel extremely vulnerable.

For whatever reason, she found herself reaching her hand out to touch Eli's arm just as he pulled the vehicle up in front of the house.

Turning off the ignition, Eli looked at her, assuming that she'd touched him to get his attention because she wanted to say something. Kasey had been exceptionally quiet all the way home. He'd just thought she was too tired to talk, but since she'd touched his arm, he figured that it was to get him to center his attention on her.

As if *all* his attention *wasn't* centered on her all the time.

Because she wasn't saying anything, he prodded her a little.

"What?" he asked her softly, deliberately keeping his voice low so as not to wake the little sleeping passenger in the backseat.

Embarrassed, she could feel color rising in her cheeks. He would probably think she was crazy. "Nothing, just proving to myself that you're close enough to touch. That you're real."

He looked at her, somewhat puzzled. "Of course I'm real. Why wouldn't I be?" he asked good-naturedly.

She shrugged, avoiding his eyes. After all he'd done for her, she owed him the truth, but she was really afraid that he'd laugh at her.

"Because sometimes I think you're just too good to be true."

Eli did laugh, but it wasn't at her. It was at what she'd just said. Turning off the Jeep's headlights, he removed his key from the ignition. "Obviously it's been a long time since you've talked to Alma."

This time, she did raise her eyes to his. "I don't need to talk to Alma to know how good you've been to me. How kind. Trust me, Eli, you're like the answer to a prayer."

And you are all I ever prayed for, he told her silently, knowing better than to say something like that out loud.

"I think you might have had a little too much to drink," he guessed, coming around to her side of the vehicle. Opening the door, he took her hand to help her out.

Shifting forward, she rose to her feet and found herself standing extremely close to Eli. So close that when she inhaled, her chest brushed ever so lightly against his.

Electricity zigzagged through her and she didn't immediately step back. When Eli did instead, the sadness within her became larger, coming close to unmanageable.

"I didn't have anything to drink," she protested. "At least, nothing with alcohol in it." She was still nursing Wayne, although he was beginning to favor the bottle. She had a feeling that her days of nursing her son were numbered. "My mind isn't clouded, if that's what you're thinking," she told him. "I see everything very clearly."

And just like that, Eli was waging an internal struggle, wanting more than anything else to lose the battle and just go with his instincts. Go with his desires.

He came within an inch of kissing her. In his mind's eye, he'd already crossed that bridge. But that was fantasy and the reality was that he didn't want to do anything to jeopardize what he had at this moment.

He pulled back at the last moment and turned toward the rear of the vehicle.

"I'd better get Wayne out of the Jeep and into his crib," he said. "He's had a pretty long day."

She said the words to his back, knowing that if Eli was facing her, she wouldn't have been able to get them out. And she desperately needed to. Her voice was hardly above a whisper. "Don't you want to kiss me, Eli?"

Eli grew very rigid, half-convinced that he'd imagined hearing her voice. Imagined her saying words that he would have sold his soul to hear.

Releasing the breath that had gotten caught in his throat, he turned around in slow motion until he stood facing her.

Looking at her face in complete wonder.

In complete surrender. "More than anything in the world," he told her.

It had to be the moonlight, playing tricks on his vision, but he could have sworn he saw tears shimmering in Kasey's eyes.

"Then what are you waiting for?"

He could have said that he couldn't kiss her because, technically, she was still Hollis's wife. Or that he couldn't because he didn't want to take advantage of her, or the situation, or the fact that she was probably overtired and not thinking straight.

There were as many reasons to deny himself as there were leaves on the tree by his window. And only one reason to do it.

Because he ached for her.

Before he could stop himself, he took hold of Kasey's shoulders—whether to hold her in place or to convince himself that she was real and that he wasn't just dreaming this, he wasn't sure.

The next moment there was no more debate, no more speculation. Because he was lowering his mouth to hers and waking up his soul.

His body temperature rose just as his head began to spin, completely disorienting him from time and space and hurling him toward a world of heat, flashing lights and demanding desires.

She tasted of all things wonderful. Unwilling to back away the way he was convinced he should, Eli deepened the kiss, thus temporarily suspending all rational thoughts and riding a crest of billowing emotions.

Tears slid free from the corners of her eyes. Eyes she'd shut tight as she focused on the wild, wonderful sensations shooting all through her like brightly lit Roman candles.

Kasey threw her arms around his neck, holding on for dear life as she followed him into a world filled with the promise of wondrous, fierce passions.

Words like *chemistry, soul mates* and *joy* flashed through her mind at the speed of light, so fast that it took her a few moments to realize that she was experiencing everything the words suggested. Experiencing it and wanting more.

Craving more.

So this was what it was like, to truly *want* to be with someone. To *ache* to be one with someone. She realized that she'd never known it before.

In all the time she'd been with Hollis, in all the years she thought she was in love with him, she'd never felt anything even remotely like this. Never had this huge, overwhelming desire to make love with him—or die.

Never felt this physical ache that something was missing.

Even though it had been.

When the kiss ended, when Eli stepped back so that their bodies were no longer pressed against one another, they looked at each other for what seemed like an isolated eternity. Each was surprised that the longing insisted on continuing.

He shouldn't have allowed this to happen. Shouldn't have given in to his weakness. It was up to him to be the one in control.

"Kasey, I'm sorry," Eli began, searching for words that would give him a way out, that would allow her to absolve him. Words that would convince her to continue staying at his ranch.

And then she said something that completely took his breath away.

"I'm not," she whispered, her eyes never leaving his. His lips might lie to her, but his eyes never would. She could tell what he was really feeling by looking at them. "I'm only sorry that it didn't happen sooner."

Did she know?

Did she realize the power she had over him? He'd walk through fire for her and gladly so. He'd been in love with her since the world began.

He wanted to take her there. To make love with Kasey with wild, abandoned ardor right here on the ground, in front of the house. But that sort of behavior was for animals in heat, not a man who had waited in silence for more than a decade.

"We'd better get him to his crib," Eli murmured, turning to unbuckle Wayne from his infant seat.

The little guy was so tired that he didn't wake as he was being lifted from the seat, nor did he wake when he was being carried into the house and then up the stairs to his room.

Kasey followed in Eli's wake, just in case Wayne woke up and needed her. But he continued sleeping.

Gratitude swelled in Eli's chest. As he gently lay the infant in his crib, he whispered to him, "Thanks, little guy, I owe you one."

He could have sworn that the baby smiled in his sleep just then. He knew that experts would claim that it was only gas, but he knew better.

Taking Kasey's hand in his, Eli moved quietly out

of the infant's room and slowly eased the door closed behind him.

The second he was out in the hallway, he could see by the look in Kasey's eyes that this was no time to tender any apologies or lay the blame for his previous actions on lack of sleep.

There was no blame to be laid.

Instead, though every fiber of his body begged him to just sweep her into his arms and carry her off to his room, Eli held himself in check long enough to ask Kasey one crucial, basic question.

"Are you sure?"

Kasey didn't answer him. At least, she didn't answer him verbally. Instead she threw her arms around Eli's neck, went up on her toes as far as she could go and kissed him even more soundly than she had just in front of the house.

She made him feel positively intoxicated.

"I guess that's a yes," Eli breathed out heavily when they finally paused because they had to come up for air.

He was rewarded with the sound of her light laughter. It rippled along his lips, making hers taste that much sweeter.

Like the first ripe strawberries of the summer.

It was all he needed. The next moment he was acting out his fantasy and this time he *did* sweep her into his arms and carry her into her room.

Anchoring herself to him with her arms around his neck, she leaned her head against his shoulder, content to remain just where she was for all eternity—or at least for the next few hours.

As he came into her room, he didn't bother pushing the door closed with his elbow. There was no one here except for them. And the baby was months away from taking his first step, so they were safe from any prying eyes.

When Eli set her down, the raw desire he saw in Kasey's eyes melted away the last shred of resistance-for-her-own-good he had to offer.

Besides, as he'd carried her into her room, she'd pressed her lips against his neck, setting off all sorts of alarms and signals throughout his body. Making him want her more than he thought humanly possible.

Eli kissed her over and over again, savoring the feel of her, the exquisite, wildly erotic taste of her and the sound of surrender echoing in his head.

Unlike the sensations she'd evoked within him, the details of what transpired were somewhat sketchy. Under oath he couldn't have recounted how Kasey and he went from being two rational, fully dressed people to two naked adults who had thrown all caution, all reason, to the winds.

Eli had always thought that if he'd *ever* be lucky enough to have an evening of lovemaking with Kasey, he would proceed slowly, affording every single part of her the time, the worship and the reverence it so richly deserved.

But somehow, even with the game plan still lodged somewhere in his brain, it had turned into a race. The eagerness he felt only intensified, growing stronger as his hands passed over her body, exploring, claiming.

Loving.

She was just as exquisite as he'd always dreamed she'd be.

And she was, at least for the night, his.

His.

If this wasn't the perfect example of dying and going to heaven, then nothing was.

With each passing moment, as each sensation fed on itself and grew, Kasey found she was having a hard time believing that this was happening. That this was actually true.

Lovemaking with Hollis had always been about what Hollis wanted, about what turned Hollis on. Her needs, when she'd still had a glimmer of them, were just collateral. The way he saw it, he'd once told her with more than a few shots of whiskey in his system, was that if she should happen to climax, that was great. If she didn't, well, women didn't really need that the way men did.

Or, at least that was the philosophy that Hollis lived by.

And she had believed him. Or, more accurately, believed that he believed.

Until Eli.

Everything she'd previously believed—that she didn't need to feel the kind of sensations, the kind of surges and peaks that a man did—they had been and continued to be all lies.

Lies.

Because what she was feeling, what Eli *made* her feel, was supremely, incredibly wonderful.

Moreover, it seemed as though the more she got, the more Eli aroused her, the more she wanted. Eli had opened up a brand-new, wonderful world for her.

A world she wasn't willing to leave that quickly.

And when he kissed her all over, leaving the imprint of his warm lips along all the sensitive parts of her body, waking them up and making them come alive, she felt eruption after eruption. They were happening all along her body, not just within her very core.

What *was* this delicious sensation, this throbbing need that he'd brought out of her? And how did she get it to go on indefinitely?

But the itch for the final peak got to be too great, too demanding.

She was primed and eager when Eli finally stopped paying homage to the various parts of her whole and finally positioned himself over her.

Even this was a far cry from the way lovemaking had gone with Hollis—especially toward the end. With Hollis, she could never shake the feeling that she could have been anyone. That in the end, his partner didn't matter to Hollis. He just wanted to reach his climax.

And, as for her, all she'd wanted at that point was just to get it over with. There was no romance, no excitement left between them. That had ended a long time ago.

Had it not been for Eli, she would have never known that her body was capable of feeling like this. That making love could be like this, all generosity, thoughtfulness—and fire.

And when they finally became one, Kasey was as eager to be with him as she sensed he was to be with her.

After the first moment, there was no time for thought at all. Because they were both hell-bent for the final climb. They took it together and shared the light show when they attained the top of the covert peak.

He made her breathless.

Chapter Ten

All too soon, the bright, shooting stars dimmed and the all-encompassing euphoria faded away.

Bracing herself, Kasey waited for the sadness to return, for the cold feeling to wrap itself around her like a giant snake.

Neither happened.

The sadness and the cool feeling were both kept in abeyance because Eli didn't turn away from her, didn't, after having her, withdraw and just fall asleep, the way Hollis, her only other lover, had. Instead, when Eli shifted his weight off her, he turned so that he was lying next to her. Tucking his arm around her, he pulled her closer to him.

A wave of tenderness made its way all through her. And it intensified when Eli pressed a kiss to her forehead with such gentleness, it brought fresh tears to her eyes. They slid out before she could stop them.

With his cheek against hers, he felt the dampness, and remorse instantly raised its hoary head, rebuking him. Taunting him that he *had* taken advantage.

Raising up on his elbow, Eli traced the path of the tear that had slipped out with the tip of his finger.

"Oh, Kasey, I'm so sorry." The words sounded so ineffectual, but he didn't know how else to apologize. "I shouldn't have pressed—"

For a moment his apology threatened to slash apart all the wondrous sensations that had just come before, as well as the happy feeling she was holding on to now. But then she realized just *why* Eli was saying what he was saying.

In her rush to set him straight as to *why* she appeared to be crying, her words got all jumbled on her tongue, making little coherent sense as they emerged.

"Oh, no, no. I'm not— You didn't— Do you think that I'm actually *regretting* what just happened here between us?" Hadn't he *been* there? How could he possibly believe that making love with him could have upset her? It was the most fabulous experience in her life.

The way he saw it, what other conclusion could he have come to? That was a tearstain on her cheek, not a stray raindrop.

He looked at her, confused. "Aren't you?"

"No!" she cried emphatically. How did she go about phrasing this? How did she make him understand what he'd stirred up within her without incurring his pity? She decided if there *was* pity, she'd deal with that later, but right now, she needed to make him understand what he had done for her.

"Oh, my God, Eli, all these years, I never knew."

"Never knew?" he echoed, not following her. "Never knew what?"

The corners of her mouth curved. The smile slipped into her eyes as it spread. "I never knew it could be like that."

She debated a moment, wondering if she should continue. She didn't want him thinking she was just an inexperienced housewife, but it was important that he understood exactly what this meant to her. To do that, she would have to tell him about what had come before.

"Hollis was never interested in…in holding me afterward. And, to be honest, he didn't exactly take all that much of an interest in my pleasure, only in his."

She paused, knowing that putting herself out there—naked—wasn't wise, but she couldn't help that. It was part of explaining what he'd made her feel and why. She didn't expect anything in return for this baring of her soul, not his commitment or even the promise that this would happen again. But she did want him to know that he had made her earth move and she was grateful for what they'd just shared.

"I think I saw fireworks going off. I definitely saw stars," she confessed with a soft laugh.

Eli threaded his fingers through her hair, framing her face, memorizing every contour, although there was no need. Every nuance that comprised her features was permanently imprinted on his brain.

Part of him still couldn't believe that they had actually made love. That his most cherished fantasy had really come true.

"Me, too," he told her.

God help her, she would have loved to believe that. Even so, she could feel herself melting again. Being stirred up again. There was something incredibly sexy about being on the receiving end of kindness.

She'd always felt that way. And never more than after she'd gotten married and learned to do without it. Hollis wasn't knowingly cruel to her and he hadn't abused her, but thoughtfulness, kindness, all that seemed to be beyond his comprehension.

"You're making fun of me," she protested.

"No, I'm not," Eli was quick to assure her. "What I *am* doing is still wondering how I managed to get so damn lucky."

She looked up at him, wondering why she'd never realized before what a knight in shining armor Eli was. Or how really handsome he was. Hollis had been a golden boy, all flash and fire. But Eli had substance. More important than his good looks, he made a woman feel safe.

"Why waste time wondering when you could be doing something about it?" she asked in a husky whisper that rippled all through him. Exciting him.

He wasn't sure if he lowered his mouth to hers, or if she pulled him down to her, but the logistics didn't really matter. What mattered was that the fireworks were going off again, in full force, accompanied by anticipation and heat.

In the end, they made love a total of three times before they lay, completely exhausted and utterly satisfied, huddled into one another in her bed.

And Wayne had come through like a trouper. The little guy had been complicit in his mother's sensual awakening by doing his part. He'd slept all through the night without so much as one whimper.

As for Eli, while Kasey might have been stunned and surprised by what she'd experienced, he hadn't been. In his heart, he'd always known it would be like this. Making love with Kasey had been every bit as incredible as his fantasies. She'd filled his soul with light, with music.

Again he wondered how Hollis could have willingly walked away from this, how he could have sacrificed exquisite nights like this because he didn't have the willpower to man up—to *grow* up. He would have crawled over glass on his knees for this, and Hollis had just thrown it all away.

One man's adversity was another man's good fortune, he couldn't help thinking, secretly grateful that Hollis had been so selfish.

Kasey finally broke the silence. "You're awfully quiet," she observed.

"That's because I'm too exhausted to talk," he told her with a self-mocking laugh. "You're a hard woman to keep up with."

Kasey pressed her lips together, knowing she shouldn't comment, shouldn't push this. But she *had* to know.

"Is that a good thing or a bad thing? You being tired," she added, just in case she'd rambled a little too much again.

He turned to her and she could actually *feel* his smile. It undulated all through her.

"A good thing," he told her. "A very good thing." He paused, savoring her closeness, content just to fall asleep holding her like this. But there was still something he needed to get out of the way, a question that he needed to ask, because he'd gotten so carried away so quickly. "I didn't hurt you, did I?" he asked. "It was just that—"

He stopped himself, wondering if his admission would push her away. Telling her that he'd loved her all this time, that he'd yearned for her even before she'd run off with Hollis, well, that could very well spook her. That was the very last thing he wanted. After finally having *found* her, after having her willingly become a part of his life, he couldn't just lose her again. He didn't think that he could bear that.

"Just that what?" she queried when he didn't finish his sentence.

"Just that I got so carried away, so caught up in the act, I was afraid that I might have hurt you. I'd completely forgotten that you had just given birth and all," he reminded her.

"Five weeks ago," she pointed out. Had he forgotten about taking her, as well as Wayne, to the doctor the other day for a dual checkup? The doctor had been pleased to proclaim that they were both the very picture of health. "And according to Dr. Davenport, I've bounced back incredibly well."

"You won't get an argument from me about the 'incredible' part," Eli told her. If his grin had been any broader, it would have come close to cracking his face.

"Good," she murmured. "Because I'm much too exhausted to argue," she told him with what felt like her very last bit of available energy. The very next moment, she drifted off to sleep.

The sound of her even breathing was like music to his ears. Lulling music. Eli drifted off to sleep, himself, within minutes of Kasey.

WITH THE SHARP RAYS of daylight came even sharper rays of guilt. After having just had the greatest night of his life, Eli woke to the feeling of oppressive guilt. As wondrous as making love with Kasey had been, it didn't negate the fact that he had taken advantage of her at an extremely vulnerable time.

He should have been strong enough to resist his urges, strong enough to hold her at arm's length rather than closer than a breath.

But he hadn't been.

Even now, he wasn't.

Looking at her now, he wanted nothing more than to pull her into his arms and make love with her all over again. And keep making love with her until he completely expired.

But that would be indulging himself again and not being mindful of her.

Dammit, he wasn't some stallion in heat. He was supposed to have willpower. That was what separated him from the horses he was training.

Or at least it was supposed to.

Holding his breath, Eli slowly got out of bed, then silently made his way across the floor and out of the room. He first eased the door open, then eased it closed again, moving so painfully slow he was certain she'd wake before he made good his escape.

Once out of the room, he hurried quickly to his own room. Throwing on the first clothes he laid his hands on, he was gone in less than fifteen minutes after he'd opened his eyes.

WORKING, HE PUT IN A full day and more, all on an empty stomach. After a bit, it ceased complaining, resigning itself to the fact that a meal wasn't in its future anytime soon. Eventually, after he'd done every single conceivable chore he could think of and had brought his horses back to their stalls, putting them away for the night, he ran out of excuses to stay away from the house. And her.

It was time to go home and face the music. Or, in this case, the recriminations.

Bracing himself, he opened the front door, hoping against hope that he wouldn't see the look of betrayal in Kasey's eyes when he walked in.

The first thing he saw when he shut the door behind him was not the look of betrayal—or worse—in Kasey's eyes. What he saw was a suitcase. Her suitcase.

Kasey had left it standing right by the door and he'd accidentally knocked it over as he came in.

Righting it, Eli felt its weight. It wasn't there by accident. She'd packed it.

She was leaving him.

The moment he realized that, he could feel his stomach curling into itself so hard it pinched him. Badly. And it definitely wasn't caused by a lack of food.

A feeling of panic and desperation instantly sprang up within him.

He knew he should just let her leave, that he shouldn't stand in the way of her choice. But another part of him wasn't nearly that reasonable or selfless. That part urged him to fight this. To fight to keep Kasey in his life now that he had finally discovered what loving her was like.

Kasey instantly tensed as she heard him come in. She'd been listening for him all day, literally straining to hear so much that her nerves were all stretched to their limit, ready to snap in two at the slightest provocation.

"You're leaving." It wasn't really a question at this point. Why else would a packed suitcase be left right by the door?

She needed to get through this as fast as possible. She should have actually been gone by now. Why she'd waited for him to come home, she really didn't know. Ordinarily, she avoided confrontations and scenes, and this could be both.

Maybe she'd waited because she'd wanted Eli to talk her out of leaving. She'd wanted him to explain why he'd bolted the way he had this morning. And, more than anything, she wanted him to tell her that he didn't regret what had happened between them.

"Don't worry, you won't have to drive me." If her mouth had been any drier, there would have been sand spilling out when she spoke. "I'll call Miss Joan." It was the first name she could think of.

"Why?" he asked, his voice barely above a whisper.

She wanted to cry, to double up her hands into fists and beat on him in sheer frustration. She did neither. Instead, in a voice deliberately stripped of any emotions, she said, "Because I thought she might let me stay with the baby at her place."

"No." His eyes all but bore into her. "Why are you leaving?"

Why was he torturing her this way? What was it he wanted from her? "Because you want me to," she cried, her voice breaking.

He stared at her incredulously. Had she lost her mind? "Why the hell would you think that?" he demanded, stunned.

"The bed was empty when I woke up," she told him. "The house was empty when I woke up."

She was shouting now, unable to harness her emotions. She felt completely betrayed by him. She'd thought that last night had meant something to him, other than a way of easing his tension, or whatever it was that men told themselves when they slept with a woman and then completely erased her existence from their minds the next morning.

"You didn't even want to talk to me. What else am I supposed to think?" she cried heatedly, then struggled to get hold of herself. She couldn't have a complete meltdown like this, if for no other reason than because Wayne needed a functioning mother. "Look, I get it. You don't owe me anything. You've been more than kind, giving me somewhere to stay, being my friend. Last night was incredible, but I don't want to lose your friendship, so I thought that it might be best if I got out of your sight for a while." She went to pick up the suitcase.

He pushed it out of the way with his foot. "You thought wrong."

He'd said it so low, she wasn't sure if she heard him correctly. "What?"

"You thought wrong," he repeated, this time with more conviction. "I left before you woke up because I needed some time to try to figure out a way to save our friendship."

"Save it?" she repeated, completely confused. Why would he possibly think that their friendship would be in jeopardy because they had made lyrical love together?

"I didn't want you worrying every time you turned around that I would suddenly pounce on you without warning."

"'Pounce,'" she repeated. As she said the word, an image of Eli "pouncing" materialized in her head. This time there was no confusion evident in her voice. But there was a hint of a smile.

"Pounce," he said again.

All things considered, "pouncing" had definite merits, she thought, relieved. Maybe she'd been worried for no reason.

"Did it ever occur to you that maybe I'd actually *want* you to pounce on me?" she asked Eli.

"What are you saying?"

She tried again, aware that she'd been more coherent in her time. "I'm saying that while I don't expect any promises—we're both in brand-new territory here—I would like to have something to look forward to once in a while." Was that really her, actually *asking* him to say that making love with her wasn't totally out of the picture? *Wow* was all she could think to say. "Or at least think it was a possibility."

"Then, just to be perfectly clear," he qualified, more for himself than for her, "what happened last night, that didn't offend you? Didn't make you feel uneasy about having me hanging around?"

"Eli, you're my best friend. How could I be uneasy about having you around? And, for the record, when have you *ever* just been 'hanging around'? You're running an entire ranch by yourself, helping me with Wayne and I *know* that you get up to tend to him when he starts to cry in the middle of the night."

She'd caught his attention with the first line. He was having trouble getting past that. "A best friend who slept with you," he pointed out.

Her smile expanded. "I don't recall much sleeping going on until a lot later," she reminded him. "Eli, if you think that you took advantage of me, let me put your mind at ease. You didn't. What you did do was make me feel alive again.

"You made me feel like a desirable woman instead of an unattractive, discarded one whose husband didn't even think enough of her to tell her face-to-face he was leaving. If anything," she said quietly, "I took advantage of you."

That was an out-and-out lie and it wasn't just his male pride that said so. But he didn't want to argue about it. Or about anything else. "Then I guess we could call it a draw."

Her eyes crinkled as she nodded. "Works for me."

Relief settled in.

"Me, too." And then, because his stomach decided to speak up again, voicing a very loud complaint, he asked, "What are my chances of getting some dinner tonight? Actually, it doesn't have to qualify as dinner. At this point, anything'll do. If you have some boiled cardboard lying around, I can make do with that."

"'Boiled cardboard,'" she repeated.

He raised his shoulders in a careless shrug, then let them drop again. "What can I say? I'm easy."

"There's easy, and then there's just selling yourself too cheap. Cheap isn't good," she said, pretending that they were having an actual sensible conversation.

"I'll have to keep that in mind," he said.

"You do that." She hooked her arm in his as she

led him to the kitchen. "In the meantime, why don't I see what I can come up with to satisfy that stomach of yours so it can stop whimpering like that."

"My stomach doesn't whimper, it rumbles."

"Whatever you say."

"It does," he protested. As if on cue, his stomach made a noise. "See, there it goes again."

She managed to keep a straight face. "All I hear is whimpering," Kasey said as she opened the refrigerator door.

Eli knew better than to argue. Besides, he was too busy making love to her with his eyes even to consider arguing with this woman who made his world spin off its axis.

Chapter Eleven

In the evenings, if Eli wasn't with her, Kasey always knew just where to find him. With Wayne. He'd either be playing peekaboo with the baby, reveling in the gleeful, infectious laughter that emerged from her son, or he'd be attending to the boy's needs. Eli had gotten better at changing Wayne than she was.

If Wayne was already in his room for the night, Eli could be found in the rocking chair, holding Wayne and reading a bedtime story to the boy. Once the boy was asleep, Eli would often just stand over the crib and watch him breathe rhythmically.

It was a scene to wrap her heart around.

That was the way she found him tonight. Staring down at Wayne as if mesmerized by the very sight of the boy sleeping.

"There you are," she whispered, coming up behind Eli. "Dinner's ready."

"I'll be right there," he promised, but he made no effort to move away from the crib.

She couldn't help herself—she had to ask. "You're

looking at him so intently, Eli. What is it that you think you see?"

Eli's smile deepened at her question—she noticed that he *always* smiled around Wayne. "That he has a world of endless possibilities in front of him. Right now, he could be anything, do anything, dream anything. He could even grow up to have the most beautiful girl in town fall in love with him." A whole beat passed before he realized what he'd just said and the kind of interpretation she was liable to put to it: that he thought she was in love with him. He knew better than to assume that. "That is, I didn't mean to imply that I thought—"

His tongue just kept getting thicker and more unmanageable as he tried to quickly dig his way out of his mistake.

But if he was afraid what he'd said would push her away again, he could have saved himself the grief. She had focused on something entirely different in his sentence.

"You think I'm beautiful?"

He slowly—and quietly—released a sigh of relief, even as he wondered why she looked so surprised. The woman had to own a mirror. "Of course you are."

"The most beautiful girl in town?" she questioned in wonder, repeating the words he'd used. She looked at him as if she hadn't seen him before. And maybe she hadn't. Not in this light. It put everything in a brand-new perspective.

"Absolutely," he affirmed, then added, "And you always have been to me."

Gently touching his face, she leaned into him and lightly brushed her lips against his. Not like a vain woman rewarding someone for giving her praise, but like a woman whose heart had been deeply moved by what she'd just heard him say.

"Dinner," she reminded him.

He nodded, remembering. "Dinner," he repeated, following her out of the room and into the hall.

Turning, he eased the door closed behind him. His sister, in keeping with her practice of always being one step ahead, had bought them a baby monitor. One of the four receivers was set up in the kitchen so that there was no need to be concerned that something might happen to the infant while they were busy elsewhere. They were able to hear every sound the baby made. Having the monitor definitely eased the fear that they wouldn't know if Wayne suddenly became distressed for some reason. It allowed them to have some time with one another without guilt and without involving diapers and spit-up.

Eli had had one of those days that seemed as if it was going to go on indefinitely. He felt completely wiped out and bone-tired as he sank into his chair in the kitchen.

"Need help?" he asked automatically.

"Sit there," she instructed. "You look like you just might fall over on your face if I have you doing anything."

Was there something she needed him to do? He tried his best to look like he was rallying.

"No, I'm good, really," he protested, going through the motions of getting up, even though somehow, he remained sitting where he was, his torso all but glued to the chair.

She turned to glance at him for a second, a smile playing on her lips that went a long way toward banishing the exhaustion from his body—at least temporarily.

"Yes," she agreed, punctuating the single word with a wink. "You are."

"Kasey?" he asked, not sure exactly what she was saying to him, only knowing that he was completely fascinated by what could only be described as a sensual expression on her face.

Ignoring the question in his voice, Kasey set a tureen on the table right between their two place mats. The contents were hot enough to emit a plume of steam.

"I made your favorite," she told Eli. "Beef stew."

She was rewarded with a look of pleasure that rose in his brown eyes.

It occurred to her—not for the first time—that they'd settled into a comfortable, familiar pattern, Eli, the baby and she. Mornings she'd get up—no matter how exquisitely exhausting the night before with Wayne might have been—and make Eli breakfast. After he ate, she'd send him off with a packed lunch and a kiss—and secretly begin counting the minutes until he walked through the front door again.

There was no point in pretending otherwise. She knew she was in love, although she refused to actually put a name to the exhilarating sensation coasting through her body. She was afraid if she neatly labeled it, love would arbitrarily disappear.

After all, she'd been in love before and it had turned out very badly. She didn't want to risk having what she had with Eli turn to ashes on her just because she'd called it by its rightful name. So, for now, she was just living each day, *enjoying* each day, and refusing to think beyond the moment or, at the very most, if she *had* to make plans, beyond the week she was in.

And each evening, Eli would walk through the door, and just like that, her heart would begin to sing. Everything seemed a little brighter, a little warmer. She didn't even have to be in the same room with him to know that he'd come home. She could just *feel* it. Even Wayne seemed to light up when he saw him. God knew, she certainly did.

And then, while she put the finishing touches on dinner, Eli would play with the baby. Or, like tonight, if Wayne was already in his crib, he'd tiptoe in just to check on him.

Wouldn't he be surprised to know how much that single thoughtful act on his part turned her on?

Once he came to the table, they'd eat and talk— sometimes for hours—then he'd help her tidy up and eventually they would go to bed. Together.

In the beginning, after that first night when they'd made love, there'd been just the slightest bit of hesitation—on his part rather than on hers.

That was due to his incredible chivalry again. He was always thinking of her, of Wayne. He never put himself first, which still astounded her because of all the years she'd spent with Hollis. Hollis had always thought of himself first. He believed that in the marriage, he was the one who really counted.

Hollis had told her once that his needs had to come first because he had to be in the right frame of mind to be able to take care of her. Looking back, she realized just how slow-witted she must have seemed, silently accepting his opinion without questioning him or challenging him.

She'd done a lot of growing in these past two-plus months, she thought. And it was all thanks to Eli.

"How is it?" she asked, watching Eli as he took his first forkful of dinner.

"Fantastic. As always," he added. "I don't think you could put together a bad meal even if you actually tried to."

She laughed at the compliment and the simple faith that was behind it. "You'd be surprised" was all she allowed herself to say.

There was no reason for her to go into detail about the first few disasters she'd had preparing meals, or how small Hollis had made her feel when he looked at her with belittling annoyance, saying that he thought she knew how to cook.

"Yeah, I would be," Eli agreed, continuing to eat with complete and obvious gusto. He seemed amazingly content. "You really outdid yourself this time," he told her with enthusiasm.

Kasey sat opposite him, taking a much smaller portion for herself. "You know what I think?" She didn't wait for his answer. "I think I probably could serve you boiled cardboard and you'd find something nice to say about it."

He was just that kind of person, she thought. Handsome, sexy *and* kind. It just didn't get any better than this.

Eli grinned in between forkfuls. "This is definitely *not* boiled cardboard," he told her with feeling. "If I'm not careful, I'm going to 'outgrow' my clothes and not in a good way. I'll wind up having to wear pants made out of burlap and tying them with a rope to keep them from falling down."

Kasey tried very hard not to laugh at the image that created in her mind. She didn't want to risk hurting his feelings.

"I don't think you have anything to worry about. You certainly don't appear as if you've gained any weight to me—and, if you remember, I *have* seen you up close—and personal," she added, her eyes dancing.

Funny, she and Hollis never had these sorts of sweet, intimate conversations. Most of the time, they really hadn't talked all that much at all. She'd been on edge around Hollis, waiting for him either to point out some failing of hers or to complain that there never seemed to be enough money around for him to do what he really wanted to do. Heaven knew she was often aware that there wasn't enough money available in their account to pay all the bills that kept cropping up.

But even she hadn't realized just how bad his gambling problem had gotten, she thought now. Not until he'd lost his family's ranch and her along with it.

"How could I forget?" Eli patted what was essentially a very flat middle. "Well, I guess if I've passed your inspection, it's okay for me to have a second helping tonight," he said, once again moving his now empty bowl up against the tureen. He ladled out another generous serving of beef stew. Tiny splashes were made by the tumbling vegetables.

This serving was even bigger than the first had been. Kasey shook her head in wonder. *Where* did he put it all? "Sure you don't have a tapeworm?"

Eli shrugged away the thought. "If I did, he'd be out of luck because I'm not about to share this food with any outsider."

What made it even better in his opinion was that she'd made the meal knowing that it was his favorite. She'd paid attention to learn what his favorite meal was. He found this to be very pleasing—and humbling, in a way. That he knew what her favorite things were went without saying, but then, he knew absolutely everything about her. To him, that was just a normal part of loving someone.

"But you really don't have to make an extra effort like this," he told her. "I'd be satisfied with anything you made—like a sandwich," he suggested off the top of his head.

"Sandwiches are for emergency trips, they're meant to keep you going. They're definitely *not* supposed to take the place of a real meal. Besides, I *like* cooking for you." They'd had this conversation before. She was determined to get her answer to register in Eli's brain this time. "Eli—" leaning forward, she covered his hand with her own "—I'm only going to say this once and I want you to listen to me. I never do *anything* because I have to, or feel obligated to. I'm doing it, whether it's cooking, or keeping house, or something else—" she paused for half a beat, allowing the last part to sink in "—because I *want* to. Because you *make* me want to. I just wish I could do more."

"That's not possible," he assured her with feeling.

He could feel his emotions surging within him. Once again it was on the tip of his tongue to tell her that he loved her. That she'd made him happier in these past two months than he ever thought possible.

And once again, he was afraid that putting his feelings into words would spell the beginning of the end. Most likely, he'd spook her, making her back away from him, possibly even *run* away from him.

Who knew? Kasey might even be considering moving out on her own right now. He just didn't know. But the one thing he did know was that if he said anything that remotely *resembled* a declaration of love, he'd find her packing her things within the hour.

He wanted to avoid, or at least to forestall, the end

for as long as possible. And that meant keeping his feelings to himself even though he was all but dying for them to finally come out.

"You are so very good for my ego," Kasey was telling him, savoring what he had just said. Rising, she took her empty bowl to the sink to rinse it out before she placed it in the dishwasher. The dishwasher was a recent purchase. She knew he'd bought it for her, even though he'd told her it was one of those things that he'd been meaning to get around to buying for himself.

Eli didn't lie very convincingly, which was another point in his favor. Hollis could lie like a pro. He did it so smoothly that after a while even he was convinced he was telling the truth. The upshot of it was, she never knew what to believe.

Whereas with Eli, she knew that if he said the moon had suddenly turned to pink cheese, she would race outside to see the phenomenon for herself. She trusted him beyond any words, any vows, any promises made between a man and a woman.

Kasey turned around to say something to him, but the words never came out. The serious expression on his face drove any and all coherent thought out of her head.

Why did he look like that? "What's the matter?" she asked in a hushed voice.

He raised his hand, silently asking for *her* silence. He cocked his head, listening intently. Then, rather than explain or answer her question, he was up on his feet, leaving the room. Hurrying to the second floor and Wayne's room.

Since he'd been listening to the baby's monitor, it had to be something concerning Wayne. The moment that occurred to her, concern and worry flooded her.

Hurrying after Eli, she ran up the stairs in his wake, trying to catch up.

"Eli, what's the matter?" she asked. "Why are you running?"

"He's wheezing" was all he had time to say, tossing the words over his shoulder. The next moment he burst into Wayne's room. Crossing to the crib, he saw the problem instantly. The baby was on his stomach, his face all but buried against the stuffed rabbit that had been propped up next to the inside of his crib.

Reaching the infant first, Eli turned the boy onto his back. Then he checked to see if perhaps the baby had gotten something stuck up his nose or in his throat.

But the passages were all clear and once he was on his back, the baby began to breathe more easily.

Eli removed the rabbit, tossing him onto the rocking chair he'd bought for Kasey to celebrate her first week on his ranch.

And then it hit him.

"Kasey, I left Wayne on his back, the way I always do." His eyes met hers. "Do you know what this means?" he asked as he picked the fussing infant up and began to gently sway with him.

"He turned over by himself." She said the words out loud, partially in amazement. She paused, thinking of what she'd found in the *Parenting During the First Year* book—also a present from Eli. He had a way of spoiling her, she thought fondly, then forced herself to get her mind back on track. "Isn't he a little young to be doing that?"

"Not for an exceptional baby," Eli assured her, then looked at the infant in his arms. "And you are exceptional, aren't you, Wayne?"

For his part, Wayne looked up at him with wide, serious eyes, as if he was hanging on Eli's every word.

"Well, since I'm here…." Eli said, pretending to resign himself to the chore. "I guess we might as well finish that story I was reading to you last night," Eli said as if the little boy understood every word.

Picking up the large, rectangular book from the top of the bookcase, he settled in to read. "Let's see what that little mouse has been up to since we left him," he said, taking a seat in the rocking chair. He arranged the baby so that he could turn the pages more easily while still holding Wayne against his chest.

Kasey lingered in the doorway for a couple of minutes, listening and wondering whether, if she prayed very hard and was the best person she could possibly be, she could keep living inside this dream for a little longer. She knew all good things came to an end, but that didn't mean it had to be right now, did it?

The sound of Eli's voice, reading to Wayne, followed her all the way down the hall until she reached the stairs. Her smile lasted a great deal longer.

Chapter Twelve

Something was bothering her.

Eli could see it in her eyes. Kasey hadn't really said anything yet and she was moving around the kitchen, getting breakfast, acting as if nothing out of the ordinary was going on.

That was the problem. She was *acting*. He could tell the difference when it came to Kasey. For instance, he'd noticed that she had paused in midmotion several times, as if wrestling with a thought or searching for the right words to use before she said anything to him.

A sliver of uneasiness pricked him.

He knew he should give Kasey space and let her say something—or not say something—when she was ready. But he would be going out to the stable soon and wondering what was on her mind would bedevil him the whole time he was gone. Not to mention that if she decided she *did* want to talk to him, she would have to trek out to the corral with Wayne since that was where he would be for most the day, training the horses.

No, asking her outright was by far the easier route

all the way around, despite the fact that he really didn't like invading Kasey's territory, or making her feel pressured.

"Something on your mind, Kasey?" he asked, trying to sound casual.

What she said in response threw him off a little. At the very least, it wasn't what he'd expected her to say. Or, in this case, ask.

"How are your training sessions with the horses going?"

"They're going well," he answered slowly, never taking his eyes off her expression, waiting for something to tip him off. She'd never asked him about his training sessions before. "As a matter of fact, I'm ahead of schedule." He paused, waiting. She said nothing. "Why?" he finally asked.

She answered his last question in a roundabout fashion, like someone feeling their away around a brand-new situation.

"Then would you mind not training them? Just for today, I mean," she added quickly. There was no missing the hope in her voice.

He noticed that she'd wrapped her hands around the mug of coffee she'd poured for herself. Her hands were shaking a little.

Something was *definitely* wrong.

"No, I wouldn't mind," he told her, watching her more intently than ever. He curbed a sudden surge of impatience, knowing that would only make her more reticent to explain whatever had prompted her request.

"Why?" he asked gently. "What do you have in mind, Kasey?"

She pressed her lips together, half-annoyed with herself for not being stronger. She'd done so much by herself in these past few years, taking care of the ranch, trying to make a go of her marriage. She should have been able to do this alone, as well.

But this was a huge step she was about to take. Heaven help her, but she wanted someone to lean on, someone to turn to for emotional support. She was afraid that if she didn't, if she went alone, she might change her mind at the last moment.

She blew out a shaky breath. "I'm thinking of going into town today."

He waited for her to continue. When she didn't, he picked up the fallen thread of conversation. "All right. I can certainly put some things off for a day. Any particular destination in town you have in mind?" he asked mildly.

She was pressing her hands so hard against the mug, he was surprised it didn't just shatter. "I thought I'd go see Olivia. The sheriff's wife."

He smiled at the addendum. "I know who Olivia is, Kasey." And then the pieces started coming together for him. "This isn't going to be a social call, is it?"

She shook her head slowly from side to side. "No, it's not."

If she was going to do what he thought she was going to do, she needed to at least be able to put it into words, to say it out loud so that she could begin getting used to the idea.

"Why are you going to see Olivia?" he persisted.

She didn't answer him right away, trying to get comfortable with the idea. What she knew she *had* to do.

Kasey took in a deep breath. This would be her reality now. She had already forced herself to face the fact that her marriage was over.

Technically, it had been over for longer than just these past two and a half months. It had been over the moment she'd become pregnant. She'd only fooled herself during those nine months before Wayne was born, telling herself that Hollis would change once the baby was here. Telling herself that he'd want to finally grow up because he was responsible for a brand-new little human being and behaving recklessly was no longer the answer.

But despite her ongoing optimism, in her heart, she'd always known better. Always known that Hollis was *not* the man she'd hoped he was beneath all the bad-boy trappings.

The roof of her mouth felt like sandpaper as she told Eli, "I want to file for a divorce. Hollis isn't coming back and I need to move forward."

Although this was *exactly* what he'd hoped for, Eli didn't want her feeling pressured to take this step. Not that he had pressured her, even remotely, but maybe just the very fact that he had taken her into his home somehow made her feel obligated to take this step. Especially since they were now sleeping together.

"Are you sure you want to do this, Kasey?"

The question, coming from him, surprised her. Was he afraid that once she was a free woman again, she'd try to get him to marry her? Well, he could rest easy. She was not about to repay his kindness with any undue expectations.

She'd been blind before, blind to all the wonderful qualities Eli possessed, but that was on her. She'd missed out on a great deal—on the life she would have ideally wanted. But again, there were no "do-overs" in life and she was just grateful to have Eli in *her* life. More importantly, with any luck, the bond he was forming with her son would continue. She knew that Wayne would be the richer for it. As would she.

"Very sure," she answered.

He wanted to reach out to her, to hold her and assure her that he'd always be there for her. But, considering this step she was taking, he didn't want her to feel crowded or stalked in even the vaguest sort of way.

"All right, then," he told her. "Let me just take care of a few basic things with the horses and then I'm all yours." Finished with breakfast, he was already on his feet and heading for the back door.

As she turned away to clear the table, Kasey smiled sadly to herself.

If only.

But she knew that she had no one to blame but herself for that. And wishing for a do-over was more than useless. It was a waste of time.

A FEW HOURS LATER, Olivia Santiago, Forever's legal Jill of all trades, ushered in her first client of the morning. Eli, Kasey and Kasey's son were welcomed into the office before the lawyer asked them just what it was that had brought them to her.

"How can I help you?" Olivia asked, looking from Kasey to Eli. And then her gaze came to rest on the cooing baby.

"My daughter used to drool something awful at about his age," Olivia confided. "I couldn't wait until she outgrew it. Now I wish those days were back." And then she laughed. "It's true what they say, you know," she told Kasey. "They *do* grow up much too fast. Cherish every moment you get."

Kasey nodded her agreement, but when she spoke, it wasn't in reference to Olivia's last observation. It was to answer her initial question.

"I need to know if I can file for divorce if my—" Unable to refer to Hollis either by his name, or by what he was supposed to have been to her, she fell back on a euphemism. "If the other party isn't around."

She paused for half a second to pull herself together, searching for inner strength. The encouraging smile Eli flashed at her seemed to do the trick.

"He walked out on me. On us," Kasey amended, looking at Wayne.

The infant was obligingly drifting off to sleep, but

fighting it as best he could. His eyes had popped open twice, as if he was aware that once they really closed, he'd be sound asleep and missing out on whatever was going on here. But within moments he'd given up the fight and the sound of soft, regular breathing noises could be heard coming from his small mouth.

Olivia appeared extremely sympathetic to what Kasey had just told her.

"You have grounds for a divorce," she assured the other woman. Then she put it into a single word. "Abandonment. I can also get the paperwork going to sue him for child support and make sure that he never gets joint custody—"

The laugh that emerged from Kasey's lips echoed of sadness. "You don't have to go through the trouble of that," she told Olivia. "The last thing in the world Hollis wants is to be responsible for Wayne. That was why he left to begin with."

Olivia raised an eyebrow. "Oh?" She looked to Eli for confirmation and he gave her a very discrete nod.

Steeling herself as best she could, Kasey went over the events of the past. "He said he couldn't take the idea of being a father. And I don't want to sue him for child support." She didn't want a single thing from Hollis, other than to be left alone. "I'll take care of Wayne myself. I just don't want Hollis coming back into our lives, thinking that he could just pick up where he left off."

"I understand how you feel," Olivia assured her new client. "You do know, however, that he is responsible for at least half of your son's care and feeding. More if he can afford it."

But Kasey was already shaking her head. It was a lovely scenario that Olivia painted, but it just wasn't about to happen.

"I know Hollis. He won't pay it."

"In that case, he can be a guest of my husband's jail," Olivia told her in a no-nonsense voice.

Even so, Kasey remained adamant. She wanted to have nothing further to do with Hollis. Dealing with him was just a reminder of the kind of fool she'd been.

"If it's all the same to you," she said to Olivia, "just file the divorce papers, please."

Olivia seemed eager to talk her out of this pacifistic stance, but Kasey remained firm on this issue.

With a sigh, Olivia said, "You're in the driver's seat. I'll draw up the necessary papers and bring them on over when they're ready. That should be in a few days."

She raised her eyes to Eli, who had been quiet throughout the conversation.

Kasey nodded, relieved that it would finally be over. And yet, at the same time, there was a bit of residual sadness, as well.

"I'll have to pay you in installments."

It killed her to admit, but there was no getting around the fact that she had very little in the way of money right now. She might as well let the attorney know that up front. Paying her in installments would be the case no matter what the charge. And, no matter what the cost, she was determined to pay her own way.

It occurred to Kasey at that point that she was still missing one crucial piece of information. "You haven't told me your fee."

Olivia waved a hand at the question as she accompanied the young couple and the infant to the door of her office.

"Don't worry about it, we'll work something out," she promised. And then, curious, she asked Eli, "Will I see you at the wedding?" A second later, she laughed at her own question. The answer was perforce a no-brainer. "Of course I will. I forgot for a minute that Alma is your sister, isn't she?"

Eli smiled as he nodded. "That she is." A dozen memories came crowding back to him. He wondered if he should send Cash a condolence card. Poor guy didn't know what he was getting himself into.

"Rick thinks the world of her," Olivia confided. "And my closedmouthed husband doesn't often speak highly of people. I can't say I know much about your sister's future husband, though."

"Actually, Cash is originally from around here," Eli told Kasey's new lawyer. "He and I and Gabriel were best friends back in elementary and high school. We lost touch when he went off to college to become a lawyer." That had been Cash's doing, but it was all in the past now. Cash would be part of the family. Eli pretended to lower his voice as he said, "You know what they say about lawyers."

"That they're the salt of the earth?" Olivia interjected, tongue-in-cheek.

Eli smiled, going with her description. "I don't know about any other place, but they are around here."

Olivia smiled her appreciation at the kind words.

Extending her hand, she first shook Kasey's, then his. "I think we're going to get along fine. And don't worry," she told Kasey. "I'll be sure to handle everything. All you'll have to do is sign on the dotted line."

"Just like that," Kasey murmured a few minutes later as they were walking back to Eli's Jeep. Eli looked at her quizzically, not really following her train of thought. "Just like that," she repeated. "I sign on the dotted line and the marriage is dissolved, almost like it never happened."

Was that regret he heard in her voice? What kind of regret was it? Was it regret over the end of her marriage, or that she had married Hollis in the first place? And if it was the first, what did he do? Did he try to change her mind, or did he let her sort it out by herself, without any interference—praying that he would come out the victor?

"Having second thoughts?" he asked, watching her expression in case she chose to lie to him.

She didn't. "No, just amazed at how quickly something can be erased, that's all."

"Not everything," he assured her, slipping his arm through hers and lending her a hand.

She smiled at that, taking enormous comfort in just

the sound of his voice as well as in what he was subtly telling her. That his presence in her life was steadfast.

"Nice to know," she murmured.

Chapter Thirteen

Miguel Rodriguez was not a man who gave in to sentiment easily.

Except for the time when he held his dying wife in his arms, feeling the weak flicker of life slowly ebbing away from her, he kept his emotions tightly under wraps. It was important to him to remain on an even keel no matter whether it was an occasion for anger or for joy. The father of six always met both in the same manner. With thoughtful reserve.

But today was different.

Today his youngest born, his baby, his Alma, was getting married. The first of his children to do so. And, he realized as emotions vied for space within him, all but choking him, she looked absolutely beautiful in her mother's wedding gown.

He'd known Alma was going to be wearing it. He was the one who had offered to take it down for her from the attic.

But he hadn't seen her in it.

Until now.

He hadn't expected her to look so much like his young bride had all those many years ago.

Long-ago yesterday, he thought now, because that was what it felt like. As if he and Dolores had just exchanged their vows yesterday.

It was hard to believe that a lifetime had passed since then.

He hadn't been prepared for the kick to his gut that he'd received when he first saw Alma in the wedding dress. Popping his head into the room where Alma and some of her bridesmaids were getting ready—after first knocking to make sure he wouldn't be surprising anyone—Miguel was the one who found himself on the receiving end of a big surprise.

It took him a second to remember to breathe and far longer to tear his eyes away.

He felt moisture forming along his eyelashes.

Miguel cleared his throat, trying to sound as if nothing was out of the ordinary, but it so obviously was. "For just a moment, I thought your mother was back. That I was looking at her, not you, on our wedding day. She was a beautiful, beautiful bride," he told her. "As are you," he added reverently, patting her hand.

Moved, Alma had to take a moment before she could say anything to her father. And that was when she saw it, the glisten of unshed tears in his eyes.

"Dad, you're not going to cry, are you?" she asked in a disbelieving whisper. She didn't know whether to be horrified—or touched. What she was without thinking, was stunned.

Miguel shook his head, tilting it backward a bit, as if relying on gravity to hold his tears in abeyance.

"Of course not. A man does not cry," he told her. "I just wanted to see if you were ready yet, that is all."

She nodded, letting him have his white lie. "It must be the lighting in here," she said after a moment's speculation.

Still, as she gave his hamlike hand a squeeze, Kasey tucked a handkerchief into it—just in case.

Miguel glanced down at his hand and then back at her, a glimmer of surprise in his eyes. She merely winked at him, as if to tell him that this would be their little secret.

"I will be waiting for you outside the church doors," he told her. Then, after a sweeping glance that took in all of the other bridesmaids, all women who had grown up in Forever—except for Olivia Santiago, the sheriff's wife—he put his hand on the doorknob, ready to leave. "Ladies," he said politely, bowing his head as a sign of respect, "I will see you all inside."

"Your father looks very happy about you marrying Cash," Kasey commented.

Although not a bridesmaid, Kasey had offered to be a last-minute gofer for Eli's sister. Not encumbered by the flowing gray-blue bridesmaid's dress, she pointed out that she could move around far more easily than the members of the bridal party.

Having witnessed the exchange between Alma and

Miguel, Kasey couldn't help wondering what that felt like, having a father, much less one who so visibly approved of her and what she was doing. One who was so completely invested in her happiness.

Her own father had been nothing like that. If anything, he'd seemed resentful of her, of the attention she'd received from her mother when she was very young. Attention that he felt had been taken away from him. Some men were just not cut out to be fathers and he was one of them.

Like Hollis, she thought, although at the time, when she'd happily accepted his proposal that night and fled her father's house, she hadn't even been thinking about that possibility.

Her father was dead now, but she found herself wondering if, like the sheriff's mother, he would have attempted to make amends for his obvious shortcomings. Would he have professed to regret his actions the way she had?

The sheriff and his sister, Ramona, the town veterinarian now that her mentor had retired, had both gone through a very rocky period when their mother suddenly returned to Forever asking for their forgiveness. It had been harder on Mona than on Rick, but in the end, they had come around and softened, forgiving the repentant woman. Their mother had since become a very important person in their lives, watching their children grow the way she hadn't when they had been that age.

It was the sheriff's mother who had volunteered to

watch over all the children today so that their parents could have a few hours of enjoyment at the wedding.

Some stories did have happy endings, Kasey thought. Would hers?

"Your father looked really very moved to see you in that wedding dress," she commented to Alma as she helped her with the full-length veil, spreading it out so that it didn't get tangled underfoot.

Alma was silent for a moment, solemnly scrutinizing her reflection in the mirror. The young woman looking back was her—and it wasn't.

"I hadn't realized how much I looked like my mother," Alma said in a quiet voice. It had taken her father's shaken observation to make her see that. "Funny, growing up, I didn't think I looked a thing like her."

"That's because, growing up, you were always covered with dirt, running after all of us and trying so hard to compete," Eli said.

After running into his father just now and hearing what he'd said about Alma, Eli wanted to see the resemblance to his mother for himself. Standing in the doorway now, he could see both sides of his sister, thanks to the position of the full length, wood-framed mirror in the room.

Although he had obviously only seen photographs from that day, he could see an eerie similarity between his one-time tomboy sister and the genteel, dark-eyed woman who had been their mother.

Alma turned from the mirror. "What do you mean,

'trying' to compete?" she challenged, pretending to rise to the bait. "I usually *beat* all of you boys—especially you."

"You didn't *beat* me," he corrected. "I just felt sorry for you and didn't want to be the one who delivered a final death blow to that 'fragile' ego of yours," he informed her with a laugh. Walking into the room, Eli paused for a second, taking in the full effect of the vision his sister cast. "Dad's right. You do look beautiful, Alma," he acknowledged, becoming serious for just a moment. "Cash is a lucky guy."

Alma could feel herself growing emotional, just as her father had earlier. She'd promised herself to keep a tight rein on her more sensitive feelings. Tears just ruined makeup.

"Don't be nice to me, Eli," she chided. "You know I don't know what to do when you're nice to me." Alma blinked several times, warding away the tears that threatened to betray her.

He took her words in stride and nodded. "Okay, I'll go get a switch and beat you with it. Be right back," he promised, backing away.

Watching the exchange between Eli and his sister, Kasey realized all over again what a very special man he really was. And how very lucky she was to have him in her life, however briefly that turned out to be.

Don't go there now, she chastised herself. *Nothing good'll come of it. Just enjoy the moment and pray it continues.*

On his way out, Eli paused by her. Raising his

voice, he said to his sister, "If you're through with Kasey, I'd like to steal her back for a while."

"I'm all set," Alma announced. "She's free to do whatever she wants." Glancing in her direction, Alma said, "Thanks for your help, Kasey."

"I did next to nothing," Kasey protested.

"Nothing's good," Eli quipped, only to have his shoulder hit. "Hey, careful," he chided. "I bruise easily."

But curiosity kept Kasey from verbally sparring with him. Turning toward Eli so that she blocked anyone's visual access to him, she asked in a lowered voice, "What's wrong?" There was uneasy anticipation in her eyes as she waited for him to say something.

"Nothing," he whispered in her ear. "I just want you to myself, that's all."

A warm glow, initiated by the feel of his breath against her ear and neck and fed by his words, spread rapidly through her.

Her heart swelling despite all her logical reasoning, Kasey grinned. "Careful what you wish for," she whispered back.

That might be true, at times, in other cases, Eli thought, but not in this one. Because right at this precious moment, he was happier than he could ever remember. The girl he'd been in love with since forever was right next to him when he woke up each morning and when he went to bed each night.

And he was absolutely crazy about her son. When things settled down a little after Alma's wedding and after Kasey's divorce was finalized, he was going to ask her to marry him. And if she said yes—he didn't want to think about how he would feel if she turned him down—he would ask her if she had any objections to his adopting Wayne and making the boy his son in the eyes of the law.

He couldn't think of anything he wanted more, the perfect woman and the perfect family. That would be all he'd need.

Ever.

But for now, Eli kept his thoughts to himself, not wanting to make Kasey feel as if he was rushing her. Even without words, he was fairly certain that she knew how he felt about her. He knew it was certainly there, in his eyes, every time they made love, or laughed together, or just shared a quiet moment together. He couldn't hide his love for her, not even if his very life depended on it.

She had become very important to his world.

Hell, she *was* his world.

And he had never felt luckier.

THE ACTUAL WEDDING ceremony was simple and all the more beautiful for it.

Simple or not, Kasey was struck by the contrast between Alma and Cash's ceremony and the one that she'd had when she'd married Hollis. The whole thing had lasted five minutes—if that much—from start to finish.

And afterward, when they'd checked into a motel

that had looked better cloaked by the night than it did in the light of day, the lovemaking that followed had been conspicuously short on tenderness and—for her—long on disillusion.

But for that she had only herself to blame. After all, no one had forced her to build up fantasies that, Hollis quickly made her aware of, belonged to a child, not a woman. Certainly not one who knew what the real world was like.

It was only after she'd experienced making love with Eli that Kasey realized her fantasies *could* become a reality. To her unmitigated joy, she'd found everything she'd ever been looking for—and so much more—in Eli's arms.

There was a collective sigh, followed by applause and cheers, when the ceremony concluded and the priest pronounced Cash and Alma to be husband and wife in the eyes of God and the law.

Kasey, Eli noted, had been awfully quiet throughout the whole thing. Even at the very end when Cash had kissed Alma so long that their relatives and friends had all begun to rhythmically clap as if they were keeping time with the beat, Eli noticed that Kasey was just going through the motions as she watched the couple intently.

Her palms hardly touched as she clapped.

Was she thinking about her own wedding? Was she thinking about Hollis? Or worse, was she missing him?

He had no right to be jealous, especially since Hollis was no longer around, but he was. Hollis didn't deserve to have one minute wasted on him with thoughts of regret. Definitely not after what he'd done to Kasey. She should erect a piñata with his face on it so that she could take a stick to it, not pine for his return.

Still, he didn't want her being uncomfortable, and the wedding might be bringing up past hurts and longings for her. It wasn't like her to be this quiet this long. "Do you want to leave?" he asked.

The question startled her. Without thinking, she wrapped her hand along her neck, as if pressing the warmth of his breath into her skin permanently.

"No, why?" Was *he* the one who wanted to leave for some reason? "Do you?"

This was his sister's wedding, why would he want to leave? He shook his head in response. "No, but I just thought—" He stopped and tried again, determined to sound coherent. "You just looked like you were a million miles away."

Or however far away Hollis was these days, he added silently.

"Did I?" she questioned. "I wasn't, really. I was just thinking how happy they looked. And how happy I am for them," she added with feeling. Just because her own circumstances hadn't worked out didn't mean she wanted other people not to have a shot at happiness and attaining their own happily ever after. "Especially Alma."

She looked at Eli as they filed out of the rows of chairs, following behind the bride and groom.

"Did you know that she was once in love with Cash?" She suspected that Alma had never really stopped loving the man, but she hadn't pressed the issue when Alma had confided in her.

For the most part, Kasey was not the type to be eaten up by curiosity. She could wait for something to be told to her, no matter how long it took to own up to. But that didn't mean she didn't have her suspicions.

"It's nice to know that sometimes happy endings do happen," she said wistfully, more to herself, actually, than to Eli.

"It's not a happy ending," Eli pointed out. When she looked at him, confused, he explained. "It's a happy beginning."

"I do like the way you think, Eli," Kasey confessed. He had such a positive outlook on things, and yet it wasn't without some sort of a basis, a solid foundation. There was *logic* behind his positive thinking. Whereas Hollis always had a tendency to build castles in the sky, shooting for improbable things that hadn't a prayer of coming true. He had no solid base, no foundation.

How different the two men were, she thought now. One was charming and attractive and about as deep as a thimbleful of water. The other was a rock, someone she could trust, someone she could lean on.

Someone, she now realized, who put her first, before himself. The bottom line was that Eli was a man, while Hollis was an attractive bad boy.

But as sexy as it might initially be, the latter attraction wore thin in the real world, she mused, realizing how lucky she was and how grateful she was to have been given a second chance to do it right.

A second chance to discover that Eli had feelings for her, at least for now. Of the two, it was Eli who was the better man. She just hadn't realized it before, at least not consciously. She'd been too blind, too dazzled by a man with no substance.

Eli had substance.

Thanks to the efforts of some very skilled amateur musicians, music filled the air.

"Dance with me, Eli?" Kasey proposed suddenly, putting out her hand to him.

Reluctantly he took her hand but didn't move. "I don't dance, Kasey," Eli told her.

"Yes, you do," she insisted. "You danced with me. At the prom, remember?"

At the time Hollis had temporarily disappeared on her and when she'd come to him, asking if he knew where Hollis had gotten to, he had feigned ignorance, then asked her to dance to distract her.

He'd known that Hollis had ducked out with another girl who was very willing to gratify his more basic needs. Hollis had gone missing for approximately half an hour, then returned to claim "his date." Hollis had also accused him with a laugh of "stealing his girl."

For his part, Eli had come extremely close to confronting Hollis about cheating on Kasey that night, but he hadn't wanted to humiliate her in front of the whole senior class, so he'd kept his mouth shut and said nothing.

And Kasey went on believing Hollis's stories.

"I remember," Eli said. Then, with a shrug, still holding her hand, he led her to the small area that had been cleared for dancing. "I'm really rusty. I can't remember dancing since then, so you're doing this at your own risk. Don't say I didn't warn you."

"Consider me warned," she told him, a smile playing on her generous mouth. "I've decided to chance it," she said bravely. "Besides, you would never hurt me."

And knowing that was an immense comfort to her.

And almost a burden for him.

Chapter Fourteen

The reception, held outdoors on Miguel Rodriguez's ranch, was deliberately an informal affair. In the spirit of camaraderie, attendance was open to anyone who wanted to stop by to add their good wishes for the happy couple.

Which was how the man who wound up casting a shadow over the event had come to be there.

One moment Eli was holding Kasey in his arms, swaying to a slow dance and allowing himself to make plans for their future. The next moment a chill went down his back as he heard a familiar voice uttering a phrase out of the past.

"Thanks for taking care of my girl, but I can take over now."

It was like being on the receiving end of an upended bucket of ice water. Both he and Kasey immediately froze in place, then, ever so slowly, they turned around to look at the man who had just spoken.

Her mouth went dry at the same time that her heart rate sped up.

This can't be happening. It has to be a nightmare.

The thought pulsed in Kasey's brain over and over again, repeating itself like an old-fashioned record playing on a Victrola with its needle stuck in a groove.

"Hollis," she finally whispered hoarsely in sheer disbelief. What was he doing here? *Why* was he here?

Hollis smiled at her then, that wide, golden smile that had once captured her heart and so firmly captivated her soul. A smile that now left her utterly cold.

"In the flesh," he told her, spreading his hands in front of himself like a showman. He completely ignored Eli, looking only at her. "May I have this dance?" he asked, acting as if it were a sheer formality, that he didn't expect any resistance.

"The music stopped," Eli said, still holding Kasey to him. His voice was cool enough to freeze an ice-cube tray filled with hot water.

Hollis didn't even bother sparing his one-time friend so much as an extra glance.

"So it did." He had eyes only for Kasey. "I guess I'll just have to wait for the next song."

Eli squared his shoulders, shifting slightly so that he was between Hollis and Kasey. "I don't think so." He ground the words out between clenched teeth.

Hollis finally glanced in his direction. There was more than a little mocking contempt in his tone. "Don't get carried away, Eli. When I asked you to look out for her, I didn't mean when I was around. Your job's done here."

For two cents—less—he would have decked the pompous jerk he'd once thought his friend. But this was Kasey's call. So Eli turned to her, waiting for Kasey to say something, to tell him whether she wanted Hollis to go—or to stay.

Kasey remained where she was, making no effort to move around Eli. "Don't cause a scene, Hollis" was all she said.

"Hey, I'm not the one acting like some big super-hero," Hollis protested, dismissing Eli's presence with a sneer. He eyed Kasey, his demeanor growing serious. "I'm back and I want to make amends. I've missed you, Kasey," he told her, sounding more sincere than she'd ever heard him. "We need to talk."

She was not about to allow him to draw the focus away from Alma and Cash. This was *their* day and she didn't want it marred by a potential ugly scene. It gave her the courage to tell him, "Not here."

Kasey was willing to talk to Hollis, Eli thought, even after he'd walked out on her. Willing to hear the man out despite all the things he'd done to her. But then, Kasey was usually willing to hear a person out, willing to be more than fair no matter how poorly they'd treated her. He remembered how she used to make excuses for her father's behavior.

He had a bad feeling about this.

Hollis had a golden tongue when he set his mind to it. The gift of gab, some people called it. Gift or not, all Eli knew was that Hollis could talk a wolf into buying a fur coat in the middle of July.

While he, well, he had a habit of getting tongue-tied and not being able to say just the right thing when the time came for persuasive arguments. The right words would come to him *after* the fact, when it no longer mattered.

Eli could feel his stomach tying itself into a hard knot, but there was nothing he could say. Nothing he *would* say. He didn't want Kasey looking at him someday and accusing him of having talked her out of reuniting with her husband.

Husband, Eli thought bitterly. Whether he liked it or not, until the papers were final, Hollis was Kasey's husband.

As for him, he was just the man who'd loved her forever. In silence.

The bad feeling he had grew.

"Where and when?" Hollis asked, his grin widening. "You just name the time and place, Kase, and I'll be there, waiting with baited breath." He watched her for a long moment, his grin fading, his voice growing serious. He lowered it as he said, "I didn't mean to hurt you."

Kasey gave no indication that she'd even heard the last words he'd said. Instead she addressed the question he'd put to her. "I'll let you know."

"I'll be waiting," he promised, then added for good measure, "My fate is entirely in your hands." No doubt feeling himself to be on solid ground, he glanced at Eli and said magnanimously, "You did a good job looking out for her. Thanks."

Eli knew he should just ignore Hollis altogether. He shouldn't let the man get under his skin like this, but he couldn't make himself just stay silent, either. "I didn't do it for you."

Hollis surprised him by quietly acknowledging, "I know."

"Problem?"

The question, mildly put, came from Rick. His manner was nonthreatening as he asked the simple question, but there was no doubt in anyone's mind that Rick could become all business at a moment's notice if necessary.

Finally, Eli spoke up, taking the opportunity to defuse the possibly explosive situation. "No, no problem, Sheriff. Hollis here was just leaving." He looked at his former friend expectantly. "Weren't you, Hollis?"

Hollis had no choice but to nod, confirming Eli's statement. "I just wanted to pay my respects to the happy couple," he said pointedly.

"Then you've got your 'happy couples' confused," Rick informed him in a pseudo-expansive voice. "Alma and Cash are the ones sitting at the head table." Rick nodded over in their direction. "Just follow me, I'll take you to them." It wasn't an invitation but a thinly veiled order. "I'm walking right by them." He eyed the man expectantly, waiting for Hollis to fall into step beside him.

Reluctantly, Hollis finally did.

But just as he left, Hollis looked over his shoulder at Kasey. "I'll see you soon," he promised.

And she knew he intended to. Until they had that conversation that Hollis had alluded to when he'd said they needed to talk, she was certain that he would continue popping up when she least expected it.

Or wanted it.

If she was to have any peace of mind, she had no other choice but to get this over with sooner than later. She'd hear him out and then—

"You're really going to see him?" Eli asked, snapping her back into the immediate present. Eli didn't seem exactly happy about the turn of events.

That made two of them.

"I don't think that I have much of a choice," she told Eli. He probably had no idea how much that bothered her, not to have any options, but instead to have her path cut out for her by someone whose motives were highly suspect.

Eli frowned. He took her response to mean that she *wanted* to see Hollis. *And why shouldn't she?* a voice in his head taunted. Hollis had been her husband, was *still* her husband. And during their marriage, he had managed to throw her equilibrium off so much that logic had no place in her life.

A person just had to reflect on her past. She'd gone against her parents because of Hollis, run off and married Hollis against her parents' expressed wishes.

Had he really expected her to choose him over someone as dynamic, as mesmerizingly compelling as Hollis? That kind of thing only happened in his dreams. He had a sinking feeling that reality had a completely different kind of outcome in store for him.

Kasey turned her brilliant blue eyes on him and

said something unexpected. "Unless you don't want me to talk to him."

No, don't talk to him! Don't ever talk to him. Not one single word, because he'll twist everything around, make himself out to be the victim here. And you'll take him back, warts and all.

But out loud, all Eli said was, "I have no right to tell you what to do or not to do."

If he had to tell her not to talk to Hollis, well, then it didn't really count, did it? He wanted her to come to that conclusion on her own. He wanted her to cut Hollis off without so much as a prayer. It wouldn't count if he asked her to do it.

The corners of Kasey's mouth curved just a little. The fact that Eli didn't tell her what to do was part of the reason why she loved him the way she did. But even so, a small voice within her questioned what he'd just said.

Didn't he care that Hollis was obviously trying to get her back? Had she been just a pleasant interlude for Eli? Someone to warm his sheets for a while? Didn't he *want* something permanent with her? Was she wrong about him after all?

All these questions and more crowded her mind, making her uncertain about what to expect next when it came to Eli and herself—if there actually *was* such a duo.

Expect nothing. That way, you can't be disappointed.

Kasey could feel the frustration building up inside of her.

For now, she forced herself to push all that aside and go on pretending that they were the same two people who had arrived at the ceremony just a few short hours ago.

As the music started up again, she looked up at Eli pointedly as she held out her arms to him. "We have a dance to finish."

And this might be the last time he got to hold her in his arms, Eli thought.

"So we do," he acknowledged, pulling Kasey to him again. And they danced, each determined to block out everything that threatened to rend their fragile world apart.

The reception ended by degrees rather than by any sort of agreement. Eventually there were only a few people left. The bride and groom, accompanied by a wealth of good wishes, cheers and applause, had driven off in their car some forty minutes ago, in a hurry to begin their honeymoon. The people attending the reception had begun dispersing around then.

Tired, Kasey murmured, "I think it's time to leave."

Eli reluctantly agreed, although he couldn't shake the feeling that once they left here, they would also be leaving something precious behind.

The possibility of a life together.

As if on cue, he saw Hollis approaching them.

Had Kasey's delinquent almost-ex-husband been lying in wait all this time?

Eli glanced at Kasey. If the same thought had occurred to her, she didn't show it. Instead she turned to him just as Hollis came up to her and said, "Would you mind giving us a few minutes, Eli?"

Yes, he minded, minded a hell of a lot. But again, if he voiced his objections, if he had to deliberately place himself in the way, stopping her from talking to Hollis, then what they had—what he *thought* they had—wasn't really there at all.

"I'll go get Wayne," he told her, his voice devoid of any emotion. As he walked away, he told her, "Take as much time as you need."

Kasey stared after him. *To do what? To say no? To say yes?*

More than anything, she wished Eli had said something definitive so she knew how he felt about Hollis's unexpected appearance here. Did Eli *want* her to go with Hollis, or was he hoping she'd tell her ex to get lost?

Well, either way, she would have words with the man. She resigned herself to the confrontation.

The old Kasey would have run from this confrontation, avoiding it like the plague. But the new Kasey had too much respect for herself to behave like some limp dishrag, allowing herself to be used, then discarded, only to be picked up again at will.

"Hi, this too soon to have that talk?" Hollis asked with a grin.

She had visions of wiping that smile off his face. How could she have ever been naive enough to have fallen for this shallow, shallow man? Especially when there had been a man of substance just around the corner for the better part of her life.

"No, it's as good a time as any," she told Hollis. There was no inviting smile on her lips and when he went to kiss them, she turned her head, giving him a mouthful of hair instead. "I said we'd talk. That's not code for kiss, or grope, or anything else, is that understood?"

"Okay." He put up his hands, as if pushing away any further dialogue about his aborted attempt to kiss her. "I get that."

Her eyes narrowed. "Get what?"

"That you're angry. You have every right to be angry," he acknowledged. "I made a huge mistake. I should have never left you," he told her, and he sounded so sincere, she found herself believing him. And then he *really* surprised her by saying, "I should have taken you with me."

She stared at him, stunned. Taking hold of her hand, Hollis continued, making his plea. "Come with me, Kasey. I don't belong in this two-bit, flea-bitten town. I have to be where the action is," he stressed. "I was dying here, but out there, out there is a whole big world, just waiting for us." His eyes fairly glowed as he added, "Just ripe for the picking."

She didn't ask him what that meant, although she had a sneaking suspicion she knew. But there was a far more pressing question to ask him as he spun his grand plans about escaping Forever with her.

"What about Wayne?"

His words coming to a skidding halt, Hollis looked at her blankly. "Who?"

"Wayne," she repeated a bit more firmly. When there appeared to be no further enlightenment on his part, she added, "Your son."

"Oh." It was obvious that not only had he forgotten about the child, he really hadn't even given him any thought. He shrugged. "Well, he can come, too." His mind appeared to race, searching for a way to make this all work out. "We'll get a sitter for him." Problem solved, he continued in a far more enthusiastic voice. "I want to show you things, Kasey. I want to put Las Vegas at your feet."

"Las Vegas," she repeated incredulously. What in heaven's name would she want to do there? She had absolutely no desire to spend any time in a place that revolved around pitting yourself against luck for a monetary outcome.

Hollis took her tone to mean that she needed more input on the subject to be won over. And he was more than prepared.

"Yes. You wouldn't believe the luck I had out there. I won enough money to buy back the ranch if I wanted it," he confided, then smirked. "But then I thought, why? It would only tie me down to this place, and like I said, there's a whole big world out there." He took her hand in his, coaxing her. "What d'you say, Kase? Come with me." It wasn't a request so much as a statement. He expected her to eagerly agree.

She looked at this man who thought he was tempting her. He didn't even know her well enough to understand that what he said held absolutely no allure for her.

Again she couldn't help wondering, what had she ever seen in him? Especially since Eli had always been around, there whenever she needed him. Comparing the two was like comparing fool's gold to the real thing. One's shine didn't go beyond the surface, the other had to be mined before he showed his full worth. His *significant* worth.

"You're right," Kasey acknowledged quietly. "You don't belong here—"

Hollis took her agreement to mean that he'd won. He all but beamed, triumphant. "Oh, Kasey, wait'll you see—"

Kasey cut him off. "I didn't finish," she pointed out sternly. "*You* don't belong here," she stressed. "But I do. For me, this *is* where the action is and I don't have any intentions of ever leaving it."

"Not leave?" Hollis asked, confused and unable to process the very idea that she would turn him down. That she would pick living here over living with him. Hollis looked at the woman he'd come back for as if she had just turned slow-witted on him. "How could you not want to go?"

"Because my life's here," she stated. Didn't he get it? "My son is here. My friends are here—"

"And Eli?" His tone was accusing, contemptuous. "Is he the reason you want to stay?"

If Hollis meant to make her feel guilty, he was out of luck. It wasn't going to happen. She smiled as she said, "He is a good reason for wanting to stay in Forever, yes," she agreed.

As she watched, Hollis's complexion turned red and his anger erupted. "And that's what you're settling for?" he demanded. "Being with Eli?"

"Being with Eli wouldn't be settling," she informed him coldly. "But for the record, he hasn't asked me to be with him. I just don't want to be with you—here or in Las Vegas. I don't want to be with you in any kind of setting."

Hollis seemed unable to believe her. He had never been turned down before, not by any woman. "You're just saying that because I hurt you when I left."

She had come to view that segment of her life in a completely different light.

"Your leaving me just might have been the kindest thing you ever did for me," Kasey told him. "You forced me to open my eyes, to finally see you the way you were, not the way I wanted you to be. Don't misunderstand," she said quickly, "I don't begrudge you that life you want, Hollis. I just don't want to share it with you."

As Kasey turned to walk away, incensed, Hollis grabbed her roughly by the arm, jerking her around. "You're my wife, Kasey, and you'll do as I say."

Okay, he'd seen enough. Put up with enough. This was the final straw, Eli thought, stepping forward.

He'd returned with Wayne in time to see Hollis grabbing Kasey to force her to stay.

Braced for a confrontation, he shifted Wayne to the crook of his left arm, turning his body so that he half shielded the infant.

"Let her go, Hollis," Eli ordered angrily. "You gave up the right to call her your wife when you abandoned her."

The expression on Hollis's face was absolutely malevolent. "This is none of your business," he shouted angrily at Eli.

"This has *always* been my business," Eli contradicted. "Now I'm not going to tell you again. Let her go, Hollis."

There was pure fury in Hollis's eyes. "Or what?" he challenged, then jeered, "You're a big man, aren't you? Growling out orders. Meanwhile, just look at you! You're hiding behind a damn baby. Think that'll keep you safe?" he demanded, taunting him. "Well, think again, hotshot. You holding a kid in your arms isn't going to stop me from whipping you good," Hollis promised.

Eli didn't bother answering him. At least not verbally.

In less time than it took to think about it, his fisted right hand flew out, making solid contact with what had always been referred to as Hollis's glass jaw.

Hollis never knew what hit him. He dropped to the ground like a stone.

Chapter Fifteen

Stunned, Kasey stared at Hollis, lying in an unconscious, crumpled heap on the ground, then raised her eyes to the man who had delivered the punch.

"Eli?"

She said his name as if she wasn't certain she'd seen what she'd just witnessed. As if she suddenly realized that there were even more hidden facets to this man than she'd already discovered in these past few months.

Kasey forced herself to glance one final time at Hollis, just to make sure he was still breathing. She put her fingers against his neck and found a pulse. It was then that she felt a sense of relief as well as a smattering of triumph. Hollis had finally gotten what was coming to him.

Eli found the expression on Kasey's face completely unfathomable.

Oh, damn, now he'd gone and done it, he thought, frustrated. She would probably feel sorry for Hollis.

Kasey had a huge heart and she'd always had a soft spot in it for the underdog.

Eli saw no way to salvage or reverse the situation.

"Sorry," he told her, "but there's just so much I could take."

Eli watched her face intently, watched Kasey slowly nod as she appraised the crumpled figure on the ground again.

A feather would have done it. Or even the slightest summer breeze. Either would have easily knocked him over right after he heard her say, "About time."

Had she really said what he thought he'd heard her say?

"Excuse me?"

She raised her eyes to his. "I said 'about time.'" And then she elaborated, in case he still wasn't getting her meaning. "It's about time you stop letting that walking ego order you around like you were some sort of unpaid lackey of his. Hollis never appreciated you." She came closer to him, a soft smile blooming on her lips. "And I'm ashamed to say, neither did I." She thought of the past couple of months and what he had done for her, how he had made her feel whole. "At least, not completely. Not until you gave me that letter and said it was from Hollis."

He looked at her uncertainly. "I don't—"

"Don't you think I knew that you had written it? That you were just trying to save my feelings?"

"What gave me away?" he asked, then took a guess. "The handwriting?"

"The thoughtfulness. Hollis wouldn't have said that he was at fault. Hollis always found a way to blame everyone else except himself. You were trying to spare my feelings by giving me the words I needed to read. I think that was when I started to fall in love with you," she told him honestly.

Eli said nothing for a minute. And then, still holding a very cooperative Wayne in the crook of his left arm, Eli cupped the back of Kasey's head and kissed her with all the fervor that had suddenly seized every single fiber of his being. He kissed her with all the love he was feeling and instantly sent her heart, not to mention her head, reeling.

And it was exactly *that* moment when everyone still at the reception appeared, drawn by the initial noise. They gathered around them as well as the fallen Hollis.

Sensing their presence, Eli reluctantly pulled his head back, released his hold on Kasey and looked around. His brothers and father had surrounded them, as did Rick, Joe and several other people, including Miss Joan and her husband.

"What are you all staring at?" Eli asked, doing his best not to appear as self-conscious as he felt.

"A late bloomer, apparently," his brother Gabe answered for all of them. He was looking down at Hollis's prone body when he said it.

To underscore his opinion, Gabe began to clap, applauding Eli not just for seizing the moment with Kasey, but predominantly for decking Hollis. Within less than a minute, the sound of his palms meeting one another was echoed by the rest of the remaining guests.

Eli looked at Kasey. "I guess Hollis doesn't have a whole lot of friends around here anymore."

"None that I can see," Miss Joan agreed, raising her voice above the noise. "By the way, Stonestreet's car's parked out front," she told them. "Why don't some of you boys take the man to his vehicle and just put him inside? Maybe he'll take the hint when he wakes up, and drive away from Forever. The town doesn't need some mouthy gambler stirring things up and causing trouble." She turned toward Rick. "Do they, Sheriff?" she asked pointedly.

"No, they surely don't," he agreed heartily. "You heard the lady," he said, addressing Joe and several of the other men around him. "Let's go take the trash out. No reason to leave it lying around and have it ruin a fine wedding," he emphasized.

Within a couple of minutes, Gabe, Rafe, Rick and Joe, the sheriff's brother-in-law, deputy and friend, had each taken an extremity and were just short of dragging the unconscious Hollis out to the front of the house. His flaming red sports car sat just where Miss Joan had said it would be.

The man had no sense of subtlety, Eli thought, looking at the car as he followed behind the men carrying Kasey's ex. Moving around the men, he opened the driver's side door for them, then stepped back. The other men deposited Hollis into his car, draping the unconscious man's arms over his steering wheel and anchoring him there as best they could.

The message was clear: go away.

"That's some haymaker you've got, Eli," Rick commented, dusting off his hands. "Remind me never to be on the receiving end of it."

"No chance of that." Kasey spoke up. She'd followed the others, holding her son in her arms. "It takes a lot to get Eli angry."

"You want to press charges?" Rick asked Eli. He nodded toward the slumped figure in the car. "I could hold him for a few days for disturbing the peace," he offered. "Give you two a chance to get away if you wanted to."

But Eli shook his head. "Nobody's going anywhere, Sheriff."

"You're wrong there," Kasey told him. When he looked at her, obviously waiting for an explanation, she said, "Hollis can't wait to leave this two-bit, flea-bitten town behind. His words, not mine," she clarified when Rick raised a quizzical eyebrow.

"Well, then, by all means, let's oblige him," Rick proposed. "One of you boys do me a favor and drive our former citizen to the edge of town. I'll have Larry follow and he'll drive you back," he promised, referring to his other deputy.

"Sounds good to me," Gabe declared. "I'll do it," he volunteered.

"Guess then the rest of us will be going home," Rick declared, stating the obvious. Stepping back toward Miguel Rodriguez, he shook the man's hand. "Great reception, Mr. Rodriguez. Everyone had a great time."

"Some more than others," Miguel agreed, looking at his youngest son and the woman beside him. "You two are welcome to stay the night if you're too tired to drive back to your place," he offered.

Your place.

It had a nice sound to it, Kasey thought. A nice feel to it, as well. She knew in her heart that she belonged with Eli on his ranch. But it would take words to that effect from Eli before she could even think of settling in.

And, as of yet, he hadn't actually *said* anything about their future together. She'd noticed that he deliberately kept the scope of any conversation they had in the present, never mentioning anything even remotely far ahead.

Was that on purpose or just an oversight? She wished she knew.

"Thanks, Dad, but I think we'll just be going back to the ranch," Eli told his father.

There was no reference to the term his father had used, she noticed. Was that deliberate?

Or…?

You're going to drive yourself crazy. The man stepped up to defend you. He punched Hollis out when he tried to manhandle you. What more do you want?

What she wanted was commitment. The very concept that had frightened her just a few short months ago was now something she coveted.

But hinting at it wasn't her style—and even if it was, pushing the situation might make Eli balk. Men were unpredictable at bottom and maybe his throat would start to close up at the mere thought of settling down. Of committing to one woman. To her. It wasn't exactly unheard of.

One day at a time, Kasey.

"I wasn't going to go with him, you know," she said very quietly some fifteen minutes later as they were driving back to the ranch.

Kasey said the words so softly, for a second he thought he was just imagining her voice and it was just the breeze whistling through the trees.

"What?"

"Hollis." She turned to look at him. "Just before you decked him, he wanted me to leave town with him. I wouldn't have gone." When he made no comment in response to her declaration, she nervously went on talking, not knowing what else to do. "Would you believe that he didn't know who Wayne was?"

Eli looked at her, confused. "He didn't know Wayne was his son?"

This wasn't coming out right. Since when did she have trouble being coherent? Since she had so much riding on it, she thought, answering her own question.

"No, the name," Kasey corrected. "Hollis didn't remember that we named him—that I named him Wayne," she amended. "When he said he wanted me to go away with him and when I asked him what about Wayne, he looked at me as if he didn't know who I was talking about. He never once asked about him or wanted to hold him." She looked at Eli. "You holding Wayne certainly didn't stop him from threatening to hit you." The very thought made her furious.

Kasey's hands were fisted in her lap, just as his had been earlier.

"It all turned out well," Eli said, soothing her. "Hollis is pretty clear now how you feel about leaving and I've got a feeling he won't be bothering you anymore. His ego doesn't like rejection." He wasn't saying anything they both didn't know. "You'll be erased from his memory because you don't fit his cookie-cutter mentality of what a fawning woman should be like around him."

They were home. Eli pulled up in front of the ranch house. Turning the ignition off, he left the key where it was for a moment as he shifted toward her. "Does that bother you, being erased from his mind?"

"Why should it bother me?"

"Well, you love him," Eli answered quietly, treading lightly in this obvious minefield of emotions.

"Lov*ed*," Kasey stressed. "I *loved* him, dumb as that now seems to me. But I guess everyone's allowed one really bad mistake in their lives." And he was hers. "And when you look at the total picture, it wasn't a complete disaster."

As he listened, Eli expected to hear her say something about the nice moments that she and Hollis had had together. Instead, Kasey surprised him. "If I hadn't married Hollis, then I would have never had Wayne." Looking over her shoulder to the backseat, she smiled at the sleeping little boy secured in his infant seat. He'd be outgrowing it soon, she thought fondly. "The best baby in the whole world. Funny how that is, given Hollis's temperament," she commented.

"Well, it's obvious. Wayne takes after his mother," Eli told her.

She could always count on Eli to say something sweet and reaffirming. "Thank you for coming to my rescue back there," she said. She couldn't help smiling at the way that sounded, like bad dialogue from a damsel-in-distress movie.

Eli was never one to take credit if he could help it. "I had no choice," he told her simply.

"Why not?"

"Because" was all he said out loud. *Because I love you,* Eli told her silently. *I've loved you for as long as I can remember.* "He was threatening to take you away," he continued. "And, from the looks of it, you didn't want to go with him."

"What if I had? What if I was willing to just pack up and leave Forever with him? Would you still have punched him out like that?"

He wasn't a man who liked to bare his feelings. But he'd come this far, he might as well go all the way—and besides, he felt he owed it to her. "I would have wanted to, but no, I wouldn't have."

"Why not?" she returned, curious. "Why would

you hold back?" If anyone had the right to tap-dance on Hollis's body, it was Eli. Eli who had put up with so much from the self-centered Hollis in the name of friendship.

"Don't you get it yet?" he asked, surprised that she hadn't caught on by now. "I want you to be happy. That's always been my bottom line. I would have wanted you to be happy with me, but if you would rather be with someone else—"

He didn't get a chance to finish. It was extremely difficult to talk when his lips were pressed up against another set. Especially if that other set was also wreaking havoc on his ability to think. He had no choice to do anything except to respond—physically and emotionally—to this passionate outside catalyst that completely stirred him as it effectively stripped his mind.

All he could think of was her.

Of having her, of loving her, of losing himself in her.

"Then you don't want to be with anyone else?" he asked hoarsely when she finally pulled away.

How could he even ask that question after a kiss like that? It had all but singed his eyelashes. "You're an idiot, you know that, don't you?"

"But a lucky one," he pointed out with a wide grin. "A damn lucky one."

He was riding on a crest. It was now or never. He threw down a challenge to himself. Either he asked her now, or he held his peace indefinitely. Maybe even forever.

He decided that indefinitely was more than he could bear.

"Just one thing would make me luckier," he told her.

A ripple of desire danced through her, heating her down to her very core.

She wasn't going to jump to conclusions, Kasey told herself. That would be greedy and she'd already been on the receiving end of so much. He wasn't necessarily talking about what she so passionately wanted him to be talking about.

So, very carefully and treading lightly, she asked, "And that would be…?"

He realized that she was an old-fashioned girl, after all, wanting to hear the words, go through the proper steps. She was an old soul inside of one incredibly well-rounded body.

"If you married me."

There were bells and whistles and banjos, all making wonderful music within her.

"You want me to marry you," she repeated.

"Yes, I do."

She pushed a little further—because she had to know the truth. "Because it's the right thing to do and people are talking about the 'living arrangement' we have?" Was he just trying to make an honest woman of her, or was there more involved here?

She crossed her fingers.

Eli looked at her, stunned. Since when had other

people's opinions ever meant a hill of beans to him? "When do I see people?" he asked. "When do I care about what they say?"

He sounded so defensive, she decided that he meant what he was saying. But that still left her with an unanswered question. "Then why are you asking me to marry you?"

"Best reason in the world," he said, lightly stroking her hair. "Because I love you."

There it was, she thought. The magic. The starbursts, all going off inside of her like a super Fourth of July celebration.

"You love me."

He laughed, shaking his head. "And I'd love you even more if you stopped parroting everything I say," he told her, deadpan. "But yes, I love you," he confirmed. "And when you're ready, I want you to marry me. No pressure," he assured her.

"Maybe I'd like some pressure," she told him, and then she grinned. "And I'd like to get married right away, before you realize what a catch you really are and start to have second thoughts about marrying me."

"That," he told her very seriously, "would never happen."

"How can you be that sure?" she challenged.

"Because those 'first thoughts' I'm having are just too damn sexy to give up."

Her eyes smiled at him. "Stop talking, Eli."

Had he said too much? Made her begin to have doubts? Looking at her more closely, he decided

that wasn't the case. Looked as if he was home free.
"Why?" he asked, tongue-in-cheek.

"Because I want you to kiss me."

His smile went straight to her heart. "I can do that."

"Then do it."

And he did.

Expertly.

* * * * *

Ramona and
the Renegade

Chapter One

He recognized the car immediately.

On his way home, hoping to beat the predicted flash floods, Deputy Sheriff Joe Lone Wolf brought his four-wheel-drive vehicle to a halt the moment he spotted the other car.

The rain was falling faster and harder with each quarter hour that went by. Because of that, his range of visibility was considerably shortened. It hampered him somewhat, but Joe still would have known the battered Jeep anywhere.

It was ten years old, silver, with a red door on its passenger side thanks to an unexpected, sudden meeting with a hundred-foot bitternut hickory tree one foggy night. With some effort on his part, Mick Henley, Forever, Texas's best—and only—mechanic, had managed to find an exact match to replace the Jeep's mangled door.

Well, almost exact. It would have needed two coats of silver paint to make it the same color as the rest of the vehicle. But Ramona Santiago had fallen in love with the bold red color and refused to change it once the new door was in place.

Red suited her.

It matched her personality, Joe had thought at the time.

He still did.

Mona was all things wild and bold. Far from shy and retiring, the raven-haired, green-eyed beauty had all the subdued qualities of a Fourth of July firecracker in the middle of exploding. The green eyes came from her Irish ancestors, the midnight-black hair was a gift from the rest of her heritage—Mexican and Apache.

They had the last in common.

Deputy Joe Lone Wolf was an Apache, through and through, born on the nearby Apache reservation where he spent his younger years before his uncle finally uprooted him and transplanted him into Forever proper, thereby rescuing him from an early demise.

He and Mona had something else in common—she was the sheriff's younger sister, and he was technically in Rick Santiago's employ. One of three deputies, Joe had been with Rick and on the job the longest, although only by a matter of a few months.

If Rick knew that his sister was coming back to Forever tonight, he hadn't mentioned anything. Joe had a strong suspicion that the sheriff would be just as surprised as he was that Mona was here. The last anyone had heard, Mona was due to reach Forever the day before her brother's wedding.

Why the change in schedule? Joe wondered.

The vehicle's windshield wipers were already set on maximum speed and were clearly losing the battle for visibility against the rain. He would have had better luck seeing if he just stuck his head out the side window.

But he'd seen enough, approaching on the gently inclining slope, to know that something was definitely wrong. Mona's Jeep was stationary in a place where no one would willingly choose to stop. Moreover, Mona wasn't in the vehicle but was standing outside it.

Specifically, Mona was in the process of wrestling with a tire iron, cursing the very flat front passenger tire that was, of necessity, the focus of all her attention.

Though never demure, the Mona he recalled didn't ordinarily turn the air blue around her. She'd obviously been at this for a bit and, just as obviously, been unsuccessful in her endeavor to change the tire.

Just the slightest hint of amusement ran through him, even though it made no appearance on his face. He knew better than that. Mona had eyes in the back of her pretty head. At least, she did before she'd gone off to college to become a veterinarian.

Parking his vehicle several feet away from hers, Joe got out and, braving the rain, approached the sheriff's sister from behind. She didn't appear to hear him, but under the circumstances, that was more than understandable. The wind howled, the rain pelted and made its own mournful noise, and Mona, damsel-in-distress in this scenario, was cursing.

Loudly.

With all this going on, Joe doubted if she could have heard a train approaching from a distance.

"Don't you know you have to sweet-talk a car to get it to cooperate?" Joe asked just as he came to where Mona was standing.

The next thing he knew, he was literally jumping back, out of her reach, and not a moment too soon. Startled, Mona immediately turned the tire iron in her hands into a weapon and swung it at her invisible target for all she was worth.

"Hey!" Joe cried indignantly, barely avoiding being separated from his midsection by the metal tool.

Tired, annoyed at the sudden downpour that had wreaked havoc with her schedule, and furious with the tire that had almost caused her to go careening off the road and down into a ditch, Mona was definitely not at her best. In addition to that, the knowledge that, at this moment, she bore a strong resemblance to a resuscitated drowned rat did nothing to improve her mood.

When she saw who it was, she let go of the tire iron, dropping it to the ground. After a beat. She took in a deep, shaky breath, trying not to think about what might have happened if Joe's reflexes hadn't been as good as they were.

"Joe, you scared me!" she snapped. Turning the bolt of fear that shot through her into anger and aiming it at Joe.

"Then I guess we're even." His voice was calm, but beneath the deadly still exterior he had to admit he was anything but. Moving in closer again, Joe looked down at the tire that was still very much a part of Mona's vehicle. She hadn't gotten very far in her attempt to remove it, he noted. Raising his eyes to hers, he asked, "Got a flat?"

Mona laughed shortly and shook her head. "I always did love the way you could grasp any situation at lightning speed."

His expression never changed. "It was a rhetorical comment."

She pushed her plastered wet hair out of her eyes with the back of her hand. "So was mine."

With the rain beating a faster and faster tattoo on his tan, worn Stetson as it showered down all around him, Joe gave her a long, measuring look.

For the most part, Mona had been away at college, then veterinarian school these past eight years. Although it didn't seem possible, every time she came back, she seemed even more beautiful than when she'd left. But her sharp tongue hadn't dulled a whit. He supposed that there were just some things in life you could count on.

"You want some help or not?" Joe asked, quietly eyeing her.

Mona had made it a point never to ask for help. It was a matter of pride with her. Plus, if she wasn't counting on anyone, if she didn't depend on anyone, then she would never have to go through the agony of disappointment again. It was a philosophy she was forced to develop very early in life, when she finally realized that her mother would never come back for them the way she'd promised.

The only exceptions to Mona's philosophy were her brother, her late grandmother and Doc Whitmore. Over the years, the latter had slowly became the father she'd never known, as well as her mentor. Those were the three who'd brought stability into her life.

As for Joe, well, Joe was someone she'd gone to school with. Someone who'd always managed to be somewhere in close proximity, like the air and the trees. One way or another, Joe seemed never to be that far out of range. In short, he'd been her best friend, though neither one of them had ever verbally acknowledged the role.

She might have known she'd run into him before she saw anyone else from Forever, Mona thought.

In response to his offer for help, her slender shoulders rose and fell in a careless shrug beneath her soaked jacket. "Well, since you're here and all…"

As she spoke, she stepped back from the defunct vehicle. Because of the torrential rain and the dust now swiftly turning into mud, Mona found her footing compromised. She was about to slip backward and come perilously close to ignobly landing on her butt if not her back altogether. At the last second, she was rescued from the impending embarrassment by Joe's quick reflexes. He grabbed her, pulling her forward toward him before she could slide backward. Due to his strength, the abrupt motion was a matter of over-compensation and suddenly, rather than discovering herself sprawled out on the ground and flat against the oozing mud, Mona slammed up against Joe without so much as the width of a raindrop between them.

She raised her eyes to Joe's, doing her best to re-group as quickly as possible. Her pulse raced and she didn't like it. She also didn't want him taking any note of it.

"Is that your heart pounding?" she asked flippantly, doing her very best to sound as nonchalant as she didn't feel.

"Nope," he lied. "Must be yours."

The same strong hands that had grabbed her now pushed her back by a good twelve inches, if not more. Having Mona against him like that took control out of his hands.

"You're an accident waiting to happen," he told her, his voice flat, emotionless as he tried to deflect any more attention away from the state of the organ that was betraying him.

Or *one* of the organs that were betraying him at any rate, he thought ruefully.

He nodded toward his vehicle that was parked off to the side. "Why don't you just go and wait in my car while I handle this?"

She was *not* about to take a chance on slipping again so soon. The last thing she wanted was to hear him laughing at her.

"What? And miss the learning experience of a life-time, watching you change a tire?" she scoffed, raising her voice so that the winds didn't whip it away.

"How will poor little me ever learn how to do such a big, manly thing if I'm shut away in an ivory tower?"

For emphasis, she waved toward the vehicle, which became less visible despite its close proximity.

Joe shook his head. "I see you still have a smart mouth."

The grin on her lips was deliberately exaggerated. She batted her eyelashes at him like an old-fashioned movie goddess. "It goes with my smart mind."

"Then I guess you must be brilliant by now," he commented drily.

Moving slowly, he picked his way around her Jeep, going to the rear.

"I am," Mona answered in the same tone, punctuating her sentence with a toss of her wet head. "Where are you going?"

He glanced in her direction. "Someone with your brilliant mind would know that I wanted to check the condition of your spare before going through the trouble of taking off the flat."

"I knew that," she retorted, then added in a more mellow tone, "but I didn't know if you did." She followed him to the rear of her vehicle.

The spare tire was mounted on the back of the Jeep. Testing the tire's integrity, Joe frowned and shook his head. This was not good. He spared her a glance over his shoulder and could see by her body language that she'd become instantly defensive before he even said a word. He said it anyway.

"Don't you ever check the condition of your spare?"

Her eyes narrowed beneath her soggy bangs. "Somewhere between studying for my finals—and the examination for my vet license—and juggling a part-time job to pay for little incidentals like food, it must have temporarily fallen off my 'immediately to do' list."

He ignored her sarcastic tone and answered matter-of-factly. "Well, that's a shame," he told her. "Because your spare's flat, too."

Mona closed her eyes. It figured. All things considered, this had not been one of her better days. Opening her eyes again, she looked at Joe. "As flat as the one on it?" she asked.

You just didn't substitute one flat tire for another. Flat was flat. His dark eyes would have pinned her to the wall—if there had been one around. "You know better than that."

Yes, she did. She was just desperate. And really, really annoyed. With both tires for being flat and with herself for not noticing that the spare had slowly lost its air. And most of all, right now she was annoyed with Joe for pointing it out.

Hands fisted at her waist, Mona swung one booted foot at the right front tire and kicked it.

"That's not going to make it come back to life," Joe commented.

She glared at him. "I know that." The hood she had on provided next to no protection for her at this point and when it slid off her head, she didn't bother to try to pull it back up. "Now what?"

The weather seemed to be getting more hostile by the moment. He turned so that the rain was at his back. Because he was taller, he provided a little shelter for her, as well.

He gave her options, although only one was really viable. "Well, I could call Mick and you could wait here for him to come with his tow truck—if you don't wash away first. Or I could give you a ride into town and you could talk to Mick yourself, face-to-face."

Mona was in no mood to share a car ride with him, even though she knew it was her best bet. "No third option, huh?"

"Sure." Joe raised his voice again, competing with the increasing sound of the wind and the rain. "You could wait here for the tire spirits to come and perform the miracle of the reinflating tire."

His expression was so serious that anyone not knowing Joe would have thought that he actually believed in the spirits he'd just invoked. But she had grown up witnessing displays of his deadpan sense of humor.

With a sigh, Mona resigned herself to her only real alternative. "I guess I'll have to pick option number two."

"Good choice," he answered.

Turning on his heel, he started to lead the short distance back to his parked vehicle. It took him less than a minute to realize that Mona wasn't following behind him. He stopped and looked over his shoulder. She was still next to her Jeep.

"Change your mind?"

Crawling into the rear of the vehicle, Mona hauled out a large suitcase. She had no choice but to set it down in the mud.

"No," she told him, "I don't want anyone making off with my clothes." She didn't bother looking at him as she leaned into the back and grabbed a second suitcase. This one, lodged behind the driver's seat, proved to be less cooperative and she struggled to get it out of the vehicle.

Joe shook his head at the woman's unadulterated stubbornness. He crossed back to her in a couple of long strides. Firmly taking hold of her shoulders for a second time, he moved her out of the way and easily pulled the large suitcase out. Instead of putting it down next to the first one, he held on to it, keeping it out of the mud.

Mona squared her shoulders. "I could have managed," she protested.

Arguing with her served no purpose. "No one said you couldn't," he answered. Still holding one suitcase, he deliberately picked up the other with his free hand. "This it?" he asked. "Or are there more?"

She'd never been one to be careless with her hard-earned money, but she had accumulated a few things in the past eight years. "The rest are being shipped," she told him.

Something small and hopeful zipped through him. He banked it down quickly, giving absolutely no indication of its momentary existence. Instead, he asked in what passed for a disinterested voice, "You moving back?"

She wanted to. But there were things she needed to work out. Not to mention that her brother had said he had other plans for her, plans that included having her move to a large city. She didn't want to disappoint him, but Forever was really the only home she ever knew. The only place she'd ever felt she really belonged.

"For now," she allowed.

Joe weighed her tone and made a judgment.

He was forced to raise his voice yet again as he walked to his vehicle. The wind grew louder, the rain more harsh. He felt as if his words were being snatched away even as he uttered them.

"Set your sights on somewhere else?" he asked.

She had nothing to carry but the shoulder bag that had seen her through both college and veterinarian school. Holding it tightly against her, Mona moved quickly to keep up. At this point, she wanted nothing more than to get out of the rain and curl up somewhere warm and dry. In lieu of that, Joe's car would do.

"Not me," she told Joe, then repeated the words when he looked at her quizzically. Satisfied he'd heard her, she added, "Rick."

Reaching his vehicle, Joe loaded first one suitcase, then the other into the backseat. When he turned to look at Mona, she had already scrambled into the passenger seat in the front.

He opened the driver's-side door and got in. "You want to explain that?"

Mona felt around for the seat belt. Finding it, she secured it around herself. "Rick—" She realized she was still yelling and lowered her voice. "Rick has high hopes that I'll move to the big city, open an animal hospital and be a big success."

"And you?" He put his key into the ignition, but didn't turn it just yet. "What are your hopes?"

Mona ran her hands up and down her arms, trying not to shiver. It was unseasonably cold for spring.

"To get dry again," she answered.

She glanced out the side window. The rain was getting worse, but that wasn't what was bothering her. She heard a distant muffled roar and it was getting louder. That could only mean one thing. She turned toward Joe. Now wasn't the time for any false bravado or stubborn ploys on her part. They had trouble.

"Joe—"

Joe turned the key and after what seemed like an unnaturally long moment, the engine caught and turned over.

"Yeah, I know," he answered. "Looks like we're in for it."

They both knew what he was talking about. "It" was Joe's loose reference to the flash floods that they were periodically subjected to when Mother Nature decided to be too bountiful with her supply of rain and drenched the lands far too quickly to be of any actual benefit to anyone.

Mona twisted around in her seat, looking back at

her vehicle. She knew she had no choice, but she really hated leaving it behind.

"My car," she protested.

"We'll find it once it stops raining," Joe told her with an assurance that defied argument.

She turned back around and sat facing forward again. Mona watched as his car's windshield wipers vainly battled the downpour, losing ground with every stroke they spasmodically made. To her dismay, the man beside her slowed down and began driving at a speed that would have brought shame to an arthritic turtle.

The fearless daredevil she'd once known would have laughed at the rain and gone full throttle into the storm. But that boy was gone now and in his place was a cautious man who thought things through.

She knew that any faster and they risked driving off the road and landing in a ditch.

Or worse.

Another thought suddenly struck her. She turned to look at his profile. "We're not going to make it into town, are we?"

If this had been anyone else in the car with him, he might have uttered some platitude meant to be reassuring, doling out a spoonful of hope to someone he knew was silently asking for it.

But this wasn't anyone else. This was Mona. Mona, who took every white lie as an affront, every sugar-coated fib as an insult to her intelligence. So he said the only thing he knew she would tolerate.

He told her the truth.

"Nope."

Chapter Two

"'Nope'?"

Stunned, Mona repeated the single-syllable answer Joe had just uttered. If they couldn't reach town, that meant the oncoming flash flood would cut off access to Forever.

But she knew Joe, knew him as well as she knew herself and her brother. Joe was not the type to merely give up or surrender, even if his adversary was Nature itself.

Still, the seconds ticked by and he wasn't saying anything beyond the one word he'd already uttered. Mona felt herself growing antsy, in direct correlation to the force of the storm.

If they couldn't make it to town, they would have to find shelter somewhere. They couldn't stay out in the open. Flash floods were known to sweep vehicles away in the blink of an eye.

"Say something, already," she ordered, then immediately added a warning. "I swear, Joe Lone Wolf, if I hear you say, 'Today is a good day to die,' you are going to really, really regret it."

He stole a quick glance in her direction, taking care not to look away from the road for more than half a heartbeat. Visibility was next to impossible, but at this point, he was searching for something very specific.

"So much for my one dramatic moment," he quipped. "How about, 'Let's hole up in the old Murphy place until this passes'? Will that get me beat up, too?" he asked.

"The Murphy place?" Mona repeated uncertainly. She hadn't realized that she'd gotten this disoriented. She squinted as she peered through the all but obliterated windshield. Visibility was down to approximately twelve to eighteen inches in front of the vehicle, maybe less. "Is that around here?"

The "Murphy place" was little more than a three-room cabin that by urban standards hardly qualified as a vacation getaway, much less a regular home. It was more in the realm of a shack, really. More than three quarters of a century old, it had once been the center of a dream—and a budding cattle ranch—until an outbreak of anthrax had eventually killed both. The cabin, which should have been the beginning of a sprawling ranch house, had stood empty for close to twenty years now, after the last descendent of Jonas Murphy died without leaving any heirs, just a mountain of bad debts.

Somehow in all that time, the building, a veritable feasting ground for vermin, had managed to escape being torn down or even claimed. No one cared enough about the unproductive piece of land to buy it and begin building something from scratch again. So the decaying cabin stood, enduring the seasons year after year and, like an aging octogenarian with osteoporosis, it grew steadily more and more frail.

The last time he'd passed this way and actually looked at the cabin, Joe had thought that the only things keeping the building up were probably the termites, holding hands.

He sincerely hoped that they were holding tight for at least one more night.

Instincts that were generations in the making guided him toward where he had last seen the cabin this morning on his way into town.

"It should be close by," he answered Mona, then spared her a grin and added, "Unless those pesky tire spirits decided to move it just so that they could annoy you some more."

She doubted that it was possible to annoy her any more than she already was, Mona thought. "Very funny."

The grin on Joe's face softened into a smile and then that faded, as well. He found that he had to fight not just the rain but the wind for control over his vehicle. He sensed Mona's tension. She was watching him.

"Nothing to be afraid of," he assured her quietly as he continued to stare intently through the blinding rain.

Mona bristled. "I'm not afraid," she retorted, stopping just short of snapping at him.

She hated the fact that Joe could read her so well,

that all he had to do was just look at her to sense what she was thinking. What bothered her most of all was that she couldn't return the "compliment" and do the same with him. It just didn't seem fair.

"Okay," Joe allowed. "Then why are you about to rip off my dashboard?" he asked. Without looking, he nodded in the general direction of her hands, which were gripping the aforementioned dashboard.

Mona gritted her teeth. *Damn it.*

She was completely unaware that she was gripping the dashboard. Swallowing a curse, Mona dropped her hands into her lap, trying hard not to clench them.

"Just bracing myself for the inevitable crash. You're not exactly the best driver in the world," she reminded him pointedly.

He knew what she was referring to. At thirteen, he'd been angry at the world in general and specifically at the absentee father he'd never known and his mother, who'd died suddenly three years earlier. He'd been passed around from relative to relative and raised by committee, which compelled him to steal one of the elders' cars just to thumb his nose at everyone.

For the space of half an hour, he'd felt like his own man, free and independent. But the joyride ended when he lost control of the car and ended up in a ditch.

Miraculously emerging unscathed, he'd wound up working the entire summer and half the fall to pay off the repair bill for the car. He figured the episode would always haunt him, no matter what he might go on to accomplish in life. He didn't mind. He considered himself lucky to have walked away alive, much less without so much as a scratch.

What amused him about the whole thing was that Mona had a similar incident in her past. It had happened when she was ten. Rather than a joyride, after an argument with her grandmother Mona decided to run away from home. She took her grandmother's car to enable her escape. But the adventure was short-lived. Mona managed to go down only two streets before her grandmother had caught up to her—on foot. Even at that age, the old woman had been swift.

The car sustained no damage. The same, he knew, couldn't be said for Mona's posterior or her dignity. She was grounded for a month.

"I wouldn't throw rocks if I were you," he said, leaving it at that. When she frowned, he knew that she knew exactly what he was referring to.

A second later, Mona sat up straight in her seat, suddenly animated. "I see it. You were right. The cabin *is* here."

"Nice to know you have faith in me," Joe cracked, tightening his grip on the steering wheel. It was getting harder to keep the vehicle from veering.

"It's raining horses and steers," Mona cried, gesturing at the windshield and doing one better than what she considered to be the stereotypical comment about cats and dogs. "Anyone could have gotten turned around in this storm."

"*Most* people could have gotten turned around," he

allowed. Things like that never happened to him. He took his natural sense of direction for granted.

She sighed, shaking her head. Same old Joe, she thought. "Despite what you think, you are not mystically empowered, Joe Lone Wolf."

Not for one minute did he think of himself as having any special, otherworldly powers, but he couldn't resist teasing her. "I came to your rescue out of the blue, didn't I?"

"You were just on your way home and stumbled across me," she corrected. "You've been taking the same route ever since you went to work for my brother as one of his deputies."

He turned the tables on her with ease. "Are you saying you took this path on purpose?" he asked, feigning surprise. "Just to run into me?"

"No, I'm saying that you— I mean, that I—" This wasn't coming out right. He was getting her all tongue-tied. Mona gave up. "Oh, hell, think what you want—but you *do* know better than that."

Yeah, he thought, he did. Had known it from the first moment that he'd laid eyes on Ramona as she walked into his second-period tenth-grade English class that February morning ten years ago. She'd been so beautiful to look at that it hurt him right down to his very core.

And right from the beginning he knew that girls like Ramona Santiago did not wind up with guys like him. He was an Apache through and through and it wasn't all that long ago that people regarded Native Americans like him as beneath them.

Granted, Mona, like her brother, was one-third Apache herself, but it was the other two-thirds of her, the Mexican-American and especially the Irish side of her, that carried all the weight. And those two-thirds would have never welcomed a poor Apache teenager into her life in any other capacity than just as a friend.

So a friend he was. Someone for her to talk to, confide in if the spirit so moved her. Being her friend— her sometimes confidant—he'd long since decided was what made his life worth living. And what had, ultimately, made him abandon the wild, bad boy who didn't play by the rules and take up the straight-and-narrow path instead. The guy he had been would never have pinned on a badge and sworn an oath to it. But he'd done it for her, for Ramona.

She probably hadn't had a clue, he thought now.

Just as she didn't have a clue about the rest of it. About his feelings for her. And he intended for it to stay that way.

Resisting the urge to speed up just a little, Joe slowly drove the Jeep up to the rickety cabin that had once been home to an entire family.

Silently breathing a sigh of relief, he pulled up the hand brake as he turned off the engine.

Mona, he noticed, hadn't undone her seat belt. "Something wrong?" he asked her.

"Is it safe?" she asked, eyeing the cabin uncertainly. There'd been ghost stories about the cabin when she'd been growing up. She didn't believe those for a minute, but the cabin did look as if it was about to blow away in the next big gust of wind.

Joe knew that the cabin wasn't as structurally sound as some of the newer buildings in town, but he really didn't expect it to fall down around them—unless one of the termites sneezed, he thought, suppressing a smile.

"It's standing and it's dry inside," he pointed out. "Or reasonably so," he added, figuring that time had been hard on the roof and there had to be places where it would leak. "Right now, that's all that matters." Unbuckling his seat belt, he glanced at her, waiting. "Now are you coming, or are you planning on spending the night in the Jeep?"

The latter idea thrilled her even less than spending the night in the rickety cabin. With a sigh, Mona pressed the button and undid her seat belt.

"I'm coming, I'm coming," she muttered.

Opening the passenger door, Mona got out. As she stoically battled her way to the cabin's front door, she suddenly shrieked as the cold rain whipped about her face and body, drenching her for a second time in a matter of moments and stealing her breath away, as well.

The next moment, a strong arm tightened around her waist and pulled her the rest of the way to the cabin.

Joe pushed the door open for her. The cabin hadn't

had a working lock on it for most of the twenty years it had been empty.

"I can walk," Mona protested as he all but propelled her into the cabin.

"You're welcome," he replied after putting his shoulder to the door and pushing it closed again, despite the fact that the rain seemed to have other ideas.

Steadying herself, Mona scanned the area to get her bearings. The interior of the front room looked particularly dreary, like an old prom dress that had been kept in the closet years too long. The roof, she noted, was leaking in several different spots.

"So much for staying dry," Mona muttered under her breath as she moved aside after a large splotch of rain had hit her on her forehead.

Rubbing his hands together to warm them, Joe gave her an amused look. "You just have to make sure you don't stand under any of the holes in the roof."

"Brilliant as always." Her voice dripped with sarcasm. "Did you figure that out all by yourself?"

Joe's expression remained stoic and gave nothing away. He deflected the sarcasm with a mild observation as he pointed out, "I'm not the one getting rained on."

Mona struggled with her temper. He wasn't the reason she was in this mood. She'd planned on surprising Rick with her early arrival. He thought she was coming in a couple of weeks, just in time for his wedding. She had sped things up on her end, taking her license exam earlier rather than later, so that she could come and lend a hand in the preparations. Her almost-sister-in-law was six months pregnant and most likely not up to the rigors involved in preparing for a wedding.

Mona knew that a lot of the town was probably willing to pitch in and help, especially Miss Joan who ran the diner and knew everyone's business. But Rick was her only brother, her only family, and she wanted very much to be part of all this. Wanted, she supposed, to be assured that even after the wedding, she would still be a part of his life.

It was all well and good for her to go gallivanting out of town for long spates of time as long as she knew that Rick would be there when she got back. But the thought that he might not be, that he could go off and have a life that didn't directly include her, rattled Mona to her very core.

Changing the subject in her attempt to get back on a more even keel, Mona frowned. She zigzagged across the small room and looked around at her surroundings in the limited light. There was hardly any furniture and what did exist was falling apart.

"Can you imagine living here?" she asked Joe, marveling at the poor quality of life the last inhabitants of the cabin must have had.

"I've seen worse," Joe replied matter-of-factly.

Mona bit her tongue. She could have kicked herself. For a moment, she'd forgotten that he'd spent his early years living on the reservation where poverty and deprivation had been a vivid part of everyday life, not just for Joe, but for everyone there. More than likely, she realized, he'd grown up in a place like this.

She hadn't meant to insult him.

Mona pressed her lips together as she turned to look at him. An apology hovered on her tongue.

"Joe, I didn't mean—"

He didn't want to hear it. Didn't want to glimpse the pity he was certain would come into her eyes, accompanying whatever words would ease her conscience. He wasn't proud of his background, but he wasn't ashamed if it, either. It was what it was. And what it was now was behind him.

Joe waved his hand, dismissing what she was about to say. "Forget it."

Turning his back to her, he focused his attention on the fireplace. Specifically, on making it useful. Squatting down, he angled his head to try to look up the chimney.

Curious, Mona came up behind him. "What are you doing?"

"Trying to see if the chimney's blocked. Last thing you want, if I get a fire going, is to have smoke filling this room." He leaned in a little farther. "Damn," he uttered sharply, pulling back.

Mona moved quickly to get out of his way. "Is it blocked?" she guessed.

"No," he muttered almost grudgingly, "the chimney's clear."

"Okay, I'll bite," she said gamely. "Why are you cursing?"

Disgusted, he rose to his feet for a moment. "Because I wasn't expecting to be hit with big fat raindrops." The last one had been a direct hit into his eye.

Mona laughed. "Especially dirty ones," she observed. He looked at her quizzically. With a flourish, Mona pulled a handkerchief out of the back pocket of her jeans. "Hold still," she ordered.

"Why?" he asked suspiciously. Mona was nothing if not unpredictable. Added to that she had a wicked sense of humor.

"Because I can't hit a moving target," she deadpanned, then said seriously, "Because I want to wipe the dirt off your face." Doing so in gentle strokes, she shook her head. "God, but you've gotten to be really distrusting since I was last home."

"No, I haven't," he protested.

Saying that, he took the handkerchief from her and wiped his own face. He told himself it was in the interest of efficiency and that reacting to the way she stroked his face with the handkerchief had nothing to do with it. Some lies, he argued, were necessary, even if they were transparent.

"I never trusted you in the first place." He raised his chin a little, presenting his face for Mona's scrutiny. "Did I get it all?"

"Why ask me?" she asked innocently. "After all, I could be lying."

"True," he agreed, "but seeing as how you're the only one around this cabin besides me who talks, I have no choice. You'll have to do."

"You look fine," she told him, playfully running her index finger down his cheek. "You got it all, Deputy Lone Wolf."

He held out the handkerchief to her. "Thanks." When she took it from him, Joe turned his attention back to the fireplace and getting a fire going. There was kindling beside the stone fireplace. It didn't appear to be that old. Someone had obviously been here and used the fireplace since the last owner had vacated the premises. He shifted several pieces, positioning them in the hearth.

Mona went over to the lone window that faced the front of the house and looked out. The rain seemed to be coming down even harder, if that was possible. She shivered slightly, not so much from the cold as from the feeling of isolation.

"Think this'll last all night?" she asked Joe, still staring out the window.

He hefted another log, putting it on top of the others. "That's what they say."

She didn't like the sound of that. Turning away from the window, she addressed her words to his back. "You mean, we have to stay here until morning?"

Joe fished a book of matches out of his front pocket. He didn't smoke anymore, hadn't for years now, but he still liked to have a book of matches in his possession. You never knew when they might come in handy— like now. He had no patience with the old ways when it came to making fire, even though, when push came to shove, he was good at it.

"Unless you want to risk being caught in a flash flood the way we almost were back there."

She sighed, moving about restlessly. The cabin was sinking into darkness and although she'd grown up in Forever, this setup was disquieting.

"Not exactly the way I pictured spending my first night back home," she told him.

"You mean, stranded and hungry?" he guessed.

"For openers," she agreed. Mona ran her hand along her extremely flat abdomen. It had been rumbling for a while now.

He crossed to her. It might have been her imagination, but Joe seemed somehow taller to her in this cabin.

"When did you eat last?" he wanted to know.

"This morning. I skipped lunch to get an early start driving down to Forever." It had seemed like a good idea at the time. She hadn't bothered to listen to the weather forecast. She wished she had now. "I figured I'd be in time to grab a late lunch at Miss Joan's," she added. Miss Joan, the owner of the diner, had been a fixture around Forever for as long as she could remember.

Arms wrapped around her to ward off the chill, Mona glanced around the cabin's main room again. "Doesn't look as if there's been food around here for a good long while."

"Except for maybe the four-footed kind," Joe interjected as the sound of something small and swift was heard rustling toward the rear of the room. A rat?

"I'll pass, thanks," she muttered. She wasn't *that* hungry yet, Mona thought. She preferred meals that *didn't* deliver themselves.

"You sure?" Joe asked, a hint of a grin on his lips. "I hear that squirrels and possums taste just like—"

"Chicken, yes, I've heard the same myth," she said, cutting him off. "I'll let you know if I get that hungry. I'm not there yet." And hopefully never would be, she added silently.

He looked mildly amused. "Suit yourself."

"What, you're willing to eat a squirrel?" she challenged. He couldn't be serious, she thought. Joe knew better than that. "They're full of diseases. You won't have any idea what you're swallowing," she insisted.

"Yeah, I will," he said.

Was he just trying to bait her? And then she realized that Joe was walking toward the door. He couldn't be going out—or could he? "Where are you going?" she wanted to know.

"To my Jeep to get the dinner I was bringing home from Miss Joan's."

"You had food all this time and you let me go on about the rodents?" she demanded.

"Never known anyone to be able to stop you once you got wound up," he pointed out. "I figured I'd just wait it out, like the storm. Be right back," he told her. He opened the door only as much as he had to in order to slip out.

He heard her muttering a few choice words aimed in his direction before the wind carried them away.

Making his way to the Jeep, Joe smiled to himself. Yup, same old Mona. There was a comfort in that.

Chapter Three

Wind and rain accompanied Joe's reentry into the cabin several minutes later. Mona was quick to throw her weight against the door in order to shut it again.

"Took you long enough," she commented, hoping to divert his attention from the fact that she had been right next to the door, waiting for his return. Her concern had nothing to do with hunger. But there was no way she was about to admit that.

"I'll move faster next time." Opening his jacket, he took out the prize and placed it on the rickety kitchen table. The next moment, he shed the jacket and spread it out in front of the fireplace. With any luck, it would be dry by morning.

"Any sign of the storm breaking up?" she asked hopefully. She really wanted to be in town before nightfall.

Joe shook his head. "If anything, it's getting worse," he told her.

Frowning, Mona glanced at the food he'd braved the elements to bring in.

"This is all that you eat?" she asked incredulously.

The only thing on the table was a roast-beef sandwich, perched on a bed of wax paper.

"I wasn't planning on having to share it with anyone," Joe said a little defensively.

"Share?" she repeated. "It's not big enough for one person, let alone two." The man was six-two with a far better than average build. Didn't that take some kind of decent fuel to maintain? "Don't you get hungry?"

Wide, strong shoulders rose and then fell carelessly beneath his deputy's shirt. The material strained against his biceps.

"Not really," he answered. "Eating's never been a big deal for me."

It wasn't exactly a new revelation. Thinking back, she knew that no one could ever accuse Joe of consuming too much. He's always had the build of a rock-hard athlete without so much as an ounce of fat to spare. It was the reason that so many girls drooled over him. Or at least one of the reasons, she amended. The fact that he had brooding good looks didn't exactly hurt.

Joe didn't sit down at the table. Instead, he pushed the sandwich toward her. "You can have most of it if you like. I'm not really hungry."

Well, she was. While tempted to take him at his word, Mona didn't really believe him. He was just being Joe and that entailed being quietly noble. She wasn't about to take advantage of that. Hungry or not, it didn't seem fair.

"When did *you* last eat?" she asked him, repeating the question that Joe had put to her less than a few minutes ago.

He didn't even bother trying to remember, shrugging off the question. "I don't know." He made a vague gesture with his hand. "I don't live by a clock when it comes to food. I eat when I'm hungry, I don't when I'm not."

"We'll split it," she declared, her tone saying that she wasn't about to take no for an answer and she was done discussing it. Gingerly sitting down on one of the two chairs, Mona picked up the half closest to her.

Joe ignored the finality in her tone. "You just said that there wasn't even enough for one person," he reminded her.

Was he *trying* to pick a fight? Mona forced a fake smile to her lips. "And now I'm saying that we're splitting it. Seems to me if you can listen to me say one thing, you can listen to me say the other."

He laughed shortly and picked up the half closest to him. "It's been dull without you here."

She took a bite and savored it before commenting on his statement. Miss Joan's food was plain, but it could always be counted on to be delicious. "I don't think my brother would agree, what with finding first a baby, then the baby's aunt on his doorstep."

"Technically, the baby's aunt turned up on the diner's doorstep," Joe corrected just before he took his first bite of the sandwich.

Mona looked at him. She'd known that. Rick had given her all the details—after she'd pressed him for them—when he called to tell her he was getting married. For the purpose of narrative, she'd exaggerated. She should have known better around Joe.

"I forgot what a real stickler for details you could be."

"Gotta pay attention to the facts," he pointed out mildly. "Without the facts, your story can turn into someone else's."

Too tired to unscramble his remark, she took another healthy bite of her half, but needed something to wash it down with.

"You wouldn't happen to have brought along a beverage with your 'dinner,' would you?" she asked.

"I've got beer at home," he told her.

"Doesn't exactly do us any good here, now does it?"

Setting what was left of her half down on the wax paper, Mona eased herself off the chair, taking care not to make any sudden movements that might cause the legs to separate from the seat.

Meanwhile Joe had made his way over to the sink and slowly turned the faucet. It squealed in protest just before the water emerged. The smell alone was terrible. The color was a close second.

He turned off the faucet. "Well, water's out unless rust is your favorite flavor."

Since he was conducting the search, she sank back down on her chair. Her half of the sandwich was disappearing much too quickly, she thought, silently lamenting that he hadn't brought two.

"I'll pass." She watched Joe as he opened and then closed the overhead cabinets. "Anything?"

He was about to say "No," but the last cabinet he opened contained an old, half-empty bottle of whiskey. Judging from the dust, it had been left behind a long time ago.

Turning back to face her, he held the bottle aloft. "Does this count?"

"Rotgut," Mona cried, using the word that had defined crudely made alcohol a couple of centuries ago. That wouldn't have been her first choice, but any port in a storm, she reasoned. "It'll do in a pinch."

"We're going to have to drink straight out of the bottle," he told her, crossing back to Mona and placing the bottle in the middle of the table. "Seems like the last owner didn't believe in glasses." His eyes briefly met hers. "I can't find any."

Mona scrutinized the bottle. The light from the fireplace bathed it with gentle strokes, making it gleam amber. But there was no missing the thick dust. She hesitated. "Think it's safe to drink?" she asked him.

"Only one way to find out," Joe answered gamely. Before Mona could say anything further, he tilted the bottle back and took a small swig. Even that little bit jolted him. It took him a couple of seconds to find his breath. "Hell of a kick," he told her.

Suddenly, Joe grabbed his chest and began making strangling noises. His eyes rolled back in his head. Horrified, Mona was instantly on her feet. Throwing her arms around him, she struggled to lower him to the floor. She needed to get him to a flat surface before she could start CPR.

Mona did her best to fight back panic. "Joe, talk to me, what do you feel? Can you breathe? Damn it, you shouldn't have—"

The words dried up on her tongue when she caught a glimpse of Joe's face. He wasn't choking, he was laughing.

Furious, she opened her arms and his upper torso dropped, hitting the floor with a thud.

"Idiot!" she bit off. "I thought you were poisoned." She crossed her arms before her angrily. "I should have known the poison hadn't been invented that could do away with you."

Getting up off the floor, Joe dusted himself off. "A second ago, you were worried that I was dying. Now you're mad that I'm not. You sure do blow hot and cold, don't you?" he asked with a laugh.

Mona frowned as she sat down at the table again. For a moment, she said nothing, just ate the rest of her sandwich in silence.

He supposed it was a dirty trick. Sitting down opposite her, he apologized. Sort of. It would have carried more weight if he wasn't grinning. "Sorry, I just couldn't resist."

She raised her eyes to his face, glaring at him. "That was a rotten trick."

"Yes, it was," he responded solemnly. She knew he was just humoring her.

"So? How is it?" she pressed, changing the subject.

When he looked at her quizzically, she nodded at the bottle on the table. "The whiskey."

"Pretty smooth for rotgut," he told her. When he saw her reaching for the bottle, he advised, "Go slow if you're going to try it."

He realized his mistake the moment the words were out of his mouth.

"The day I can't hold my liquor as well as you can is the day I'll admit myself into a nursing home and spend the rest of my days sitting in a rocking chair in a corner—rocking."

He didn't crack a smile. "There is middle ground, you know."

"Not for people like you and me," she told him just before she took a swig from the bottle, determined to match him.

Joe watched her eyes tear up as the whiskey hit bottom. He knew better than to laugh, or even point the fact out. That would only goad her on. For all her education, she really hadn't changed that much, he mused. She still had that sharp, competitive edge that made her see everything as a personal challenge, even when it wasn't.

She would have never made it as a Navajo, he thought. The Native American tribe was known for *not* competing. They saw competing against their fellow man as being impolite.

Mona had never been hampered by those kinds of feelings.

"How is it?" he asked, infusing just enough disinterest in his voice to sound believable.

"Smooth, like you said," she managed to get out, her voice a raspy whisper. It felt as if the whiskey had instantly stripped her vocal cords, but she wasn't about to let on. Mona deliberately took another swig.

Liquid flames poured through her body. Even so, this time it was a little less jarring than the first sip she'd taken.

He wanted to tell her not to overdo it, but he knew better. Mona was nothing if not contrary. When she set the bottle down, the look in her eyes wasn't hard to read. She dared him to take another swig himself.

So he did.

And then it was her turn again. Joe caught himself thinking that he was grateful the pint bottle was half-empty when they found it. The damage caused by the whiskey wouldn't be too great.

Worst case, Mona would get light-headed and giddy for a bit, but since she was with him, she was safe.

Lucky for her, Joe thought rather grudgingly.

Yeah, you're a regular Boy Scout, aren't you?

The bottle was passed back and forth between them, traveling faster with each handoff. Before either one of them realized it, nothing was left.

With a sigh, Mona tilted the bottle all the way over, trying to coax another drop out, but without success.

She felt oddly relaxed and revved up at the same time, as if sliding around in a bright, shiny echo chamber.

Setting the bottle down on its side, she planted her hands on the tabletop and pushed herself up into a standing position. The chair behind her fell. There was a crash accompanied by a cracking sound as parts splintered against the floor.

Mona glanced behind her, mildly surprised. "Oops," she murmured. "Don't make them like they used to, do they?" Drawing herself up to her full height, she turned to her left a bit too quickly and found herself wavering unsteadily on her feet.

The sudden action had intensified her dizziness. "I think the wind is pushing the room around," she told Joe just before she tilted too far to the right.

Jumping to his feet quickly, Joe managed to grab her before Mona could fall over. "Guess that must be it," he agreed.

Her eyes narrowed as she forgot what had brought her to her feet to begin with.

"What are you doing over here? You were just over there." She pointed to his chair as if it was located on the other side of town.

"Wind blew me over here, too." He figured she'd accept that, thinking that if the wind was responsible for moving the room around, it could just as easily have moved him, too.

He should have known better.

Grabbing the front of his shirt with her hands in an effort to really steady herself—or the room—Mona stared up into his face rather intently. "Know what I think?" she asked him.

The woman was entirely too close to him, Joe thought. Her sweet breath mingled with the distinct scent of the whiskey she'd consumed, creating a very odd combination that reeled him in. He was acutely aware of every single supple inch of her. As well as his own body. Struggling, he did his best to appear indifferent.

He wasn't, but in her present state, he hoped Mona wouldn't notice. If she pressed up against him, all bets were off.

"What?" he finally asked her.

She was really trying to focus and not doing an overly good job of it. "I think that you're trying to take advantage of me, Joe."

That was when she moved in closer to him, as if that could somehow help her read him better. She pressed all her curves against the hard contours of his body and in turn threatened to create Joe's own personal meltdown.

"Are you trying to take advantage of me?" Mona asked.

He did his best to try to make her turn toward the rear of the cabin. Hands ever so lightly on her shoulders, he maneuvered her toward it. "Right now, I think you should lie down. There's a bed in the other room."

"Ah-ha! I was right. I knew it," Mona declared triumphantly, swinging around so that she could grasp hold of his shirtfront again, crumpling it beneath her fingers. "You *are* trying to take advantage of me. Oh, Joe—"

Every fiber of his being wanted to give in, but he continued to fight it. "No, I'm—"

The rest of his adamant protest went unspoken. He found it impossible to speak when Mona's lips were suddenly and firmly pressed against his.

She was quick, he'd give her that.

She was also damn intoxicating, far more potent than an old, half-empty bottle of aged whiskey, Joe caught himself thinking—while he could still think.

But that ability quickly faded as the taste of Mona's lips steadily got to him, weakening his resolve. Making him want Mona with a fierceness that jarred him.

The will to push her away, to do the right thing, was not nearly as strong as it should have been. As strong as it had been only moments ago.

His lips worked over hers, deepening the kiss.

He tasted her moan and felt the blood surge through his veins as if it had been set on fire.

Maybe it had been.

He needed to put a stop to this.

In a moment. Just one more moment.

He promised himself that he would do the right thing in a moment. Right now, just for this erotic half a heartbeat, he wanted to enjoy this completely unexpected turn of events.

Wanted to enjoy the feel of her warm body pressed so urgently against his.

Wanted to savor the taste of her mouth as it drained his soul away. With the least bit of encouragement, he would have fallen to his knees, silently begging her for more.

But that wasn't going to happen for a whole host of reasons, not the least of which was pride.

His.

So, realizing that this was a once-in-a-lifetime occurrence, like Halley's Comet, he took his time ending it.

Took full enjoyment of the moment—and her.

The very act, even as it was occurring, left him vulnerable, unmasking the secret that he had tried to keep, even from himself. That he wanted this woman with the laughing eyes and the sinful mouth. Had always wanted her and would, most likely, go to his grave wanting her.

In silence.

Because a man had his pride and any admission as to the depth and breadth of his feelings—his *unrequited* feelings—for Mona would expose him and leave him open to ridicule and pity, neither one of which he could endure.

With a jolt, Joe realized that he was very close to the edge of the vortex. To the point of no return. Any second now, it would suck him in, rendering him a prisoner of this feeling and leaving him incapable of cutting off this kiss.

Incapable of walking away.

He already didn't want to. Fiercely.

If he didn't back away in a moment, there would *be*

no backing away. Because he was only a man, only flesh and blood, and his flesh and blood craved hers.

Now! Stop it now! Before you can't!

Inflamed, Joe went on kissing her.

And she was kissing him back just as urgently.

Chapter Four

The sound of her own groan rudely nudged Mona into semiwakefulness.

An elephant tap-danced on her head. A heavy elephant that threatened to crush her skull any second now.

Mona curled up into herself, trying to hide from the creature, from the pain that his lumbering movements created.

But there was nowhere to hide.

As the haze lifted, scraping slowly along her awakening consciousness, she realized that she was squeezing her eyes shut. Squeezing them shut in self-defense.

Why?

Was she afraid of seeing something? Someone?

Very cautiously, Mona pried her eyelids open. The moment she did, she instantly shut them again.

The sunlight hurt her head.

Sunlight?

Her eyes popped open and she jackknifed up into a sitting position. The pain doubled but she valiantly struggled to ignore it as urgent messages telegraphed themselves to her throbbing brain.

The incessant, heavy rain had stopped. As had the moaning wind. The world was still.

She was on a striped, bare mattress that smelled as if it had been used every day for the past two centuries, all without being cleaned.

She'd gotten drunk, she suddenly recalled.

Drunk with Joe.

Joe! *Omigod, Joe!*

Shock raced through her aching mind as bits and pieces of last night came back to her, jumbled and completely out of order. The only thing she specifically remembered was throwing herself at him.

Hard.

And then nothing.

She covered her mouth in growing agitation. She couldn't remember what happened after she'd hermetically sealed her mouth to his.

Had he—

Had they—

"Oh, God," Mona groaned more loudly this time as her distress mounted. She dragged her hand through her hair. The roots hurt. Her skull hurt.

Did that mean that she…?

That he…?

"Oh, God," Mona groaned again, confused, embarrassed and absolutely, unequivocally miserable.

"He's busy. Will I do in a pinch?" Joe asked.

The sound of her groaning voice had drawn him

in. The expression on her face as she looked up at him told him everything he needed to know. She remembered last night.

That made two of them.

"You—you—" She couldn't bring herself to finish the sentence, hoping against hope that nothing had happened. Afraid that it had. And worse, not knowing how to bluff her way through this to get him to tell her the details—or the lack of any—without admitting that there was a huge void in her aching brain.

"It stopped raining," Joe informed her mildly as if he hadn't noticed her sudden inability to form a complete, coherent sentence. "Hell, it looks as if it never even rained at all." There were only a few small puddles to hint at the rising waters that had encroached around the cabin yesterday. "I can get you into town now."

And then, because he wasn't entirely a plastered saint and because he couldn't resist teasing her just a little, he stood in the doorway of the tiny bedroom where he'd deposited her passed-out body last night and grinned wickedly at her.

"Unless, of course, you'd rather stay here for a while longer…." His voice trailed off, leaving the rest to her imagination.

Mona instantly stiffened. Something *had* happened last night. "No, I don't want to stay here a second longer," she informed him woodenly, scrambling off the sagging, weathered mattress. "Not *one* second longer."

Feet planted firmly on the floor, her head still

throbbing like a war drum pressed into use, Mona raised her chin pugnaciously, ready to go toe to toe with him in order to get at the truth.

"What happened last night, Joe?"

The wicked grin remained. "You weren't yourself," he answered.

There were *so* many different ways to take that, and from where she stood, none of them were good. "Exactly who *was* I?" she demanded.

Enjoying himself, Joe played it out a little longer. He turned on his heel, ready to leave the room and the cabin. "Maybe we'd better leave that to another time." He kept his voice deliberately vague.

He figured she owed him, seeing as how he'd been the personification of honorableness last night. Turning a deaf ear to the demands that his body fairly shouted at him.

Stunned that he wasn't answering her, Mona launched herself at the doorway, making it half a step before he reached it. Hands on either side of the doorjamb, trying not to wince from the pain in her head, Mona blocked his way.

"Maybe we better not," she countered. Damn but her head was killing her. Any sudden movement on her part just intensified the crushing pounding. "*What* happened?" she asked again, enunciating each word slowly, her teeth clenched.

Silent, Joe watched her for a long moment. She didn't remember anything. Hadn't witnessed his superhuman struggles with himself to finally separate her lips from his and hold her at arm's length. Didn't remember that she'd pushed his hands away and snuggled up against him again, her soft, inviting body promising him a time he wouldn't soon forget—and she wouldn't remember.

That had been just the trouble. Whether it was just the liquor talking, or the liquor dissolving the inhibitions that kept her from him, he didn't know. What he did know was that if he made love with a woman, she would damn well be conscious of her decision to meet him halfway, not slide to meet him on a slick path of mind-numbing alcohol.

"Nothing happened," he finally said.

If it was nothing, then why had it taken him so long to say the word? And why couldn't she remember anything beyond—

Oh, God, she'd kissed him.

Kissed him? She'd all but swallowed his mouth up whole, she realized as the memory came vividly crashing back to her, heating her blood at the same time. Heating all of her.

Embarrassed, Mona could feel her cheeks suddenly blazing. It took everything she had not to try to cover them up with her hands.

She tried diversion. "Don't lie to me," she snapped angrily.

His eyes captured hers, making a soul-to-soul connection, the way he used to back when he would walk her home from school and dreams were cheap.

"When have you ever known me to lie?" he asked her quietly.

Mona shrugged, struggling to recapture the dignity she felt she'd forfeited by allowing her old, and secret, girlhood crush on Joe to come out last night.

"For the most part, I've been gone these past eight years." Although she had come home almost every summer. "I don't know. You could have changed."

But even as she said it, Mona knew she didn't really believe that.

"I didn't," he replied flatly.

"So what did happen after I glued my mouth to yours?"

"You passed out."

Mona froze inside. This was worse than she'd thought. No wonder she didn't remember anything. She wasn't conscious for it. "And then what?" she asked in a quiet voice.

"And then I carried you into this room and put you to bed," he told her matter-of-factly.

"And?" she asked, her voice hitching in her throat as she waited for the rest of the details. Joe never said all that much, but he had a way of stringing it out, and right now, he drove her crazy. It was hard not to let her irritation just jump out at him.

"And I slept on the couch."

Mona drew in a shaky breath, trying to do it quietly. Was he really saying nothing happened? "And that's all?" she questioned.

"That's all." He cocked his head. "Why, what else did you want to have happen?" he asked innocently.

"Want?" she repeated indignantly. Did Joe suspect that she'd had feelings for him? No, how could he? She'd never given him any reason to suspect—until last night, she thought ruefully. "Nothing. Absolutely nothing," Mona retorted with emphasis.

One dark eyebrow arched higher than the other. "That why you kissed me, Mona?"

"I didn't kiss you!" Mona shot back. And then, because he was grinning at her knowingly, and because she actually *had* kissed him, she added, "Like you said, that wasn't me."

"Sure looked like you," he told her.

He got a real kick out of watching her squirm. Since he'd played the noble guy while everything inside of him screamed not to allow this one once-in-a-lifetime opportunity slip through his fingers, she owed him a little entertainment at her expense. After all, he'd been noble even though it had cost him.

Joe had taken off her boots, she noted, grabbing them from the floor. Going out into the main room, she hobbled over to the sofa. Overall, she was grateful to him, but right now, the humiliation of her unscheduled transformation into a passion-laced woman haunted her and she wanted nothing more than to divert his attention from that image.

Planting herself on the sofa so she could pull on her boots, she addressed Joe in a clipped voice. "Can we just get going?"

He nodded. "The rain didn't sweep away the Jeep, so whenever you're ready, we're good to go."

Boots on, she jumped up to her feet. "Ready," she announced. The next moment she winced again from the pain shooting through her temples.

"Bad?" he asked sympathetically.

"What do you think?" She eyed him accusingly. They had both had the same amount to drink last night, that much she remembered. So why wasn't his head splitting in two like hers was? "Why didn't that whiskey affect you?"

"Oh, it did," he told her, thinking of how his resistance to her had been lowered. Had the whiskey not affected him, he wouldn't have let things go as far as they had. If nothing else, his background had taught him how to stoically do without. Not having her was part of that. "I just handle it better."

Had she not been feeling sick, she would have taken that as a challenge to her own capabilities when it came to tolerating alcohol. But that was a catch-22 situation, she thought. So she said nothing as she lowered herself into the passenger seat and buckled up.

The less said, she decided, the less her head hurt, and right now, that was all that counted.

It DIDN'T TAKE THAT LONG to get into the heart of Forever. Joe made the decision to go there instead of stopping at the house that Mona shared with her brother. He'd already gathered that her main purpose was to see Rick first, and at this hour, the sheriff was most likely in his office.

The additional benefit of going straight to town was that he could get Mick moving. The sooner he got the mechanic to tow in her vehicle and fix the flat, the sooner life would begin to get back to normal for Mona, he reasoned.

As for him, well, the memory of last night and what had *almost* gone down would linger in his mind for a very long time, as would the revelation that, just as he'd always believed, her lips had tasted incredibly sweet. That, too, would have to sustain him for an indefinite period to come. He knew there would be no replays, instant or otherwise.

Joe brought the Jeep to a halt before the sheriff's building, parking it in the only space still available. Turning off the ignition and pulling up the hand brake, he was surprised that Mona remained beside him. He'd expected her to hop out. Under ordinary circumstances, he'd have to grab her to keep her inside the vehicle until it stopped moving.

"Something wrong?" he asked her.

Mona sat looking straight ahead, as if debating answering or just quietly getting out of the vehicle.

With a suppressed sigh, she turned toward him and said, "I'm sorry if I took your head off back there."

The apology was even a greater surprise than her silence. He wondered what was going in her head. To his recollection, Mona had never been the type to tender her apologies.

She would have to have gone a long way before she measured up to anything he'd endured after his mother had died, leaving his welfare up in the air and at the mercy of a host of relatives who all had better things to do than raise a homeless boy.

"You didn't," he told her.

Mona knew better. She'd been rude and short with him and none of it had really been his fault. But she was trying to work certain things out in her head and, through no fault of his own, he had been a handy target.

"And about last night…" She wanted him to know that it wasn't the thought of being with him that had horrified her this morning. It was the idea of not remembering, of believing that she hadn't had control over her actions.

"There's nothing to talk about," Joe told her. Nothing had happened beyond the one soul-searing kiss and she didn't need to agonize over and regret. They would continue the way they always had, as more than friends, less than lovers. "Now, why don't you go inside and see your brother before someone does start talking about you sitting out here with me in my Jeep?"

Other than playing poker, gossip and rumors were the number one diversion for a lot of the citizens of Forever. She didn't want to give them any more fuel than they probably already felt they had. She was in no mood to be forgiving right now and probably wouldn't be until she'd worked out what was bothering her.

"Right."

Unbuckling her seat belt, Mona got out of the vehicle. The heels of her boots made rhythmic, staccato sounds as they hit the pavement before the short, squat office's front door.

She didn't bother knocking before she entered. The door was unlocked, which meant that at least one of the four-man team was in.

From the sound of it, the entire crew was present except, of course, for Joe, who for some reason hadn't followed her in. She didn't have time to wonder why.

The first to see her was Alma Rodriguez. Glancing up from her desk, the slender, dark-haired deputy was on her feet, running across the room to Mona with her arms outstretched. The next second, Mona found herself caught up in a fierce hug. For a small woman, Alma was exceptionally strong. She'd said it had something to do with growing up with five brothers and trying to hold her own.

"Hey, Mona, what are you doing here?" Alma cried, her voice muffled against Mona's shoulder. "Rick told me that you weren't coming in until the day before his and Olivia's wedding."

Mona hugged the woman back, partially in self-defense to keep from being smothered and partially because Alma, Larry and Joe were family to her. Coming to the office felt more like a home to her than the house where she'd grown up. Without her grandmother there and with Rick at work, the old building just felt like a shell with memories.

She pushed aside the sudden pang that sought to entangle her.

"I decided you guys needed my help getting everything ready," Mona told her with a laugh.

Alma released Mona only to have her place taken by Larry Collins, the third deputy. Older than Joe and Alma, the tall, blond-haired man treated Mona as if she was *his* little sister and not the sheriff's.

"Good to see you, little girl," he said with feeling, stepping back. He smiled at Mona appreciatively. "You just keep getting prettier every time I see you. Good thing you came early. With you around, the sheriff's fiancée can get to see that there's a pretty side to his family after all."

"What the hell's all this noise?" Rick asked, coming out of his office. "It sure better have something to do with seeing to all the damage caused by yesterday's flash flood—"

Rick stopped talking when Mona swung around to face him. Grinning, she threw up her hands like a gymnast jumping off the uneven bars after completing her program, waiting for applause.

"Surprise."

Rick's mouth dropped open. His sister was two weeks early. "Mona, what the hell are you doing here?"

"Surviving being hugged by your deputies," she deadpanned as she crossed over to him. And then she answered him seriously, leaving out the part that a sense of anxiety had prompted her to come early. That was her problem to work out, not his. "I decided that

I wanted to be more than just a spectator at my only brother's wedding."

Because he was glad to see her, alive and well and in one piece, he paused to hug her. Then stepped back, as all the things that could have happened to her took over his thoughts. A disapproving look mingled with the deep love for his younger sister.

"You should have waited until I came up for you." That had been the plan, for him to fetch her and bring her down here the day before the wedding. They'd left it at that, with her agreeing. He should have known better. Mona was far too impetuous for her own good. "You know how I feel about you driving at night. Especially in a storm," he emphasized.

"I didn't drive through the night—or the storm," she told him. "When I left Dallas, it wasn't raining. I stopped when it started getting bad." For now, she left out the part about the flat. No sense in giving her overprotective brother more ammunition.

His eyes narrowed. "Where'd you stop?"

She sighed, shaking her head. When she looked to Alma for help, the woman conveniently retreated to her work. She was on her own here.

"Do you have to play twenty questions now?" she asked her brother. "I haven't even been here two minutes. The least you can do is pretend like you're happy to see me."

"I *am* happy to see you, you know that." But he pinned her down with a look, the way he'd seen his grandmother do more than once. The old woman had been the only one who had ever managed to make his sister toe the line. "I'm just curious how you managed to avoid getting caught in the storm."

"She didn't avoid it," Joe said, aware that all eyes turned toward him as he walked into the office. He'd stopped by Mick's garage and given the mechanic directions as to where to find Mona's Jeep. Mick had put the sheriff's sister up to the head of his list and taken off before any of the other customers he had coming in today could complain. "Mona spent the night at the old Murphy place halfway between the reservation and town."

"I *know* where the old Murphy place is," Rick told him.

"That moth-eaten old cabin?" Alma cried in surprise, then looked at Mona. "You poor thing. What a way to spend your first night back."

Rick had a more important question. He addressed it to Joe. "How would you know about that?"

"'Cause I was there, too," Joe told him.

Crossing over to his desk, he acted as if he didn't know that he'd just detonated a major bomb right in the middle of the room.

Without pausing to stop, Joe picked up his mug, which was in desperate need of cleaning, and went to make himself some coffee. Ordinarily, he wasn't awake before the first cup. But today, watching Mona sleep had done a lot to get his blood moving.

Still, he had a feeling he was going to need more. He usually wasn't wrong when it came to feelings.

Chapter Five

Mona saw the look that entered her brother's green eyes as they shifted from her to Joe and then back again. She could almost hear the thoughts and questions sprouting like weeds in his mind. Thank God he didn't know anything about the bottle of whiskey they'd found. Or the kiss.

"Don't go all 'big brother' on me, Rick," she warned. "If it wasn't for Joe, I would probably have been swept away to who knows where," she informed her brother. "Joe came to my rescue."

Ordinarily an easygoing, laid-back sort of a man, all sorts of protective instincts rose to the fore when it came to his sister. Subconsciously, he always felt he had to step in for the father who had died before she was even a year old.

Rick took her answer with more than a degree of skepticism. "Oh? Would either one of you care to elaborate how this rescue wound up with you two spending the night together in the old Murphy cabin?"

Coffee mug in hand, Joe crossed back to the sheriff. All eyes were now on him. Stoically, he recited the facts as if he'd just been sworn in on the witness stand. "Her Jeep's front right tire was flat—so was her spare. I was on my way home, saw her cursing at the tire and offered to take her back to town. The storm was getting worse and visibility next to impossible, so when we drove by the cabin, I decided it was better if we just waited it out there instead of running the risk of getting caught in a flash flood."

"So you picked the cozy cabin," Rick interjected, his tone far from satisfied.

"Cozy?" The incredulous utterance came from Alma, who hooted at the very thought of what her boss was suggesting. "Hell, Rick, have you *seen* that cabin lately? Not even a raccoon in heat would call it 'cozy.' Staying there's like spending the night in a Dumpster."

"How would you know that?" Larry asked, curious.

"That's not the point here," Alma pointed out evasively.

The cabin hadn't been that bad, Joe thought, taking a deep sip of his coffee. But for the sake of putting Rick's mind at ease, he decided it best to keep his observation to himself.

For a moment, it looked as if the sheriff would subject them to more probing questions. But then, mercifully, Rick shrugged, letting the matter drop.

He nodded toward Alma. "Yeah, I guess you're right. Nobody would willingly spend the night in that place."

Her brother might be willing to let the matter drop,

but Mona wasn't. She took umbrage with his line of questioning.

"Alma might be right," Mona allowed, "but you seem to be forgetting that I'm twenty-six." She saw Rick's eyebrows narrow, a sure sign that he wasn't pleased with what he was hearing, but she pressed on. He had to be made to respect her as an adult, not a child. "Don't you think it's about time you stopped acting as if I was fifteen and still needed someone to guard my virtue?"

"Time to get back to work," Larry announced loudly, turning away and clearly indicating that he had no intentions of taking sides in what looked to be a possible war between his boss and Mona.

Alma took her cue from Larry and glanced at her watch. "My turn to go on patrol," she said to no one in particular.

Strapping on her sidearm and picking up her hat, the petite woman was out the door before any more words were exchanged.

Rick stood there for a moment as if debating two lines of thought. Coming to a conclusion, he turned to Joe. "Sorry, Joe. I should have just thanked you for bringing her in safely."

Joe brushed off any real need for an apology. "That's okay."

She wasn't exactly thrilled with that wording, either. All she wanted was to be treated as an equal, not an afterthought that needed special tending.

"Bringing me in safely?" Mona asked, incensed. "What am I, a stray mare to be 'brought in safely'?"

Rick allowed a smile to curve his mouth. "No, definitely not a mare. Mares can be gentled. You're more like a burr under a mustang's saddle."

Mona decided to take his comment as a compliment and smiled.

Though a great deal more vulnerable than anyone suspected—or possibly because of it—she'd made a point of never coming across as meek and mild. The meek and mild were stepped on and pushed around on a regular basis.

"Now that that's out of the way," Mona said, the edge gone from her voice, "you have any aspirin around here, Rick?" she asked hopefully. "My head's about to split open."

"Why didn't you say so earlier?" Rick asked. "I've got a whole bottle of the stuff in my office." Leading the way back, he grinned. "I stocked up when I knew you were coming home."

"Very funny," she retorted. But there was affection in her voice as she said it. And a smile bloomed on her face when he put his arm around her shoulders, guiding her into his glass-walled office.

"BE WITH YOU IN A MINUTE," Dr. Henry Whitmore, affectionately referred to as "Doc" by everyone who knew him, called out from the back room. His words were addressed to whoever had just walked into the front of his clinic, setting off a series of chimes that corresponded to the beginning notes of "How Much Is That Doggie in the Window?" He'd had the chimes ever since he'd opened his animal hospital in Forever more than thirty years ago.

There was something incredibly comforting in hearing the chimes, Mona thought as she walked in. It connected her to her childhood and all the years she'd spent here, apprenticing Doc, learning from experience what no textbooks could have possibly conveyed nearly so well.

From the time she was eleven until she went off to college, Doc's animal hospital had been like another home to her. She'd felt comfortable here. Useful. And so in her element. She couldn't always communicate with people, her emotions getting in the way. But animals were a different story. She had an affinity for animals. And they responded to her in kind, as if sensing the compassion she had for them, the respect with which she regarded all of them.

She'd loved animals ever since she could remember. Animals were loyal. If you showed them affection, they stayed. They didn't just take off one morning, promising to be back but never meaning to keep their word, the way her mother had.

Her grandmother had solemnly called her an animal whisperer. The old woman had said that this was her calling. Her "gift." It was obvious that animals seemed to be attracted to her. She could get them to do things that other people couldn't. Mona was gentle with them, patient, and they trusted her even when they were sick or hurt.

She decided early on that her mission in life was to help these creatures that looked at her so trustingly, to make them well and to generally improve their quality of life. Because she was so determined to help every sick animal she found, it was only natural that her path would cross with Doc's. From the time she was a little girl, he took a special interest in her and invited her to his clinic to be his "assistant."

In time, she actually became one. She worked for him after school and on weekends. She would have done it for free just to be around the animals, but he insisted on paying her. Told her to save the money for her schooling, which she did, religiously.

That was how her college fund initially got started. Even so, it still wouldn't have been enough for more than a year's worth of tuition and expenses if Doc hadn't come through again.

He insisted on giving her the money she needed to fund the rest of her education. Never married and childless, with no known relatives, Doc told Mona that she was the daughter he would have wanted to have if things had worked out differently for him. At the time he'd told her, she had the feeling that he'd loved someone once who hadn't return that affection, but he never elaborated any further and she didn't pry.

What she did do was promise to pay him back as soon as she was able. He'd answered that he wasn't worried about getting his money back. He considered what he was doing to be a sound investment.

After her brother, Doc was the first person she went to see after she got into town.

Henry Whitmore came out of the back room where he performed his surgeries as well as his examinations on the smaller animals brought in either as beloved pets or wounded strays. He saw them all and treated them all. No animal was turned away because of the owner's inability to pay. Neither did he turn out the strays. In his book, a suffering creature needed to be helped. It was as simple as that for him.

Gray-haired with deep blue eyes, Doc was a robust-looking man in his late fifties. He wore his glasses on the tip of his nose, making it easier for him to see his patients up close and look at the owners at the same time.

Walking out into the reception area, Doc was wiping his hands on a worn white towel, an indication that he had just completed an operation. Preoccupied with details pertaining to his last patient, he apologized before he even looked at his visitor.

"Sorry, my assistant's been under the weather the past couple of days. I told her to stay home and get better. Hope you haven't been waiting too long. What can I do for…?"

Doc stopped dead in his tracks as he got his first look at the person who'd walked into his clinic.

"Ramona?"

"You don't have an assistant, Doc," Mona reminded

him with a smile. At least, he hadn't had one the last time she'd been by. He'd told her that she'd spoiled him for anyone else and he wasn't even going to attempt to replace her.

She'd rather liked that, even though she did acknowledge that it was a little vain on her part. "Do you?" she tagged on.

"Just Linda. She juggles my appointments," he explained, "but she doesn't like to be called a secretary. Says it's outdated. So I call her my assistant. It makes her happy." He tossed the towel aside on the reception desk and took hold of both of her hands in his wide, capable ones. "Here, let me look at you," he cried, as pleased as any father would be when his only daughter was finally home from college. "You look good," he declared. "But then, you always looked good," he amended.

And then he seemed contrite. "I'm sorry I missed your graduation, Ramona. I wanted to come, but Jake Sloan's mare was having trouble giving birth to her foal and I couldn't just leave her like that—"

"I know," she told him, cutting his unnecessary apology short. He wouldn't have been Doc if he'd left the mare in distress. And she wouldn't be where she was if he hadn't been that man. No way would she ever find fault with him. She dismissed the graduation ceremony with a few words. "It was just a couple of hours in a day. You were fighting to save the mare's life. Rick told me," she explained in response to the quizzical look the veterinarian gave her.

"Don't get me wrong, Doc," she continued quickly, in case he misunderstood. "I would have loved to have had you there, but I understand why you weren't. You're like a father to me. If it wasn't for you, I would have never been able to go to college, much less on to veterinary school. And you gave me my edge. I was ahead of the class because you allowed me to trail after you, letting me learn firsthand how to successfully treat sick animals. I'll never be able to even begin to pay you back for that."

He gestured to a seat beside the receptionist's desk and he sat down behind it. "You really want to pay me back?" he asked, studying her expression.

"You know I do."

"Then come join my practice."

Mona's mouth dropped open. This was what she'd been secretly hoping for all along, but they had never discussed her coming to work with him after she graduated. She'd thought that maybe he would have preferred working on his own.

She had to ask before she let herself begin celebrating. "Do you mean it?"

Doc chuckled. "Why do you think I sent you to veterinary college? I'm getting on in years, Ramona," he confided, leaning over the desk. "I'm not as young as I used to be—"

She cut him off. She didn't want him dwelling on age, didn't want to think about his ever getting old. She'd come to depend on the fact that he would always be there. Like Rick. It had been hard enough on her when her grandmother had died. There were times when she couldn't get herself to accept that. It felt too much like being abandoned.

"Sure you are, Doc," she told him with feeling. "You're the youngest man I know."

Doc grinned and it made him appear at least ten years younger. "Be that as it may, being the only vet in the area is really beginning to wear me down. I don't mind saying that I could use help. The right kind of help." He looked at her pointedly. "Your help. How about it? Are you game, Ramona?"

Unabashed enthusiasm throbbed in her voice as she told him, "Try and stop me."

Amused, pleased, he laughed at her challenge. "You're a force of nature, Ramona. I wouldn't dream of ever getting in your way."

Mona moved to the edge of the seat. "So when can I start?" she wanted to know.

He would have wanted her to begin yesterday. He really was swamped.

"I'd say 'now,' but realistically, how about right after your brother's wedding? I'm assuming that you want to pitch in with the preparations," he said knowingly. "From what I hear, Miss Joan's got the food covered, but there are still the decorations and all that stuff I have no idea about that needs doing. I'm sure that Olivia and Tina will appreciate the help."

Olivia and Tina. That would be her future sister-in-law and Olivia's sister. She'd met them both just once, at her graduation. Both were initially from Dallas and, according to the brief explanation she'd gotten, Rick had met Olivia when she'd come looking for her runaway sister. Rick had brought them to her graduation, then dropped the little bombshell on her that he was getting married. *And* that Olivia was having his baby.

In all honesty, she was excited about the prospect of becoming an aunt, but not so much about becoming a sister-in-law. Or, more specifically, if she was being really honest with herself, she wasn't all that thrilled about Rick getting married. Though she would never tell him as much, she didn't want to lose him, or lose the connection they had. And wives had a way of doing that, cutting their man out from the herd and keeping him all to themselves.

For as long as she could remember, Rick had been part of her life. Even this morning's protective big-brother display was all part of the deal, even though she bristled and made noises that she was irritated and that he was cutting into her independence. But if Rick wasn't there to care about what she did, or who she did it with, she knew she would miss that terribly. Miss having him worrying about her.

Miss being the center of his world.

But now he was going to have a new center. Olivia was going to be his center. And she would be out in the cold.

Mona wasn't all that sure how she would handle that reality in the long run. That was what she needed to work out. But even as she thought about it, she could feel a loneliness seeping in.

"And," Doc was saying, "there's something else to consider."

She blinked. How much had she missed with her mind wandering? "What?"

"Well, it's no secret that Rick was hoping you'd open a practice in Dallas or Austin. There's a lot more money to be made in big cities like that. People have a lot more money to spend on their pets," he told her. "I know Rick's hoping that you'll become financially secure. That won't happen if you work with me."

Money had never been her primary concern. She wanted to stay in Forever, wanted to work with her mentor. "Don't worry about Rick. I doubt if he even remembers that he had any plans for my future," she said dismissively. "My brother's got more important things on his mind these days."

Doc watched her for a long moment. Something about his expression told her that he'd heard more than she'd been willing to say.

"Rick always struck me as a very capable young man," Doc said. "I'm sure he can handle having a wife *and* a sister."

Was she that transparent, or was Doc just that good at reading people as well as animals?

Mona shrugged, doing her best not to look as if her brother's ability to be a husband and a brother mattered to her one way or the other.

"We'll see."

Just then the chimes in the doorway sounded, interrupting the flow of the conversation. Mona turned around in her seat, fully expecting to see another of Doc's patients being brought into the clinic.

Instead, Joe walked in.

"Thought you might be here," he said. And then, as an afterthought, he nodded at the veterinarian, muttering Whitman's title by way of a greeting. "Doc."

"Why are you looking for me?" she asked. Suspicion crept into her voice. "Rick send you?"

"No, Rick left the office to see Olivia. Something about having to drive her to the next town for a doctor's appointment. I just thought you might want to know that Mick towed your car in and he's finished fixing your flat—and putting air into your spare," he added. "Car's waiting for you at his shop anytime you're ready to pick it up."

Mona nodded her thanks, then looked back at Doc. "Why would I want to go anywhere else?" she asked the older man. It was a rhetorical question. "Everyone takes such good care of me here. Besides, I do have that loan to pay back," she reminded him pointedly.

Doc waved his hand at her words, dismissing them. "Wasn't a loan, it was a gift. A scholarship, if you will. You don't pay back a scholarship."

"Doc, you don't charge your patients much. You're hardly rolling in money. You can't afford to just give that kind of money away—even to me."

"Now, there you're wrong," Doc told her. "It's my money, which means that I'm at liberty to spend it any way I want. And what I wanted was to be part of creating the best damn veterinarian that this part of

Texas has ever seen. You wouldn't begrudge an old man his dream, would you?"

"I already told you, I don't know any 'old man,' so there's no way I could begrudge him anything. As for you, I know that I owe you so much more than I can ever pay back. The money's the least of it."

"If it's the least of it, there's no point in even concerning yourself about it. Good, that's settled," Doc pronounced. "You're not paying me back."

Mona blinked, feeling a little dazed. Doc had somehow managed to twist her words. But this wasn't the end of the matter. She would find a way to get money into Doc's bank account without raising any red flags. Once it was there, he couldn't just hand it back to her. She wouldn't let him. His mentoring had been priceless and no way could she ever pay him back for sharing his time and himself with her.

But money was something she *could* return. And would.

"We'll see," she murmured.

Turning toward Joe, she asked, "Want to give me a ride over to Mick's Garage?"

"That's why I'm hanging around," the senior deputy told her.

That said, Joe turned on his heel and led the way out.

"See you later, Doc," Mona called out, following Joe.

"Later," Doc echoed. And smiled to himself.

Chapter Six

They looked good together.

Sitting at one of the tables set up for the reception, Mona felt a pang. She was watching her brother and his brand-new bride dancing together. Wearing a beautiful floor-length gown with an empire waist that softly swirled about her as she moved, Olivia looked radiant. The statuesque blonde had a double glow about her because she was not only a bride, but a mother-to-be, as well.

It was ordinarily not the best of combinations, but Mona had to admit that Olivia carried it off with aplomb. When she first met her sister-in-law last month, Mona was completely prepared to dislike the woman who was taking her brother away from her. But Olivia was smart, sharp and witty—and obviously very, very much in love with Rick.

It was the last quality that carried the most weight with Mona. If she had to lose Rick, lose the man who'd been brother, father *and* mother to her as far back as she could remember, she wanted it to be to a woman who had stars in her eyes every time she looked at him. That described Olivia to a *T.*

And Rick, well, Mona had to admit that she'd never seen him look so proud, so happy. Oh, he'd displayed both emotions at her recent graduation, but this, this was something different, something more. This demonstration of pride and happiness came from a man very obviously in love, who clearly felt that the sun rose and set around the woman he had just promised to love and cherish in sickness and in health until death reared its dark head to part them.

She knew that her brother had never thought true love was in the cards for him—honest-to-God, gut-twisting love. And now, here he was, dancing before the whole town and seeing only the woman in his arms.

Here he was, Mona thought, in love and a husband.

Not just a husband but a father-to-be, as well. He was taking on a great deal in a very short amount of time. And while she was glad for him, truly, truly glad because Rick deserved every bit of happiness that came his way, deep down she was still very sad for herself.

She'd done her very best not to show it, to throw herself wholeheartedly into festively decorating Doc's backyard—the veterinarian had generously thrown open his house because his was the largest backyard in the area and there were a lot of people who wanted to celebrate their sheriff's nuptials—so that no one would suspect that she struggled to keep this growing feeling of loneliness from consuming her.

It wasn't an unfamiliar feeling.

Mona had struggled with it before. This was the same loneliness that had come for her when their grandmother had died so suddenly when she was in her second year at college. At the time, Rick had unknowingly made the loneliness retreat by promising that she'd always have him to rely on, that he would always be there for her, no matter what.

But today, his first priority had become his wife, as it should be.

However, who did *she* have? Mona wondered, suppressing a sigh as she twirled the stem of her champagne glass, hardly aware of what she was doing.

Yes, technically, to the outside observer, her family had just increased. She'd gained not only a sister-in-law, but Olivia's sister, Tina, and nephew, Bobby, as well. Yet that gain was just on paper. In her heart, she hadn't gained, she'd lost. Lost a very, very important person in her world.

She hated feeling like this, hated not being able to simply celebrate Rick's happiness and just be *happy* for him.

Rick and Olivia had each other and she…she had Doc and the practice, Mona consoled herself. Doc had no other family. *She* was going to have to be his family, she reminded herself. And maybe, in time, that would become enough. For her, as well.

Rick caught her eye as he twirled Olivia about

on the floor. He was grinning from ear to ear. Mona smiled broadly for his benefit, silently telling herself to stop being so maudlin. She loved Rick and she wanted him to be happy.

Larry looked from his friend, to the sheriff's sister. Mona was sitting several tables away from theirs. With an annoyed sigh, Larry shook his head.

"So when are you going to make your move?" he finally asked Joe.

Preoccupied, Joe realized that the deputy beside him had addressed the question to him. Not that the question made any sense.

He blinked and stared at Larry. "What?"

Larry appeared ready to hit him upside the head. "Your move, man," he ground out between clenched teeth. "When are you going to make your move?"

He was *not* going to encourage this. Turning away from Larry, Joe said, "I don't know what you're talking about."

Larry did not cease and desist, the way Joe had hoped. Instead, he asked another question, one that was just as annoying as the first.

"God, you're even thicker than a bale of hay, aren't you? You've been staring at Mona for the last half hour," Larry hissed. "If you stared any harder, your eyes would have fallen out of your head by now. She's alone, you're alone. *Do* something about it."

He was going to do something about it, Joe thought. He would go home in a few minutes, but not yet. Right now, he just wanted to look at Mona a few minutes longer. Dressed in a deep green cocktail dress that accentuated her small waist and clung invitingly to her curves, she was a vision he was sealing into his memory. A vision he couldn't get enough of.

"Maybe she wants to be alone," he pointed out to the blond deputy.

"Then she'd be smiling, wouldn't she?" Larry asked, gesturing toward Mona. "Is she smiling?"

Joe had a clear view of her profile. The corner of her mouth was not curving and she wasn't given to lop-sided smiles. "No."

"I rest my case." Larry eyed him expectantly. When Joe gave no indication of moving from his seat, Larry shook his head and mumbled something about "hopeless." "You're going to die alone," the deputy said to him. "You know that, don't you?"

Frowning, Joe rose from the table. It wasn't clear whether he would take the advice he'd been given or if he just wanted to get away from the giver, but Larry went with the positive and nodded his approval.

"Good, now just put one foot in front of the other until you reach her table. When you do," Larry continued to coach, "you ask her to dance with you." Joe shot him a dark look. "The band's playing a slow dance. Everyone is capable of a slow dance. Even you," he insisted. "Just pretend to move your feet. The object is to have an excuse to take her into your arms and hold her."

But Joe remained in his spot. Larry's thin grasp on his temper snapped. "Damn it, Joe, if it all depended

on you, there'd be no Apache nation." Larry scowled
in frustration, but he was not about to give up. "Do I
have to drag you over there?" he asked.

As close as Joe could figure, his friend had had
three drinks at the reception so far and while that
didn't make the tall deputy drunk or dangerous, Larry
grew agitated.

Afraid that the man might do something that would
wind up embarrassing him or worse, embarrassing
Mona, Joe weighed the options and decided that it
would be more prudent just to ask Mona to dance.
If she turned him down, he could tell Larry to back
off. If she took him up on it, well, so much the better.

Like Larry had said, he knew how to move his feet
back and forth and sway in time to the music. Not
much more was required in a slow dance. And it *did*
give him the opportunity to hold Mona without any
consequences.

"Stay put," Joe growled in a low voice. There was
no missing the command in his tone. The last thing
he wanted right now was a wingman, something he
could see that Larry was more than ready to become.

Crossing from his table to Mona's, he searched his
mind, looking for words that wouldn't instantly trans-
form him into a fool.

Mona saved him the trouble.

Aware of the slight shadow that had fallen over her
from behind, Mona turned in her seat and found herself looking up into Joe's ruggedly handsome face.

If her heart leaped just a little, she told herself it was because he'd startled her.

"Hi," she murmured.

"Hi," he echoed.

So much for groundbreaking conversation.

Glancing over his own shoulder, he saw that Larry watched him intently and that the deputy was moving his hands in a gesture meant to urge him along. To get on with it already. Joe had a feeling that if he didn't progress any further, Larry would hurry to his side and take over like a frustrated puppeteer.

He turned back to Mona. "Feel like dancing?" he asked her.

No, what I feel like doing is sitting here, feeling sorry for myself. But maybe dancing might help me get rid of that feeling, she thought.

"Sure," she answered. Her quick answer, she could see, surprised Joe. "Why not?"

Rising, she put her hand into his. Joe wrapped his fingers around it, turned on his heel and led her to the dance floor.

As he passed Larry, Joe deliberately refrained from making any eye contact with him. He sensed that the deputy probably congratulated himself on getting them together, as well as flashing some kind of sign meant to cheer him on. Larry had absolutely no handle on what was embarrassing behavior and what was acceptable.

They came to a stop on the edge of the dance floor.

Mona turned her face up to his. "You sure your date won't mind you dancing with me?" she asked.

"I didn't bring a date—unless you count Larry." He looked down at her as if to probe her thoughts. "You're not counting Larry, are you?"

"No, I'm not counting Larry," she said with a wide grin. "You don't strike me as a couple."

She laughed and the light sound instantly burrowed under his skin, the way it always used to whenever he heard it. Though he wasn't prone to poetic thoughts by any stretch of the imagination, the sound of Mona's laughter always made him think of bluebells growing wild in the field. He wasn't sure as to why that was, but felt it was safer if he didn't explore his reaction.

The less he thought about Mona in general, the better. Except that since she'd returned two weeks ago, and especially since that first night in the cabin, he couldn't seem to make himself *stop* thinking about her. Mona was one of the reasons he'd allowed himself to get roped into decorating the outside of Doc's place.

One? Hell, Mona was *the* reason he'd agreed to lend a hand. Sure, the sheriff was a man he not only admired but also liked, and he wished Rick nothing but the very best with this marriage, but in general, outside of his job, Joe made it a rule to keep to himself whenever possible. Keeping to himself didn't include picking up a hammer and hanging up streamers or building a dance floor or the trellis where the happy twosome and one-quarter—if you counted the baby—exchanged their marriage vows.

But the sheriff was Mona's brother and pitching in with the decorating allowed him to be around her. He'd assumed, rightly so, that she would be in the thick of it, at least working if not actually ordering people around, telling them what to do and, more likely than not, how to do it.

"Something wrong?" he asked her as he threaded one hand through hers while lightly placing the other around her waist. He tried not to think how good she felt in his arms.

And how much he wanted to kiss her again.

Mona gazed up at him, cocking her head as if she was trying to understand. "No. Why? Do I look like there's something wrong?"

"Well…" Backtracking, he reconsidered his assessment. "You don't exactly look like there's something right."

She pretended to shake her head as if she was trying to clear it. "Is this something new? I don't remember you talking in riddles."

"I don't remember you sidestepping and being evasive," he countered. He told himself to remember to sway to the music. The natural rhythm within his body took over. "C'mon, Mona, this is me. You used to be able to tell me what was bothering you," he reminded her.

"I also used to be able to skim rocks along the surface of the lake," she answered flippantly. "I can't do that anymore."

He stared at her for a moment. The sun was still

in the sky, allowing him to look into her eyes, to see the things that she wasn't saying. "When was the last time you tried?"

Shrugging, Mona deliberately looked away. "I don't remember."

Just as he thought. "Then how do you know you *can't* still skim rocks on the lake?" he challenged. He saw the exasperation that entered her eyes as she turned back and raised her chin. He knew that stance. She was on the brink of picking a fight. "Tell you what, after your brother and his wife make a break for it to go on their honeymoon, why don't you and I go down to the lake and test that theory of yours?"

She shook her head, rejecting the suggestion. "It's not that important."

He surprised Mona by agreeing with her. "No, but maybe if you find out that you can still skim rocks over the lake, you'll think of me as your friend again and tell me what's bothering you."

He was making sense. She had no use for sense right now and just wanted to be agreed with and left alone.

"Shut up and dance," she ordered in barely suppressed exasperation.

"There's that winning personality of yours again," he declared with a grin. If looks could kill, he'd be lying on the floor, dead on the spot, he thought. He feigned ducking her glare. "I'm dancing, I'm dancing," he told her.

The silence between them lasted less than thirty

seconds. The look she flashed him when she leaned back was apologetic. "I'm being prickly again, aren't I?"

"Yeah, but your brother just got married, so I'm cutting you a little slack."

Mona eyed him sharply. "Get out of my head, Joe."

A so-called contrite expression on his face, he danced her in a semicircle. "Yes, ma'am."

Mona closed her eyes. "Oh, God, I'm not a 'ma'am,' Joe. Don't call me that," she told him sharply. "It makes me feel totally ancient."

"Every female above the age of ten in this part of the country is politely addressed as 'ma'am.' You know that. You also know that you're not ancient," he pointed out. The song came to an end and, reluctantly, Joe released her. Or at least he dropped his hands. But his eyes held her in place far more effectively than his hands could ever do. "You want to go somewhere and talk?"

The suggestion did not meet with her approval. She knew that if she went with him, she'd say far too much, and right now she didn't like herself, didn't like how she was feeling. It didn't point to the person she really was. What it did was make her out to be a spoiled, self-centered child and it was bad enough that she knew that. She didn't need anyone else aware of the fact.

"No," she answered much too quickly, then shrugged as she looked away. She tossed him a bone, hoping it would get him to back away. "Maybe later."

"How much later?" he pressed. "A couple of hours? A couple of days? A couple of decades?"

She sighed. "Just later."

By then she hoped to have worked out what was bothering her. Hoped to finally react maturely, the way she knew in her heart she should.

The way she knew that right now, she wasn't.

That was what bothered her. That she should be putting Rick first, the way he'd always done with her. She should just be happy for him with his new life.

But all she could think was that their paths had suddenly diverged and he was going off in another direction. A direction she would never be able to follow. Not even with his example leading the way. Because in her heart, she knew she would never trust anyone else, never give them her heart the way Rick had given his to Olivia.

Mona knew, as surely as she was standing here on this temporary dance floor, that someday, the person she gave her heart to—if she was ever so foolish— would desert her. Would leave her behind as surely as her father had, as surely as her grandmother had.

As her mother had.

Except for Rick, none of the important people in her life had remained. Granted she'd never known her father and both he and her grandmother had died, but the bottom line was that they were gone.

As gone as her mother was. Her mother who had left both Rick and her with Abuela, promising to be back "soon." And "soon," it seemed, had no end, no finite definition.

At least not to Elena Santiago.

"Okay," Joe was saying to her gamely. "You got it. Later it is."

She sighed. "You're like some kind of a pit bull, aren't you? Latching on and refusing to let go."

If she thought she was insulting him, she miscalculated. He grinned at her instead. "You don't know the half of it."

"And I don't think I want to know," she told him. She saw a strange, alert look come into his eyes as he glanced past her. "Okay, now what?" she asked.

Instead of Joe answering, she heard a woman behind her say, "Hello, Ramona."

Curious, not recognizing the voice, Mona turned around. And found herself looking up into a face that was familiar to her even though she couldn't really place it.

A face that looked like an older version of hers.

"Hello," she replied guardedly. No name came to her as she appraised the dark-haired, dark-eyed woman. "I'm sorry. Do I know you?"

"No, not really," the woman answered. "But I'm hoping to change that." Before Mona could ask how she intended to do that or why she wanted to, the woman said, "I'm your mother, Ramona," and promptly generated an earthquake in her world.

Chapter Seven

Joe knew that Mona hated having anyone butt in to her business. She took it as an insinuation that she was incapable of handling her own affairs, of dealing with whatever curve nature happened to throw at her. A smart man would have just kept to the shadows and let things play out without interfering.

Maybe, when it came to things that concerned Mona, he just wasn't smart.

Because, despite all he knew to the contrary, he could feel that same protective instinct that had kicked in the evening of the flash floods.

Mona had visibly stiffened when the woman said she was her mother. He knew this would not turn into a happy reunion complete with tears of joy. Mona had told him a long time ago that she wanted nothing to do with the woman who had been able to walk away from her and her brother without so much as a single qualm.

He also knew that Elena Santiago had come back to Forever once before. She'd shown up on Rick's door-step eighteen years after she'd disappeared out of her children's lives. The way he'd heard the story, Elena had wanted to make amends, but Rick would have none of it. He had deliberately sent her away before Mona came home from school. He hadn't wanted his sister to be upset by the reappearance of a mother who didn't know the meaning of the title.

As far as Joe knew, Mona never met her mother that day. Judging from the way she'd blankly stared at the woman, before Elena had told her who she was, he was right. Mona had no idea what her mother looked like.

Until now.

Taking his cue from Mona's stiff posture, Joe moved forward, ever so slightly placing himself between her and the woman claiming to be her mother.

In her day, Elena had been a very beautiful woman who turned the heads of men and women alike as she passed. Even now, she was still a very attractive woman and it was obvious that she was accustomed to getting by on her looks and using those looks.

After giving him a flirtatious smile, making no secret of the fact that she took full measure of him, Elena turned to Mona. "Is this your man?"

Mona's eyes narrowed into angry slits. "You don't have the right to ask me anything or know anything about me."

It was obvious that Elena didn't think her daughter meant what she said. With a tolerant smile, she tried again. "Ramona—"

Mona was not about to be won over. Her brother and his wife had gone to change into their traveling clothes. She wanted this woman gone before they returned. "You gave up that right a long time ago. Now, please leave before Rick sees you."

"Protective," Elena said with a nod. "Like your brother. Your brother's wedding is why I came back."

"Why?" Mona demanded, struggling to keep her voice down. For her brother's sake, she wanted no undue attention drawn to this woman. "So you can ruin that, too?"

Elena appeared a little hurt by her daughter's accusation. Joe noted that she rallied, keeping her smile in place.

"No," Elena told her. "So I could make amends. A wedding is a celebration of a new beginning. I thought Enrique might want to make that new beginning knowing he had a mother in the background who wanted—"

Mona cut her off. She didn't want to listen to theatrical rhetoric.

"Don't you understand? You have no right to want anything," she informed the other woman coldly. "Now, I'm asking you nicely, please leave. If you care anything at all about Rick the way you claim, you'll go without causing a scene. Rick doesn't need to know that you're here."

Joe could see that the woman struggled between her own desire to put the sins of her past behind her and doing as her daughter requested.

In the end, Joe took over. He politely but firmly took hold of Mona's mother by the arm and escorted her out of the backyard.

"This way, please, Mrs. Santiago," he said, gesturing toward the front of the two-story house.

Elena gave him no opposition, allowing herself to be led away.

"Ruiz," she corrected him, regally walking toward the front of the house as if all eyes were on her. "It's Mrs. Ruiz now."

"You got married again?" Joe asked, not because he was curious but because he saw that the woman wanted him to ask. It cost him nothing to play along.

Elena nodded. "Twice." She leaned her head in toward him and lowered her voice as if she was sharing something in confidence. "Men keep dying on me," she said with a deep sigh. "I seem to have the worst luck."

"Not as bad as the men," Joe commented without a hint of humor.

Elena laughed anyway. In contrast to her daughter, Elena's laugh was deep and throaty, as if she had spent a good deal of the past eighteen years sipping whiskey at the elbows of fawning men.

But something about the way she cocked her head and her stance, that reminded him of Mona. Like it or not, the two women were connected.

Elena pressed her lips together, clearly debating asking him a question. She decided to put it to him. "Think that Ramona will ever forgive me?" she asked without preamble.

He considered the question in light of what he remembered about Mona's character when they were much younger.

"She's stubborn, but she's got a good heart. But getting Mona to come around won't come easy," he warned the other woman.

Elena barely suppressed a sigh and nodded. "I didn't think it would, but I knew I had to take that first step."

In her eyes, Joe saw a sadness that transcended the bravado she presented to the world.

"Be good to Ramona and protect her," she instructed him.

Joe could just see the way Mona would react if she overheard her mother telling him that. "That's not my call," he answered.

Elena watched him for a long moment and he could almost feel her eyes burrowing into him.

"Oh, but I think it is," Elena contradicted. She slipped her hand into his and then shook it. "Tell her I'll be seeing her again." She flashed a broad, telling smile. "And maybe next time, we can work things out."

I wouldn't hold my breath if I were you, Mrs. Ruiz, Joe thought. But he kept his opinion to himself. No sense in getting the woman upset.

She squeezed his hand, as if they had made some sort of a pact, and then walked away, making her way to her black sedan.

He didn't waste any more time watching her. The noise from behind the house picked up and that could only mean one thing. Rick and Olivia were about to leave on their honeymoon. He didn't want to miss saying goodbye to the couple.

Or being there for Mona when they finally left. He had a feeling she'd need him.

Joe made it around to the back just in time. Rick and Olivia had all but come to the end of the line of people who wanted to wish them well.

Rick glanced his way as he approached and grinned, looking somewhat relieved. "Thought maybe you decided to back out on me," Rick said.

Joe thought it was an odd choice of words. But the sheriff's flippant tone told him that Rick *hadn't* noticed his mother crashing the party, which, all things considered, was a good thing. He was careful, though, not to look relieved. He didn't want to trigger any questions. It wasn't in his nature to lie outright.

Instead, he picked up the thread of what Rick had just said. "Back out?" he echoed.

"Yeah. I'm leaving the office—and the post—in your hands." Rick seemed pleased with the decision he made earlier while making arrangements to book his honeymoon. "You're going to be the sheriff of Forever for the next three weeks."

Joe looked at the bridegroom, stunned. "Sheriff?" he repeated numbly.

Rick laughed at the completely stoic expression. "Yeah. Sheriff. What's the matter?" he asked. "You forget you're the senior deputy?"

He hadn't forgotten, he just never thought it put him at the head of the line for anything. He wasn't the competitive type. "No, but I just thought that Larry—or maybe Alma—would be your first choice to fill the position."

But Rick shook his head. "Larry and Alma are good people, but you're the head deputy and it's about time you tried out your wings to see if you can fly, Joe."

"Flying" held no appeal to him. He liked being under the radar. Liked just doing his job, taking care of what he was responsible for and not worrying about any big pictures that might be lying around, needing to be considered.

"Maybe I don't want to fly," he told Rick. "Maybe I just want to walk to wherever it is that I'm supposed to be going."

"Sorry." Rick clapped him heartily on the back. "Decision's been made. Right now, you've gotta fly." He gave his senior deputy an encouraging look. "I'll see you when I get back."

"*We'll* see you when we get back," Olivia corrected, slipping her arm through his and smiling up at her husband's face with the eyes of a woman who was head over heels in love.

"Right. *We'll* see you when I—when *we*—get back," he amended with a quick grin to Olivia. "This 'couple' business is going to take a while for me to get the hang of," he confided more to Olivia than to the reluctant deputy standing before him.

"You'll get used to it," Doc assured him with a hearty laugh. The veterinarian had come up behind Joe as Rick was telling the deputy that he had been temporarily promoted. Doc curled his fingers about the letter-sized envelope he was holding. "Of course, I wouldn't know about that from firsthand experience, but that's what people tell me."

"Yeah, that's what I hear, too," Rick told him, looking at his bride with a boundless affection. And then he turned toward Joe again. "In the meantime, I want you to look after Mona for me."

That made two people who were entrusting him with Mona's care in a short amount of time. Mona would have been fit to be tied if she knew.

"I'll try," Joe promised honestly. "But it won't be easy." Rick looked at him quizzically. "She doesn't like anyone hovering over her," Joe pointed out.

"Then don't let her see you hovering," said Rick. He looked around the immediate vicinity and frowned slightly. "Speaking of my sister, where is she? I kind of thought I'd see her before we left."

"Maybe she doesn't like saying goodbye," Joe suggested.

The two men looked at one another, as if communicating in silence what they couldn't in words.

Mona had never been much for goodbyes.

"Yeah, maybe," Rick agreed vaguely.

Doc moved forward, taking both of Olivia's hands in his and managing to secretly slip the envelope he'd been holding into them. It was a little something to help out with expenses when they got to their Southern California destination, a charming little bed-and-breakfast just north of San Diego.

"You two have a safe flight. Now *go*," Doc ordered, releasing Olivia's hands and taking a step backward away from the couple. "Before someone decides they just have to talk to you before you leave."

"Good advice," Rick agreed.

He took Olivia's hand in his and together they made a run for it through the house and out front to his Jeep. The vehicle stood waiting for them, already gaudily decorated to announce to the world at large that they had gotten married today.

A crowd of well-wishers were at their backs, pelting them not with rice but with choruses of good wishes and orders to enjoy themselves and not to come back too fast. Forever, like the town's name promised, would be here waiting for them.

Turning away from the speeding vehicle as it disappeared down the road, Joe scanned the faces that had poured out of the backyard with him.

Mona wasn't among them.

As he looked second time, his eyes met Larry's. Joe made his way over to the other deputy to enlist his help.

"You seen Mona around?" he asked Larry, trying his best to keep the impatience gnawing away at him out of his voice.

Larry didn't even have to pretend to think. "You mean, just a few minutes ago? Yeah, she was heading your way." He pointed to the encroaching darkness, indicating the infinite vastness that stood at the back of Doc's property. "I thought that maybe you were taking

my advice and the two of you were rendezvousing."
Larry drew out every one of the four syllables, making the word sound as if it had twice as many letters
in it as it did. "Guess I thought wrong." But he found
himself talking to Joe's back. Joe headed toward the
rear of the yard, a purpose to his gait. "You know
where she is?" Larry called after his friend.

"I've got a hunch," Joe tossed over his shoulder,
moving quickly. In a few seconds, he was out of ear-
shot.

Twilight crept in and, as it approached, systemati-
cally erased any decent visibility. If he didn't find her
soon, he might not be able to until the next morning.
The city proper had streetlights, but if Mona had gone
where he thought she might have, there weren't any
streetlights to illuminate the way for her.

Or him.

He had a flashlight in the glove compartment of
his vehicle, but he hadn't thought to get it and he was
already too far out on the road to the woods to double
back for it now.

He moved quickly, the way he'd learned as a boy.
Back then he'd had to jump aside to get of the way of
his uncle's long, powerful reach as the latter swung
his fisted hand at him. The man had only done that
when he got drunk, but he'd been drunk pretty much
most of the time.

And eventually, alcohol did the six-foot-five man
in, and indirectly, alcohol had taken his mother, as

well. She was run over by a drunk driver who didn't even realize that he had hit her.

As for him, Joe took what he could from every life experience and his uncle's drunken temper had taught him how to move fast, how to *be* fast. And while his tolerance for the substance for some reason was unusually high, he never tried to uncover his limits. He didn't want to know. But his uncle's substance abuse had at least enabled him to become a fast runner.

Most nights Joe would be down the road, running for the shelter of the woods behind his house before his uncle even rose to his wobbly feet.

Joe ran now, ran toward the lake where he'd guessed Mona would be, since they'd talked about it earlier.

And he'd guessed right, he saw, as the lake came into view.

The full moon was seductively bouncing its beams off the water. Competing, it seemed, with Mona, who was skimming flat, smooth stones along the lake's surface.

Joe stopped running and slowed down to a walk. A languid one. He didn't want to startle her.

And he did like looking at Mona when she thought that she was alone. Some of the tension in her face and body had faded and she became more like the girl he'd once known.

The girl he'd once thought about in the wee hours of the night.

He'd been right, Joe thought as he continued observing Mona. She hadn't lost her touch. The stones that left her fingers skimmed along the surface of the lake as if it was solid, made out of spun glass rather than liquid.

She didn't seem to notice. The look on her face was one of preoccupation. He guessed that it had little to do with skimming stones along a lake and everything to do with the woman who had returned, uninvited, into her life.

Chapter Eight

Several minutes slipped away as Joe continued to stand there, watching her as she skimmed stones. If Mona turned around now and saw him, she might think he was stalking her.

So he resumed walking, and as he came up to her, he announced his presence by saying, "Told you that you hadn't lost your touch."

Lost in conflicting thoughts that assaulted her from all directions, Mona jumped at the sound of Joe's voice. She spun around, ready to pelt whomever with the stones in her hand. She let loose with two, aiming them at the source of the voice like a modern-day David firing rocks at Goliath. All that was missing was the slingshot.

Joe instinctively ducked and dodged to the left as one smooth black stone flew by his head, missing contact by less than an inch.

"Hey, whoa!" he protested, holding his hands up in semisurrender. "I come in peace."

Recognition sank in. Swallowing an oath, Mona

dropped the last three stones, the sound of contact with the ground muffled by the grass.

Realizing that she could have seriously hurt him had he not moved, fear instantly morphed into anger. "Damn it, Joe, you should know better than to sneak up behind a person."

"I wasn't sneaking," he pointed out, joining her. "I was talking."

She dusted off her hands. Joe couldn't have been more than a few feet away when he spoke, which meant that he had to have soundlessly crossed over several yards to reach her.

"You didn't make any noise when you came up behind me," she accused. In her book, that qualified as "sneaking."

"I'm not supposed to," he answered glibly. "Moving around without making any noise is incorporated into my genes, remember?"

Mona frowned, grateful that she hadn't really hurt him. "I don't care about your genes, wear noisier boots," she ordered.

He liked the way the full moon scattered its light along her hair. She wore it loose and long. It flowed past her shoulders like black steam.

Joe roused himself, focusing on the conversation. "I'll look into that as soon as your brother comes back from his honeymoon." Mona glared at him as if she didn't follow. "I'm not going to have time for anything else right now. He made me temporary acting sheriff."

"Good for you," she said with more enthusiasm

than he thought she would feel, hearing the news. He hadn't thought that she cared what he did, as long as he stayed on the right side of the law, a fact that had been in some doubt in his earlier years.

Right now, she seemed more pleased with this temporary appointment than he was. "Yeah, well, we'll see," he said with a careless shrug.

He was definitely not comfortable with his new role, but he hadn't thought it right to mount an argument with a new husband driving off on his honeymoon. He doubted if Rick would have heard a word he said in his own defense.

Joe took in the surroundings. Listening, he could hear the stealth movement of several creatures that called the immediate area home. Looking at Mona, he doubted that she could run very fast in that tight dress should the occasion arise.

"You shouldn't be out here alone like this," he said.

"I know everyone in town," she argued. Nobody would try to hurt her, or take advantage of the situation. Besides, Rick had taught her enough defensive moves when she was younger.

"Not the drifters," he told her. "Forever gets its share."

She knew that there were women—probably more than a few—who liked the idea of a big, strong man protecting them. But she didn't number herself as being one of them. If you depended on no one, then you weren't disappointed when they didn't come through.

"I wasn't aware that there was a databank somewhere, distributing drifters. What *is* our share?" she asked flippantly. "One and a half a year? Maybe two?"

He wasn't about to let himself get sucked into a mindless argument for no reason. Besides, he knew she picked fights when she was upset. Not that he could blame her for feeling the latter. Having her mother appear out of nowhere was tantamount to a sucker punch.

"How are you?" he asked quietly.

As they started to walk back to Doc's, she plucked a wildflower growing in the grass and began to pull off its petals one by one. No singsong rhyme involving love accompanied their individual descent. Just nervous energy.

"I'm coming to terms with it," she answered with a sigh. "Things can't stay frozen forever, I know that. And if I decide to move to Dallas or Austin the way Rick wants me to, I'll feel better about leaving him if I know he has someone to watch over him. I guess that it's just going to take me a bit longer to ad—"

Joe interrupted her before she got any further. "I'm not talking about Rick getting married."

"Oh?" Mona responded innocently, avoiding his eyes. "What are you talking about?"

Her voice always got a little higher when she was lying. "You know what I'm talking about. Don't play dumb, Mona. You're smarter than that."

She resumed walking again, still avoiding his eyes. But there was no point pretending.

"I don't know about that," she said. "If I were smarter, then I wouldn't let it bother me at all."

He knew what she was saying, that she would be devoid of any emotions. He'd been that route himself. Hell, most of the time, he still opted for that route. But that wasn't Mona's way. "Then you'd be a brick wall," he told her.

Maybe that was for the best. "I can handle that." The wildflower had been plucked clean. She let the stem fall from her fingers. "Brick walls don't hurt."

Everyone hurt sometime, even if they didn't let on, Joe thought. "Unless someone takes a wrecking ball to them."

"They still don't hurt," she insisted. "They just crumble, but they don't hurt."

"Do you?" He placed his hand on her shoulder, stopping her from taking another step. Very gently, he turned her around to face him. "Hurt?" he added when she said nothing.

Mona shrugged off his hand and continued walking. He noticed that she'd raised her chin stubbornly. Another typical move for her. "Why do you care if I do or not?"

"Because I'm your friend, Mona. That's what friends do, they care. Even when they want to strangle their friends, they care," he told her evenly.

His answer coaxed a half smile out of her. It was his first indication that he had reached her.

"That's better," he said.

She let out a long breath and slowed her pace to match her cadence.

"Not really," she responded. "Why did she have to turn up like this? And now, of all times. What does she want, Joe?"

Maybe he was wrong, but he didn't believe there was an ulterior motive involved. "I think she—" he carefully avoided using the label *mother* "—wants what she said. To make up. To show you she's sorry."

Mona closed her eyes for a second, shaking her head. "It's too late for that."

He thought like that once, thought his life was set on a course to eventual destruction. And then a friend of his uncle pointed out that he was the master of his own destiny—and that nothing was written in stone. That had been his turning point.

Looking back, it probably saved him from a premature death.

"It's only too late if one of you is dead," he told her firmly.

"Well, then it's too late," she answered with finality. "Because she's dead to me. And if you're my friend the way you claim, you'll stop talking about it. Talk about something else."

"Okay." Joe looked up at the stars, thinking. And then he asked, "Think the Dallas Cowboys have a shot at the Super Bowl this year?"

She laughed and felt some of the tension drain away. "You don't like sports."

"No," he agreed. "But I was looking for a topic that wouldn't make you want to bite my head off."

She felt a flash of embarrassment. "I'm sorry, Joe. I'm a little edgy, I guess. This whole wedding thing was really unexpected and then *she* blows in from nowhere. I guess I got a little out of sorts."

He looked at her. "Mount St. Helens was a little out of sorts when it erupted. This is something a whole lot bigger."

She stopped walking again. Wrapping her arms around herself, she looked up at the sky. The darkness peaceful.

"Show me the Big Dipper, Joe," she asked, glancing toward him. "I always have trouble visualizing it when you're not there to point it out to me."

"There never seem to be as many stars in the big city as there are out here," he told her. "Maybe they just don't like all the noise."

She laughed and realized that she felt a lot better. Joe always had a way of making her feel better.

"That has to be it," she agreed, tongue in cheek.

He moved directly behind her, to get the same perspective as she had. The breeze shifted just then and the scent of her hair seemed to fill his senses, making him dizzy. But he didn't step back. Instead, he pointed to a group of stars, drawing imaginary lines between them with his index finger.

"It's right there," he told her.

She saw it then. Joe always made it seem so easy.

"Oh, you're right," she cried, turning her head toward him as she spoke.

Mona was acutely aware that she had brushed against him, not just with her hair, but with parts of her body, as well. Parts that felt as if they were shooting static-electricity pulses all through her.

She drew in her breath slowly and then took a tentative step back. If she didn't, she would do something stupid. Like kiss him again. This time, there was no half-filled bottle of aged whiskey to blame it on.

He could feel the tension. Feel the attraction. He did his best to block both and didn't quite succeed.

"Want me to take you home?" Joe heard himself asking.

Home.

It would seem really empty tonight, she thought sadly. Without Rick, without her grandmother, it was just an old building with old memories. Rick wouldn't return for twenty-one days. And once he did get back, her brother would be sharing the house with Olivia. And, very soon, with their baby.

There wasn't a place for her in this house. Never mind that there was a third bedroom. She would still be the fifth wheel.

The thought pressed down heavily on her.

Mona pushed it aside, unable to deal with it just now.

She'd come to the wedding with Rick, but he had taken his car in order to drive himself and Olivia to the airport several towns away. That meant that she would either need a ride or have to walk home. Joe, she was certain, would lecture her if she chose the latter. It was simpler to accept the offer for a ride.

"Sure," she answered. "Might as well go home while it still is home."

Joe wasn't sure he understood her meaning. "You want to explain that?"

Did he need a road map? "Well, when they come back from their honeymoon, Rick and Olivia are going to be living there." Doc's house was coming into view in the horizon. She hoped that most of the people at the reception had already gone home. She didn't feel like talking to anyone. Except for maybe Joe. He somehow seemed to lure the words right out of her.

"Last I heard, three's a crowd unless one of the three is a product of the other two, like the baby," she continued. "I'm going to need a place to stay." Her mouth curved. "Maybe I can buy and fix up the old Murphy place."

To her surprise, Joe didn't laugh that off the way she'd expected him to. Instead, he managed to throw her completely by saying, "Well, that's something to think about."

The cabin smelled of the past and creatures that had crawled in there to die. She couldn't see herself staying in the Murphy place, except in an emergency, the way she had that first night when the storm hit. "I was just kidding, Joe."

"I'm not," he replied matter-of-factly. "It's not as if there's a handy apartment building in town. Or even a hotel where you can stay indefinitely. Taking that into consideration, I'm sure Rick and Olivia won't mind having you around—"

There was no way she was going to impose on her brother and his wife unless both her legs were broken. Which they weren't. "Right. A couple just back from their honeymoon really *love* having an extra person hovering around."

Ordinarily, she would have considered moving in with Miss Joan, who had room to spare. But that was no longer an option. "Tina and Bobby have already moved in with Miss Joan," she murmured, voicing her thoughts.

The owner of the diner had taken a real shine to Tina's baby and enjoyed having her quiet home finally filled with the sound of voices. In exchange, Olivia's younger sister was taking care of the house for the older woman, gladly doing all the things that Miss Joan found exceptionally tedious.

"You could move in with me," Joe suggested, catching her completely off guard with his suggestion.

Mona started, then regained her composure. "Yeah, that'll go over really well." And then she smiled, amused. "It'll certainly give the town something new to gossip about."

Gossip had never bothered him. No matter where he was, he'd always thought of himself as an outsider. Living in Forever and working as a deputy was the closest he'd ever come to being part of something.

"Doesn't bother me if it doesn't bother you," he told her.

She stopped walking and looked at him for a long moment. Was Joe saying what she thought he was saying—or was he completely oblivious to the way his offer could be interpreted?

"If you're still living where you were when I went away to school, you've only got one bedroom," she said pointedly.

She wasn't exactly telling him something new. "I am and I know. You take the bed, I'll take the sofa— like in the cabin," he added, humor entering his voice, as well as his eyes. "Anyway, it's just until we get the Murphy cabin fixed up." There was also another possibility, he reminded himself. "Or you decide to move away."

She didn't hear the last sentence, or the forced nonchalance that he'd woven through it. "You're serious about the cabin, aren't you?" she asked.

The more he thought about it, the better the solution seemed. "Why not? The foundation's solid. We can go to the county office and find out who owns the property and make a bid for it."

There was one little thing wrong with his reasoning now that she gave it some serious thought. "I'm not exactly flush at the moment. I've got about two hundred dollars to my name," she calculated, then amended, "Maybe less."

"That's okay. I've got more."

For as long as she'd known him, Joe had never had

much. In high school he'd worked odd jobs on weekends in order to pay for things like clothes and whatever else he needed. He never had any extra money to throw around, the way a few of the more privileged kids did.

"How much more?" she asked now, curious.

"More," he repeated. When she looked at him quizzically, he said, "I've got simple needs. Don't need much," he emphasized, "so I've been banking the rest." He spared her a glance, allowing himself a smile. "Waiting for a rainy day."

"And I qualify as a rainy day?" she guessed.

"You qualify as a whole storm on the horizon," he corrected her. They were almost at Doc's property, so Joe tabled the discussion. "We'll talk about this on Monday," he promised. "Right now, let's just get you home."

That was when she remembered.

"Can't just yet." Joe looked at her, waiting for an explanation. "I just remembered that I volunteered for the cleanup committee." She felt she had to, since she was, after all, the groom's sister.

"I can wait," he told her.

Knowing that Joe would be taking her home made her feel a great deal better without her really understanding why. Right now, it was just too much to deal with, she told herself, mentally shoving all of it to the side for the time being.

She grinned at Joe. "You can do better than that. You can help me with the cleanup."

When she had gotten him to "help set up" he'd found himself pulled into a frenzy of work that had only ended in the early hours of this morning. This had the makings of the same thing. He didn't want her to think that he could be won over so easily. It might make her guess how he really felt about her.

"Do I have a choice in this?" Joe wanted to know.

Mona gave him a look that clearly said, "Not really," even though out loud she said, "Yes."

"But if I make the wrong choice, you won't be happy about it," he wisely guessed.

The smile on her lips had made its way to her eyes. He remembered how much he liked to see her that way. If he wasn't careful, he could lose himself in her eyes.

"Something like that," Mona answered.

"You know," Joe said with a reminiscent note in his voice as he entered Doc's side yard directly behind her, "I forgot how peaceful things were without having you around."

She sniffed. "The word is *boring*."

Joe inclined his head and said in a voice that was devoid of emotion, "If you say so."

Miss Joan was still there at the diner, overseeing her waitresses who bussed the tables and stacked dishes in Doc's kitchen. Some of the men were taking down the different-sized tables that had been donated from various households, giving the reception a very unique look.

Still another group, coed this time, took down the

gaily colored crepe lanterns and other decorations that had been made just for the occasion.

A wave of nostalgia hit Mona as she looked around. All of this struck her as a beehive of activity. There was nothing like this to be found in the big city, she thought with a touch of pride. People were just not that invested in their neighbors.

"Hey, Doc," Miss Joan called out, crossing back to the yard. The large man currently supervised the dismantling of the trellis used in the wedding. As he turned in her direction, graying tufts of unruly eyebrows raised silently in response to his name. "Where do you keep your dishwasher?" Miss Joan asked.

The veterinarian held up his wide, hamlike hands and wiggled them in the air. "At the ends of my wrists," he told her.

The girl who had come out with Miss Joan groaned. "No dishwasher?"

"It's all in how you look at it." Doc Whitman chuckled.

"I'll do them," Mona volunteered.

Miss Joan eyed at her skeptically. "Careful what you raise your hand for, honey. You know how many dishes there are?" the woman asked.

Mona grinned. "I was at the reception, remember? The place was packed. Everyone had at least one dish if not two or three. I know what I'm up against."

"You're going to be washing dishes into the middle of next Tuesday," Miss Joan warned.

"Not if she has help," Joe muttered under his breath.

He pretty much knew what was coming. If he had to pitch in, then he might as well be doing it on a joint project with Mona.

"Nice of you to volunteer," Miss Joan declared with a vigorous nod of her head. After stripping off her apron, she held it out to Joe.

Try as she might, Mona couldn't picture Joe doing something so utterly domestic. "You don't have to do this," Mona told him.

He shrugged. "Gotta do something, waiting to take you home."

"You could come back," she suggested, feeling guilty for having roped him in. "Or I could get a ride from someone else."

"Shut up and wash," he instructed, nodding toward the house.

"Yes, Joe," she answered meekly as she walked into the kitchen.

He wasn't buying her meek act for a second, Joe thought, following her inside. But he really did like the way it sounded.

Chapter Nine

The two-story house looked unusually dark to Mona as she and Joe drove toward it. As if the life, the heart, had been siphoned out, leaving the shell.

That morning, as she and Rick had driven away from the house on their way to Doc's and the wedding, the sun had been bright overhead and the air had been pregnant with the promise of a new beginning. Rick had been so nervous that she'd volunteered to drive.

She was happy for him while sad for herself. But the main thing was that Rick deserved to be happy. He'd always put her and their grandmother first, becoming the man of the house way before a male should have to even consider taking on the role.

In all the excitement and rush this morning, she hadn't thought to leave a light on for tonight when she returned alone. Hadn't thought about how dark and gloomy it would seem to come back to a house where there was no one to respond to the sound of her voice.

She thought about it now.

Joe drove his Jeep up to front of the old house. Stopping, he pulled up the hand brake, put the vehicle into Park and turned off the ignition. Only then did he look in Mona's direction. He sensed rather than saw the tension roaming through her.

"We're here," he said when she made no move to get out.

She glanced at him. "You really didn't have to tell me that. I do recognize the house."

Mona took a deep breath, not wanting to go inside just yet. Once she shut the door behind her, that was it. She would be alone with her thoughts, and right now, especially with her mother's sudden reappearance, she really didn't want to have time to think. Tired, she still felt way too wound up to fall asleep.

The night loomed before her like an unfriendly stranger.

She supposed that she could find something to do to keep busy until she felt ready to go to bed. There were still boxes that she'd shipped from Dallas when she'd relocated. This would be a good time to unpack them.

Settling in at Doc's Animal Clinic had gone far better. She'd already shelved all her references books and brought in a few things to personalize her space. But when it came to this house where she'd been raised, she had only unpacked the bare necessities.

Subconsciously, she supposed that pointed to her feeling that she was just a temporary guest and that she needed to be ready to leave at a moment's notice.

She was lost in thought, not reaching for the door handle. Joe interpreted it the only way he could. Mona didn't want to be alone tonight. "You want me to go in with you?"

Joe's low voice cut into her thoughts, bringing her back to the Jeep and the fact that she was still sitting in it. Shaking free of the mood that had all but wrapped itself around her, she looked at Joe, doing her best to appear bright-eyed and alert. But she still didn't know what he'd just said to her.

"What?"

"Inside." Joe nodded toward the house. "Do you want me to go into the house with you?" he asked pointedly.

There was no pity in his voice, but she could swear that it was implied. Mona squared her shoulders. "I'm not needy."

"No one said you were needy," he told her. This defensiveness was getting old. He was ready to be sympathetic, to talk or to listen, or just be there with her in total silence. But she had to stop beating him back every time he made a gesture. "Hell, Mona, I don't remember the chip on your shoulder ever being this big before."

Green lightning flashed from her eyes. "There *is* no chip on my shoulder."

Okay, he'd had enough. Unbuckling his seat belt, Joe shifted in his seat and gave it to her full blast.

"The hell there isn't. You could ram a hole in a brick building with that chip and still keep it in one piece. We're friends, remember?" he reminded her tersely. "Friends from way back. I was just offering you company if you wanted some."

"Well, I don't," Mona fairly snapped, then felt guilty about it. This was becoming an unfortunate pattern. Snapping, feeling guilty and then apologizing. If she could just manage to control her temper, she wouldn't be dancing this boring two-step with Joe over and over again. For some reason, he seemed to be the only one who could set her off like this, but that was no excuse for her acting like such a shrew.

"But I appreciate the offer," she said in a far more even tone. She didn't apologize to him outright, but she did try to explain her behavior. "A lot has happened in a short amount of time," she told him. With a sigh, she looked up at the sky outside the windshield. "I guess I was really hoping that nothing had changed while I was away. That I could just come back, pick up the reins of my life and slip back into it as if I'd never been gone—except that I'd be a lot better at diagnosing and taking care of animals," she added with a glimmer of a self-deprecating smile that came and went from her lips.

"That's not possible."

She closed her eyes and nodded. "I know."

No, she didn't, Joe thought. She'd misunderstood him.

"No, I mean, the part about you being a lot better at taking care of animals. If anyone ever had a gift for it, you do. Sometimes, I'd swear you even speak their language. You're better at it than any Apache

I've ever known—but then," he remembered, "you are one-third Native."

His low-keyed praise made her smile. "You always did know how to make me feel better about things, even when you weren't trying." Smiling her appreciation, she said, "Thanks." Opening the door on her side, Mona climbed out of the Jeep, then turned to look at Joe one last time. "See you around, 'Sheriff.'"

He frowned. He'd forgotten about that for a moment. The title made him uncomfortable. It wasn't that he didn't think himself equal to the task. Ever since he'd turned over a new leaf all those years ago, he'd always done what needed to be done. He'd been a deputy for a number of years now and knew all the basic fundamentals of law enforcement in Forever.

The problem was he just didn't look forward to interacting with some of the citizens in Forever. The people who clung to drama and made mountains out of proverbial molehills. The ones who needed special kid-glove treatment. *Rick* was good at handling them, at returning Joanna Mendoza back to her home when she went for one of her moonlight walks in her flannel nightgown, sleepwalking with her eyes wide-open.

Rick was equally as diplomatic tucking Charlie Halpern in for the night when the senior citizen had consumed more than he could comfortably imbibe and still walk a straight line. Rick had patience and knew how to talk to people like that.

Him, he hardly talked at all, unless it was to Mona and look how well *that* was going tonight. She snapped out every second sentence at him. That didn't exactly attest to his people skills.

"Offer still stands," he told Mona as she closed the passenger door behind her and began to walk away.

"I know."

And she did. She knew he was there for her, her own personal human safety net. That more than anything else urged her to behave like an adult. She didn't want Joe to know she needed him. Or to suspect the depths of her loneliness.

In response to his assurance, she didn't even bother turning around. Instead, she raised her hand over her head and waved at him as she continued walking up to her front door.

Had she been alone, she might have started whistling to keep herself company, but if she did that now, she knew Joe would take it as an indication that she was not up to facing the empty house. He had an annoying habit of being able to read her and guess what she was thinking. She didn't want to add this to his tally.

After letting herself in, Mona locked the door and began the process of turning on all the lights on the first floor. Granted it was a waste of energy, but it made her feel better. The light chased away the eerie shadows on the walls.

She was about to turn on the TV and leave it on a channel running an old movie—the voices would provide a form of company—when she heard someone knocking on the front door. Since the house was located on the outskirts of town, she doubted if this was a neighbor who had a sudden urge to call on her at this hour of the night. Or borrow a cup of sugar.

It had to be Joe.

Mona looked at her watch. It hadn't even been five minutes. She hadn't even had the opportunity to change out of her cocktail dress and get comfortable.

"I'm still fine, Joe!" she called out, raising her voice to compensate for the distance.

"Yeah, but he's not," she heard Joe say through the door.

"He?" she repeated. Mona quickly crossed the rest of the way to the door. "Who is 'he'?" she wanted to know as she unlocked the door and pulled it open. The next moment she had her answer.

Joe was holding a dirty, pathetically skinny, shaggy dog of dubious parentage in his arms. The dog looked frightened and far from happy. The whining sound he emitted wrenched her heart.

Mona never hesitated. All her better instincts instantly rose to the foreground. She took the dog from Joe and held the frightened animal against her chest, allowing the stray to absorb her warmth, to "sense" that he had nothing to be afraid of.

Speaking to the dog in a low, soft, soothing voice, she gently stroked his head. The whining subsided by degrees.

"Where did you find him?" she asked Joe.

"Right outside your house, in the street. Maybe he was coming to pay you a visit," he quipped, then grew a little more serious. "He was almost roadkill. I came this close—" he held the thumb and index finger of his right hand barely two inches apart "—to hitting him. He walked right in front of my Jeep. I swerved at the last second. I didn't see him before then." The downtrodden animal had been slinking by right in front of him, as if trying to avoid being noticed. "He doesn't have any tags and he's pretty dirty, so I'm guessing he's a stray. I thought that maybe you could check him out."

She was already won over. "Poor little guy," she murmured to the dog, still stroking him.

Though he'd stopped whining, he continued to shake even though she held him against her. Because he was severely underweight and seemed so frightened, Mona was fairly certain that someone had abused the animal severely. People like that, she thought angrily, should be filleted.

"You want to adopt him?" she asked Joe, since he'd brought the dog to her and asked her to check him out.

The question surprised him. Why would she think that? He liked his life simple. He believed that if a man had too many possessions, the possessions really had him. That especially applied to pets.

Joe wanted to own nothing. That way, there were no expectations, no disappointments. No ties to be severed if he wanted to pick up and leave.

"No," he answered. "But I thought that maybe you would."

Mona looked at him curiously. "Me?"

"Yeah."

From where he stood, it only made sense. Currently, Mona had no pet roaming around the house, a condition that he considered rather unusual for her. Growing up, Mona was constantly bringing home strays, nursing them back to health. Having a pet right now would definitely take the edge off of being alone.

"It's only logical," Joe argued. "How are people going to trust a vet with their pets if that vet doesn't even have a dog or a cat of her own?"

Mona laughed and shook her head. "Always looking out for me, aren't you?"

It was a teasing remark. She wasn't prepared for the seriousness of his expression—or of his tone—as Joe answered, "Yes, I am."

He meant it, she thought. The next moment she told herself not to make a big deal of it. He said a lot of things with that solemn look on his face. It was just his way. It didn't mean anything.

In any event, it wasn't so much a case of what Joe had just said, that people would regard her with suspicion if she didn't have a pet of her own. He probably believed that if she was busy nursing the dog, she would stop dwelling on the things that made her unhappy.

He was probably right, she mused.

Besides, she'd been on the lookout for a new pet ever since Lloyd, her beloved Labrador, had died six months ago at the age of thirteen.

Still cradling the stray against her, she looked up at Joe and quietly said, "Thank you."

And then she turned her attention to the animal. The mongrel was badly in need of a bath, but from what she could see at first glance, the dog didn't appear to be injured. Right now, her first order of business was to see about feeding him. Cleaning him up could wait.

"You hungry, Apache?" Mona asked her newfound friend.

Joe frowned, looking from the dog to her. "Apache?" he questioned. "You're actually going to call the dog Apache?"

Her smile widened. The smile infiltrated her eyes. "Yes."

"Why?" he asked, mystified.

"Because he *looks* like an Apache." Before Joe could say anything in protest to the comparison, she added pointedly, "Just look at the nobility in those eyes." She turned slightly so that the dog's face was more visible to Joe. "He's had his share of troubles and managed to survive and still come out whole. Still able to hold his head up high." She scratched the dog under his chin as she continued. The dog looked as if he'd just crossed over to heaven. "If that isn't a good description of an Apache, I don't know what is."

"You know, if you ever decide to stop being a vet, you could always become a politician."

Mona met his suggestion with a pronounced shiver. "God forbid. Anyway, I just got started finally putting all that veterinarian schooling to work. I don't plan to stop for another fifty, sixty years."

Mona didn't know the meaning of the word *stop,* Joe thought. She was relentless when she wanted something or had her mind set on an idea.

"If I know you, you'll just be getting your second wind by then," he said.

Tickled, Mona laughed, really laughed. As always, the sound got under his skin, doing things to him with an increased urgency that could easily turn out to be his undoing.

Time for him to get going. Before the temptation to stay grew to be too big to resist. Or conquered.

"I'll see you later," he said to Mona, then pet the dog's head. The dog didn't even seem to notice. His entire focus was on Mona. "You, too, 'Apache.'"

Just for a second, the dog shifted his eyes toward him, as if the animal sensed that was his new name. God, now Mona had him attributing a complex thought process to a dog.

With the dog still in her arms, Mona accompanied Joe the short distance to the door.

"Thank you for this," she said warmly, affectionately leaning her cheek against the top of Apache's caramel head.

Much as he would have liked to take the full credit for this, it was all just happenstance. The animal had picked the right time to cross his path. Two minutes either way and the dog would have still been roaming the streets.

Moving Apache over to her left side, Mona impulsively rose up on her toes and expressed her gratitude with a kiss.

She'd intended to kiss Joe on the cheek, but just before she made contact, Mona swayed, her balance shifting, and she suddenly wound up brushing her lips against his mouth instead. Memories of the first night she'd returned to Forever flashed through her head. The next second, heat pulsed through the rest of her.

The identical kind of heat, it turned out, that now wound its way through Joe. He'd felt it the instant her lips had touched his. Had there not been a dog between them, he might have been seriously tempted to push things further. Might have anchored her in place by taking hold of her upper arms with his hands and then brought her closer to him as he did his damndest to deepen the kiss.

To bond their souls a little more.

But the dog had started whining again, the jarring noise shattering the moment and the things that might have been.

Know just how you feel, Apache, he thought as he stepped back. It was obvious to him that the old adage about no good deeds going unpunished was true. Just as well. If he'd gone ahead and done what he'd wanted to do, there would be no end to the consequences.

The yearning he felt refused to go away. He did what he could to ignore it.

"If you need anything," he said to Mona, "just give me a call." Then, in case she took that to be some sort of open invitation to follow up on that fleeting kiss, he added, "I am the acting sheriff until your brother gets back, so it's my job to look out for everyone in Forever. You included."

She smiled at him. The smile seemed to pierce his chest and go straight into his heart. It was a damn silly notion considering the way he felt about complications.

"Nice to know." She raised Apache's paw and pretended that the dog was waving goodbye. Assuming a light-pitched voice she said, "'Thanks for not hitting me with your car, Sheriff Joe.'"

Joe said nothing. He merely rolled his eyes, turned on his heel and walked out.

The sound of her laughter, even after she closed the door, followed him down the short walkway, and he could have sworn he heard it even as he got into the Jeep.

With determination, he started his car and pulled away, knowing that if he lingered even a second longer, he wouldn't be going anywhere except inside her home again.

And this time, the stray he'd be bringing to her would be him.

He had a feeling that this more than anything else was why Rick had left him in charge. The position was a safeguard against his acting impulsively. In other words, being acting sheriff was supposed to keep him on the straight and narrow. And that in turn meant that he couldn't allow himself to follow any basic instincts that reared their heads while Rick was gone.

"Think of everything, don't you, Rick?" he murmured under his breath, addressing his words to the man who was not there.

Chapter Ten

"Morning, Sheriff."

Alma and Larry's voices blended together in a sing-song cadence as Joe walked into the office the following day.

He had never cared very much for Mondays and this Monday promised to be a trying one.

Today was the day he assumed his new—albeit temporary, he silently emphasized—post.

Going toward his desk, he muttered a barely audible, "Morning, Alma. Morning, Larry," in response. He made his way around Larry.

Just before he was about to sit down, Alma placed herself between him and his chair.

Joe sighed. He'd already braced himself this morning, expecting to be the target of a great deal of ribbing today and probably for the next few days. Hopefully this wouldn't last the entire time the sheriff was gone, but to be honest, he wouldn't bet on it.

When Alma continued to place herself in his way even as he tried to move around her, he raised a quizzical eyebrow. "Yes?"

"You can't sit here," she told him, her heart-shaped face the picture of innocence.

It was going to be a *long* Monday. "And just why is that?"

"Because this isn't your desk right now." Turning, Alma pointed toward the small, crammed, glass-enclosed area that served as Rick's office. "That's where the sheriff sits," she informed him brightly.

Joe knew that if he gave even so much as an inch and allowed her to win this round, Alma and Larry were seriously going to ride roughshod over him. He intended to hand Rick back the office just the way that he had found it—running smoothly.

"That's where the sheriff sits when the sheriff is Rick," Joe corrected, then nodded toward his own desk. "And this is where the sheriff sits when the sheriff is me." He looked from one deputy to the other. Maybe it was better to cut to the chase right from the beginning. "Look, I don't like this any more than you do. Maybe even less, but leaving me in charge is something that Rick decided on his own, so let's just all try to get through it, okay?"

Larry grinned. "Who says we don't like it?" he asked. And then he laughed when Joe looked at him in confusion. "This gives us one hell of an opportunity to hold your butt to the fire."

Joe closed his eyes as he took his seat. "Now, there's a pretty image," he muttered.

Alma grinned wickedly. "Depends on what side of the fire you're on."

When he opened his eyes, Alma was still watching him.

"You do wear your jeans a whole lot better than Larry does," she told him, a wicked grin on her face.

"I take exception to that," Larry protested.

"Don't you two have work to finish?" Joe asked.

He heard the front door opening behind him and was grateful that Pete McKay chose that moment to walk into the sheriff's office.

For about ninety seconds.

It turned out Pete was there to file a complaint regarding the "noise pollution" he was forced to endure. Joe knew from experience that it wasn't the first time, but this time, he was in charge.

He listened to the retired hardware-store owner rant for a couple of minutes, sprinkling twenty-dollar words in between two-dollar phrases.

"You know, Pete, you might try talking like a regular person," Joe suggested patiently. He displayed no emotion one way or another. "It's not 'noise pollution,' it's a damn dog barking."

"It's a lot of damn dogs barking," the old man corrected angrily. "And it's getting worse."

Joe was fairly certain the problem wasn't getting worse because the noise was increasing. The reason lay elsewhere. "That's because you retired, Pete, and you're home all the time." He saw a reasonable solution. "Ever think of going back to work?"

"Can't," the old man bit off bitterly. He blew out an annoyed huff because he apparently had no one to

blame for this but himself. If there had been someone else, Joe knew the old man would have loudly
informed him of it. "I sold the hardware store to Jim
Phelps last month."

Joe was aware that Larry and Alma were taking in
every syllable while pretending to be busy.

He paused for a moment, thinking, then said, "Well,
you could try offering to go back as a consultant." He
saw Pete's sour look deepen. "I'm sure Jim could use
you. There's a lot of stored-up knowledge in that head
of yours, Pete," Joe said, laying it on thicker than he
might have normally. "Why don't you ask him?"

Joe had a feeling that this display of even worse
temper than usual was because the man, a lifelong
bachelor with no family to speak of, had just recently
retired and, devoid of hobbies, he had nothing to do
with his days and nights. Every minor irritation grew
to the size of a pending war.

Pete's frown grew so deep, it created ruts in his
forehead. The old man waved an impatient hand, dismissing the suggestion. "Why bother? Phelps won't
want me hanging around."

"Not hanging around, mentoring," Joe told him. He
saw a flash of interest enter the man's dark gray eyes.
"You could give advice, show people how things are
done. Maybe even hold some do-it-yourself classes in
the back of the store once in a while. I'll talk to Jim
about it," Joe promised. "And in the meantime, I'll ask
Doc if he could do something about the noise. Does
that work for you?" he asked.

"Yeah." The snow-white head bobbed up and down as Pete appeared to consider what had just been said. "That works for me." Satisfied, Pete turned on his well-worn heels and headed for the door. He paused only long enough to say, "Thanks," before he closed the door behind him.

The moment the door clicked into place, Joe exhaled. He felt as if he'd just run a marathon. A long one. It took him a second to realize that instead of mercilessly tag-team ribbing him, Alma and Larry were applauding and giving him a standing ovation.

Alma stopped clapping and dropped her hands to her sides. "You know, I think that's the most I've ever heard you say at one time."

"At one time?" Larry echoed with a hoot. "Hell, that's the most he's ever said in a week. A month," he corrected.

Joe decided that he could do with some air—and some time away from his deputies. Getting to his feet, he reached for his hat that he'd tossed on the edge of his desk.

"Where're you going?" Larry asked.

Joe had never liked being questioned. Now was no exception. "I told Pete that I'd have a talk with Doc, so I'm going to go have a talk with Doc. That all right with you, Larry?"

Larry held his hands up as if he were surrendering and pretended to back away. "You're the boss, Joe."

"Ha!" was the only comment Joe made as he left the office.

He knew that Larry and Alma didn't really mean anything by the ribbing. They, and Rick, were as close to family as he had these days and this was what families did: they drove each other crazy. Except for his real family. They had gone out of their way to ignore him when he had been thrust into their midst, a recently orphaned ten-year-old boy.

Foregoing his Jeep, Joe opted to walk to the vet's. It was too beautiful a day not to enjoy at least some of it.

With his long stride, he got to Doc Whitman's fifteen minutes later. Years ago, Doc had bought the old Sutherland house and converted the bottom floor into an animal clinic. The veterinarian lived on the second floor. It had three bedrooms, but he kept two locked up for the most part, claiming to need very little in the way of space.

They had that in common, he and Doc.

McKay's house bordered the animal clinic on the left. There was enough room between the two buildings for any loud sounds coming from the clinic to be fairly muffled by the time they reached the old man's walls. Joe suspected that McKay had lodged the complaint because he just needed an excuse to come into the sheriff's office and interact with another human being.

Some people couldn't handle loneliness without it changing them. Joe had gotten fairly used to it himself. Until Mona had come back.

Joe blocked the thought and went up the front steps to the animal clinic's front door. As he did, he noted that McKay's 1983 Impala wasn't in his driveway. Hopefully, the old man had taken his advice and gone to see Jim Phelps about helping out at his former hardware store.

Knocking on the door, Joe walked into the clinic just as Shirley Hoffman exited one of the exam rooms, one arm draped over her daughter, Celeste's, shoulder. Celeste, twelve, was carrying her pet guinea pig, the obvious reason for the visit.

The visit had to have come out all right, Joe judged. The little girl was smiling.

Shirley paused at the empty receptionist's desk. The receptionist had decided last week to move to Seattle with her boyfriend and Doc had yet to find someone to take her place. Shirley put her purse on top of the desk and rummaged for her checkbook.

"How much do I owe you, Doctor?" she asked.

Her question was directed to Mona, who had come out behind her. Mona joined the woman, still making notes in the very thin folder she carried.

She wore a white lab coat and looked exceedingly professional—for Mona. The image of her, wearing the lab coat, high heels and nothing else, flashed through his mind.

The image stirred him.

"Nothing," Mona answered. When the woman looked at her quizzically, Mona explained, "The first visit is free."

"But this isn't our first visit," Shirley protested, although even from where he was standing, Joe could see that the woman looked hopeful.

"I meant, the first visit for me," Mona told her. She nodded toward the animal in the carrier that Celeste was holding. "Just make sure Ginny takes the medicine I gave you. She needs to take it until it's all gone," Mona emphasized.

That was when Shirley released the breath she was holding. "I don't know how to thank you. Celeste is so attached to that animal."

"No need for thanks, that's what I'm here for," Mona assured her, walking the pair out the front door.

"You're here to drive Doc to the poor house?" Joe asked after Shirley and Celeste were gone.

Aware that he was there, she'd acknowledged him with a nod until her business with Shirley and her daughter was finished. Now that they were alone, Mona was mildly curious what he was doing here.

"Shirley's husband lost his job last month," she told him. "They're having a tough time of it." She'd gotten that information from her brother as a quick review of what had been going on since she was last home. "Besides," she said with a careless shrug, "I'm only doing what Doc would do if he were here."

Joe realized that he'd missed that little fact. Ordinarily, Doc would have come out by now, drawn by the sound of voices if nothing else. "Doc's not here?" he questioned.

As she spoke, Mona began neatening the reception

desk. With mail, flyers and folders scattered about, the surface currently resembled no-man's-land. "No."

"Where is he?" Joe pressed when she didn't elaborate beyond the one-word answer.

At times, he got the distinct feeling that she enjoyed pressing his buttons. All of them. At the same time.

"He drove over to the Jessup ranch first thing this morning. One of Drew Jessup's prize stallions is acting colicky."

Thinking of something she forgot to put down, she opened the folder she'd been writing in previously and made another notation. Finished, she left the folder neatly lying on top of the others. She intended to file them all away the first chance she got.

Joe was still standing there. Why? "I take it this isn't a social call."

"Pete McKay tried to lodge a formal complaint against Doc," he told her.

She'd been working here with Doc since the day after she'd arrived in Forever. That was a little over two weeks ago. And in that time, she'd noticed McKay standing in his yard, glaring over toward the clinic several times. Each time he wore an angry expression on his face.

"That grumpy old man would lodge a complaint against Mother Teresa if he got it into his head that he didn't like what she was doing," she said in disgust. His words replayed themselves in her head. She looked at Joe, confused. "Hey, wait a minute. You said 'tried.'"

"I did," he agreed, his voice giving nothing away.

"So why didn't he?" Mona asked.

He wasn't about to go into details, explaining that he'd suggested that McKay see the new owner of the hardware store and offer to give customers the benefit of his years of experience. Instead, Joe gave her a quick summary.

"Long story, but part of it is that I said I'd talk to Doc about seeing what he could do to keep the dogs from barking." Joe looked at her pointedly. "I figure now that you're around, that might not be such a problem anymore."

"And why is that? You think I'm going to gag the dogs?"

The image of her rushing about, slipping multicolored bandanas over the dogs' muzzles amused him, although he kept that image to himself. No sense in getting her annoyed. "I think that you're going to do whatever it is you do that makes them obey you and you're going to get them to keep quiet."

Her grandmother had called her an animal whisperer, but that had been just between the two of them. She doubted that Joe knew about that. "You're giving me a lot of credit."

"Only where it's due," he answered. She was good at getting animals to do what she wanted and they both knew it.

Joe took a look around, noticing the outer office for the first time since he'd gotten there. Scattered about the walls were framed photographs of a variety of animals, most of them with Doc standing beside them. He didn't recall ever seeing the photographs before. Not that he frequented the place all that much, but he'd been here a couple of times with Rick on business. The walls had been bare then.

"This your work?" he asked, turning back to her.

Over the years, as she'd worked with and learned from Doc, Mona had brought her camera along. It was an inexpensive, simple one but it accomplished what she wanted. It took pictures and captured memories. At the time, the photographs had been for her album. But recently, she decided that they also made good decorations.

"You might say that," she answered evasively.

"You took them?"

She smiled and nodded. "Yes."

"You framed them and hung them?" he continued.

"Yes," she answered, observing him carefully.

"Then, yeah, I 'might say that.'" He looked around again, taking in the whole effect. "Nice touch," he told her.

She had no idea why his approval pleased her. Granted he was her friend, but she had always done her own thing without needing a seal of approval from anyone. Why did his create this warm glow inside of her?

"Thanks." She did her best to sound blasé. "I like it." She had to get back to work. There was a dog in back she needed to prepare to be neutered. Mona looked at him. "You want me to give Doc a message for you?"

She was telling him to leave, he thought. Just as well. He needed to get going. There was a patrol around town to make.

"No, I'll be back." One hand on the doorknob, he looked at her, reluctant to leave just yet. "How's Apache doing?" he asked.

The mention of her new pet brought a smile to the corners of her mouth. "Well, he didn't like getting a bath."

"Wouldn't think so." Although, the thought suddenly occurred to him, if he was the one being bathed by her, it wouldn't exactly qualify as a hardship.

He slanted a look in her direction, more than a little relieved that even though Mona was pretty intuitive, she didn't have the ability to read minds.

Mona had brought her new pet with her to the clinic, not wanting to leave him alone his first full day in new surroundings. For a moment, she thought about inviting Joe to come to the back and see the dog for himself. But he looked as if he wanted to get going and she did have a patient waiting for her, so she just told him about Apache rather than showed him.

"And he looks even thinner right now with all that dirt off, but he's eating," she said with affection.

Joe had no doubt of that. "Probably like the starving dog he is."

"Was," Mona corrected. "He can't possibly be

starving after all the food he consumed between last night and this morning."

The dog had jumped up to reach the counter in the kitchen and wound up capturing what was left of a pot roast she'd made earlier in the week. She'd taken it out of the refrigerator to make a sandwich to take to work for lunch. She had to physically separate Apache from his "prey."

What amazed her was that the dog had allowed her to take the food away from him. It was proof that at bottom, Apache had a gentle nature. It also told her that she'd guessed right, he'd been abused and was fearful of punishment.

"The trick was to get him to stop eating before he exploded or ruptured something," she concluded.

"Not much of a trick for you," Joe said matter-of-factly. "Getting animals to behave and listen is right up your alley."

As far as she was concerned, getting animals to behave was just a given so she took no credit for it. "Thanks for bringing him to me." She had no doubt that the poor dog *would* have starved to death if Joe hadn't had the presence of mind to bring the animal to her.

Joe shrugged as if what he'd done was a no-brainer. As if he'd been thinking only of the dog and not her when he decided to unite the two of them. "You're the town vet. Or one of them."

Mona had a strong suspicion that it had been more than that simple fact that made him decide to bring the poor thing to her, but she also felt that neither she nor Joe was comfortable exploring what had prompted him to do what he did. So she left his statement alone.

Instead, she cut the conversation short with words meant to send him on his way. "I'll tell Doc you were looking for him when he gets back."

He nodded. "No hurry." Joe opened the door. "I just wanted to let him know that Pete was complaining, but I think I handled it."

Now he had succeeded in arousing her curiosity. The dog awaiting surgery could wait another couple of minutes. "Oh? How?"

"Pete sold his business a short while ago. He's got more time on his hands than he's used to and nowhere to go now that he doesn't have to work. I got him to offer his services to Jim now that Phelps owns the hardware store. This way, he's got something to do and isn't hanging around his house, listening for the next dog to bark."

She nodded, impressed that Joe actually put himself in someone else's shoes. He was more intuitive than she remembered. "Doc'll be relieved to hear that. He doesn't like dealing with complaints."

Joe was about so say something else, but any further conversation was curtailed by the arrival of a frantic Dana Richards who clutched what sounded like an asthmatic cat to her more than ample bosom.

"Mr. Boots stopped breathing twice this morning," she cried. The Siamese cat seemed to have great difficulty getting in air.

It looked like Dakota, the mixed-breed dog in the back, had just gotten a stay of execution for his manhood, Mona thought.

"I'll see you, Joe," she said, before turning to the distraught woman. "Let's go to exam one," she coaxed Dana, placing a comforting arm around the woman's shoulders.

Joe left then. As he closed the door, the same unbidden thought he'd had earlier flashed through his mind. Mona, in the white lab coat, wearing high heels and nothing else but a smile.

He felt his blood heating as he walked back to the sheriff's office to get his Jeep. The fast pace he'd assumed had nothing to do with it.

He made a mental note to start taking cold showers instead of warm ones.

Chapter Eleven

"There she is," Miss Joan declared with a broad, satisfied smile as Mona came into the diner. The unofficial town psychologist beckoned her over and then pointed to the only empty table in the place. "Pull up a booth and sit down," she coaxed, tendering the invitation as if she hadn't said the exact same thing last night, and the night before that.

Mona had shown up at the diner for dinner that first Monday that Rick and Olivia had left for their honeymoon. Her appearance had been prompted by her decision that she preferred grabbing a bite to eat at the diner and listening to the snatches of various conversations around her to going directly home. The house still mocked her with its emptiness.

Although it wasn't exactly empty. Apache did come home with her every night after spending the day at the animal clinic. And once across the threshold, the scrappy dog made enough noise for three. It was obvious that he was happy to be away from the animals that were brought to the clinic. She'd quickly learned that Apache preferred humans to his four-footed brethren.

When she came into the diner, initially Miss Joan had told her to leave Apache outside, tethered to the first handy stable item she could find. But that was because Miss Joan was accustomed to dogs behaving like her own pet, an enormous dog who had an appetite for the convertible tops of sports cars and whatever else he could sink his teeth into—literally.

But Apache, with his desperate need to be loved, had won Miss Joan over within the space of an hour. By day two, he was allowed—invited, really—to come inside the diner with no hesitation.

"So, what can I get for you and your fierce guard dog today?" Miss Joan asked, abandoning the cloth she used to massage her clean counter.

Mona spared a glance at the dog who followed her like a short, fuzzy shadow, running her hand over his head affectionately.

"Just some soup for me and the usual for Apache," Mona told the woman.

Miss Joan smiled. "The usual it is."

"The usual" was the biggest bone that was available to gnaw on. Miss Joan took it upon herself to serve the dog personally, amused by the way the animal first licked her hand when she set the bone in front of him before settling in to enjoy his feast.

After bringing today's offering to the pet, the woman chuckled to herself as she rose again to her feet.

"If my first husband, Clyde, had reacted that way

when I gave him dinner, we'd still be married." About to go back behind the counter, Miss Joan paused as she scrutinized Mona. "Not feeling well, honey?" the woman asked, lowering her voice as she put the question to her. When Mona eyed her quizzically, the woman explained, "Most folks don't ask for soup unless they're feeling kind of under the weather."

"No, I'm fine." Mona deliberately put a little bounce in her voice. "I just felt like having some of your chicken soup. It really is good."

Miss Joan beamed, pleased despite the fact that she wasn't fooled. "Flattery'll get you everywhere," she said, and went back to the kitchen to bring out a bowl of the soup.

Mona watched the older woman go through the swinging door into the kitchen and slowly sighed. She wasn't being strictly honest with Miss Joan. She wasn't ill, but it was more than just good taste that prompted her to order soup for dinner. She hoped that the warmth of the soup would somehow ease the emptiness that she felt inside.

She'd thought—hoped—that she had finally conquered the feeling, because it had disappeared for several days. But then, just like that, the emptiness returned, coming out of nowhere and threatening to swallow her up whole if she didn't find a way to beat it back again.

In the midst of work—and today had been a particularly hectic day—she felt alone. Even here, in the diner, she felt the emptiness eating away at her despite the fact that this was dinnertime and a great many people, travelers as well as town citizens, were clustered here, filling every available seat in the place except for her table.

She had a feeling that Miss Joan had saved the booth for her and she was grateful. She knew if she said anything, or made any mention of her gratitude, Miss Joan would tell her that she had no idea what she was talking about.

Miss Joan was like that.

The woman returned with her soup, steam curling from the bowl and melding with the air above it, and placed it on the table in front of her.

Mona smiled as brightly as she could as she fought back the crippling ache. What *was* the matter with her? she silently demanded, annoyed with herself. "Thank you, Miss Joan."

The woman nodded, sweeping away the thanks. "Anything else, honey?" she wanted to know.

Mona shook her head. "Nothing I can think of." After all, Miss Joan could do nothing about this feeling eating away at her the way Apache was eating away at his bone.

But rather than make her way back behind the counter and other customers, Miss Joan looked at her for a long moment. Looking, it felt, right *through* her.

"You sure about that, honey?" Miss Joan finally asked her.

Mona forced a very worn smile to her lips, doing

her very best to make it seem spontaneous and natural. "I'm sure."

Just then, the door to the diner opened and Joe walked in. He removed his hat the moment he crossed the threshold, then slowly looked around, searching for a seat. All the stools that lined the counter were taken and so were, it appeared, all the booths.

With a resigned sigh, Joe began to put his hat back on. But before he could leave again, Miss Joan saw him and picked up her voice by several decibels.

Raising her hand to catch his attention, she called out, "Over here, Joe." Miss Joan shifted her glance toward Mona and asked what anyone could easily see was a rhetorical question as far as she was concerned. "You don't mind sharing a table with Joe, do you, honey?"

Actually, she did. Right now, Mona wasn't feeling at her best. She felt dull tonight and she couldn't put her finger on exactly *what* had triggered this feeling, but she felt that she would make awful company.

However, she knew that it would do no good to protest or worse, take exception to Miss Joan's seating plan. Miss Joan was one of those people who always knew best, or so the older woman liked to believe.

As for her, Mona had too much regard for the diner owner to even make an attempt at refusing her.

"No, I don't mind," Mona murmured, more to herself than to Miss Joan.

"Here, boy, take a load off," Miss Joan instructed, gesturing him into the booth seat opposite Mona.

"So what can I get you, Joe?" As she had done with Mona, Miss Joan peered closer at his face. "You look tired, Joe. Some kind of crime wave hit Forever?" the woman asked, an amused glimmer in her eyes.

"Not tonight," he told her, deliberately not going into any details regarding why he looked as if he hadn't slept much the past few days.

The woman was, among other things, not just the owner of the diner and a budding psychologist, but what amounted to the town crier, as well. A person with that many so-called hats to wear had no need to know that the woman she just sat him with was the one responsible for his sleeplessness.

Things were getting worse in that respect, not better. Rather than taking her presence in stride the way he thought he would, having Mona around like this, interacting with her a little almost every day, just made him acutely aware of the fact that he wanted her. A great deal.

And Mona, undoubtedly, had other plans for herself. There wasn't an endless supply of men in Forever, but there were enough and he'd seen several coming by the clinic with pets or borrowed animals, obtained from helpful friends or well-meaning relatives, just to have an excuse to confer with the sexiest veterinarian east of California.

It was only a matter of time before one of those guys put a lock on her affections, and then that would be the end of it. He would have to terminate his own longing at that point. Hell, maybe *then* he'd start getting a decent night's sleep.

Or, if not by then, he definitely would by the time Mona became Mrs. Somebody-or-Other because then he would go on being just Joe, good at his job and undistracted by extraneous things—like the laugh of a beautiful veterinarian who popped up in his fantasies with frustrating regularity.

"Just get me a ham and cheese on rye, black coffee and a piece of that cherry pie of yours," Joe requested in response to Miss Joan's query.

Mona glanced toward the counter and saw the empty cake container where the cherry pie was usually kept on display for the customers.

"Looks like they're out of cherry pie, Joe," she commented.

Miss Joan placed a hand on his shoulder and gave it a squeeze. "Don't you worry that handsome head of yours," she told Joe. "I figured you'd be coming in tonight and I set a piece aside for you." She looked at Mona. "He orders the same dessert every night. I'd do the same for you if you were predictable—or ate dessert," Miss Joan threw in over her shoulder as she walked away from them and toward the counter again.

"If you'd rather eat alone," Joe began, "I can just get mine to go."

"And disappoint Miss Joan?" Mona asked. "I don't think so. The woman looked as if she was a fairy godmother at loose ends, doing her best to make something 'happen' between us," Mona said with the first smile she felt like offering today.

He did that for her, she thought. Joe made her smile for no reason at all. To counterbalance that, he could also arouse her temper faster than anyone else, a temper whose magnitude she wasn't even aware of until Joe popped into the picture.

"I don't think she needs to make anything happen," Joe told her quietly, his eyes on hers.

Mona looked at him sharply. Was he saying that she was wrong in her supposition, or that something was *already* happening between them and they didn't need Joan to stir the pot?

Joe's tone, as well as his reply, confused her, and for the life of her, Mona couldn't sort out what he actually meant.

Or maybe she was afraid to.

So she answered him with as much evasiveness as possible. "I'm fairly sure that Miss Joan wouldn't be of the same opinion as you if you asked her."

"Miss Joan marches to the beat of her own drum," he agreed. There was a faint smile in his voice as he added, "But then, so do you."

She was about to ask him just what he meant by that when he turned his attention to the dog at her feet. Apache appeared oblivious to everything and everyone around him as he went wholeheartedly at the bone Miss Joan had placed before him.

"How're you doing, boy?" Joe asked, leaning down to scratch the animal behind the ears.

Apache paused for less than half a second to look up at the intruding human before resuming his determined gnawing. Joe straightened up and faced Mona again.

"He looks happier," he told her. "Also wider." He laughed, amused. "You did a good job with him."

Mona was about to point out the very obvious fact that she was *supposed* to be able to do a "good job" getting the dog healthy again considering that she was, after all, a vet, but somehow, that sounded pretty argumentative even to her own ears. So instead, she just rendered a careless, one-shoulder shrug and murmured a simple, "Thanks."

Miss Joan returned with Joe's dinner, offering the temporary sheriff a wide smile, then shifting her keen gaze to include Mona.

"Here you go. Sandwich, coffee and pie," Miss Joan announced as she slide each plate and cup from the tray she'd brought onto the table. Finished, she tucked the tray under one arm. "All right, now get to it," the woman instructed. Again she spared a glance in Mona's direction. "Both of you."

And just like that, Mona could feel her cheeks heating, taking on a hue all their own. To her recollection, she'd never blushed before. Not even when she'd had what she now freely admitted was a *stupid* fling with Steven James during her second year in college. She'd known from the beginning that she wasn't in love with the extremely good-looking senior, but it was college and she was away from home, free to test the waters of independence. So she had.

Besides, like most of the girls around him, she'd found herself exceedingly attracted to Steven.

Or so she'd thought at the time.

But the attraction she'd felt back then was an empty one involving merely Steven's looks and nothing of a deeper substance. Steven James, it turned out, didn't *have* a deeper substance. What she saw was not only what she got, but it was apparently all there was to the pre-med student.

It took coming home and running into Joe over and over again to make her see the difference. There was no denying that she was attracted to Joe, that she felt more than just a spark of electricity whenever she was around him. But that attraction encompassed not just his dark good looks, but the man, as well. Though she wasn't about to voice it out loud, Joe Lone Wolf was a good, decent man with qualities that made him good-looking inside, as well as out.

"Heard from Rick?" Joe asked her after several seconds of silence wrapped in the surrounding din had ticked by.

Mona nodded. She had, earlier in the week. "Just a postcard that said, 'No offense, but glad you're not here.'" She nodded toward him. "You get anything?" she asked.

He took a long sip of his bracing coffee. Resting his cup, he shook his head. "No, but then, I didn't expect to. A man on his honeymoon doesn't spend his time thinking about the job he left behind. Right now, he's probably squeezing the last drop of pleasure out of the honeymoon. He's due back in a couple of weeks," he added matter-of-factly.

"I know."

And once Rick and Olivia and the almost-baby were back, she was going to have to figure out where to go. Pronto, Mona thought.

So far, the whole thing was up in the air. She'd shelved it and promptly forgot about looking into the matter. She hadn't thought about having to move since the evening of the wedding.

The evening Joe had brought Apache into her life, she remembered with a fond smile, glancing down at her dog. Apache was making short work of the bone.

Mona supposed that she had better *start* thinking about it, about finding a new place to stay, and soon. The Murphy place might be an option, but only after it was fixed up.

Maybe she could crash at Doc's for a while, she thought. He had that big old house and lived in only the kitchen and one bedroom. She could easily rent one of the free bedrooms.

Most likely, she'd have to threaten him to take the money. Doc was like that, charitable to a fault. He'd probably say that at his age, he didn't have a whole lot of use for money. She'd have to remind him that the clinic could always use more expansion, or a new MRI machine. He couldn't turn down the money then, she thought confidently.

Joe broke into her thoughts by asking her out of the blue, "What are we doing here, Mona?"

She blinked, confused by the question. Wasn't it obvious? "What?"

He didn't say anything to enlighten her about his meaning. Instead, he just repeated his question. "I said, what are we doing here?"

"Eating?" she guessed, her voice going up a little the way it did when she felt herself on unsafe ground. "Talking a little," she added. She cocked her head, looking at him and waiting for him to elaborate.

What he meant was what were they doing, sitting around playing games, pretending that this "something" shimmering between them didn't exist. But instead of saying as much, he got to the heart of the matter because it was time to get things moving and there would never be a better time.

Setting down his fork on the near-empty plate, he dove in.

"Mona, I'd like to ask you out for a date."

"A date," she repeated incredulously. Her pulse suddenly accelerated into triple time. She tried to tell herself that it was because the soup was hot and she'd just almost burned her tongue. But even she realized just how lame that really sounded.

"Yes, a date," Joe underscored. He wondered if he'd just made a stupid mistake he would live to regret, or if the regret would come because he hadn't taken this chance.

"You mean, like when a man and a woman go

someplace to eat and talk?" Mona asked innocently, deliberately shifting her gaze to the food between them and then back up to his face.

"Yes," he answered tersely, refusing to back away. You never knew what you were missing if you didn't try. His mother had said that to him the day before she'd died. "The only difference is that they go in together and leave together. And the guy pays," he added as an afterthought.

"Not always," Mona contradicted, clinging to her perverseness as if it was a protective shield. "In this day and age—"

Exasperated, Joe rose in his seat, leaning into her. Taking her startled face in his hands, he kissed her. Long and hard.

When he drew back again an eternity later, the diner had tilted a little. But he wasn't paying attention to the diner. He was paying attention to the woman who had begun to haunt his dreams. Again.

Stunned, a little shocked, Mona waited for the electricity to stop shooting through her veins. It didn't seem to want to.

"What did you do that for?"

"The primary reason was to shut you up—it worked beautifully," he pointed out needlessly. "The other reason, well, I think you know what the other reason is. And if you don't," he added, settling back in his seat, "then I did it wrong."

This was where a flippant answer would fit in

nicely, she thought. All she had to do was say it and things would go back to the way they'd been.

Not a single flippant statement occurred to her.

"No, you didn't do it wrong," she told him quietly, her eyes on his. "You did it exactly right."

Mona realized that she said what she had, messing up her chances for a successful retreat, because she didn't want things to go back to the way they'd been.

At least, not yet.

Chapter Twelve

She had a date.

A date with Joe.

The thought still mystified Mona the next day. Joe would swing by after work and pick her up at the house. And they were going to Miss Joan's—because it was the only available place to go—to have dinner.

Nothing they hadn't done before. Singularly. The difference this time was that they would do it together. On purpose, not because Miss Joan had suddenly taken it upon herself to seat one of them with the other for lack of space. Or because she'd suddenly decided that they would make a good couple.

Joe wanted to take her out.

Mona caught herself humming more than once during the course of the day. When her stomach wasn't tied up in knots.

Neither reaction made any sense to her. This was Joe she was going out with. Joe, whom she'd known since she was a teenager. Going out with him, date or not, should be a piece of cake. Old hat. Nothing to get excited about. Certainly nothing to get nervous about.

And yet she was both.

Because this was also Joe, the guy she'd had a crush on all those years ago.

Work had always helped her cope with mental unrest. Today was one of those days where being busy would have been a blessing. But unfortunately, no blessings in the offing today. There had been only two appointments that morning and only one walk-in.

As a result, the minutes dripped away slowly. That afternoon, Simon Taggert had called Doc about his quarter horse, Wildfire. The animal had gotten tangled in some barbed wire, panicked and cut up two of his legs trying to get free. Doc had left for Taggert's ranch immediately.

"Hold down the fort, Mona" were Doc's parting words to her, thrown over his shoulder, as he hurried out to his truck.

The problem with that was that there was nothing to hold down. The "fort" was almost painfully empty. There was only one animal, a cat, in the hospital area. The pet was staying overnight. Mittens was recovering from yesterday's emergency surgery. The willful feline had apparently decided to snack on a long section of wool that was originally intended to become part of a sweater Mittens's mistress was knitting. The wool had gotten entangled around her intestines. The surgery had been exceedingly challenging and, thankfully, successful.

But that had been yesterday. Today involved periodic checking to see how the cat was doing. Mittens was doing fine, which was more than Mona could say for herself. Attacks of antsiness had her all but climbing the walls.

There was no reason to feel this way, she kept arguing. This was the same Joe she'd always known. The only thing that had changed since she'd gone away to college was that he had grown handsomer and just possibly more silent.

The only actual "business" that had transpired at the animal clinic today occurred when Greta Wilson had come in to buy Alec, her border collie, his six-month supply of heart medicine.

Mona hated being at loose ends and not accomplishing anything. She knew she had to act fast or wind up going crazy before her date even started. So, with Apache following her around like an extension of her shadow, Mona set about straightening the clinic and washing and cleaning everything in sight— whether it needed it or not.

The frenzy took her a little over two hours. Finished, Mona sat back, waiting for Doc to return. Since there was only the cat in the back to occasionally monitor, she decided that she'd go home early and get ready. Maybe take a hot bath in an attempt to take the edge off her nerves.

She glanced at her watch. Doc had been gone for some time now. Since he hadn't called her, she felt that the injured quarter horse must be in good shape. And that in turn meant that Doc should be back pretty soon.

Just then, the floorboard directly overhead creaked.

Mona looked up and stared at the ceiling. The floor didn't creak unless someone was walking on it. Had he gotten back earlier and gone directly upstairs for some reason? Was he sick?

Ordinarily, when Doc returned from a call, he walked into the clinic. Maybe he'd taken the side stairs and gone up to take care of something. She was pretty certain that if he wasn't feeling well, he would have called by now.

If he was here, that meant she could go home. But Mona didn't want to leave without telling him that she was going.

She gave it a few minutes. But when the time passed and Doc still hadn't come down into the clinic, she decided it was time that Mohammed went up the stairs to see the mountain.

She picked up her purse and checked to make sure she had her keys.

There was a staircase in the back just to the side of the operating area that led to the second floor. Rather than hang back behind her as she made her way up, Apache crowded her on each step, reaching the landing at the same time she did.

"Doc? Are you up here?" Mona called out when she didn't see him. He didn't answer. Curious, she ventured forth a little farther. She didn't like the idea of invading his privacy, especially if he wasn't there, but she was *sure* she'd heard footsteps overhead. "I thought I heard you walking around and I wanted to let you know that I was leaving early today. Doc?"

she called again, raising her voice when he still didn't answer.

The house was old and sections of boards beneath the neutral-colored carpet creaked. If Apache hadn't stayed at her side all day, she would have blamed the noise on him. The dog had gone exploring around the building a couple of times and he'd managed to wander into the living quarters twice. Doc had brought him down, chuckling and telling her that she had an explorer on her hands.

The "explorer" was still right here, next to her.

Feeling unaccountably uneasy, Mona went from room to room. Since Doc hadn't answered her, she decided that he wasn't in his rooms. But what—or who—was?

When she tried to open the door to the third and last bedroom, she discovered that it was locked. From the inside. Something cold and icy slid down her spine. Unless raccoons had suddenly learned how to lock doors, someone had broken into Doc's house. And whoever it was was hiding in the bedroom.

Thank God she was the one who'd discovered this. She couldn't bear the thought of Doc stumbling onto the intruder and possibly getting hurt or shot by him. Knowing Doc, he'd be tempted to feed the thief and give him a place to sleep. Kindness wasn't always repaid with kindness. Doc was entirely too trusting.

Angry at this intrusion, Mona raised her voice. "I've got the sheriff downstairs," she informed the person she was certain was on the other side of the locked door. "All I have to do is call out and he'll be up here in a second. With his gun. Why don't you just unlock the door and tell me what you're doing here?"

After a moment, she heard the lock being turned. And then, ever so slowly, the door opened. The person in the room answered her question as she walked out. "Waiting for Doc to come back."

The world around Mona went in and out of focus twice, alternating between just blurred edges and a complete blur. She tried to tell herself she was seeing things.

Except that she wasn't.

"Why are you here?" she heard herself asking the dark, petite woman with the large brown eyes. She struggled to keep her voice low.

Mona felt as if the other woman's eyes were all but devouring her. "I just told you, I'm waiting for—"

Mona cut her off impatiently. "No, why are you *here?* Here in Forever? You were supposed to leave. At the wedding, you said you were leaving."

"No," Elena Ruiz corrected softly. "*You* said I was leaving. I just walked away because I didn't want to cause a scene at Enrique's wedding."

As if her showing up hadn't already lain the groundwork for that, Mona thought angrily. "He goes by Rick," Mona informed her curtly. Anger melded with contempt as she said, "You don't even know that."

"How could I?" Elena cried, frustrated. "He won't talk to me. *You* won't talk to me."

And she didn't want to be talking to her now. "All

the more reason for you to go," Mona pointed out in exasperation.

Elena almost pleaded as she said, "But I can't make amends if I go."

"There's nothing you can do to make amends so you might as well go," Mona told her coldly.

She hated this, hated confrontations, hated being in the same room with a woman who hadn't cared for anyone but herself for so long. And now she was back, expecting to be forgiven and embraced? Just like that?

"Doc thinks I can make amends," Elena told her. It was evident that hope was all she had to cling to. "He thinks that you and Enr—Rick will come around."

"Not for at least a hundred years—" And then she stopped as Elena's words replayed themselves in her head. "What's Doc got to do with it?" she asked. "And what are you doing in his house?" The strays Doc dealt with were the four-legged kind, not two-legged. Why was this woman in his house? In one of his bedrooms?

"Doc's letting me stay here until I can find a way to prove to you and your brother how deeply, deeply I regret walking away from you." She reached out to place her hand on Mona's arm, but Mona jerked back, putting herself out of reach.

"Rick said you didn't walk away, you ran," Mona corrected. Her eyes narrowed as she got down to what was bothering her about all this. "Doc's a good man, he knows how I feel about the situation. About you." He wouldn't hurt her like this, sheltering Elena when he knew how much the woman's rejection had hurt her. "What did you threaten him with to make him let you stay in his house?" Mona demanded.

Elena pressed her lips together. For a moment, it appeared as if her thoughts were elsewhere. "Yes, I know he's a good man. A very good man." She let out a shaky breath. "I should have realized that a long time ago, too. And no matter what you think of me, I didn't threaten him. I couldn't. Staying in his house was Doc's idea."

Her mother's tone suggested things that she didn't want to hear. Didn't want to think about. But despite her denial, Mona knew that it would eat away at her until she had the truth. Right now, her imagination made her think the worst.

"Is Doc a friend of yours?" Mona couldn't bring herself to add to the question, to give Elena an alternative to choose from. As it turned out, she didn't have to.

"Doc would have been the best thing to happen to me—if only I had let him."

Mona shattered inside. She wanted to scream at Elena, to accuse her of lying. But the look on the woman's face verified everything for her. Mona didn't want to hear anymore. She felt angry and betrayed. Betrayed by one of the few people she'd ever allowed herself to trust.

How could he? How *could* he?

She ran out of the room. Behind her, she could hear Elena calling her name, but Mona didn't turn around.

She flew down the stairs with Apache anxiously right behind her.

Mona didn't stop running once she got to the first floor. Instead, she kept going, blindly making her way out the front door. That was when she plowed right into Doc. Because he was so much larger and heavier than she was, Mona found herself stumbling backward from the impact.

Stunned, Doc caught her by the shoulders to steady her. "Mona, where are you going to in such an all-fired hurry?"

She angrily shrugged him off. "Let go of me!" she ordered.

Concern leaped into his eyes. "Mona, what's wrong? What happened? Why are you running away from the clinic?" Doc glanced through the open door and toward the rear of the clinic as he tried to understand her strange behavior. "Did something happen with Mittens?"

"The cat's fine," she bit off. "But I'm not." There was hurt and anger in her eyes as she glared at him. "I trusted you, Doc. I *trusted* you," she repeated with angry emphasis. "You were the father I never had. How could you?" she cried. "How could you do this to me?"

For a moment, he seemed completely confused. And then he understood. "You went upstairs."

"Yes, I went upstairs," she spat out. "How long has that woman been hiding here in your house?" Mona asked. "Since the wedding?"

"Yes," Doc answered in a heavy, solemn tone. "Mona, she's your mother. Please, give her a chance. For both your sakes."

"She's not my mother," Mona cried. "Abuela was my mother," she insisted. "That woman you took into your home is a complete stranger. I don't know her—"

"Then get to know her," Doc interrupted, trying to get through to her. "You have to try, Mona. Elena's been through a lot—"

He was taking *her* side. Mona went numb inside. "Yeah, well, so have I."

She didn't want to hear anymore, didn't want to argue about this. Didn't even want to think that this was happening. Mona spun around on her heel and ran away from the clinic she'd been more than ready to work in for so long. Without making a sound, Apache ran out the door right behind her.

Mona didn't stop running until she got to her car. Getting in, she waited only long enough for the dog to jump into the backseat. Mona slammed the door shut and peeled out of the small parking lot.

In her rearview mirror, she saw Doc standing where she'd left him, watching her go. He appeared upset.

"That makes two of us, Doc," she whispered.

Hot tears stung her eyes as she drove away.

SHE HAD NO IDEA HOW LONG she'd been standing there, in the cemetery, talking to the headstone that she and her brother had bought for her grandmother.

Pouring out her heart to the memory of the woman the way she hadn't since she was a little girl.

On automatic pilot when she'd left the clinic, she didn't realize she was driving in this direction until she'd almost reached the cemetery.

Ordinarily, whenever she was upset, whenever something was really bothering her, coming out here to talk it out with her grandmother seemed to help. Right now, as she talked to the headstone, Mona could almost envision her small, gray-haired grandmother sitting there, a solemn expression on her face, listening to her. When she was done, Abuela would advise her. The old woman's advice was sparingly given out, but it had always made her feel that everything was going to be all right.

But now there was no low-key, gravelly voice to tell her what direction to take, or to say just the right words that would put her dilemma into the proper perspective.

Mona felt incredibly lonely. Incredibly lonely and betrayed.

"What do I do, Abuela? How can I ever forgive her for what she did? How can I forgive him?" Doc knew how she felt about the woman he'd taken in. How could he have done that? And how could he now ask her to give her a chance? Especially since what he was asking her to do was forgive the woman and start fresh?

"You know, this wasn't what I pictured when I suggested we go out on a date."

A second ago, she was the only one in the cemetery.

The voice, coming out of nowhere, made her jump and gasp. The next second, she looked down accusingly at Apache. At the very least, she would have expected the dog to bark and warn her of Joe's approach.

No bark, no warning. All Apache did was run up to Joe and enthusiastically wag his tail as if he hadn't seen his rescuer in at least a hundred years. The dog's tail thudded against the neighboring headstone, beating out what sounded like a rhythmic tattoo.

Joe blew out a breath, proceeding very cautiously. Despite all her bravado, he knew that Mona was very fragile right now. When he hadn't found her at home, he thought she was still at the clinic. He assumed some kind of emergency had come up. No problem, he was willing to wait.

But when he arrived at the clinic, he discovered that she had fled. Doc had filled him in on what had happened. It wasn't all that hard finding her after that. When Mona felt as if her world was coming apart at the seams, she always came here, to the cemetery, to talk to her grandmother. And search for peace.

Averting her face, afraid that another tear might betray her, Mona murmured, "I'm sorry. I forgot about our date."

"Good thing I don't have an ego to bruise," he said lightly, poking fun at himself in an attempt to get her to come around. He'd just given her a straight line. When she said nothing, he gave it one final beat, then said quietly, "Doc told me what happened."

Tears all but choked her. Mona looked in his direction, struggling not to cry. But her eyes were welling up anyway.

"How could he, Joe?" she cried, wanting desperately to understand, to come up with a reason she could understand and forgive. "How could he do that to me? How could he take her in, knowing how I felt? I *trusted* him and he took her side."

Very slowly, Joe drew closer to her by degrees, approaching her the way he would a wounded animal. Because that was what she was. Wounded. And he wanted nothing more than to help her heal.

"Doc wasn't taking sides, Mona, you know that. You know *him*. He just wants to help the two of you heal a rift."

"This isn't a rift," she retorted. "Friends have arguments, they get mad, they don't talk for a couple of days. That's a rift. *This* is a chasm," she informed him with emphasis. "You don't put a Band-Aid on a chasm and hope it'll all get better."

"Not unless you have one hell of a Band-Aid," he quipped. And then he looked at her pointedly. "Or one hell of a heart, willing to forgive."

"My heart's the usual size," Mona answered, still struggling not to cry. "And right now, it's not feeling very forgiving."

Joe had managed to cut the distance between them down to a mere couple of inches. Enough to be able to put his arms around her and hold her to him just as the dam broke open inside her.

"I'm not supposed to cry," she sobbed against his shoulder, unable to stop.

"Don't worry," he told her softly as he tightened his arms around her, willing her to be comforted. "I'm not going to tell."

She broke down completely at that.

Chapter Thirteen

Mona hoped that if anyone from the town drove by and saw her crying like this in the cemetery, they would think her tears were for the woman whose body rested in peace beneath the headstone.

There was no reason why anyone would guess that it was because she felt so betrayed by both the man she'd thought of as her surrogate father and the woman who had given birth to her, then took herself out of her life.

But no one drove by and no one knew she was crying except for the dog that stood like a sentry right beside her.

And Joe.

Desperately trying to get a grip on herself—crying never solved anything—and feeling as if she was dehydrated, utterly drained of any and all moisture, Mona drew her head back. She gazed up at Joe, whose arms were still very much around her, creating a shelter for her to cling to.

It was merely an illusion, she told herself, trying

not to allow herself to believe it was anything more than that. But still, the idea helped her cope.

By degrees, she became aware of the front of his shirt and what she'd done to it. "I'm sorry, I got your shirt all wet."

The price to pay was infinitesimally small for having her in his arms. He just wished that she wasn't so terribly distressed. Ordinarily, he left people their dignity, allowing them to cope with whatever it was that upset them. But this was Mona. There was no such option here.

"Fortunately, it's wash-and-wear," he quipped, then added, "Don't worry about it."

Joe knew what this was about, what had made her crumple this way, and he wanted to make it all better. He wanted to make her see what he assumed Doc saw, as well. That by allowing her mother back into her life, by forgiving her, Mona would be a great deal happier and it would help to erase her residual pain and resentment.

But this wasn't a time for lectures, however well-intentioned. She wouldn't be receptive to any speeches about her mother right now. Mona was about to pull away, like one of the wounded animals she treated.

"C'mon," he urged, slipping his arm around her shoulders and turning toward the front of the cemetery. "I'll take you home." They could go out to dinner some other time. Mona came first.

She shook her head, although she didn't pull away from him. Having him here soothed her. With Rick gone and Doc's betrayal, Joe was the only one she could still trust. The only real friend she could count on.

"You don't have to," she told him. "My car's parked out front."

Joe really didn't want her driving anywhere in her present condition. She was far too overwrought to be by herself.

"I'll have Larry or Alma bring it over tomorrow morning in time to get you to work," he promised. With his arm still around her shoulders, he gently steered her toward the cemetery entrance.

Too drained and exhausted to argue, and more than a little afraid to be alone with her thoughts, Mona let him guide her.

"I don't know if I'm going to work tomorrow," she told Joe, struggling to keep her voice even. To keep the tears out. If she began to cry again, she wouldn't be able to stop.

Joe made no comment until she got into his vehicle. Taking care to get Apache into the backseat, he then rounded the Jeep's hood and got in on his side.

This was serious, he thought. Mona had wanted to be a vet ever since he'd known her. Was she thinking of giving it all up because Doc had taken her mother in? He couldn't let her throw everything away like that.

"Why not?" he asked as he buckled up.

"Why not?" Mona repeated. She shoved the metal tongue on her seat belt into the slot. The click echoed within the vehicle. "Why not?" she said again, this time her voice swelling in volume.

"That's the question," Joe said, his tone level, nonthreatening. "Why wouldn't you go in to work tomorrow?"

"How can I go in there tomorrow and act as if nothing happened?" she asked incredulously. "It *did* happen. Doc lied to me, Joe. He *lied* to me. The man I trusted, looked up to, *believed* in, thought of as my father, for God's sake, lied to me. How could he do that? And how can I face him now? That woman was there, in his house, all along. She'd been there since the wedding."

Turning the key in the ignition, Joe put the Jeep into Drive and released the hand brake. "No, Doc didn't lie," he contradicted in the same emotionless voice.

Mona fisted her hands in her lap. "How can you say that?" she cried.

There was no moon out tonight. He turned on his high beams and picked his way back to the main road. The road that would take him to her house. "Did you ask him if your mother was staying with him?"

"No," she spat out, exasperated, "but—"

"Then he didn't lie." He glanced at her for a moment, then looked back on the road. "He just didn't tell you she was there."

"All right, then it's a sin of omission," she insisted, her voice breaking as she uttered the last word.

Damn it, she upbraided herself, she wasn't supposed to be this weak, this vulnerable. She was supposed to be able to say the hell with everything, everyone, keep her eyes front and just keep going, not fall apart this way like some delicate flower.

"Maybe," Joe allowed. He made a sharp right as they cleared the chapel. "Way I see it, he figured he'd get around to telling you once he felt you were ready to listen."

Mona stared straight ahead. Her reflection in the windshield bounced back at him. "Listen to what?"

"To your mother's side of it."

Mona could feel her resentment flaring all over again. "She doesn't get to have a side. She dumped us and ran off to have fun."

"Maybe," Joe agreed, although he thought there might be more to it than that. Doc was a good man, but he wouldn't have taken the woman in if there wasn't more to Elena Ruiz's story. "But I doubt she wound up having it."

"How the hell did you come to that conclusion?" she demanded.

"Because she's here, asking you to give her a chance. Because she didn't leave after you told her to go." He paused a moment, debating adding the next sentence, but if Mona was going to come around, she needed to know this. "Because she came back even after Rick told her to go that first time."

Mona stopped staring out the window and looked at him. What was he talking about? "What first time?"

"Your mother—"

"Elena," she corrected fiercely. The woman didn't deserve to be referred to as her mother.

"Elena," he amended for her sake, "was here before," he told her. "When you were around eighteen. She went to Rick to try to make things up to him and you. He told her that she was eighteen years too late and sent her away before you could see her. He didn't want you to be hurt," he added.

Just like she hadn't wanted Elena's return to spoil Rick's wedding day, Mona thought. She and Rick were protective of each other.

"Someone who keeps coming back like that," Joe was saying, "*really* wants to make amends."

"How do you know all this?" Mona asked. "That she came back before?"

"Elena told me when I escorted her out of Rick's wedding," Joe said. For a long moment after that, Joe said nothing. But then he decided that he had to. Otherwise, by his silence, he would contribute to the mistake Mona was about to make and eventually, that mistake would haunt her. And when it did, it would be his fault.

"We only get one mother in our lifetime, Mona. Mine died when I was a kid and I would give anything, *anything,* just to be able to spend one more day with her. You're getting that chance. Don't turn your back on it."

Mona's expression hardened. "Your mother didn't abandon you. Didn't just leave you with the first person she thought of and then take off. Big difference," she insisted.

"No, not really," he contradicted. "Not to me at the time." She, of all people, should understand this, he thought, considering how she'd felt when her grandmother had died. "I felt as if she'd abandoned me and I was pretty mad at her for about two years. Maybe even longer." As he was passed from one indifferent distant relative to another, the resentment had been pretty intense at times. "Never mind that she hadn't wanted to die, bottom line to me was that she did. And she left me behind, ten years old and scared, handed off from relative to relative like one of those cakes people try to get rid of at Christmas."

She supplied the name he couldn't remember automatically. "Fruitcake."

"That's the one." He could see her house in the distance and began to slow down. "Be the bigger person, Mona. Give Elena a chance to talk to you. If you don't like what she has to say, you haven't lost a thing. But if her apology is sincere, if you decide to forgive her for leaving in the first place, the way I see it, you're both getting a second chance."

She shook her head.

He knew that she could be the most stubborn person ever created and he understood that she was hurt, but he'd never known her to be unfair.

"Don't say no," Joe advised. "Say you'll think about it."

"I'm not saying no," she told him.

She'd been through a lot today. Maybe she was operating on the hairy edge. The corners of his mouth curved slightly. "You're supposed to nod your head, not shake it, if you're agreeing with me."

"I'm just stunned," Mona explained. He raised a quizzical eyebrow. "I don't think I've ever heard you say that many words at one time. Hell, I don't think I've ever heard you say that many words in a single day," she amended.

"It's the job," he commented, remembering that Alma and Larry had said almost the same thing the first day he was acting sheriff. "It makes you talk."

Hardly hearing him, Mona blew out a long breath, as if she was centering herself. "Okay," she finally agreed, "I'll let her talk to me." She raised her eyes to his. "I'll do it for you."

"No," Joe corrected her firmly. "You do it for *you.*"

After pulling up in front of Mona's house, he put the Jeep into Park and turned off the ignition. He still wasn't certain if she was actually all right. Moreover, her vulnerability affected him. It made him want to wrap her up in his arms and just protect her. From absolutely everything that gave her pain.

That would go over like the proverbial lead balloon if he so much as hinted at it. Still, he wanted Mona to know that she wasn't alone. That he was there for her if she needed him and he always would be.

"Want me to come in?" he asked quietly.

"Yes."

She said the word so quickly, it sounded as if it had

come out riding on the end of his sentence. The moment he'd begun to ask, she realized just how much she wanted him to be with her. How much she didn't want to be alone tonight.

Her eyes met his and in what she hoped was a more sedate voice, Mona repeated the single word. "Yes." But even as she said it, it sounded more breathless than the first time.

Unbuckling, Joe got out of the vehicle on his side and came around to hers. By the time he reached her, Mona was already out, getting out her keys. She had the door unlocked and open just as Apache bounced out of the backseat. The dog ran between them, dashing into the house as if seeking shelter.

A lot of that going around tonight, Mona thought.

She walked in ahead of Joe. The moment he was inside and closed the door behind him, she turned around to face him. Everything inside of her was tingling. Set to go off.

He could feel the charge in the air, could feel his capitulation shimmering despite all his noble intentions only to comfort her and then leave. He could feel his body wanting hers. Could feel the heat flaring between them.

If ever there was a need to lay ground rules, it was now.

"Mona—"

He got no further. She had captured his lips, rendering them useless. At least when it came to forming any intelligible words. They were pressed against hers, lost in a deep kiss. She literally took his breath away. Unable to resist, he wrapped his arms around her, held her close to him and kissed her with all the passion that he'd stored up over all these years.

Later he might tell himself that it was in self-defense but that would be a lie. Yes, she'd been the one to initiate this, but he was kissing her because he wanted to. He kissed her back with complete reckless abandon. Because what he was doing, what he was letting himself in for, *was* reckless. Acting on suppressed desires always was.

Up until this moment, he had been holding himself relatively in check. But the moment her lips had touched his, he couldn't do that any longer.

His reaction to her kiss wasn't born of the moment. It was, instead, the culmination of years of desire. If he'd thought that he'd outgrown it, the moment he'd seen her that first day, standing beside her car in the rain, it had overtaken him full force. All the time they'd spent together, everything they did together since then had only reinforced it.

Last week, he'd brought her to the reservation where he had been born and his mother had been buried. Brought her there so he could show her, without words, what had shaped him. It was meant to be just a short trip but it hadn't turned out that way. They had wound up staying far into the night.

Several of the children on the reservation were down with a particularly strong strain of the flu. There was no doctor to treat them, no medicine available to them. It was all too costly and far away. So Mona had rolled up her sleeves, falling back on her initial basic medical training and done what she could. And he had been there, right by her side, lending support and aid.

It was an education in more ways than one. He learned that the antibiotic that she prescribed for ailing canines could also be given to ailing children.

"And I won't grow a tail or anything?" one of the little boys weakly asked her, even as a fever raged through his small, thin body. When she'd assured him that he wouldn't, he'd been crestfallen. And she had struggled not to laugh.

At that exact moment Joe was certain that he was in love with her. And just as certain that nothing would ever come of it.

But here they were, in her house, and she was kissing him. All of his noble resolve never to let her know how he felt, never to touch her like a lover, had just gone up in flames. Because if he *were* noble, he would gently but firmly break the connection.

Instead of embracing it. And her.

His blood rushed hot through his veins as his hands molded her to him, caressing her curves, caressing her. Each time his mouth left hers, it was only to return from another angle, kissing her over and over again, each time more deeply than the last.

He'd never felt like this, like some wild-eyed kid with his first girl. She made him feel that anything was possible. She made him feel reborn.

Reality, never far away, waited for him at first light.

But right now, in this place, he could pretend that *this* was his reality, one that began and ended with her. With Mona.

A frenzy had descended over her. There was no other way to describe it. Mona felt as if she was on fire and she couldn't stop herself, not while the flames burned so brightly within her. She wasn't able to back away.

The more he kissed her, the more she wanted him to. She could feel the demands increasing inside her, ready to burst. Arching into him, she began to fumble at the buttons on his shirt, undressing him while her mouth was still sealed to his.

An eternity later, when all the buttons had finally been released, she pushed the shirt off Joe's shoulders and then struggled to get the sleeves off his arms. Progress was impeded by his rock-solid biceps.

Her breathing grew audible, each breath shorter than the last because the air in her lungs was rapidly being consumed in direct proportion to her increasing passion.

Time became a blur but everything was crystal clear to her. She was acutely aware of every pass of his hands, the feel of his warm breath along her skin. Aware of his hands as he slowly stripped her clothing away from her.

There were calluses on his fingers and palms. That only intensified the delicious feel of them as his strong hands came in contact with her bare skin. It heated immediately in response to his touch, heated until she thought she would burn away to a small, black crisp.

She wanted him, wanted him to make love with her now, this instant. Wanted to be one with him before something happened and made the moment go away.

They tumbled onto the sofa, locked in an embrace, oblivious to everything else.

With each pass of his lips, the intensity within her gathered, making her ache for release even as she struggled to perpetuate the moment. She had never known she could feel this way, ecstatic and yet, in part, afraid. Afraid that, in the end, disappointment would be waiting for her. Disappointment just as there always had been in her life.

But if, at the last moment, she wanted to postpone the inevitable, she realized that she couldn't. The matter was completely out of her hands. Her body had taken command and, like a speeding train, it was hurrying to its culmination.

And around each bend, there was another surge, a surge that built upon the last and reached out to the next.

She arched and bucked, wanting to absorb it all while it lasted.

IT WAS JUST AS HE'D thought it would be. Only better. So incredibly better. This was where all his fantasies about her—when he allowed himself to have them— had promised to lead him.

There was just a micron of control left to him, a

slender thread that allowed him to, at the very end, go slower than he would have ordinarily wanted to. Go slower so that he could share with her and give her the same pleasure she gave him.

But he was only a man and in the end, even he had his limits.

His mouth sealed to hers, Joe moved his body until it was directly over her. With an agonizingly slow movement, he entered her, sealing their union. Holding fast to his resolve, Joe tried to move to a tempo that built up bit by bit, but that lasted less than a moment. Going slow was no longer an option.

They moved in harmony, faster and faster until he sensed she was almost at the final plateau just before the fireworks. Releasing himself, he joined her at the last second and as the atmosphere around them filled with the splendor of skyrockets bursting all around them, they shared the exquisite joy of reaching fulfillment together.

There was no denying it. He loved her.

Chapter Fourteen

Mona caught herself wanting to curl her body into his.

Now that the glorious shower of pleasure had subsided, she wanted to hold on to Joe, to enjoy the simple pleasure of feeling his warmth, feeling his body beside hers. Feeling him drawing breath next to her.

But that would be taking things for granted. That would be leaving herself wide-open for disappointment, if not now, then soon. All too soon. She had learned a long time ago that you couldn't depend on people. Even people you gave your trust to.

And if that hadn't been driven home right from the beginning, or with the death of her grandmother, well, all she had to do was look to today. She would have sworn on a stack of bibles—if she was given to swearing—that she could trust Doc completely. That the man who'd been her mentor, who had funded her college education, would come through for her no matter what. That she could count on him to be there for her and to always, always be honest with her.

But in the end she couldn't rely on him. He had sided with the woman who had now decided to call herself her mother. God only knew why, but it had taught her a lesson. *No one* could be counted on if for some reason it went against their own interests.

So if she gave in to these feelings that she had for Joe, these feelings that he had skillfully aroused as sure as the sun would rise again tomorrow, she would crash and burn. Maybe not tomorrow, maybe not even the day after that, but crashing and burning would definitely happen and it would be sometime soon. Which meant that she would be left stricken again.

The only way around that was to brace herself for the inevitable. To rally by withdrawing into herself and to not expect *anything* from Joe.

Not even a replay of the physical experience that had just taken place.

For all she knew, she'd disappointed him. She wasn't exactly experienced. Joe, she had no doubt, had had a great many partners even though he didn't allude to them or bring up so much as one name. It was still something she was certain of, deep in her bones, and it made her worry that when measured against these nameless others, she came up short.

So, rather than curl up into him the way she longed to, Mona curled up into herself, assuming what amounted to an adult fetal position. It was not an easy trick within the confines of her sofa, which was barely wide enough to accommodate their two bodies, much less granting a separation between them.

Even so, Joe was aware of what she was doing.

Aware that she was trying her damndest to pull away from him. Why?

He thought of pretending that he didn't notice. Thought of getting up and getting dressed as if what had transpired between them was just part of a greater whole, but he liked lying here beside her. Liked the fact that, despite her efforts, their two bodies were still touching.

So he took the simplest route. He asked. "What's the matter?"

He felt her stiffening. "What makes you think there's something the matter?" Mona fired back.

"For one," he observed, "when you just answered me, you sounded like a machine gun going off in rapid succession. For another, you're pulling back into yourself like a bedsheet that's attempting to fold itself into a handkerchief."

Why was he always able to read her as if she was an open book? "Colorful," she said sarcastically. "Ever think of writing poetry?"

"No. Ever think of giving a straight answer?" Joe countered, his eyes on hers, pinning her down. He was tired of her blowing hot and cold whenever she was around him. The only thing worse would be *not* having her around him at all.

"I give straight answers all the time," Mona shot back indignantly.

"Maybe. To other people. But not to me, not this time," Joe pointed out quietly. "What's wrong, Mona?" he asked again, propping himself up on his elbow and looking down at her face. How many times had he dreamed of this moment? *Wished* for this moment? He couldn't allow it to end badly. "Did this scare you?" he wanted to know.

Digging into the sofa with her elbow, she rose up, her face a couple of inches from his. "No!" Mona cried angrily.

Joe continued as if she hadn't said anything. "Because it sure as hell scared me," he admitted.

And it had. Because he'd felt things he wasn't supposed to. Things he'd never felt before. Longings that went beyond the moment. Longings, he knew, that were beyond his reach.

He was willing to enjoy the interlude. But he wasn't willing to get even more tangled up inside over someone who he ultimately hadn't a chance with, especially not when he was looking at forever.

He was certain that, if Mona thought of him at all, to her he was Joe-the-friend, or Joe-the-deputy, not Joe-possible-husband-material. Not in her world. In her world, she was completely out of his league. She'd never said it, but she didn't have to. His earlier life on the reservation, intentionally or not, had taught him what his ultimate place was. And that place wasn't with someone bright and fresh, witty and intelligent, like Mona.

Mona blinked. "You, scared?" she repeated in a mocking tone.

The Joe she knew wasn't threatened by anyone or anything. She didn't think that she'd even ever *heard* him use the word *scared* in reference to himself. Joe was *never* scared. It was one of the givens of life. He was different than the rest of them. And that difference had always made him special to her, even though she would never admit it to him.

"Why would you be scared?" she questioned.

His eyes held hers for a long moment, hypnotizing her. Hypnotizing himself.

Joe swept back the hair from her face, cupping her cheek gently. "You ask too many questions, woman," he murmured just before he kissed her.

The questions remained, but for the time being, they faded away, replaced by the fiery sensation that once again leaped to the foreground the moment his lips touched hers.

He wanted her. That was all she needed to know right now.

MONA LONGED TO REMAIN in that nice warm cocoon that they had woven together in the night, but morning arrived with its own ideas.

She wasn't the type to run away from problems, even though a large part of her wanted to. If she did, setting a precedent, the very action would make her disgusted with herself. She prided herself on the fact that she wasn't a quitter, that she didn't run. She was a fighter. And somehow, although she wasn't sure as to the exact logistics that had been involved, Joe had convinced her to hear her mother out and allow her to make amends.

So, Mona showered and got dressed—actions that took her longer than usual, given that she was doing neither alone—and had Joe drive her and Apache back to the cemetery so that she could retrieve her vehicle.

From there, she would to drive to Doc's. Without Joe.

"You sure you're going to be all right?" Joe asked, unaware that he was allowing his concern about her to show through so strongly.

He was worried about her, she thought. That gave her the exact push to see this through. It was the reverse of a dare, but it had the exact same effect.

"Of course I'm going to be all right," she told him with feeling comprised mostly of sheer bravado. "I'm always all right."

"If you say so." She couldn't tell by his tone if he was mocking her or being doubtful.

Or just being Joe and thus completely unreadable.

In any case, she needed to get going before her courage deserted her. Mona patted the seat beside her in the Jeep. The next moment, Apache leaped into the vehicle. She leaned over to close the passenger-side door.

Time to see this through and make everyone else happy, she thought, lumping Joe and Doc into the same group.

They both drove into town with Joe turning right and going on to the sheriff's office, while she turned left and drove to the animal clinic.

Doc was already there when she walked in. He was

doing something at the receptionist's desk and looked up when the door opened.

"Mona." Relief washed over his broad face only to give way to a look of uncertainty and concern. "I didn't know if you were going to come in today."

"Why wouldn't I come in?" she asked, forcing her voice to sound cheerful. "Delia Morales is bringing in her cat to be declawed today. I made the appointment for her myself. Wouldn't exactly look right if I didn't show up and the cat did. I'm guessing that your agenda's full today."

He nodded, but it was obvious that his mind wasn't on the day's appointments. He trod lightly.

"Mona, about yesterday, I'm sorry. I should have told you that she—" he prudently refrained from referring to his houseguest as her mother "—was staying with me. Elena and I go way back," he told her. "Back to even before she married your father. She wasn't exactly what you might call disciplined. Unharnessed energy was the way I used to think of her."

He appeared to be unaware of the fond expression that slid over his face. But Mona wasn't. She refused to allow her thoughts to go any further and explore the reason for his look. There was only so much she could handle at one time.

"You should have seen her back then," Doc was saying, "before she was even your age. She was the most beautiful sight God ever created."

Mona listened to him, to the man she had always had such respect for, such affection, and despite her attempts to block the thought, she realized that he wasn't just giving shelter to a distraught soul, he was doing it because he'd had feelings for the woman. Feelings for Elena. Strong feelings.

He still did, her mind whispered.

She didn't know if that made her feel angrier—or feel happy for Doc, who, as far as she knew, never had anyone in his life to care about in that way.

"I'd take it as a personal favor if you heard her out, Mona," Doc appealed to her. "She really wants another chance to be the mother she couldn't be before. I know that in your eyes she's done nothing to deserve another chance, but—"

"Are you in love with Elena?" Mona asked abruptly.

The unexpected question appeared to jar him for a moment. She knew she'd never spoken to him like that, but then, he'd never hurt her like this before, never taken someone else's side against her before.

"What I feel for her doesn't matter," Doc replied in his quiet, even voice. "What does matter is your relationship with her—or lack of one. Some day, Mona, she won't be around. I don't want you to look back then and realize that you're feeling guilty about your behavior toward—"

"What makes you think I'll feel guilty?" she asked. For the moment, she decided not to tell him that Joe had already driven home the point he now tried to make.

Doc paused for a moment, as if wrestling with an issue. When he began to talk, he told her something about himself he'd never shared with anyone. "Because I had an absentee father and had the same feelings about him as you do about your mother. And when he came back into my life suddenly some twenty years later, I didn't want to have anything to do with him."

She could see by his expression that this was hard for Doc to talk about. Doc, who had always been able to talk about anything without hesitation. She realized that by telling her this, he tried to spare her the same kind of guilt.

"He left," Doc was saying, "and I never saw him again. I didn't know at the time that he was dying and he'd wanted to make amends so that he could die in peace."

Doc paused, taking a long breath. "I didn't give him that peace and sometimes, when I sit back and take stock of my life, that comes up to haunt me." His eyes peered into hers. "It's on the minus side of the tally."

She wanted to put her arms around him, around the young man he'd been, feeling abandoned just as she had. "How old were you when he left?"

Doc shrugged, the white lab coat he wore moving about his wide, powerful shoulders. "Six, seven, I don't remember exactly. What I do remember was the look on his face the last time I saw him. He was anguished and heartbroken. And I had done that to him, to another human being. To my father." His voice was kind, supplicating. "I don't want you to feel the same way, Mona."

It suddenly occurred to her that maybe Doc was trying to tell her something covertly. She felt a chill go zigzagging along her spine. "Are you telling me that she's dying, Doc?"

Her question seemed to throw him for a second. "What?" He then realized she might have picked that up from his own story. "No, but that doesn't change anything. If you send her away, you'll carry that look in her eyes around with you for the rest of your life." He took her hands into his. "I don't want that for you."

Mona blew out a breath. She loved Doc and didn't like these mixed emotions. In her heart, she *knew* that he was only thinking of her. But a part of her still resisted what he asked her to do. Resisted and nursed hurt feelings.

If she was honest with herself, she knew that Doc and Joe were both right in their urgings. It wasn't her nature to harbor a grudge. Bearing one against her mother was like a dark force that ate away at her soul, and she'd kept it inside of her for a long time now. Long enough.

With a nod of her head, Mona gave in. "Is she still upstairs?"

"Yes," he told her. "Upstairs and packing."

Packing. Elena was leaving. That meant that all she had to do was keep busy and out of the way. By the end of the day, her problem would be gone and life would go back to the way she knew it.

Kind of, she amended, thinking of last night and Joe. After experiencing that, nothing would ever really be the same again. There was another factor to consider. She was now a sister-in-law, as well as a sister. That changed a lot.

It wasn't just Rick and her against the world anymore. Their family was expanding. Within a couple of months, she'd be an aunt. And Rick would be a father. She supposed that it would be a good thing for the baby to have a grandmother, and Olivia's parents were both dead.

Mona made up her mind.

"I'm going to take a break, Doc," Mona informed the senior veterinarian.

Without waiting for Doc to comment on the fact that she hadn't begun to work yet, she went toward the rear of the clinic and went to the back stairs. Gripping the handrail, she made her way slowly up to the second floor and Doc's living quarters.

When she came to the landing, she stood there for a second, waiting for her heart to settle down again. It had gone into double time as she tried to anticipate the words that would pass between her and her mother.

She hadn't a clue.

Taking another breath, she made her way to the last bedroom. The room she had found her mother the previous time. The bedroom door stood ajar. Rather than push it open, she knocked on it lightly and waited.

"Come in, Henry," she heard her mother respond. "I'm almost finished."

Mona opened the door and stepped over the threshold. Her mother's back was to the doorway. She was bent over an opened suitcase that was on the bed, trying to arrange what went inside.

"I'm not even good at packing," she said, still thinking she was talking to Doc. "I can't seem to get everything back into the suitcase. It all fit when I came," Elena lamented, shaking her head. "Don't see why it won't go back in now."

"You're leaving." It was a question hidden in the guise of a statement.

She saw her mother stiffen, then turn around, a look of tentative disbelief on her face, as if she thought her ears were playing tricks on her. When she saw who was in her bedroom, the look of stunned surprise froze for a moment on her face.

"Yes," Elena finally answered, "I'm leaving." She took a breath, as if to steady her voice, which trembled. "I thought it would be better that way. Whether you believe me or not, I don't want to cause you and your brother any more pain than I already have, and it seems that having me around does that, so I'm leaving."

Mona took another step closer to her mother. "Where will you go?"

The shrug was careless. And hapless. "I don't know yet." The smile that came to Elena's lips seemed forced. "It's a big country and there are a lot of places I haven't seen yet."

"They'll still be there later," Mona told her quietly, seriously. "I mean, if you don't go now."

Elena looked at her uncertainly. The question she

asked was uttered very carefully, as if she was afraid of hearing the answer. Of being wrong. "Are you asking me to stay?"

"Well, if you go," Mona told her, "then neither one of us will ever know if this has a chance in hell of working, will we?"

Her mother's deep brown eyes were searching hers. "Are you saying that you forgive me?" Her voice rose at the end of the question as joy and hope wove their way through it.

Mona couldn't jump into it that fast, even though a small kernel inside of her wanted to. The small part that belonged to the little girl who had lain in bed, night after night, wondering what it would be like to have a mother who loved her.

"No, I'm not saying that. I'm saying that I'm leaving myself open to the possibility of forgiving you. If I feel that you deserve it," Mona qualified. "Doc seems to think you do and Joe thinks I should give you a second chance and I've always had a lot of respect for both their opinions." Pausing because she was afraid her voice would break, Mona pressed her lips together before going on. "So, I suppose what I'm saying is that I'm willing to give this relationship a try—if you're really serious about making amends."

"Oh, I'm serious," Elena said quickly, tears gathering in her eyes only to come spilling down her cheeks. "I'm very serious," she assured Mona with enough feeling to fill a stadium. There was silence for a moment, and then Elena said, "I need you to know that leaving you and your brother here with your grand-mother was the best thing I could have done for ei-ther of you. I wasn't stable. After your father died, I couldn't take care of you, either of you. I wasn't a fit mother. I wasn't even a fit person."

"You don't have to explain right now."

"Oh, but I do. It took me a long time to forgive my-self. Forgive myself for being alive when your father was dead. By the time I worked things through, years had gone by. I didn't know how to come back. And when I finally did, Enri—Rick sent me away. It took me eight more years to work up the nerve to try again."

"I won't send you away this time," Mona told Elena quietly.

Elena steepled her fingers together before her lips to keep the sobs from escaping. And then, in a shak-ing voice she struggled to keep even, she had to ask, "Am I allowed to hug you?"

Mona said nothing. Instead, she silently held out her arms. Elena fell into them, sobbing loudly.

Mona struggled valiantly not to do the same. In the end, she lost.

Chapter Fifteen

"Your brother's coming back tomorrow."

Joe's quiet voice broke through the echoes of sub-siding euphoria within her bedroom.

They were lying together in her bed, the way they had been every night since that first time. This was a new frontier he'd crossed. The women he'd bedded before had one thing in common. He rarely saw them twice, certainly not more than a handful of times. This was entirely different. Different and amazingly satis-fying, although he tried not to explore as to why. He knew the danger in that. Mona would bolt.

He had his arm tucked around her, keeping Mona close to him. He knew all this was temporary, the way someone reluctant to wake up from a good dream knew without being told that it couldn't last forever. Dreams never did.

"I know," she murmured, loving the way her body curled into Joe's. Lying beside him like this was al-most her favorite part of their lovemaking. The opera-tive word being *almost*.

Funny how her perspective on things had changed

in such an incredibly short amount of time. When her brother left with Olivia for their honeymoon, she'd felt gnawingly alone again, like someone forced to remain on the train platform while her life pulled away, locked tightly inside the train that was departing from the station.

And now, now things were different. So very different.

Mona turned into Joe, tilting her head so she could look up at him. "I wonder what's going to surprise Rick more, that I'm actually talking to our mother or that you and I are…"

Her voice trailed off as she realized she didn't know what to call what she and Joe were now. Lovers? That was too solid a word. She was going to say "together" but that might scare him away, as well, and besides, he'd never actually come out and said anything to make her believe that this was more than a pleasant interlude for him.

"Are more than friends," Mona finally said for lack of another, better term to describe where their relationship had now gone.

And even that, she thought, looking at Joe's impassive face, seemed not to be the right thing to say. So what *were* they? What did he think their togetherness meant?

She waited for him to speak, to jump in and tell her what he was feeling.

"You're going to tell Rick about…this?" Joe questioned.

He was being deliberately vague because Mona appeared to have gone out of her way *not* to label what was going on between them. He especially avoided the word *relationship* because he knew how Mona didn't trust relationships.

"No," she replied, sensing that that was the answer Joe was after. "I'm not going to go out of my way to specifically mention it. Why?" At the last moment, she'd decided to confront him. This playing games couldn't continue indefinitely. Either he was committed or he wasn't. And if he wasn't, she needed to know now, not six months down the road after she'd irretrievably lost her heart. "You don't want my brother to know you're…'seeing' me?"

God, but it was hard second-guessing what she wanted to hear. He went with a traditional excuse, even though, as far as he was concerned, it carried no weight with him. If he believed that Mona actually cared about him, about them, he would go up against Rick in a heartbeat.

As he spoke, Joe watched her face for a reaction. "Rick's my boss. Bosses usually don't like their employees sleeping with their sisters. Besides, you said this was no big thing."

She'd said that for his benefit—and, she supposed, in part to keep from scaring herself. It was, she knew deep in her heart, a lie right from the very beginning. This was a *very* big deal. At least, it was to her.

But obviously not to Joe.

"Right," she said, keeping her tone matter-of-fact

to hide the hurt all but exploding inside her. "It isn't. No big deal at all." She sat up, holding the sheet to her. She wanted him gone—before he could see her cry. "Look, since Rick and Olivia are coming back tomorrow, maybe I should clean up a little bit." She kept her face averted, avoiding his eyes. "Would you mind letting yourself out?"

The cool tone jarred him, but then, maybe that was what he needed, he told himself. Something to shove him out of the fool's paradise he'd constructed for himself. He'd foolishly created it despite all his self-imposed warnings that she was out of his reach. He'd known from the beginning that giving in to his feelings would make retreating back to his life that much harder.

It was coming to an end a lot faster than he'd thought, but then, it served him right for letting his guard down.

"Sure thing," Joe said. Sitting up, he grabbed his jeans from the floor and slid into them. He put on his shirt just as quickly.

Sure thing, her mind echoed bitterly. No objection, no "Why so quick?" No protest on his part. If she really listened closely, she might even be able to detect relief in his voice. Relief because now he didn't have to go through some kind of a scene as he broke it off with her, she thought angrily. He had his fun and now he was going to be free.

And she had fallen in love with him.

How could she have been so stupid?

Just because her mother finally returned didn't mean that the pattern that had haunted her life for so long was broken. One way or another, she was still the one who got left behind, physically or emotionally. By everyone who mattered.

Mona felt the bed shifting. Joe was on his feet. "See you around," she heard Joe say to her back.

Mona didn't bother to turn around, didn't suddenly jump up, the sheet wrapped around her, and implore him to stay. She didn't even answer his parting line with some kind of banal response. She just wanted him gone. Now. Before she *did* do something stupid. Like beg him to stay, to make love with her and make her feel that the magical moment would last forever.

And when, less than a couple of minutes later, she heard the front door close, she let out the shaky breath she'd been holding. But instead of getting up to clean, the way she'd told him she intended to, Mona fell back on the bed, curled up and cried what was left of her jagged, scarred heart out.

UNABLE TO SLEEP, HER BODY almost bruised from all the tossing and turning she'd done, Mona finally got up a little after one in the morning. It was then that she finally turned her attention to cleaning the house. She judged that maybe, if she was busy enough, the pain would fade for a little while and leave her in peace.

And maybe, your next trip out of Forever will be to Oz, she silently mocked herself.

Feeling dead inside, she got busy.

MONA LOST TRACK OF TIME.

All that mattered was cleaning, cleaning everything within an inch of its life. She kept up a steady stream of conversation, talking to Apache as if the dog was diligently absorbing every word she said. Several times during her cleaning frenzy, Apache came up to her and licked her hand, but not as if fishing for treats. She could have sworn she saw a look of empathy in the soft brown eyes as the animal looked up her.

He knew, she thought. Knew her heart was breaking. Animals could be eerily intuitive at times.

"Too bad the guy who brought you to me doesn't have some of your skills," she said out loud.

It was time to stop feeling sorry for herself and start making plans for the rest of her life. If Doc felt as if he had the situation under control, she might see about setting up a practice in Dallas the way Rick had suggested when she'd returned.

She paused, one window shy of finishing her task, letting the sponge fall into the dirty water in the bucket.

"What do you think, Apache? Would you like to go live in Dallas?"

The dog didn't bark. Instead, cocking his head he just looked at her, his eyes mirroring the deadness in her soul.

The dog definitely had more on the ball than Joe did. She sank her hands into the bucket again, squeezing the sponge, ready to keep going until the house sparkled and she dropped from exhaustion. Hopefully the two wouldn't be mutually exclusive.

"YOU'RE WHAT?" LARRY echoed, looking at Joe as if the latter had just lost his mind.

Joe took a breath. After the way things had ended last night, he knew he couldn't remain in Forever. The town was too small for him not to keep running into Mona. Seeing her and not *being* with her would just be too painful for him. He had to leave. As soon as possible.

He'd decided to break the news to Larry first in preparation for telling Rick. So far, this wasn't the reception he'd anticipated.

"I'm thinking of trying my luck someplace else," he repeated in the same monotone voice he'd used to tell Larry in the first place. Anything else and he was afraid he'd give his feelings away.

"Like as in leaving Forever?" Larry asked incredulously.

"Like as in leaving Forever," Joe confirmed with a quick nod of his head.

Larry frowned and shook his head. "You and Mona had a fight, didn't you?"

Joe maintained his stoic look. "No, no fight."

Larry moved so that he was directly in front of him, leaving only inches between their faces. "Then what?"

"Then," Joe continued in the same emotionless voice, "this is none of your business."

Beneath Larry's perpetually tanned face hints of

red brought on by frustrated anger appeared. "It is if it means suddenly having the team cut down by a quarter. If you two *did* have a fight, just go say you're sorry. Women love to hear that."

Larry had been unattached for as long as Joe had known him. "And you'd be the expert on what women want, right?"

Larry looked as if he was about to defend himself, but then he switched directions. "We're not talking about me, we're talking about you. If we were talking about me," he couldn't resist tacking on, "you'd know that I don't brag about my interactions with the fairer sex." The blond deputy reverted back to the main topic. "Now, whatever it is that's going on between the two of you, it can be fixed. You just have to—"

"There's nothing going on," Joe denied. "And nothing to fix." He drew a fortifying breath. "I just realized that I was right."

Larry shrugged carelessly. "First time for everything." He pinned his friend with a look, waiting. "What is it you were right about?"

Ordinarily, Joe kept his own counsel. But Larry was his friend. If this was one of the last conversations they had, he might as well let the deputy know and appease his vociferous curiosity.

"That Mona's out of my league." He tossed Larry a bone. "It was fun while it lasted, but now it's time to get back to reality."

Larry eyed him, clearly annoyed at his reasoning. "And reality's in another town?"

Joe shrugged. "Maybe. Because it sure isn't here."

"You're making a big mistake."

"No," Joe contradicted, "I already made one and now I'm trying to move on." He was done explaining himself. Joe crossed back to his desk. "Now, leave me alone for a while. I've got a resignation letter to put together."

RICK SENSED SOMETHING was wrong the minute he saw his sister. Despite the fact that Mona threw her arms around both him and Olivia when they stepped out of the hired car, the forced smile on her lips didn't sit right with him.

He was even further convinced that he was right when, several minutes later, as he shut the front door behind them, Mona suddenly told them that she intended to take his advice and go back to Dallas. She planned to set up an animal hospital there.

His own advice was coming back to bite him, Rick thought, looking at Mona. When he realized that she wasn't even faintly excited about the prospect she'd just outlined, he decided to try to get at the real reason for this sudden change of heart.

"Just like that?" he asked. "Five weeks ago, you didn't want to hear about it when I tried to talk to you about it."

"What can I say? I bow to your wisdom," Mona said flippantly, then flashed a grin at her sister-in-law. "He'll make you crazy being right," she confided.

"I already know that." Olivia laughed, her hand

resting protectively on her abdomen and the swell created by their unborn child.

"Besides," Mona continued, quickly glancing at Rick, then away in case he saw the doubt in her eyes, "a girl's got to think of her future."

He exchanged looks with the woman who'd won his heart. Olivia appeared as mystified as he was. "Exactly what happened to change your mind?" Rick asked, trying to pin his sister down.

"Nothing," Mona insisted stubbornly. "Like I said, I just decided that you were right. There's no future for me here."

Mona's acknowledgment that he was right just aroused his suspicions further. Mona *never* admitted that he was right—about *anything.* She lived to argue and loved a good verbal sparring match more than anyone he knew. He needed to get to the bottom of this and it wasn't going to be by asking Mona. First chance he got, he would talk to Miss Joan.

BUT TIME WAS IN SCARCE supply that first day. He and Olivia had only begun to unpack when Doc dropped by to tell them that he was holding a welcome-home party for them that evening. With a twinkle in his eye, the vet told them that he wasn't about to take no for an answer.

The party would be as good a place as any, Rick thought, to corner Miss Joan.

But it was Doc who cornered him first, as well as Olivia, at the party. Acting more mysterious than Rick could remember the older man ever behaving, Doc took them both aside and informed them that, "Your mother's in town, Rick, and she wants to meet with you and your lovely bride here."

Rick felt Olivia's hand tighten comfortingly on his arm. But he wasn't thinking about himself. This could be the reason for Mona's sudden decision to leave. If it was, he wouldn't allow it. Mona meant a lot more to him than an absentee mother.

"Does Mona know?" he asked Doc.

Doc nodded, his blue eyes crinkling kindly. "Mona knows."

He was right, Rick thought. "And?" he pressed, wanting to hear further details so he could decide whether or not he was actually right.

Doc smiled. "She's coming around. It took her a bit, but I think Joe convinced her."

"Joe?" Rick repeated uncertainly. "What does Joe have to do with it?"

"Everything." The smile had turned into a grin. A large, amused grin that instantly traveled up to Doc's eyes and took over his whole countenance. "A lot of things've been happening since you two went on your honeymoon."

"Things," Rick echoed. "What kind of things?" Then, before Doc could answer, he had another question for the man. "Did Mona tell you that she wants to leave Forever?"

Doc nodded. "For Dallas. Yes, Mona told me this

morning. If you ask me, her leaving has something to do with Joe leaving."

Rick stared at Doc in disbelief. He hadn't been to the office yet and this was the first he'd heard about his deputy's sudden plans. He would have bet that Joe intended to stay in Forever, well, forever.

Confused, Rick held his hand up to stop Doc. "Hold it. Now Joe's leaving? Since when?"

"Since today, from what I hear. Miss Joan saw him this morning. First time he'd stopped by for breakfast in a couple of weeks, according to her," he added subtly. "She said Joe seemed pretty set on going."

Rick sighed. In the short time they'd been gone, all hell had broken loose.

He looked at Olivia. "That does it. I'm putting you on notice. We're not going on another honeymoon. Too much happens when we're away."

Olivia smiled. "That's okay with me," she said, then whispered in his ear. "We can create our own honeymoon wherever we are."

Rick felt his heart swelling and thought for the umpteenth time that he was one lucky man. He hadn't realized this kind of happiness existed until Olivia had come into his life.

"Now, what are you going to do about Mona and Joe?" she wanted to know, asking the question loud enough for Doc to hear, too.

As much as he didn't want either one of them to leave, Rick didn't think there was anything he actually *could* do. Considering how independent Olivia was, he was surprised that she'd even ask.

"Nothing. They're both adults. I can't tell them what to do. They can make their own decisions."

The answer didn't please Olivia. She leaned her head into his.

"Look at them," she insisted, first indicating Mona, who was walking away from Miss Joan, and then Joe, who was apparently doing the same thing as he put distance between himself and Larry. "They look miserable," Olivia pointed out—as if she needed to. "As miserable as you and I were when I went back to Dallas and you stayed here," she reminded him.

He had to agree that neither his sister nor his senior deputy seemed very happy. On the contrary, they both appeared angry and annoyed. He had a hunch Miss Joan and Larry had urged each to stay in Forever and give love another chance.

He knew his sister well enough to know that she instantly chafed whenever someone told her what to do. When she was a little girl, she would always do the exact opposite just to show that she was master of her own destiny. It led to a lot of clashes with Abuela.

And as for Joe, the deputy was far more laid-back than Mona, but the man had worked for him for five years. Long enough for him to discover that in his own way, the full-blood Apache was every bit as stubborn as his sister. He displayed his mindset more quietly, but the "destination" was the same.

A union between these two would be pretty damn interesting, Rick mused. Not to mention fiery.

Olivia was right. He had to keep Mona and Joe from going off to the opposite ends of the earth, and find a way to get them back together again. And make them think it was their own idea. That part was crucial.

That would also be the tricky part.

"Enrique?"

About to attempt to approach Mona, Rick stopped dead when he heard the woman's low voice coming from behind him. Only one person ever called him that.

Turning around, he found himself looking into the face of the woman whose features he had tried so often to erase from his mind.

He realized that he didn't feel that same urgency anymore. He was married now, and somehow that state had expanded his range, made him see things that he'd been oblivious to before. Made the concept of family that much more important.

The woman watching him anxiously looked thinner than he remembered. Also smaller in stature somehow. But she still had the flowing midnight-black hair, pinned back now. Hair that he and Mona shared. She also didn't seem nearly as confident as he recalled.

"I don't want to bother you," she said hesitantly. "I just wanted to say hello." Wetting her lips, her eyes darted fleetingly to Olivia and then back to him. She looked as if she was ready to retreat quickly if he rejected her. "I can leave if you—"

He didn't let her finish. He didn't want her to leave. The time for retaliation, for revenge and giving back as good as he felt he'd received, was behind him. So instead, he slipped his hand around the back of Olivia's widening waist and said, "Olivia, I'd like you to meet my mother, Elena Ruiz."

Rick couldn't recall ever seeing anyone's smile as wide as the one gracing the woman his wife was meeting for the first time. It warmed his heart.

Chapter Sixteen

"Hi, Mona, how's it going?" Larry asked brightly when she reluctantly walked into the sheriff's office the next morning.

"Lousy," Mona replied, saying the first thing that came to her mind. It aptly described the way she felt.

She didn't want to be here where she could easily run into Joe. But when her brother had called her less than half an hour ago, Rick had insisted that it was pretty much a matter of life or death that she get herself over to his office immediately.

Ordinarily, she'd balk at having her brother order her to make an appearance, but the tone of his voice made her feel that something was wrong, something he assured her he couldn't discuss over the phone. For leverage, he reminded her that within a matter of days, she'd be gone and they wouldn't see one another for who knew how long.

Guilt was always a sharp, handy tool because it worked.

"Sorry to hear that," Larry commented on her reply. He seemed sincere. "Sorry, too, to hear that you'll be leaving us again so soon. Sure you want to go? You've only been back a little over a month," he said as if she wasn't aware of how long it had been since her arrival.

"Rick told you I was leaving?" Mona asked, thoroughly surprised. Her brother had never been one of those talkative types who shared family business. But then, maybe her new sister-in-law had an effect on him, changing him for the better. Still, she would have preferred if she hadn't been the topic he'd used to wet his feet after his transformation.

Mona looked around, but Rick wasn't in the outer room. Maybe he'd changed his mind about this life-or-death emergency after all. "Is my brother around?" she asked Larry.

"Yes, that he is," Larry told her with fanfare she found rather odd. "He said, when you got here, I should bring you right into his office."

As he spoke, Larry took her arm, slipping it through his as if they were going on a long stroll and he was to be her guide.

"I know where the office is, Larry," she told him. But as she tried to reclaim her arm by slipping it out again, she found that Larry had tightened his hold on her. Just what was going on here?

"I know you know, but the sheriff was very clear. He told me to bring you right in, not 'send' you right in, so I'm doing just that. I'm bringing you in," he declared with an easygoing grin. As if sensing her resistance, he explained. "Man signs my paychecks, I try to follow his instructions down to the letter. No sense in giving him an excuse to fire me. Times are tough," he concluded with a deep sigh.

Larry was acting strange, she thought, even for Larry. She glanced around, hoping to spot Alma and appeal to her. But the female deputy was nowhere around.

They'd just reached Rick's tiny inner office. Because of the glass enclosure, she could see right in. Rick wasn't alone.

Mona dug her feet in and stopped moving.

"He's got Joe in there," she protested.

Larry did a double take and appeared properly surprised. No one's acting career would ever be threatened by Larry, she thought darkly.

"Why, I do believe you're right. But he's just finishing up, so you can go on in," Larry coaxed, tugging on her arm to get her to cross the last few feet. He opened the door to the sheriff's office and announced, "Brought her right in just like you wanted, Sheriff."

Mona absolutely refused to budge. With a mumbled, "Sorry," Larry placed the flat of his hand against her back and gave her just enough of a push to get her across the threshold.

The moment she was in, he quickly closed the door behind her.

For a split second, as she was being propelled into the room, she noticed that Joe looked as surprised as she did that they were in the small enclosed space together.

Rick had called him in five minutes ago to ask why

he was so hell-bent on leaving Forever after all this time. And so suddenly, too.

"No reason," Joe had answered, determined not to say anything about getting together with Mona while the sheriff was on his honeymoon. The less Rick knew about that, the better. He didn't believe in completely burning his bridges behind him. "Just thought it was time for me to move on."

"Got a job lined up?" Rick had asked, giving him one of his penetrating looks.

Joe knew that it would be better all around if he just pretended that he had landed a job in another town. He debated even saying that he'd been offered a position as a state trooper.

But being Joe, lies did not rest easily on his tongue, so what he'd wound up saying was, "Something's in the works," letting it go at that. It was sufficiently vague to assuage his conscience and yet sounded viable. There was no reason for Rick to know the truth.

He'd just mumbled his answer when the door to Rick's office had opened and Larry had all but shoved Mona in. She'd stopped a couple of inches away from him.

For once, he managed to recover before Mona did. "Well, I see you're going to be busy, Sheriff, so I'll just go—"

Rick rounded his desk and presented his body before the door, guarding it with his back. "No, you won't," he cut his deputy off sternly.

"All right, then I'll go," Mona informed him haughtily. She was nothing if not angry at being ambushed like this. It just proved that she really *couldn't* trust Rick anymore.

"Stay!" Rick ordered, freezing her in her tracks.

Mona turned from the door, anger flaring in her eyes like twin green flames. Just who the hell did he think he was?

"I'm not a dog, Rick," she said between clenched teeth.

"Damn straight you're not," Rick fired back. "Dogs are a hell of a lot more obedient." His stern gaze swept over Joe, as well as his sister. "Look, I just have something to say to both of you and then you can go running off your separate ways," he tagged on in barely controlled disdain. "I figure after all this time, I've earned five minutes from each of you."

Mona glared at her brother, hating that he was making her feel this awkward, this uncomfortable. "Get on with it," she snapped, far from happy about having to listen to anything while standing so close to Joe.

"Go ahead, Sheriff," Joe said in a far more genial voice. "I'm listening."

There wasn't even the slightest hint of a smile on Rick's face, nothing to give away the true nature of his thoughts. "I just wanted to tell you that I think both of you are doing the right thing, leaving Forever."

"What?" Mona asked, stunned.

She'd expected just the opposite from Rick after the scene last night. Despite the fact that he'd been the one to try to convince her to pursue her future in the big city, he'd been very upset when she'd told him that she'd made up her mind to leave Forever as soon as possible.

"You heard me," Rick said, the first glimmer of a smile surfacing. "I thought it over and it's the best thing. I mean, whatever it is you two thought you had together, well, that's clearly not going to work out," he pronounced with a laugh. "If you think you're in love, you're just deluding yourselves. I never met two people who were so wrong for each other.

"She'll drive you crazy in less than six months," he told Joe, "and you'll wind up strangling her just to get some peace and quiet, and I'll have to arrest you. Trust me. I'll miss you both, but I for one am really glad you came to your senses before it was too late." He looked from one to the other, as if assuring himself that his words had sunk in. "Okay, that's all." He moved back behind his desk again and sat down, ready to get to work. "You can go now," he said, gesturing for them both to leave.

If he thought she could be dismissed like some errant schoolgirl, Rick was sadly mistaken, Mona thought, working herself up.

"I'm not going anywhere," Mona declared angrily, her hands on her hips as she glared at her brother. "And no, that's not 'all.' Not by a long shot. Who the hell do you think you are, making assumptions like that about me? About Joe and me?" she wanted to know.

Palms spread out on his desk, she leaned into her brother's face. "I can love anyone I choose—without your damn approval. And if I want to be with Joe, or not be with Joe, that's *my* choice to make, not yours, understand?" she demanded. Not waiting for an answer, she continued. "And if I want to marry Joe, then I'll marry Joe, and while it would be nice to have you happy about it, contrary to anything you might think, I don't need your blessings, big brother. Understand?"

He took so long to answer, Mona thought her brother hadn't heard her. Just as she was about to repeat her words, he said, "But you're just talking hypothetically, right?" Rick asked, slanting a look toward Joe as he addressed his words to his sister. Joe, he knew, needed to have a fire lit beneath him.

"No, I'm not talking hypothetically. Does this look like I'm being hypothetical?" she snapped. Spinning around on her heel, she grabbed hold of the front of Joe's shirt for leverage and raised herself up on her toes. The next second she was pressing her lips against Joe's, delivering a kiss that was more fire than passion.

The passion showed up a split second later, like a giant wave breaking over her head, soaking all of her and taking her breath away.

She'd gotten caught in her own trap.

Mona stumbled back, realizing belatedly what she'd just done—and with her brother looking on, too.

What the hell was she thinking?

Thoroughly stunned, Joe only allowed her to take a single step back. His arms had closed around her in an instant, holding Mona in place before she could run. He'd anticipated her flight because she had that look in her eyes, the look that told him she was about to take off as if that would somehow negate what she'd just done in an unguarded moment.

Not by a long shot, he thought.

"Did you mean what you just said?" Joe asked.

Stalling, realizing that in her flash of temper, she'd said far too much, *done* far too much, Mona asked, "What part?"

"All of it," Joe said with emphasis, and then his voice softened. "Especially the part where you said you'd marry me."

Okay, she was in too deep to backpedal. She tossed her head. "If I wanted to. I said I'd marry you if I wanted to," she reminded him, as if that somehow covered up what she was really feeling for him—that Joe was the other part of her soul.

Not this time, Joe thought.

He wasn't about to let Mona worm her way out of this with fancy rhetoric and fancier footwork. As for him, maybe leaving quietly wasn't the way to go just yet. Since Rick had forced this face-to-face confrontation on them, he either had to fish or cut bait.

He didn't want to cut bait. He would ask her for a direct answer. If Mona told him that she didn't love him, then he *would* leave town and never bother her again. But right now, he needed that shove to get him out the door. Because leaving silently would just be the coward's way and he wasn't a coward.

"And do you want to marry me?" he asked pointedly, his eyes pinning her down, holding her to the truth.

Mona felt antsy inside. She didn't want to go first, didn't want to admit that she loved him if he kept his emotions a secret.

"You haven't asked me," she challenged.

He hadn't asked because he wasn't getting the feedback from her that would have encouraged him to take that final leap over the abyss. He'd had enough pain in his life, he didn't want to willingly subject himself to more.

But imagining the rest of his life without Mona amounted to the greatest pain of all. He didn't want that kind of life, filled with nothing but routines and emptiness. He'd already experienced that for far too long.

It was time to ante up and bet everything on the turn of that one all-important card.

Taking her hand in his, Joe asked quietly, "Mona Santiago, will you marry me?"

Her flight instincts fought for control of her. But as she began to pull her hand away, Joe tightened his grasp, holding her in place. Excitement and panic grabbed equal shares of her.

Was he really serious, or was this some elaborate joke on his part? "Why are you asking me that?" she asked breathlessly.

"Because I'm taking a survey," Joe snapped out in disgust. "Why do you think?" He was fairly shouting now and for once, he didn't care. His emotions were all spilling out. "Because I love you. And I'd rather spend the rest of my life fighting with you than having a peaceful relationship with anyone else." Still holding her hand tightly in his, he gave her a moment to absorb his words. "Now, what's your answer, Mona? Will you marry me?"

She struggled to fight back the panic. This was for forever and she knew it. "Don't rush me," she told him.

Was she serious? he thought incredulously. "I've been waiting for you all of my life, Mona. Even a snail wouldn't call this 'rushing.'"

She blew out a breath, then looked at her brother, who had been a silent witness to all this. Much as she loved him, she didn't want him here. This was just between her and Joe. For now.

"Do you mind?" she asked Rick.

His lips pulled back into a grin that threatened to split open his face. "Hell, no," Rick answered.

Did she have to explain everything? "I'm not asking your permission, I'm asking you to leave the office," Mona told him irritably.

"Silver-tongued as always." Rick shifted around the side of his desk and crossed to the door. He glanced back at Joe for a split second. "I'd think about this long and hard if I were you, Joe. This is her good side."

"No, it's not," Joe murmured as Rick closed the door behind himself. "I've seen the good side," he continued, his eyes on Mona's, "and that's the side that'll keep me coming back for more."

The door was closed now. For all intents and purposes, they were alone, although he was aware that Alma, Larry and Rick were all outside, only a few feet away and only marginally pretending not to be looking into the inner office.

"I'm still waiting for an answer, Mona," he told her softly. Maybe this *was* too much pressure for her. He relented a little, not wanting to back her into a corner. "If you don't want to give me one now—"

She didn't wait for him to finish. "Don't tell me what I want or don't want, Joe."

Rather than comment on what she'd just said, he looked at her for a timeless moment. "I'm afraid, too, Mona."

Her back went up. To be afraid was to be vulnerable. She refused to appear to be vulnerable. People lost everything that way. The weak had their feelings trampled on. "I didn't say I was afraid."

"You didn't have to," he answered. He resisted taking her into his arms. First, he was going to say his piece. "It's there, in your eyes. You're afraid that if you let your guard down, if you let yourself actually expect something, it's all going to blow up on you, leaving you with nothing."

She wanted to deny it, to tell him that he was letting his imagination run away with him. But there was no hiding from the truth.

"Maybe," Mona allowed with a careless shrug of her shoulder.

Unable to stand back any longer, Joe slipped his hands around her waist, holding her to him. He saw the battle to resist take place in her eyes. She remained where she was.

He was wearing her down, he thought in subdued triumph.

"I'm not going anywhere, Mona," he promised. "No matter how much you push me away, I'm not going anywhere."

"You just were," she pointed out.

His eyes smiled at her. His lips followed. "That was before I knew you loved me."

Her shoulders stiffened. "I didn't say that."

"Yeah, you did," he contradicted. "I'm as afraid as you are for the same reasons that you are," he assured her. "But if we love each other, then we can make this work."

Mona pressed her lips together. A single word escaped. "Yes." She made no effort to rein it in, to explain it away.

Joe was both surprised and pleased. "You're agreeing with me. This *is* a special day," he teased.

Ever contrary—it was a difficult habit to break—she shook her head. "No, I didn't say yes I agreed with you."

His head began to hurt. "Was there an instruction manual that came the day you were born?" he asked. "Because if there is one, I'll do anything to get my hands on it."

You'll have to be satisfied with getting your hands on me, she thought, suppressing a grin of her own.

"I said 'yes' to your marriage proposal," she told

him. "And there's no manual," she went on to inform him. "You're just going to have to keep learning through hands-on experience."

Joe's face lit up like the sky on the Fourth of July. It made him look like the kid he'd been when he first saw her. "I can live with that."

"You'd better," she told him, threading her arms around his neck. "For a long, long time."

"I'll do my very best," Joe promised, lowering his mouth to hers.

And in so doing, he opened the door to their very own private paradise.

Neither one of them heard the three people outside the small office applauding, or Larry loudly declaring, "Finally." They heard nothing because they were lost in their own world and weren't about to try to find their way back anytime soon.

* * * * *

COMING NEXT MONTH from Harlequin®
American Romance®
AVAILABLE AUGUST 7, 2012

#1413 COLTON: RODEO COWBOY
Harts of the Rodeo
C.J. Carmichael

Years ago Colt Hart made a big mistake. Now he's fallen in love with single mom Leah Stockton. Can she accept what he did? More important, can he forgive himself?

#1414 A COWBOY'S DUTY
Rodeo Rebels
Marin Thomas

Gavin Tucker wants to do right by Dixie Cash after getting her pregnant. But Dixie's past has taught her that she and her baby are better off on their own!

#1415 A SEAL'S SECRET BABY
Operation: Family
Laura Marie Altom

When navy SEAL Deacon Murphy learns a long-ago affair produced a daughter, guilt nearly destroys him. At least until he opens himself to loving Ellie...

#1416 HONORABLE RANCHER
Barbara White Daille

Bound by a promise to watch over his best friend's widow, what can Ben Sawyer do when Dana fights him at every turn?

You can find more information on upcoming Harlequin®
titles, free excerpts and more at www.Harlequin.com.

HARCNM0712

REQUEST YOUR FREE BOOKS!

2 FREE NOVELS PLUS 2 FREE GIFTS!

♦Harlequin®

American ★ Romance®

LOVE, HOME & HAPPINESS

Angie Bartlett and Michael Robinson are friends. And following the death of his wife, Angie's best friend, their bond has grown even more. But that's all there is…right?

Read on for an exciting excerpt of WITHIN REACH by Sarah Mayberry, available August 2012 from Harlequin® Superromance®.

"HEY. RIGHT ON TIME," Michael said as he opened the door.

The first thing Angie registered was his fresh haircut and that he was clean shaven—a significant change from the last time she'd visited. Then her gaze dropped to his broad chest and the skintight black running pants molded to his muscular legs. The words died on her lips and she blinked, momentarily stunned by her acute awareness of him.

"You've cut your hair," she said stupidly.

"Yeah. Decided it was time to stop doing my caveman impersonation."

He gestured for her to enter. As she brushed past him she caught the scent of his spicy deodorant. He preceded her to the kitchen and her gaze traveled across his shoulders before dropping to his backside. Angie had always made a point of not noticing Michael's body. They were friends and she didn't want to know that kind of stuff. Now, however, she was forcibly reminded that he was a *very* attractive man.

Suddenly she didn't know where to look.

It was then that she noticed the other changes—the clean kitchen, the polished dining table and the living room free of clutter and abandoned clothes.

"Look at you go." Surely these efforts meant he was rejoining life.

He shrugged, but seemed pleased she'd noticed. "Getting there."

They maintained eye contact and the moment expanded. A connection that went beyond the boundaries of their friendship formed between them. Suddenly Angie wanted Michael in ways she'd never felt before. *Ever.*

"Okay. Let's get this show on the road," his six-year-old daughter, Eva, announced as she marched into the room.

Angie shook her head to break the spell and focused on Eva. "Great. Looking forward to a little light shopping?"

"Yes!" Eva gave a squeal of delight, then kissed her father goodbye.

Angie didn't feel 100 percent comfortable until she was sliding into the driver's seat.

Which was dumb. It was nothing. A stupid, odd bit of awareness that meant *nothing*. Michael was still Michael, even if he was gorgeous. Just because she'd tuned in to that fact for a few seconds didn't change anything.

Does Angie's new awareness mark a permanent shift in their relationship? Find out in WITHIN REACH by Sarah Mayberry, available August 2012 from Harlequin® Superromance®.

HSREXP0812